LORD DARKNESS

Beastly Lords Book Four

SYDNEY JANE BAILY

cat whisker press
Massachusetts

ISBN: 978-1-938732-38-6
Published by **cat whisker press**
Imprint of JAMES-YORK PRESS

Cover: **cat whisker studio**
In conjunction with Philip Ré
Book Design: **cat whisker studio**

DEDICATION

For Pandora and Jasper

You make me the happiest mom!

OTHER WORKS
by
SYDNEY JANE BAILY

THE RARE CONFECTIONERY
Series

The Duchess of Chocolate
The Toffee Heiress
My Lady Marzipan

THE DEFIANT HEARTS
Series

An Improper Situation
An Irresistible Temptation
An Inescapable Attraction
An Inconceivable Deception
An Intriguing Proposition
An Impassioned Redemption

THE BEASTLY LORDS
Series

Lord Despair
Lord Anguish
Lord Vile
Lord Darkness
Lord Misery
Lord Wrath
Eleanor

PRESENTING LADY GUS

A Georgian-Era Novella

ACKNOWLEDGMENTS

Thanks to my editor, Violetta Rand, also a historical romance writer in her own right. And a big thank you to my mom, Beryl Baily, always there for me and lovingly sending care packages of chocolate and biscuits to have with my tea.

PROLOGUE

1850, London

Nothing but blackness as dark as pitch. How was a man supposed to know if it was day or night? How was a man supposed to care if he lived?

Without his sight, every hour ran into the next with nothing to tell him whether it was time to wake or sleep.

Perhaps it was time to die.

CHAPTER ONE

Three months earlier

Lord Christopher Westing surveyed the crowded black-and-white tiled ballroom from the upper-floor balcony of Marlborough House, searching for his friends. Since there was no royal currently in residence, someone with ties to the queen was always throwing a ball at the spacious brick residence on the Mall just north of St. James Park.

And the Marquess of Westing, heir to a dukedom, eligible and handsome, was at nearly every one.

In the flamboyantly Baroque room below, under the wall paintings of the victorious Duke of Marlborough accepting the surrender of the French armies, Christopher spotted Lords Burnley and Whitely, both already drinking champagne and also clearly scouting the room for their next conquests. Not French armies, of course, but English females.

Champagne and lovely ladies—he ought to be in heaven.

Turning, he left the balcony and headed down the staircase lined with more wall paintings depicting resounding French defeat at the hands of Marlborough. At the bottom of the stairs, Christopher entered the ballroom and was instantly beset by a veritable brigade of young ladies.

He was not so ungrateful as ever to say this was a tiresome matter, for there wasn't a man in the ballroom who wouldn't enjoy having such a bouquet of loveliness tossed at his feet.

At least, he would never be such a boorish cad as to say it out loud. Still, in his heart of hearts, he was weary of being "that good catch Westing," as he heard murmured by mothers and daughters wherever he went, as if he were a large striped bass.

He was not simply a potential husband for every single miss looking for a titled lord with a large fortune. He was a man with his own ideas of whom he wanted for a wife, and so far, he hadn't found her.

He'd danced with many sweet and lovely ladies over the course of three seasons, he'd kissed at least half of those, and he'd developed a *tendre* for none. He was starting to worry about himself.

A few years back, he should have fallen for Margaret Blackwood, who ended up marrying Lord Cambrey, after creating a glorious spectacle at their public engagement at the Sutherland's Stafford House ball. And they did so before Queen Victoria and half the peers of the realm. Unfortunately, Christopher liked Margaret only as a friend despite her wit and beauty.

He wanted spark.

Or perhaps he should have developed an attachment to Lady Adelia Smythe, a lovely girl, but he couldn't seem to make the effort to break through her quiet manner. Again, he'd danced with her and she was intelligent, but he felt no spark.

Spark, spark, spark—he wanted it, but maybe it didn't exist. At least, not for him. Perhaps he would remain a bachelor forever and have to content himself with friends for company and with Cyprians discreetly met in one of London's many bowers of Venus for physical relief.

Wrists with dance cards were being held out to him, and dutifully, he penciled his name on most of them. He could never keep track, so hopefully, the ladies would come find him when it was his turn.

As he snatched up the last card, a firm hand grabbed his wrist.

"That won't do, brother dear," his sister, Amanda, said. "Everyone knows we are a close family, but dancing together goes beyond the pale."

He glanced at her slightly smirking face surrounded by soft brown ringlets with one of her perfectly sculpted eyebrows raised in amusement. He shrugged.

"I admit I wasn't paying attention. I would have noticed it was you eventually, probably during the first few steps of the waltz."

They both laughed, and then her attention was caught elsewhere.

"I'll see you later when it's time to leave." She winked one of her lovely blue eyes, the same Westing light blue as they shared with their father.

"Don't dodge Mother all night, or she'll make me come after you," he reminded his sister.

Amanda was already disappearing into the crowd with a backward wave of her hand.

And then Christopher pushed through the rest of the debutantes and the more seasoned girls to reach his chums and enjoy a drink. He would rather have brandy, but, as usual at these affairs, champagne or lemonade were his only choices, so he snatched up a glass of the former along the way.

Also reaching for a glass from the same tray was Lady Jane Chatley, who offered him a polite nod, which he returned, before she took a drink and walked away.

She was one of the few women of his acquaintance who was not really a friend, nor a romantic possibility. True, she was pretty enough to pique his interest with her deep blue eyes and her light brown hair always in the current style. However, she was also standoffish, at least with him, always busy with tasks that made the rest of them feel useless, and sometimes considered a little too perfect.

"A snout-looker," his sister declared her after one event, which apparently meant Lady Jane looked down her nose at others.

He knew Margaret's husband, Lord Cambrey, was on friendly terms with Jane, as their families had hosted a charitable event together two years earlier. In fact, Christopher had comforted a tearful Margaret and given her a ride home after a cricket match when it seemed the Earl of Cambrey preferred Jane. However, it all worked itself out.

Besides, who could prefer Jane over Margaret, who had a dazzling smile, follow-me-boys curls, and something sensual in her gaze?

He stopped a second and searched his feelings. *Was he in love with Margaret, Countess of Cambrey, another man's wife?* He sipped the champagne and felt not a whit of jealousy. *What a relief!*

"There you are, old boy," Burnley said, and Westing found himself welcomed into the small cluster of bachelors. "I suppose your name is already on a dozen cards."

"At least that many," he quipped. "I think there were some new faces."

"Assuredly so," said Whitely. "I see a very pretty maiden with blonde ringlets."

"Do tell, which one? There are so many of them." Christopher remarked. "There are ringlets here to spare, I'm sure. Only think how many used to be on some poor servant girl's head or a factory worker's, sold to adorn the thinner locks of a viscount's daughter."

"Rather cynical," Burnley said, despite wearing an amused expression. "Anyway, if the servant girl or factory worker couldn't come in person, at least her hair can." He grinned at his own jest.

"Better cynical than unkind," Christopher admonished him. "And on behalf of unfortunate girls who cannot attend, I say your statement was blatantly unkind."

"There's always that awkward moment, too," Whitely lamented, "usually the morning after, when you find the extra locks have come unfastened and lie like snakes on the pillow."

All three of the men shuddered. Then Christopher said, "Hardly usual for it to be the morning, though, George. I'd be shocked if you spent an *entire* night with any of these husband-seeking misses. Surely, none of them would risk their reputations at sunrise."

"True enough," Whitely agreed. "In any case, those pinned tresses come out as easily in a gazebo, a cupboard under the stairs, or even in a carriage."

They all nodded, and then the first dance and the grand march were about to begin. Each bachelor found himself claimed by the correct young woman.

Off we go, Christopher thought.

The next hour passed and then another. At some point, they stopped serving champagne, so he knew it was about two-thirds of the way through the evening. Everyone was supposed to dry up at this point so no member of the *ton* disgraced him or herself by stumbling out into the streets of Marlborough Road or Pall Mall.

For his part, he had made polite conversation and feigned interest nearly as much as he could bear for one evening with both the men and the women in attendance. This was his training for Parliament, he reminded himself, where one must listen and be perceived as diplomatic and fair-minded.

Moreover, he did need to settle down sometime in the foreseeable future, and his best chance of finding a suitable wife was, unfortunately, at one of these events. But certainly not the last lady he'd just released from his arms as he vacated the dance floor. She was far too young and could hardly string two sentences together coherently while not missing a dance step. And she thought the House of Lords was where many of London's nobility lived together, like knights of King Arthur's mythical round table.

He had tried not to laugh and failed.

Time for fresh air, while many of the attendees were becoming frantic to squeeze the last bit of enjoyment out of the evening or, if they'd had offers, then to attach themselves to the best match they could hope for to secure a long and happy marriage. Sometimes, it happened that quickly in the span of a single ball.

He headed across the crowded room toward the south entrance and the expansive lawn, knowing he'd have to deal with romantic couples, who would eye him suspiciously if he were alone.

What's more, it was entirely possible his name was on some lady's card, and to his knowledge, he'd never left a lady without a dance partner, although he couldn't be certain. Tonight might be the first time, for Christopher had simply had enough. The lady with no understanding of their nation's government had soured him.

Making his way past the hopeful debutantes and their even more hopeful mothers, he heard his name whispered and was certain he could feel them feasting their eyes on a duke's son. Then he stepped through the tall double doors to the fresh air. Or, at least, as fresh as London could produce, with its excess of coal fires. Tonight, they were lucky. There was a breeze blowing the foggy smoke out onto the Thames, and they probably wouldn't need guides with torches to lead their carriage horses home.

There was no true veranda at Marlborough House, no sturdy stone railing to lean on and overlook a pretty garden—only steps to a small tiled area before the expanse of grass and more grass. Regardless of the small, rather plain, and even, some said, ugly, terrace, couples had gathered as expected for a little privacy. Their backs were firmly to any newcomers.

Christopher wasn't interested in embarrassing any of them anyway or in ruining reputations by gossiping about those he saw.

Now what? He strolled from one side to the other, trying to keep his gaze on the tiles in front of him. Even so, he recognized Burnley's tall form by a planter pot, leaning into the shadows of the building with his arm draped around some young woman displaying those blonde ringlets they'd discussed. Moreover, he heard his friend's deep-timbered laugh.

Rolling his eyes and hoping for Owen's sake the lady's mother didn't come outside and find them, Christopher had nearly reached the end of the terrace when he spotted a lone female figure looking out over the lawn. She remained on the tiled edge, smartly cautious of stepping onto the grass as the dewy night air would undoubtedly ruin her kid-skin dancing slippers at once.

A female alone spelled one thing: a trap. The last thing Christopher wanted was a debutante at her first ball to cry 'seduction' in order to become his marchioness.

No, thank you. Pivoting on his heel, he'd taken but a single step in the opposite direction when he heard, "Lord Westing."

A familiar voice, yet he couldn't quite place it. He sighed and halted.

Don't be an idiot, he reminded himself. However, he was a gentleman, so he turned.

"I am vacating the area should you like to have it to yourself," said the lady.

The full moon, which was playing hide-and-seek behind tattered clouds, happened to come out, and the shadows dropped away from the woman enough for him to see who it was.

"Lady Jane. I'm sorry, I didn't recognize you at first, or I would never have been so rude as to turn away without a greeting."

She nodded. "Quite all right. What brings you out here?"

"Tedium," he said frankly, watching her nod in agreement. "And you?"

"Similar, I suppose. I know it is the height of foolishness to be out here alone, and I'm positive I have a frantic mother inside asking everyone if they've seen me."

As if she didn't care a fig for her mother, she stayed put, and he decided to stand with her, knowing in his gut she was not the deceitful kind. After all, Jane Chatley could have snagged a man over the past three seasons if she'd wanted. He'd heard rumors more than once about some spark being hopeful with regards to earning her affection, but she'd always let them down gently. Or so the wagging tongues said.

"I have been to enough of these I no longer care," her tone was soft as a whisper, and he frowned.

"Lady Jane, are you in distress?"

She laughed then. *In rather brittle fashion for a young woman,* he thought.

"Yes, Lord Westing, I believe I am. I don't care if I ever come to another ball. Or dinner party. Or matchmaker's breakfast, boating expedition, or picnic, for that matter."

His sentiments exactly. "Then why do you?"

"Oh, obviously for the champagne," she shot back, and he realized she had a glass in her hand at that very moment. She must have bribed a waiter for everyone else was gulping lemonade or even switched to the last offering of the night, water.

Then Jane laughed again. "Actually, I do love a glass of cold champagne, except if I have more than one, it seems to affect me more than anyone else I know. Thus, even that small pleasure is usually restricted."

Usually?

"And how many have you had?"

"I've lost count," she admitted. "But I feel out of kilter, so probably three. This one is not cold, alas, and it has been so long since the previous glass, it has not made me giddy with happiness. Quite the opposite."

She was silent again for a moment, then she turned to face him, the light catching her eyes, and he thought they might be glistening. *With tears?*

"Why do *you*?" she asked. "Come to these impressively awful events, I mean?"

He considered. "I come to see friends, I suppose."

She shrugged. "I don't have friends here. I have competitors."

He tilted his head. "Competitors?"

"Or so my mother tells me. We—all of us females—are competing for the eligible men, are we not?"

"Yet surely some of the ladies are friendly."

"Not with me. As an earl's daughter, I've always been considered a desirable match, so none of the untitled girls or even daughters of viscounts on down the line really care to befriend me. They think even if a man prefers them for their greater beauty, he'll turn to me as the preferable choice."

"I had no idea it was so calculating."

She stared at him, blinking slowly.

Christopher smiled. "All right. I did indeed know it was extremely calculating as I am on the other end of those untitled females and viscounts' daughters, and their mothers. But I believed you all stuck together."

"Oh, no, no." Jane Chatley shook her head. "The largest dowry or the best title wins. Or loses, as I see it, because it has meant years standing alone at these wretched affairs. The short answer to your question is, I come because I am ordered to come. My mother is confident one day a man will sweep me off my feet. I am equally confident I will end up on the shelf. I can only hope she will give up in the next year or two so I can shelve myself with a modicum of dignity, rather than being the oldest woman still dancing during a Season. Soon, I'll be able to chaperone myself."

She huffed and downed her warm champagne. As a gentleman, he took the empty glass from her, her gloved hand briefly in contact with his. For want of a better choice, he placed it on the tiled terrace a few feet away from her. As he turned back, she laced her fingers behind her, twiddling her thumbs and staring out into the darkness.

Most peculiar.

"I must be missing the obvious," Christopher said, returning to her side. "You are lovely, and I know from your accomplishments with your charitable work, you are smart. You seem perfectly well spoken. And you are, as you say, an earl's daughter. Why is it you think you should be shelved? In fact, why *hasn't* a man swept you off your feet?"

She still didn't look at him. Instead, she shrugged again. He waited. Perhaps she wasn't going to answer.

Finally, in a tight voice, she said, "I have had a few men pursue me."

"*Ah ha.*" He felt quite triumphant. She had tried to make it seem as if she were a wallflower, when he knew for a fact, she was considered a . . . O*h! A snout-looker!*

"I wasn't interested in them," she continued. "It was all too clear I was being chosen for *what* I am, not *who* I am. My mother says I'm a hopeless romantic. And I confess, sometimes I do feel hopeless. A few times, though, she nearly pushed me hard enough to get her way."

In all likelihood, his sister was incorrect about Jane Chatley—she wasn't looking down her nose at her suitors so much as looking into her own heart and hoping for more. She wanted at least some modicum of kindred feeling.

He felt precisely the same way.

"We are more alike than not, I think," Christopher mused. "Neither of us enjoys these social events, nor think them a very good way to find someone with whom to spend the rest of our lives."

Jane shook her head. "No, Lord Westing, we are *not* anything alike. You have freedom. You can pick a spouse or choose to wait another decade. You can come out here without risk to your reputation. You can refuse to dance and be deemed mysterious and brooding, whereas if I don't dance with every man who asks, I'm called proud and finicky—and *worse* behind my back."

He experienced a taste of guilt on his tongue at having discussed her with the other men and with Amanda.

She faced him. "You also have all the power. Unless you ask for the hand of a lady who refuses you, and that is very unlikely, don't you think?"

Then she crossed her arms. "Besides, you are incorrect. This is exactly the sort of place one finds the person with whom one will spend the rest of one's life—and most likely, unhappily at that."

He considered. "That's not always the case. I know of a few who've found love matches during a Season."

"A few, I suppose." Jane paused and seemed to study his face. "*I* shall not, however." She tilted her chin. "And what of you? After all the balls we've both attended, do you really think some young woman is going to appear on the tile or parquet, and you will stare at her," she moved a step closer, "and she will stare back," she looked up into his eyes, "and you will feel something—*really feel something*—finally, at long last?"

What in blue blazes was she doing?

They were only inches apart, and he could feel something all right—her warmth radiating from her. This close, he could see the slight rosiness to her cheeks in an otherwise pale, cream-colored complexion. A lovely face, to be sure. He'd always thought that, although in a detached, impartial way.

Now, he could see how her upper lip lifted and dipped in a pleasing manner and how full her lower lip was. Nicely plump, the kind a man wanted to run his thumb over and then soundly kiss. And her eyes were not simply blue. They were truly as blue as lapis lazuli, even in the moonlight.

Who could prefer Jane over Maggie? Why had he ever asked such a ridiculous question? They were as different as chalk and cheese, and with Jane he felt . . .

Spark!

His mouth suddenly dry, Christopher swallowed. And she must have seen something in his expression, for she uncrossed her arms, dropping them to her sides. Cocking her head, she sunk her straight, white teeth into that pleasingly plump lower lip of hers and frowned.

"Lady Jane," he began, but he didn't know exactly what he wanted to say. In any case, he wasn't given a chance to find out.

"There you are!" It was Jane's mother, Lady Emily Chatley.

His worst nightmare had happened. He'd been caught standing alone with an unaccompanied young miss by her overbearing mother!

CHAPTER TWO

Utterly captivated by Jane, Christopher had forgotten the existence of Lady Emily Chatley, along with every other inhabitant of London for a few scintillating moments.

Thankfully, Jane didn't jump back as if guilty. It would have done no good anyway, since her mother must have watched them from the top of the steps and had a good view as she descended and walked toward them.

In any case, the countess could see for herself they'd been merely standing looking at one another. She knew they had done nothing inappropriate. Except be alone.

Of course, that hadn't stopped many a determined mother from wresting a marriage proposal out of a stammering, blindsided single man.

"Jane, what on earth are you doing out here? Dance partners have been asking for you. Yet here you are with . . . Lord Westing." And the countess gave Christopher her broadest smile as if only just noticing him.

"Good evening, Lady Chatley," he said, offering her a polite bow.

"Good evening, my lord." Her tone becoming thickly sweet like honey as she sunk into a curtsey.

How could all the air have left this area of the outdoors, and so quickly?

It couldn't. Nevertheless, this overprotective, pushy woman might possibly be his downfall at last. For if she said anything untoward about his and Jane's actions, Christopher would defend the young lady and even ask for her hand if necessary.

If necessary! He was, above all, a gentleman.

"Mummy," Jane began, but she was cut off, as her mother turned back to her.

"I find you out here alone with a man," Lady Chatley pointed out, her tone changing to one of outrage. "You know what this means, don't you?"

If it weren't so serious, Christopher would have rolled his eyes at the sheer glee in the woman's voice.

And then rescue came from an unlikely source—quiet, reserved Jane.

"Don't be absurd, Mummy. We were not alone for a moment. There are other couples here." She gestured as if those fifteen feet of distance between them and other couples were negligible, as if company was right at her elbow. "What's more, I am twenty-one, quite old enough to stand where I want."

"But, Jane, only think—"

"Only think how your *friend*, the Duchess of Westing, would appreciate the way her son kept me safe out here." She took a step away from him at last.

Then with a glance at him, Jane said, "I bid you good night, my lord."

He was almost too shocked to speak, but she offered him a quirky smile of triumph and an arched lift of one lovely eyebrow, and he recovered.

"Good night, Lady Jane, and you, too, Lady Chatley," he added to her mother.

Jane walked away, seemingly assured her mother would follow. It appeared she was not going to cower or let herself be pushed into a marriage, not even with him, a marquess.

Bravo! But would she hate being married to him so very much?

Her mother gave him a long, lingering look, her lips pursed with disapproval as if she'd expected him to step up and offer for her daughter, even though he hadn't done anything wrong.

With a loud sniff and a tilt to her chin even higher than Jane's, Lady Emily Chatley marched off.

The terrace seemed quite empty without Jane. Christopher stared after her, glad at having the opportunity for their first long talk, and he wondered why he'd never really noticed her before except in the most superficial way, to nod at politely in passing, even to dance with once or twice.

Strange. Was he seeing her differently or had she changed?

Deciding to go back inside lest some other young lady and her mother approach with less than desirable consequences, Christopher decided to find Jane again and see if there was any space left on her dance card.

"I REFUSE TO DISCUSS Lord Westing," Jane said, feeling as if her backbone had never been stronger. She would not give her mother even a hint she liked Christopher. Her *tendre* for him, just a gentle preference for the man above all others, had been her small secret for years, and she liked the fact no one else on earth knew it. Her mother would make her life intolerable if she knew, for she would start to throw Jane at him upon every occasion.

Instead, by confiding in no one, Jane could be near him when she pleased, could watch him, even speak to him, without anyone tittering behind her fan or whispering behind his glove. And up until that evening, it had meant the lack of pressure from her mother.

At Marlborough House, Jane had allowed herself the pleasure of approaching Christopher and taking a drink from the same tray precisely when he did. He'd been forced to look at her and acknowledge her presence. And she'd taken the moment to make eye contact, letting the pleasure of seeing him permeate her being as it always did. Then she'd moved away.

She'd never dreamed he would come outside when she was staring at the stars and wishing herself far away, never imagined they would share a moment—not an extremely romantic one, but intimate all the same. And then, when it was getting even more interesting, her mother had shown up and ruined it all.

They climbed into Jane's father's carriage, a man she saw infrequently. It used to bother her, long ago when she was a young girl, yet it no longer did. She was more upset on her mother's behalf because everyone knew the Earl of Chatley had a wandering eye. It was his love of women—*many women*—that kept him away from home, sometimes for weeks at a time, in France, Spain, and sometimes, somewhere in London with a mistress.

Love was probably the wrong word for it.

More and more, when he was home, he enjoyed a large quantity of gin at all hours. Or maybe he always had, and Jane hadn't realized until she grew older and understood what the pleasant scent always clinging to her father really was.

In any case, he was an earl and a wealthy one at that, so he could do what he pleased, and the *ton* turned a blind eye.

As for her mother, the countess acted as if her husband didn't exist. She lived for Jane, her only child who'd survived infancy. And she devoted all her energy first into her daughter's upbringing, and for the past few years, into getting her well-married.

"But, Jane dear, he is a *marquess*, heir to a dukedom. You had him alone. You could have said anything at all had happened, and he would have been yours for the taking if he had even a modicum of decency, which I've heard Lord Westing has in spades."

At first, Jane didn't say anything as they headed home. After the scene on the terrace, she had walked straight to the coat room and gathered her coat and street shoes, regardless of any names still on her dance card.

In the spacious carriage, she let her mother prattle on, wondering if it were too late to still make a claim of impropriety against him.

"To what end?" Jane asked at last.

Her mother stared at her as if she were a simpleton.

"So you can marry him, of course! Why else would we go to these events?"

Jane nearly swore with exasperation. The very idea she would coerce Lord Westing into marrying her—how humiliating! And him, of all people, whom Jane actually admired. He spoke intelligently and thoughtfully, whenever she heard him. He made people around him laugh in a kind way, not with spiteful comments. Of course, he was ridiculously handsome, and those gorgeous blue eyes!

She sighed. Tonight, she'd had the pleasure of gazing into them for the longest period of time ever.

"Not another word on this matter, Mummy. I will not let you sully my brief encounter with Lord Westing. Besides, his mother is your friend."

Her mother crossed her arms, looking sullen, and Jane felt a moment's sympathy. Her mother was only trying to get her settled.

"I certainly hope *you* enjoy yourself a little because one of us should for all the expense you and Father put into each Season. And you know how I loathe each and every ball."

"I liked dancing when I was young," Lady Chatley said before giving a profound sniff.

"You secured your husband during your second Season," Jane pointed out, "and thus could dance or not dance. You chose to dance and had a steady partner."

At least, her father, by all accounts, had been steady at the time. Only *after* the wedding and the begetting of his heir, did he start to wander. She was a little surprised he hadn't pressed for another boy after their only son died a month following his celebrated birth. Yet Charles Chatley had, by all accounts, abandoned his family for whatever pleasures he could find nearly as soon as Jane was out of the womb, appearing lusty with health and beauty.

How could her mother not want to take a whip to the Earl of Chatley?

"You could have had the Earl of Cambrey last year," her mother continued. "Or was it the year before?"

"Mummy, John Angsley and I never had feelings for each other. That was entirely in your own head."

"*Bah!* Feelings!" her mother grumbled. "You two made a splendid couple."

"We never did. John always had his eyes on Margaret Blackwood and his heart was entirely hers."

"Blackwood," Lady Emily scoffed. "A baron's daughter."

Jane rolled her eyes. Her mother's generation saw only the ranks of the peers and not the people behind the titles. She could as easily be happy if she fell headlong in love with a banker, tailor, or even a footman. However, since she never spent time with anyone other than the cream of London's society, that was highly unlikely.

Moreover, Jane knew it would mean extreme ostracism, even banishment from all she'd ever known. Not to mention how emasculating it would be for a man of the lower classes to marry a woman of the highest level of aristocracy.

"What if I never marry?" she mused.

"Jane!"

"Why is that so terrible, Mummy? You seem to take it as a personal failure should I decide to live the life of a bluestocking or perhaps open an orphanage or a home for wayward girls. Or what if I choose to do absolutely nothing except enjoy my life?"

Her mother opened her mouth, then closed it. Then, finally, when she could speak, she asked, "How could you *enjoy* life if you were unmarried?"

Jane supposed she would keep company with other spinsters or hire a companion so she could freely go to the theatre and concerts and riding. It sounded rather wonderful.

"How much joy has your marriage brought you?" she asked her mother in return.

The countess was too self-aware of her own marital disaster to let that barb even touch her.

"I have you," her mother said, "thus I enjoy my life very much."

"By living it through your hopes for me? Then I should think you wouldn't want me to marry at all. What would you do with yourself if I marry?"

"If? What has got into you, Jane? *If!* You shall, and then you will have lovely children. Hopefully a large brood."

"And then I shall find myself sitting at these same awful social events watching my offspring dance and try to snag their own husband or wife. That sounds like perpetual hell."

"Jane!"

"Mummy, what will you do with yourself if—sorry—*when* I marry?"

Lady Emily Chatley got a dreamy look on her face, not at all what Jane had expected.

Hm. Jane couldn't begin to fathom what that look meant. And then they were home, on Hanover Square. As soon as their butler opened the front door, Jane knew her father had returned for the distinct scent of his pipe filled the air.

Why this caused anxiety, she couldn't say, but her stomach tightened. She wanted to love her father, although she certainly did not like him. She knew one flight up, probably with his legs and boots upon the sofa in the drawing room, her father would be stretched out, his once-handsome now ruddy face smiling at whatever private thoughts crossed his mind, a large glass of gin in one hand, and his pipe in the other.

Glancing back, she saw some inscrutable expression flash across her mother's face, before the look of acceptance was fixed in place.

And then, as they climbed the stairs, they heard the booming voice of the Earl of Chatley after being told they were home.

"Where are my lovely ladies?"

CHRISTOPHER COULDN'T GET JANE Chatley off his mind. He'd seen her differently the night before and wondered why it never occurred to him she was more than a good mind and a pretty face. She had personality to spare.

And, of course, she had a shapely figure. Most of the girls at the balls did. It wasn't until *after* the wedding they began to loosen their corsets and eat more than air. However, he'd seen Jane's mother, and she hadn't let herself go. She was still fair of face and svelte, not a big bear of a woman as many of the mothers were.

Shame about her husband. Even his generation, who generally only whispered and gossiped about one another, knew of the excesses of the countess's profligate husband, Charles Chatley.

Since Lady Chatley was attractive, he wondered what drove the earl to stray like an alley cat.

Undoubtedly seeing a father behave thusly had colored Jane's view of men. Plainly speaking, she had no tolerance for simply marrying a titled man and hoping for the best. That clearly hadn't worked for her mother.

Christopher maintained he and Jane were rather like-minded, despite how she'd protested. True, the men at those infernal events of the Season had the power, at least initially. Yet if a man fell for a woman, suddenly, she could lead him about by his heartstrings. He'd seen it happen, but not with his friends Burnley and Whitely. Not yet anyway.

He grinned. That would be something to witness with Burnley, who seemed to fall in love on a weekly basis, although it always turned out to be mere temporary infatuation. As soon as some divinely feminine creature blew her nose too loudly, he was finished with her.

The next day, to the sound of banging, he went downstairs, following the noise to the basement level and into the kitchens. It looked like a battlefield. In the middle of it, his father stood proudly surveying the workmen around him.

"What the devil are you doing, old man?" Christopher asked him.

"The future, my boy."

Christopher glanced around. "The future is a wrecked kitchen, is it?"

"The future is a pristine kitchen without dirty coal."

"I see. What is the cook going to use? You do know wood has been scarce since the sixteenth century, Father." He smiled, wondering if his mother had seen this yet. The Duchess of Westing's perfectly coifed hair would undoubtedly stand on end.

"Wood?" his father repeated, then he laughed. "Oh, a joke, I see. *Haha*, my boy. No, not wood, gas!"

"As in street lamp gas?" Christopher asked.

"Exactly. You know my friend Soyer."

"The chef at your club, yes."

"Smart man. He's redone his own kitchen over with a gas stove, says it's quick and clean. Remarkable. I went and saw it myself. Even lit it. Fabulous."

Christopher took a closer look at the rubber lines that were in place, lying in trenches, where they'd torn up the floor.

"And Mother knows about this?"

"Well," the duke hesitated. "She knows I'm remodeling a little."

Christopher grinned again.

"Like when you decided to add a *little* bathroom upstairs and added two of them with hot-water pipes and separate water closets, or spend a *little* money to revamp the mews behind the house or—"

"I take your meaning. But a happy cook is a happy house."

"I think that saying applies to a happy wife, Father."

His Grace shrugged and looked around again. "It will be wonderful."

"But no one will even see it," Christopher pointed out.

His father frowned. "Of course they will. Just like with the bathing rooms, I'll take every guest on a tour."

Christopher shook his head. "And how are we to eat in the meantime?"

"*Ah,* well, I'm going to the Reform Club."

"Where Soyer is the chef? Perhaps he suggested this remodeling to get your patronage at the club. Maybe they charge extra for people who've destroyed their own perfectly good kitchens." But he was hungry. "I guess I'll come with you. What about the rest of the family?"

"They will go to your aunt's home. Every morning and evening until this is finished. In fact, I think your mother said something about taking your sister and staying there until . . . *hmm,* come to think of it, her words weren't very friendly, and she has left already."

By this time, Christopher couldn't contain his mirth and was laughing uproariously.

"You may have gained a gas stove and lost a duchess."

"Don't be absurd," his father said, but he didn't sound too sure of himself. "Anyway, let's go. Are you ready, my boy?"

"Always, Father."

IN A SHORT WHILE, Christopher found himself dining at the Reform Club, the political headquarters of the Liberal Party, and a masterpiece of architecture in the Italian palazzo style. Even if it had looked like an ugly hovel, Christopher would have gone to the club for Chef Soyer's cooking was sublime. If the new gas stove in his family home caused their own cook to turn out dishes anything like the brilliant French chef's, the nuisance of installation would be worth it.

While his father was socializing with some of the others, most of them members of Parliament, Christopher sat down to eat. Then, when he realized his father had taken a seat with Sir William Molesworth, one of the club's esteemed founders, he knew he'd be dining alone.

It gave him a chance to listen to many conversations at once, as he was interested in both the Whigs and the Radicals who frequented the place. What's more, he also had time to think, and what he thought about was Jane Chatley. For some inexplicable reason, he couldn't get her out of his head. Nor did he want to.

Why not pursue the sentiment and see where it led? Indeed, why not pursue the lady?

CHAPTER THREE

Jane found herself looking forward for the first time in a long time to a ball. Moreover, it was one without cards as some hostesses were doing now. For many young women and men, it was terrifying—utter chaos. Jane, however, liked it.

It meant one could dance or, better yet, *not* dance without anyone accusing eligible ladies or gents of not doing their duty. And as long as it wasn't obvious, one could even dance with the same partner more than twice. That had never been her hope. Until tonight.

As she stood by a potted fern wearing a new gown in rich, purple satin that made her feel beautiful, she found herself watching the main entrance to the ballroom. Her mother always insisted on arriving early at these infernal events in order to stake a claim to a good table on the edge of the dance floor, where she could watch all the comings and goings. That had never bothered Jane before. An extra half hour of watching people or chatting with gentlemen who had an interest in charitable work, or at least feigned one, was neither here nor there.

However, for the first time, Jane felt the unpleasant sensation of anticipatory nerves tingling in her stomach. She found herself watching and waiting, and feeling disappointment each time a gentleman who wasn't Christopher Westing entered the room.

Previously, she'd always kept her small crush on him tamped down, buried under the practicality of life. Her thinking had been logical—if they'd been meant for a great love, surely, it would have happened already. Instead, during the past couple of years, she'd seen the marquess occasionally appear interested in one lady or another. One time, an exotic creature came among them, a Scottish debutante, and, for a few weeks, he seemed mildly interested in her. Before that, lovely Miss Blackwood kept company with him until she became Lady Cambrey. Lord Westing had never looked heartbroken by any of them.

Nonetheless, she didn't like this unnerving feeling. Never before had she sought out Christopher or imagined dancing or speaking with him. It had been easy to keep a warm sentiment without letting it bother her or interfere with her calm state of mind.

Except for the day of her successful banquet and cricket match to benefit orphans two years prior. She recalled how she felt seeing Christopher Westing with Margaret Blackwood that day, all the while knowing her mother wanted her to insinuate herself into the Earl of Cambrey's future.

Jane and Lord Cambrey, as host and hostess of the event, had eaten with the prince consort, but she would have preferred to dine at Christopher's table. She remembered thinking he and Margaret looked as though they were having great fun.

She had drunk too much champagne and dissolved into tears in front of Lord Cambrey. Christopher had never even noticed her existence.

And then, miraculously last week, something had crackled between her and the marquess while they looked at each other at Marlborough House. She was certain she hadn't imagined it. At the same time, she acknowledged, it would sting if it turned out it was all in her head.

Finally—*it might have been twenty minutes or twenty hours*—she saw him enter. He looked fabulous, but he always did. The marquess had a valet who was undoubtedly the envy of all gentlemen of the *ton*. His cravat was impeccably tied, his waistcoat straight and pressed, his jacket fit his broad shoulders like a second skin, and his pants—she tried not to think of anything below his waist. She was a lady after all, but she couldn't help noticing how the fabric of his pants molded itself to his long, muscular thighs.

Jane heard herself sigh and looked around to make sure no one was watching the direction of her glance. How terrible to be caught mooning over a man. *Pathetic!*

When she peeked in his direction again, she noticed two things. Firstly, young ladies flocked to him like birds to breadcrumbs. And secondly, he was moving through them like a ship's bow cutting through the ocean.

Then, to her delight, he looked her way and smiled. Moreover, he changed his path from the obvious one toward the group of his friends whom she recognized, and headed in her direction.

Was he actually crossing the room to speak with her?

Jane nearly looked behind her to make sure there was not a more desirable destination somewhere close. And then suddenly, he was standing there, within touching distance.

"Good evening, Lady Jane." He took her hand and bowed over it before releasing her. "May I say you look positively ravishing tonight?"

She felt the heat in her cheeks. *How strange!* She was not one given to blushing, and never had been, being neither coy nor bashful. Most people saw her the way she wanted them to, as confident and able. She was out in the world, rather than remaining in the female domain of the drawing room, and she had no qualms about meeting with the director of an orphanage or renting a tent or discussing a contract with musicians for an event.

So, why, at that moment, did she feel tongue tied and self-conscious?

She sipped her champagne and let it loosen her tongue.

"You may say it, Lord Westing, as long as you are being sincere."

His smile transformed his handsome face into a Greek god's visage.

"I am using my eyes," he reminded her, "and I assure you of my sincerity. Will you dance with me?"

Sheer pleasure filled her from head to toe at his invitation. But she looked past him to the empty dance floor and felt the urge to laugh.

"That would be odd, indeed, since the musicians have not started playing and no one else is dancing."

For the first time, he looked unsure of himself. Glancing over his shoulder, then back at her, he smiled.

"I believe you are correct. While I don't mind being in the forefront of new ideas or even standing out in a crowd, I would not shock the *ton* by taking you onto an empty dance floor."

She smiled back at him.

Cocking his head, he considered. "You already have a glass of champagne, so tell me how I may serve you?"

"I suppose we can talk," she said, then nearly rolled her eyes at her awkward lack of enticing banter.

Instead of looking put off, however, Lord Westing actually seemed pleased.

"Yes, we can. What are you interested in?"

"It would be easier to list what I'm not interested in," she said truthfully.

"I already know you have a soft spot for orphans."

"Well, who doesn't?" she asked, then considered the many stories she'd heard of people of her class preferring to turn their heads and look away when faced with children in the gutters or begging. Sadly, many wouldn't go to the East

End at all, preferring not to see poverty and, thus, pretend it didn't exist.

"I'm also interested in the general welfare of us all, meaning our air quality in London, and particularly the health of the working classes. The public health act of a few years back was a promising start, although it didn't have enough teeth, if you know what I mean. The same with the central Board of Health. And don't get me started on the drinking water crisis."

"On the contrary, I would love to hear your input on drinking water," he said. "Cholera is still one of our nastiest contagions."

Therefore, in the light of crystal chandeliers and close to the bejeweled, silk-clad offspring of the wealthiest members of society, they passed an hour discussing public welfare and what could be done to ease the plight of those who inhabited London's slums.

By the time they began discussing the merits of the current prime minister, admiring Lord John Russell while wishing he were less of a theorist and more of an activist— "Like you, Lady Jane," Christopher said—they then decided it was time to dance.

"A polka," Jane exclaimed. "How fun!" She was surprised to realize she meant it, and even more surprised by the sizzling sensations that coursed through her when Christopher took her in his arms.

An exhilarating dance, she had always handled it with aplomb, concentrating on performing the steps to perfection. That evening, she didn't worry too much about her feet and felt all the joy the dance entailed as they whirled about the floor with the other couples.

When the polka music died down, almost at once, a waltz began. Without releasing her for an instant, Lord Westing led her into the dance. And then the next.

Jane couldn't remember an evening when she'd enjoyed herself more. Not ever. And when Christopher finally brought her to her mother's table and offered to go procure refreshments, she knew she was smiling like a fool.

"I'm glad to see you so happy," Lady Chatley said.

"I am," she confessed, hoping her mother wasn't going to spoil it by saying something untoward about pushing Lord Westing into marriage.

"I think it's a masterful idea to dance with Lord Westing. You have caught the eye of many other young men while doing so. They are taking a fresh look at you."

Her smile died. Stale Jane had been given a fresh appearance by dancing with one of the most eligible bachelors in London. *How contrived that sounded!* Three dances in a row if anyone was counting. And knowing the *ton*, everyone was counting.

After their last conversation on the terrace, she hoped Lord Westing hadn't done it for the purpose of pulling her clinging fingers from the shelf on which she'd been attempting to climb this Season.

She hoped he simply liked her. Even then, he was at the refreshment table, chatting with Lord Burnley, who was gesticulating. They both turned in her direction. Luckily, she was able to turn just before they spotted her watching them.

When Christopher returned with her champagne, he leaned close for the briefest moments and whispered in her ear, "Do not drink any more than this one glass, or I shall have to take you to task."

"I won't," she promised, thinking it sweet he was worrying over her. Then she noticed he did not have a drink.

"Will you sit with us?" she invited him, already knowing by his stance, he was about to walk away.

"Alas, I cannot. I have other obligations. When they are fulfilled, I hope to see you later."

She'd stopped listening at "other obligations." *Had Lord Burnley warned him away from her?*

"Perhaps," Jane murmured, hoping she sounded mysterious and not utterly disappointed.

He bowed to her and then to her mother and hurried off. Too quickly.

All evening up until that instant, she'd felt like the luckiest, prettiest, most interesting woman at the ball. Now, she felt simply foolish. Moreover, it did hurt, as she assumed it would, to realize she'd been merely another dance partner and had imagined a deeper connection.

In any case, he'd dashed away so quickly, he left her in no doubt she was not the woman with whom he wished to spend the rest of the evening.

Jane soon realized her mother's observation was correct. No sooner had Lord Westing left her side than a steady stream of other men appeared at their table inviting her to dance.

It certainly wasn't on account of the purple gown, no matter how attractive. It was the new sheen of having been favored by a marquess for a long discussion followed by three dances, marking her as a desirable companion.

She looked past the first man in line and saw Christopher leading another lady onto the floor, along with his sister, Lady Amanda Westing, who was in the arms of another young lord, new this Season. A quaint foursome of friends.

So be it. In a flash of realization, Jane thought she might want to take pity on her mother's diligent efforts and remove herself from being a burden to her parents. If she entered into courtship with some eligible man, she could put this whole era of her life behind her. She could become engaged and decide never to attend another ball.

And there was no better time to start sifting through the pack than by dancing tonight with all those who asked.

CHRISTOPHER WONDERED WHERE LADY Jane Chatley found the energy. She hadn't been off the dance floor since he'd left her to fulfill his familial duty as his sister's chaperone. He'd promised his parents they needn't come to the Linwald ball, an event they both found tedious, and in return, he would watch over Amanda. He'd done a poor job of it earlier in the evening, being so entranced by Jane.

Eventually, he had been taken to task by his best friend, Lord Burnley, and roped into dancing with one of his sister's friends while Amanda chose her partners.

The comparison of talking with Jane, who was clever and well-informed, and the other ladies with whom he kept company that evening was a chasm of insipid ignorance. And while he twirled with a blonde, curly-haired miss who kept asking about his family's holdings in the country, he saw Jane on the arm of Lord Fowler. He sat out the next few dances, keeping his eye on Amanda, while also noticing Jane with Lord Welkes, Burton, and even Whitely, and a few others he knew by face but not by name.

It seemed to him she usually spent more time off the floor than on it, or he would have noticed at previous dances the elegance of her step, the graceful way she held her head, and the comeliness of her figure.

Had she always worn gowns showing so much of her décolletage?

At that instant, Lord Reggie Linwald, the son of the hosts, was blatantly looking down Jane's dress from the advantage of his great height and undoubtedly seeing the top swell of her bosom.

A rush of irritation burned a swath through him. At least, Christopher supposed it was only irritation he felt, but it might be jealousy. In either case, it rubbed him the wrong way.

What cause did he have to be irritated or jealous for that matter? He'd been at countless balls, and Jane Chatley's doings had never meant a thing to him.

Truthfully, he'd never spared her a second thought, but now, she was filling his mind. All because he'd encountered her alone and given her a second glance. And then a third.

Extraordinary when he considered it. If he hadn't spent a few precious minutes with her on the Marlborough House terrace, he wouldn't notice tonight with whom she was dancing or even that she was dancing at all.

It seemed hard to credit he could ever have ignored her presence because he couldn't take his gaze from her. Captivating, beautiful, looking as comfortable on the parquet dance floor as she did hosting a banquet. *What an appealing woman!*

He stood up as the music ended, and Jane left the floor on the arm of another dapper gentleman.

"Where are you going, brother dear?" Amanda asked. "We were about to dance again. Surely, you're not so ancient, you're giving up."

The girl with his sister snickered. He barely paused.

"Behave yourselves, children, or I'll send you home like the spoiled brats you are."

In a moment, he was at Jane's side, and no cards that evening meant freedom to change partners on a whim. Or to stop dancing entirely.

"Lady Jane, are you ready for a break and to resume our conversation?"

She looked wary for the first time, at least the first time he'd seen such an expression directed at him. *Had he offended her in some way?*

She glanced around, perhaps seeking an excuse. He decided to give her some options in case she really didn't want to speak with him.

"That is, unless you were going to dance with someone else or were leaving?"

Jane frowned at him. "Why should I leave before it's over? I'm not an utter bore, you know."

He knew his mouth fell open, as that was the farthest thing from his mind. After this evening of getting to know her, he found her company preferable to any other lady there. She had all the qualities of a friend with the extra wondrous layer of potential for an amorous association, like the lovely polished luster of well rubbed beeswax on his favorite writing desk.

He smiled, then he snickered.

Her blue eyes grew as large as doorstops.

"What is so humorous?" she asked tightly. "Do share, Lord Westing."

"In my mind," Christopher began, and then he chuckled. "I had a silly notion," he added but couldn't continue for laughing. The idea of Jane as a writing desk, gleaming with fresh polish, and of him sitting down before her . . . putting his hands on her. He sobered instantly.

"You wouldn't have liked what I was thinking," he said, staring into her eyes which had now narrowed considerably, examining him as if he were a lunatic. "It was rather irreverent."

"Tell me," she insisted. "No one likes to be laughed at."

"Not *at*," he promised.

"You weren't laughing *with* me since I do not, as yet, know the jest."

"Shall we take a walk?" he asked abruptly.

She raised an eyebrow, considering. Then she glanced around. They'd already ended up at the edge of the dance floor, on the opposite side from the chaperones' tables.

"Where?" she asked finally.

He lifted his forearm to her and she took it, threading her arm around his. He somehow knew she would be game, not the mincing, retiring type any more than she was brash. She was rather perfectly in the middle, up for adventure but not going out of her way to flout society.

And at that moment, she was keeping her head down and attempting discretion as he led her out of the great hall and into the connecting corridor. From there, they went farther into the heart of the Mayfair mansion. At the end of a long hallway was the type of shadowy alcove the *ton* used for quick passionate kisses and, occasionally, the more daring like Burnley used for an actual skirt-raising tryst.

Christopher glanced at the tufted velvet divan, considered the lady he was with, and turned away from its sordid implication. Instead, he set his hand on the first latch he encountered and pushed open the door.

A server's area, filled with chafing dishes and glassware. He pulled her in behind him and closed the door. The only light came from a window letting in moonlight and lamplight from the street. Quickly, he lit a lamp on the counter, next to a pile of napkins. The situation still seemed sordid and somewhat ridiculous.

What on earth was he doing?

"I'm sorry," he said, turning to Jane, but she was gazing at him seriously with luminous eyes and parted lips, and suddenly, he wasn't sorry at all.

CHAPTER FOUR

"I've never done anything I'm not supposed to," Jane confessed, looking around at the shelves of teacups and plates.

At that moment, with Christopher Westing looking devilishly handsome, she was thrilled to be in the server's room with him.

He cocked his head and surveyed her.

"Then it's about time, don't you think?"

She felt like giggling, and she absolutely never giggled.

He only had to take two steps to be right in front of her, and he took them, standing close but not yet touching her. Instead, he gazed down into her face, forcing her to look up at him.

"I am both surprised and honored," he said. "Only think of all those social events, and you are saying you never . . . ," he trailed off.

Lest he think her a total drab Nelly, an utterly lifeless fool, she confessed, "I have let a few gentlemen kiss me. Out of my own curiosity."

He smiled slightly at her. "And the other night, when I came upon you, instead of being indoors dancing respectably with your designated partner, you were wickedly on the Marlborough House veranda."

"*Alone*," she reminded him, then felt embarrassed. That didn't speak well of her allure or appeal, if she could stand alone, unchaperoned, and not be bothered by even one overly forward male.

"Alone or not, it was rather daring of you," he pointed out.

"But not to this extent." Jane shook her head. "Never something like sneaking away from a ball and into a small room. With a man."

"We are friends," Christopher said.

Were they? Is this what friends did? "Are we?"

"I hope so, and more, too, perhaps." He moved even closer until she could feel his legs against the satin of her skirts. "If not in a room such as this, where did these gentlemen have the pleasure of kissing you?"

She paused, hardly able to form a thought.

"On the lips," she murmured, making a small joke.

However, looking more serious than amused, he glanced at her mouth, taking careful study of the very lips she'd mentioned. Then his eyes seemed to darken, and she realized his pupils had grown larger, practically filling the blue of his irises.

How interesting.

Suddenly, the Marquess of Westing's hands were on her waist, and strongly but slowly, he drew her against his warm body until their thighs were pressed close, and her breasts began to crush against him.

"Tell me," she asked, wondering at her own breathy voice. "What was so amusing to you earlier?"

He frowned slightly, then as he recalled something, he smiled again.

"I was only thinking what a rare creature you are. Something about polish and luster and laying my hands on you," he said, his tone husky.

Her heart raced, and Jane couldn't do anything but stare up at him, silently, waiting, hoping. This was not her first kiss, but it was the first one that mattered.

As he bent toward her, she closed her eyes until she felt his mouth upon hers. Firm yet gentle, then downright scorching, his kiss seared her lips, and instantly the heat of it reached her heart.

She had yearned for him, refusing to acknowledge even to herself precisely how much.

And the warm feelings didn't stop at her heart. Her body was tingling and prickly hot—certainly like nothing she'd experienced before.

When Christopher raised his head, his expression was one of . . . astonishment, and her spirit soared. He'd felt it, too. It was written all over his fine-looking face.

Without a word, he swooped in again for another kiss, tilting his head until their lips fit perfectly, and then he teased hers with his tongue until she opened her mouth to discover what came next.

What followed was equally surprising and stirring. His tongue slipped between her parted lips, and it wasn't disgusting to have someone else's tongue in her mouth. It was quite lovely. In fact, it was exciting.

Boldly, she touched his, and he touched hers, and it sent little shivers through her, which ultimately concentrated in the now-thrumming place between her thighs.

Gracious!

She realized her hands had crept up his shoulders and were behind his neck, and her gloved fingers were touching his thick hair, which curled at his collar.

She was touching a man's hair! Through her sheer silk gloves, she could definitely feel its softness.

And then he pulled away again, and she nearly protested. Instead, she let her hands fall away from him. However, Jane couldn't think of a thing to say.

A slow smile spread over his face making him, if at all possible, even more attractive.

"The other kisses," he began, "where did you say they took place?"

She blinked, simply staring into his lovely eyes. She could happily gaze into them for a lifetime. Moreover, her brain couldn't pull up the face or name of a single man she'd let give her a terribly bland peck on the mouth.

"What other kisses?" she asked finally, and they both laughed.

"We should return to the ballroom."

"We should," she agreed, not wanting to leave the cocoon of the server's room. "Would you like to dance again, or do you have other obligations?"

His face took on a pained expression. "I'm supposed to be watching over my younger sister."

"Oh dear!" she said, and her practical side reared up. "I could not live with myself if she came to harm or her reputation were sullied because of . . . ," she trailed off.

"Because I was busy sullying your reputation," Christopher supplied.

They shared a foolish grin.

"Besides, your mother is undoubtedly frantic," he reminded her. "She may even be on the other side of that door."

They both glanced at it.

"Since we may be about to face ruin and damnation, may I kiss you again?"

She nodded.

He was careful not to mess up her hair as he took her face in his hands and melded their mouths again. It didn't last as long as the first kiss, most probably because he was distracted by the thought of his sister and her mother.

However, as he pulled away, he gently tugged at her lower lip with his teeth. It was shocking and wonderful, and it sent a sizzle to her womanly parts. Before she could stop herself, she moaned softly at all the sensations coursing through her.

In response, Christopher slid his hands down her back and drew her close again, holding her against his body for a long moment. Then he released her.

"I needed to hold you like that," he explained. "You are so warm and soft."

She smiled. This had turned out to be the most delightful evening of her life.

"SLIPPING AWAY LIKE THAT was very wrong of you, Jane," her mother admonished her when she reappeared in the ballroom—alone—a few moments later. Christopher had gone the long way around to come in an entirely different entrance. Jane looked past her red-faced mother, who purported to have been searching *everywhere* for her, and saw Lady Amanda perfectly unscathed, talking with a group of other debutantes.

Jane sighed and relaxed, knowing her own pleasurable indiscretion had not harmed anyone else. Except her mother.

"I went to the ladies' retiring room and fixed my hair," she added, drawing her mother's attention to it and hoping it looked *fixed*. If it didn't, she could explain it away.

"I danced so much tonight with so many agreeable men, I had lost a few pins. Does it look all right now?"

"You did dance a lot," the countess agreed, tucking an errant wisp behind Jane's ear. "I'm pleased you found some company acceptable for a change."

"Quite acceptable, yes," Jane said, seeing Christopher enter from the main doorway, meaning he must have gone outside. Clearly, he was looking for her. When their eyes met, even from across the room, she saw him wink. Then he nodded and headed toward his sister's table.

"GOOD MORNING, FATHER." JANE heard a ridiculous sing-song quality to her voice and helped herself to tea and breakfast from the sideboard.

Strange enough to see Lord Chatley up early and sitting at the table with newspapers spread around him. Stranger still to feel a bubble of happiness from the previous night's activity. Of course, she had never been kissed by Christopher Westing before and, thus, had not ever had such activity to ponder.

Her father lowered the paper he was perusing as she sat down.

"You look well, Jane."

He usually didn't comment on her appearance. Ever. They normally existed in realms that didn't overlap.

"Do I?" she asked, leaning over to see what papers he had, reaching out for the *Times*.

As her fingertips brushed it, he tugged it out of reach, and her gaze flew to his.

"Not very feminine of you to immediately read the dirty newspaper rather than to attend your father. You should practice your conversational skills so we can get you married."

So much of what he said surprised her, she could do nothing but stare at him.

Then he added, "The bloom will be off you soon, dear daughter, and then where will you be?"

The bloom, indeed! He should look in the mirror at the red veins on his cheeks. Moreover, she could smell the juniper perfume of his previous night's imbibing—assuming he hadn't had any gin before breakfast.

"My marital state and my appearance have never concerned you before," she pointed out.

"Of course they have. From the moment we lost James and then had a girl baby, I knew our lives were going to be very different from what I'd hoped. Instead of building the earldom, I could spend the hell out of it before my nephew gets his hands on the title."

Jane regarded her father over her teacup. "I'm sure cousin Bernard will appreciate it if you leave him a little something." *And what about her mother?* If her father predeceased her mother, it would be nice if he left her something to live on. Jane, too, for that matter.

"*Bah!* He'll be an earl, he'll get the country estate, which he can have with my blessing. Unfortunately, he'll also get this house if he wants it."

Jane glanced at where her mother usually sat. *Where did her mother plan on living in her dotage?*

"In fact, I've been thinking about this more and more," her father interrupted her musings. "I believe we should discover if Bernard has any interest in marrying you."

She choked, coughed, and sent tea spraying across the tablecloth.

"Jane!" her father reprimanded.

"Pardon me. I was simply unprepared for that announcement. Moreover, I reject it entirely."

At that moment, her mother entered the dining room, bristled visibly at the sight of the earl, and then took her seat, which happened to be farthest from him.

"What are you rejecting, Jane dear?"

"Father's notion that I marry cousin Bernard. We have nothing in common, and he has never shown the slightest interest in me."

"Your cousin might be interested," her mother said, sounding thoughtful, and Jane feared marrying Bernard was going to become the new daily battle. Then her mother added, "However, I reject the idea as strongly as Jane."

The countess stared at her husband.

"Why?" he asked, his tone neutral.

"Bernard seems dull, far below our daughter in intelligence. That will make him resent her. Moreover, when he was younger and we visited your brother, I witnessed

Bernard being cruel upon more than one occasion, to a horse and to their dogs. I don't want him having dominion over our Jane."

"That's absurd. Boys will be boys and play roughly."

"It was spite not roughness. He was mean-spirited, and he was a few years out of childhood." Her mother helped herself to tea.

They argued a little longer while Jane quietly ate. She didn't particularly care about the outcome as she would not marry Bernard Lowther no matter which of her parents prevailed, although she greatly appreciated her mother's support.

Lady Emily Chatley had always been indulgent when it came to her only daughter, and Jane had assumed her father had no interest one way or the other. That he suddenly had not only an interest but a keen position was unsettling. Ultimately, if he gave his consent to a proposal of marriage from Bernard, then neither Jane nor her mother's opinion in the matter would be considered relevant or even important.

If told she had to marry Bernard and thereafter turn her body, mind, dowry, and her life into his hands, she would resist. It was enough of a leap into the fearful void to become the property of a man one admired and to lose all protection under the law, basically all existence as a separate entity. To do so with someone one had no interest in, a man who might be cruel or daft, was downright terrifying, especially since Jane could be assured her cousin would marry her only so none of the Chatley money left the estate by way of her sizable dowry.

Her alternative as she saw it, on this sunny morning, as she finished her eggs and sausage, was simply to flee. Jane would take the generous allowance she'd saved and go wherever it pleased her to go. Perhaps to the Continent, perhaps simply to the countryside.

Or perhaps she would receive an offer from someone more powerful and wealthier than her cousin, and thus a more desirable match in the eyes of her father.

Thus, she let them debate, and she finished a second cup of tea before excusing herself. She was busy putting the finishing touches on a letter to Angela Burdett-Coutts, asking if she could assist with that great lady's philanthropic endeavor, along with Mr. Charles Dickens, at Urania Cottage. Despite their home for fallen ladies being all the way out in Shepherd's Bush, Jane hoped perhaps there was something she could do.

Alternately, Mrs. Burdett-Coutts was also active in the Royal Society for Prevention of Cruelty to Animals. If Jane couldn't help the women who'd turned to a life of prostitution, perhaps she could help raise the awareness of animal cruelty, particularly in the cities.

She only hoped Mrs. Burdett-Coutts didn't dismiss her outright. Whether helping orphans, women, or animals, Jane considered anything better than sitting idle with nothing but her own self-centered situation to ponder. Even her mother had a gardening club to which she dutifully went if only to sip sherry and discuss the best ways to hire a capable gardener.

Pushing all thoughts of Bernard Lowther out of her head, she returned to her writing desk in the library. The only other distraction, of course, was Christopher Westing and his glorious kisses, and when she might see him again.

TWO NIGHTS LATER, FOR the first time in . . . well, ever . . . Christopher went to a dinner party and its subsequent dance with the express hope of seeing a certain lady. He supposed he could have sent a missive asking Jane whether she would be there, but he had a feeling she would. After all, it was a party for singles of the highest echelon.

Without doubt, they both would be expected to attend.

Even better, there would be no Lady *Emily* Chatley, since this party was chaperoned not by mothers or guardians but by professionals, and without a whiff of scandal ever having occurred.

If Jane didn't turn up, he had a long-standing arrangement to meet Burnley at White's club on a Thursday night, where they would play cards and eat a fine meal. Their political persuasion was neither asked nor assumed, even though everyone knew his father was a member of the Reform Club and White's was more conservative.

In any case, Christopher had assumed correctly. Jane was at the Mulberry corner townhouse that night. When he entered, he immediately hunted for her, spying her graceful form across the room, clad in verdant green satin.

Pausing to watch her speaking with others, probably on some matter good for society at large, he was eager for the opportunity to have another long discussion with her, and then to dance with her. Mostly, he needed to determine if he had truly felt something unique during their previous encounters, something which had his pulse pounding at the sight of her.

God, he hoped so.

Before approaching her, he went to their hosts, both of whom were well-known to his family. Lady Mulberry was only too pleased to comply with the young lord's wishes, and, as if by magic, he was assured he would be partnered with Jane for the meal, which occurred before the dancing.

It was sometimes very useful to be a marquess.

As he advanced upon her, he overheard Jane mentioning the plight of overworked horses, while being barely heeded by another young woman and man. It didn't seem to bother her at all to be a third in a group. He liked that confidence about her, along with her clear, direct voice, which didn't pretend to silly, girlish breathiness.

He preferred the genuine breathlessness he'd created by kissing her senseless.

When at her elbow, he said, "Frankly, Lady Jane, I'm shocked you're here."

CHAPTER FIVE

Silence befell the small group, but Jane turned to Christopher, looking entirely nonplussed.

"Frankly, I surprise myself sometimes," she confessed.

As if they already shared a private joke, they laughed together, and the other two wandered off.

Good. He was already entranced by the shape of her perfect pink lips and wanted to have her all to himself.

"On the terrace at our first meeting, you said you would be pleased never to attend a social event again, but then at our second encounter, you danced with every willing gentleman, including me. And now I find you at another social event, perhaps once more forced by your formidable mother?"

Jane shrugged slightly, telling him nothing, as was her right. He hoped she had come out again on his account, wishing to spend more time with him.

"On second thought," he teased, "I believe I know the right of it. You came tonight because this is an event *without* your mother in attendance."

She blushed.

"*Ah-ha,* I am right," he crowed.

"Perhaps." Her blue eyes sparkled. "And what about you? Are you here to meet with your friends or to chaperone your sister?"

"Neither." Since the feeling of liking her had not diminished one whit, he decided to be honest from the start. "I am here to see you."

Her mouth formed a perfect O for a moment, and then she recovered.

"To what end, Lord Westing?"

What could she mean by asking him that? Did she want him to tell her immediately he liked her?

"I beg your pardon?"

"I'm sorry. That was unforgivably rude of me," she confessed, her hand fluttering up to her throat, drawing his attention to her elegant neck and shoulders where a few soft tendrils of pale brown hair rested.

"I only hope by 'seeing' me, my lord, you don't mean anything other than dining and dancing. I wouldn't want to place you in that category of men who buzz around a female for nefarious purposes."

He had said he liked her directness, and apparently, she was going to give it to him. He could give it back to her.

"I enjoyed *talking* with you the other night, as well as dancing, and thus, I hoped to repeat both those pleasures, with the additional one of dining with you, as we have never done that before. In fact, when we danced the other evening, I don't believe we'd done so at all this Season."

She looked at him a long while, the smallest of frowns furrowing the space between her lovely eyes. He couldn't discern her thoughts but believed she was taking his measure. He hoped she found him up to snuff.

"You are correct," she said finally. "The last time we danced was the previous Season, at the end of May. I was quite finished with having Lord Pomley tread upon my toes and went seeking a glass of lemonade. You were at the refreshments table, speaking with your friends. You asked how I was, and then, out of sheer politeness, I suppose, you asked if my next dance was free. It was a quadrille."

She had rendered him speechless.

Why hadn't he felt this spark at that time? What a lot of wasted opportunity. It seemed he'd never truly given her his entire attention before.

"I suppose you recall precisely what I was wearing and what music was played," he teased.

Her serious expression vanished, and she laughed, appearing entirely delighted by having impressed him.

"I know your waistcoat was a rich blue because it happened to be a similar shade to the dress I was wearing, only darker. Also, we danced six parts that night instead of five because the hostess chose the Viennese quadrille, and so, *La Trénis* was added before *La Pastourelle*. It certainly made for an amusing dance since a few couples were unfamiliar with the extra figure."

Christopher shook his head. "You have a remarkable memory."

She cocked her chin to one side, which he found a charming motion. "Some things make an impression on me, I suppose."

And then they were called in to the meal.

"I must find Lord Welkes. I believe he is my dinner companion tonight."

"No, I don't think so." He held out his arm for her so he could escort her into the dining room.

A moment later, they watched Lord Welkes frowning as their hostess, Lady Mulberry, introduced him to another young lady.

"Why do I think this is not happenstance you and I are seated together?" Jane asked, looking not the least bit displeased when Christopher pulled her chair out for her.

"I told you, I came to see you and to dine with you. I certainly didn't intend to merely look at you from across the table."

JANE WAS PRACTICALLY VIBRATING with delight. *He* had sought *her* out. *Her!*

Lord Christopher Westing had arranged to sit with her at dinner, which meant he would also be her partner for the majority of the dances. What's more, she was certain her mother had nothing to do with it. Lord Westing simply liked her.

How glorious! She felt positively giddy. He was the only man whose attention she gave a fig about, and at long last, he was paying it to her. And she hadn't changed a thing about herself. Nor had he seemed to change from the man she knew over the past few years.

To her way of thinking, the only alteration was he had finally noticed her, precisely when she wasn't even trying to be noticed.

As soon as they were seated and their wine was poured, the first course was served, predictably mussels. She'd been to enough of these, she could almost tell by look on the servers' faces what each of the five courses would be.

Tonight, the food tasted better. Even the mock-turtle soup wasn't as revolting as she usually found it. However, if she never had it again, it would be too soon. Through each plate or bowl, she and Christopher conversed.

By the time the fish and fowl courses had been cleared and they were enjoying egg custard tarts and chocolate-smothered berries, she felt as if they were becoming fast friends, the way she had with Lord Cambrey while organizing their banquet.

The difference in that case was she hadn't felt the least bit romantic toward the Earl of Cambrey. However, the man seated beside her caused all sorts of interesting sensations in her mind and body.

"And do you *want* to take your father's position in Parliament?" Jane asked, after he said it was his destiny to sit in the House of Lords.

"Strange question," he said, "like asking the queen's eldest if he wants to be king?"

She grinned, but he didn't seem to be boasting, merely stating a fact of heredity in his position as a member of their government.

"It's not quite the same thing, is it?" she asked, hoping not to offend but knowing sometimes sons didn't have the same calling as their fathers.

"I believe it is my duty as much as any military officer does his duty to his country. To that end, I went to Eton and Trinity College, I go to political clubs and read the papers, and I attend Parliament weekly to hear the proceedings."

"Not only to listen," she said. "I'm aware you have spoken out for reform and have written some very thoughtful articles for the papers about the best way to help the poor."

"Thank you." He looked pleased and even slightly embarrassed. "I believe we are both people of action. I'm interested in charitable work and was very impressed with what you accomplished for the orphans with your fundraising efforts at Lord's Cricket Ground."

She felt her cheeks warm at his words. "I did what I could and would be happy to do more. It seems impossible to live in London and not see the suffering on the very doorstep of our most affluent. One certainly need not go to Ireland to see those who starve."

He set down his wine glass. "I hope it doesn't seem glib or insincere to discuss the poor while we eat. Yet inside many a dining room and drawing room, the actual deals are made, usually in the Whig houses, if I may say, to help those less fortunate."

"I understand. Without the support of the wealthiest donors who enjoyed the cricket match and the banquet, we wouldn't now have two new orphanages."

She was rewarded with Christopher bestowing a handsome smile upon her, and it made her toes curl inside her satin slippers. Staring at his mouth as he spoke, she had trouble entirely focusing on what he was saying.

Suddenly, despite her interest in charitable work, all she could think of were his kisses.

"I wholeheartedly support our diminutive prime minister," he agreed, referring to the man's stature, "and what he has done for the working class. Lord Russell demonstrates to one and all that intellect and the ability to get things done do not depend upon brute strength, but only a strong will and a supple mind. Having said that, I don't think his Factory Act went far enough."

"Agreed," Jane said, at once, which engendered another smile from him.

He nodded. "Moreover, my political interest gives my father and I something to discuss and, sometimes, to argue over."

"Do you get on well with the duke?"

"Another strange question," Christopher said.

Jane sipped her wine slowly—the only glass she would have so as not to lose her good sense—and thought of how very little she respected her own father.

"You wouldn't think it so if you knew the Earl of Chatley."

Then, by Christopher's oddly uncomfortable expression, she could tell he did.

"*Ah,*" she said.

He shrugged. "I'm sorry. I mean no impertinence. I don't know your father personally, only *of* him. Quite famous."

"Infamous, you mean."

"Just so," he agreed.

"Whereas your father is considered perhaps a little eccentric, but very stable and reliable. A good man." Jane had met the Duke of Westing on occasion, although exchanging little more than a low curtsey from her and a polite nod from him.

"Yes, my father is all of that and more. Still, he drives my mother to distraction."

Jane considered her own parents. "Better than ignoring her altogether."

"Truly. No woman should be ignored or treated badly, especially by the man who has taken a vow to stand beside her throughout their lives."

Goodness! What a wonderful concept. Christopher was even more forward-thinking than she'd given him credit for. If only English law—and the very Parliament he loved—would see it the same way.

"My mother will soon be impossible to ignore in any case," he continued, "as she is organizing a showing of her art."

"I had no idea Her Grace was an artist," Jane said.

He nodded enthusiastically. "It is not widely known outside of her own circle of friends. I am biased, naturally, but I think her watercolors are sublime. She's a member of the New Society of Painters in Water Colors, and as I said, soon, she'll have her first exhibit."

"How wonderful!" Jane said, and meant it.

Not long after, they were dancing, a quadrille as it turned out. And then, as if a marquess magically could arrange things others couldn't—and perhaps he could—she found herself alone with Christopher in the Mulberry's second-floor library, down the hall from the great room.

Standing in the center of the thick rug inside the darkened room with floor-to-ceiling shelves, Jane wrapped her arms around herself and waited while Christopher lit a lamp.

"I've never done anything I'm not supposed to," she said.

When he turned back, locking his gaze with hers and obviously recalling how she'd said the same thing in the server's room, he started to laugh.

"Then it's about time, don't you think?" he repeated his words from that night, before brushing his thumb across her lips. "I think what you meant to say is you've never done anything you're not supposed to with anyone *except* me."

Jane nodded, and he took her in his arms. As her body began to hum with anticipation, she felt quite serious.

"Yes," she agreed, looking up at him. "Precisely." *Not with anyone but him.*

Dropping his mouth to hers, Christopher claimed her lips without delay, as if he'd been waiting all night. She certainly had been. Everything up to this moment had been a bother, keeping her from experiencing this stirring elation.

At once, her body's gentle humming turned to a roar of flames, as his mouth set her senses on fire.

Low between her hips, she grew molten and didn't flinch as his hands began to roam her body. The only irritation were her gloves. Jane wished she had left them on her lap at dinner and let them fall on the floor when she stood. Then she could truly touch him.

Christopher, though, was gloveless, and she could almost feel the warmth of his hands through her satin gown and silk corset, skimming down her back, pulling her against him.

His kiss deepened; her lips parted to admit his searching tongue. She sucked gently at it, hearing him groan into her mouth. Then his right hand brushed her waist and before moving steadily up toward her . . .

She gasped as he cupped her breast, despite being barely able to feel his palm against the underswell encased by her corset. However, when his thumb smoothed over the sensitive skin of her exposed upper curve, her nipple tightened. It was a heady sensation. Moreover, it seemed to be directly linked to the apex of her thighs.

For the first time, instead of thinking of her clothing as feminine and attractive, she felt sheathed in medieval armor. Shocking herself, Jane wanted her layers to drop away so she could better feel his fingers on her skin.

If only she could stand before him unclad and let him touch all of her. She grew damp at the idea. Surely, she would combust.

Ignoring her growing frustration, she focused on another exciting kiss. He must have experienced the same sense of yearning, for his mouth left hers to trail along her jaw and down her exposed neck, his teeth eventually nipping at her throat and collarbone.

Grasping his jacket with her hands to steady herself, Jane leaned back as his wicked lips kissed a path farther down her bare skin until he was blowing warm breath upon the valley between her breasts. Both her nipples were now firmly peaked, and it was bliss when he touched the tip of his tongue to her skin again.

In silence, with heavy breathing and heated bodies, they continued as best they could. He managed to slide his fingers down the front of her gown, and when he touched her nipple for the first time, she gasped and bit her lip. The ache between her legs intensified unbearably.

His other hand curved under her bottom, to squeeze one of her soft cheeks and pull her against the hard swell she could feel in the front of his pants.

Gracious! She wished he could ease the throbbing low in her body, knowing he could—although obviously not here, not now.

For a moment, he held her to him, their lower bodies pressed tightly, his fingers still down her dress, softly stroking her bosom. When she dared to glance at his face, his eyes were closed, his jaw clenched.

Then his eyes snapped open, and he focused on her face.

"This is madness," he said, startling her and withdrawing his hand from her gown. "I vow I never meant to take such liberties when I brought you in here. I only wanted to kiss you again."

"Kiss me again," she repeated his words as an order.

"Gladly," he said and complied. Taking her face in his hands, he lowered his lips to hers and ravished her mouth with a firm, plundering tongue.

When he pulled away, he tugged at her lower lip with his teeth, as he had once before, and her most private area tingled with appreciation.

And then Christopher drew back.

"We had best return to the dancing. Even a marquess's influence can only gain so much private time."

Her cheeks heated at his words. *What must their hosts think of her?*

Oh dear! She raised her hands to her flaming face, glad of the dim light, for certainly, she must be berry red.

"Please, don't worry," he said. "I told Lady Mulberry you are special to me."

She froze. *Special?*

"Besides," he added, "our mothers are acquaintances who sometimes take tea together."

"And that signifies what?" Jane asked, hurrying toward the door, feeling the urgent need to run along the hallway into the small ballroom where everyone could see her. Alone.

This trespass against decorum was far worse than the one at the previous ball. Everyone who'd taken notice tonight would know she and Christopher had fled the party together.

What had she been thinking? She had *not* been thinking. Not at all, too befuddled by sensations of desire for this handsome man beside her.

His humorous tone reached her, "Perhaps our parents have been at each other's homes so much, we were raised as siblings."

"That's ridiculous!" she said.

"Jane." Her name on his tongue sent a thrill racing through her, and she halted at the door. "In truth, don't worry," he said. "We've only been away a few minutes, and Lord and Lady Mulberry were about to have the servants carry in a champagne-filled glass tower, something she said she'd seen on the Continent. Everyone's eyes and attention will have been on that spectacle."

She breathed a sigh of relief.

Then Christopher's hand touched her chin. "May I ask you something?"

Her stomach fluttered, and it didn't have anything to do with the horrid mock-turtle soup.

"Of course."

"I would very much like to call upon you at your home. Would you be amenable to that?"

Happiness spread through her again like warm treacle. *Was this really happening?*

"Yes," Jane said. "I would be pleased to receive you."

CHAPTER SIX

With his mother and younger sister living at his aunt's townhouse, and his father dining at the Reform Club, Christopher had the house to himself. No meals were being prepared, however, and who knew what the cook was doing with his time.

Would anyone notice if he went downstairs to examine the progress? He was rather hoping once again, sometime sooner rather than later, meat pies and sponge cakes, roast beef and puddings were going to be coming out of the Westing kitchen.

He could hear plenty of racket from below stairs, and so, he let his curiosity take him to the scene of the renovations.

Making his way past the butler's and housekeeper's rooms, the laundry, store room, and housemaid's closet, and a sleeping room for two male servants, he ended up in the back section of the house, past the lift for sending food upstairs. There, the still and beer room, scullery, pantry, larder, cleaning room, and kitchen were usually set up and functioning perfectly. He whistled when he saw the state of the disarray. His mother would be livid. The kitchen floor was still torn up, and two of the counters, both top and shelving, were missing. The copper pans and jelly molds hanging along one wall were covered in dust. Even the bells next to the larder, one for each of the upstairs rooms, were covered in filth.

The mess looked as if it were still weeks from being finished.

"Good day, Lord Westing. Have you come to assess our work?"

It was Mr. Elms, the builder, who'd been peering over the back of the gleaming new appliance which had caused all this mayhem. Standing, the man gave a short bow of his head.

"Good day, Mr. Elms. I'm not assessing so much as I am looking for a biscuit, hopefully in the pantry, if we still have one."

The man laughed. "I've no knowledge of the whereabouts of biscuits, my lord."

"And all the kitchen staff have vanished," Christopher pointed out, with only a mason doing something to the outer wall next to the stove and another man measuring a hole in the floor.

"I believe your father sent them somewhere to be out of our way." He smiled. "In order for us to work faster."

"And are you?"

The man laughed heartily again, a generally jolly fellow, it seemed.

"One can't work too quickly with gas, my lord. However, I am ready to give the stove a try."

"But the—" Christopher began, eyeing the gaping hole and general mess.

"Just going to make sure it's working correctly before we get everything put back together, sir. We'd only have to tear it all up again."

"I see. Well, I'll leave you to it." Christopher returned the way he'd come, even as the man pulled out a matchbox.

"Don't you wish to see the beautiful blue flames?" Mr. Elms inquired.

Looking back, Christopher shook his head. "While I have a curiosity for many things in this world, watching a stove turn on isn't one of them."

He had taken only a few steps along the passage, not yet even passing the door to the housemaids' sitting area, when he both heard and felt the explosion at the same time. The blast sent him flying along with pieces of debris at his back until he ended up in a heap on the floor. Then, he heard a groaning sound above.

With time only to throw his hands over his head, the ceiling collapsed along with, he feared, the entire four stories above him. And then he knew nothing more.

JANE FELT LIKE LIGHTNESS itself, as if she could float, perhaps the way a butterfly flitted between spring blooms. Sheer and utter joy.

For at least three years, she'd noticed Lord Christopher Westing, noticed him and found him to be desirable, thought him exceedingly handsome, and believed him to be entirely out of her reach, for he'd never shown her an ounce of attention.

And then, everything changed. In a single evening, she went from lonely Jane, melancholy Jane, even resigned Jane to happy, hopeful Jane.

What's more, very soon, Christopher would be on her doorstep. Her pushy, albeit well-meaning, beloved mother and her mercenary, self-centered father would find out she was considered worthwhile by a man outside of her family. Jane was going to have the life she previously hadn't even dared to dream about, without her mother needing to trick some young man, and without her father's money, which her marquess didn't need.

She hadn't told her mother any details of her spectacular evening at the Mulberry's—not about the long discussion over dinner that made her feel as if she were speaking to an old friend and a kindred spirit, nor about the dancing, which allowed her to be held in Christopher's arms for hours, feeling both comfortable and entirely on the edge of excitement at the same time. And she certainly hadn't mentioned anything that had come later.

She had no idea how long they'd stayed in the library, secluded, exploring each other's mouths while their hands roamed each other's bodies, but for the first time in her life, she'd caused a raised eyebrow.

She'd seen a few glances when they'd returned to the party, despite the ingenious tower of glasses filled with champagne.

Their absence had been noticed and marked, and even caused a few whispers.

How thrilling! It would have been entirely terrifying if it weren't Christopher with whom she'd been alone and who'd practically made a declaration.

Christopher, who'd deliciously used her given name.

He had said he intended to call on her. So, while her reputation might be slightly tarnished, thankfully as yet unknown to her mother, word might reach her at any moment from some other dinner guest or even from Lady Mulberry, herself. By that time, she hoped Christopher would already be considered her exclusive suitor.

For she truly didn't care if other men now considered her sullied. She didn't care if another man ever spoke to her again.

"Jane, you are whistling," her mother said, startling her.

"Am I?" She had been staring out at the street, rather hoping one of the Westing carriages would appear.

"You know I think it a crass thing for a young lady."

"I didn't realize I was doing it, Mummy."

"You sounded happy," her mother pointed out the anomaly.

Jane nearly laughed.

"But also like a stage performer." This time, the countess shuddered. "Why are you standing here, looking out the window?" Her mother's tone was both sour and unhappy, and instantly, Jane felt sorry for her.

She could only imagine how awful it would be if her mother had felt about the Earl of Chatley the way Jane did about Christopher Westing, and then he—

"Shall we do something together, Mummy? Perhaps go shopping? We could stroll along Bond Street if you like."

Her mother frowned. "Is there something you need? Did you lose another pair of gloves?"

"No. I merely thought you might like to spend time together while *not* at a ball."

Lady Emily Chatley narrowed her eyes at her daughter, who'd never suggested anything of the sort before.

Finally, she nodded. "I would, indeed. And there is a tea room we could go to, if you like."

Jane smiled. "I would."

"And you won't whistle anymore?"

"Not when you can hear me. I promise."

"Very well." Her mother's sour expression vanished. "I'll go change into something suitable."

While Jane had hoped Christopher would be there that morning, or at least his calling card would, it was already past noon, and she decided she needn't wait indoors for him. He was a man of his word, she felt that in her gut.

He would come. Soon.

CHRISTOPHER OPENED HIS EYES. Nothing. *What the hell?* What room was he in that not a crack of light was entering?

He yawned and stretched, knowing he was on a soft comfortable bed. Yet the bed seemed unfamiliar. The mattress was not his mattress, nor was the pillow. He was certain.

Fumbling to the side, feeling for a lamp, his fingers touched both an unfamiliar table and then a strange lamp. *Had they gone to their country home in Surrey?*

Strange, he didn't recall going to bed in the country. He was certain he had last been in London.

Paying close attention to what he could hear, expecting the nighttime sounds of bugs, he heard instead carriage wheels and horses' hooves on cobblestones.

Hm. It certainly sounded like London.

A frisson of trepidation shot down his spine. Something wasn't right beyond the fact his head ached and he didn't remember drinking too much the night before. In fact, he couldn't remember the night before at all, now that he tried.

If he were at their country home, it would explain the utter obsidian blackness. However, he should hear wheels and hooves on gravel, or naught at all except the occasional owl if it were the middle of the night.

Besides, the air had the distinct scent of London—coal fires. The moon must be behind thick clouds, but why were there no gas lamps to light the street outside? Usually they were lit until dawn.

Sitting up, after further exploration, he found a box of matches at the lamp's base. *Wonderful!* He would light it and solve whatever mystery was afoot.

Striking the match as he'd done hundreds of times before—nothing.

A scream gurgled up in his throat, but he quelled it. Perhaps he was dreaming.

He shook his hand with a quick flit of his wrist to put out the match if it had, indeed, been lit. Then, by feel, he lit another one and held it steady.

Was it lit?

He moved his other hand toward it and—*ow!*—burned himself.

There was a match directly in front of his face yet he couldn't see it. For the life of him, he couldn't figure out why.

Again, he shook the match out, testing to make sure it was no longer alight. Then he blinked, touching his face with his hands to make sure he, indeed, still had eyes and they were open. Then he laughed slightly at his own fantastical notions, even though it made his head ache a little to do so.

This must be a dream, for none of it made sense. And then he heard a terrible sound.

It took him a few long moments to realize he was making it—he'd given in to the dread of the inexplicable utter blackness and begun to scream.

He yelled until he heard footsteps, until the door slammed open on its hinges, and he saw . . . nothing!

"Who is there?" His voice sounded ragged with terror.

"What do you mean? Chris, it's me."

"Mother?" *Thank God!* "It's dark as pitch in here. Why is it so dark?"

She gasped. Then in a shaky tone explained, "It's half past noon, my love."

And thus, full daylight. He swallowed. "Where are we?"

"I'm here, too, laddo," came his father's voice.

"Where are we?" Christopher asked again, hoping that snippet of knowledge would make all of this become crystal clear, both in his brain and before his eyes.

"We're at Aunt Tabitha's," his mother answered, her voice hesitant and tremulous.

He remembered at that moment how his mother and Amanda had gone to stay with his father's sister and her husband because of the kitchen renovations.

Something about the kitchen was important, but he didn't know what exactly.

"We are at Lord and Lady Forester's home?" he asked.

"Yes," his mother said.

"I can't see anything," he admitted, feeling as if it was a personal failing. He must simply not be trying hard enough because he'd never had to try before to see. "It is light in here, you say, correct?"

"Yes," his father said from directly beside the bed, and he could hear his mother crying softly.

"Why can't I see?" He might as well ask.

"I don't know." The duke hesitated, but Christopher knew he was going to say more. "We didn't know you couldn't see until this moment. The explosion knocked you out, debris smacked your head, but—"

"What explosion?"

His mother cried more audibly now, and he felt responsible, even guilty for upsetting her.

"Send for the doctor at once," he heard his father order someone, probably their butler, and then footsteps hurried away.

Christopher started to get up, trying to swing his legs out of bed, and immediately got tangled in the bedclothing, dragging it with him.

"Stay in bed," his mother said, and then he felt his father's hands on him.

Christopher let the duke help him back into bed and remove the matchbox still clutched in his hands. Then he felt his father sit on the edge of the bed.

"I'm sorry," his father said. "This is all my fault."

The statement stunned him. As far as he knew, his kind, indulgent, and loving father had never done anything to harm him.

"There was a gas leak according to the inspector. When the stove was lit, the entire kitchen was consumed."

"Dear God!" Christopher had a memory of going down there, of speaking with . . . "Mr. Elms?"

"Dead," his father told him. "And two workmen, as well. Thankfully, all our staff had been vacated."

"I remember," Christopher said, recalling a conversation with the builder. "In order for the work to progress more quickly."

"Exactly. What on earth were you doing down there?"

Was that a hint of irritation in the duke's voice?

"I don't know. I went down to take a look." If he had stayed above stairs where he belonged, he wouldn't be in this bed and, apparently, blind.

He touched his face. "Am I disfigured? Was I burned?"

"No," his mother insisted. "Except for some bruising and a cut to your forehead, you appeared unharmed. Except you wouldn't wake up."

"I am rather thirsty and hungry," he confessed, now that he could think of something besides not seeing. It seemed he was going to have plenty of time to consider that grim fact. He simply couldn't focus on it at the moment.

"What do you want?" his mother asked. "Anything you like, you can have. The cook here is very good. Tea or coffee, or maybe something stronger? Although it is early in the day, still, no one would mind if you want wine. Or brandy even or—"

"Helen," his father cut her off gently. "Let him speak."

What did he want besides the obvious? Jane came to mind. *Where was she at that moment? Did she know about the explosion?*

He could hardly ask his parents to send a message to a woman he'd never even mentioned to them before, although they certainly knew her and her family. His mother and her mother occasionally took tea together.

"I would like tea," he began. "And water, too. And I think I will start with breakfast. Eggs, toast, sausages, bacon, some porridge. Whatever can be brought immediately would be best, as I feel sick, I think from hunger. And the water, bring it up first, please."

With those words, he heard more scrambling feet and realized there must have been a maid or two in the room. He would have to start asking his parents who was present.

That thought was followed quickly by another one: *Was this blindness permanent?*

In less than five minutes, he had water and toast in hand with his mother helping him. None of them spoke while he munched the buttered squares and drank the entire glass.

And then the rest of his food was brought in. His father set a pillow on his son's lap and then a tray was set onto that.

Immediately, Christopher reached out and knocked something over. Luckily, it turned out to be an empty tea cup, with the pot of tea safely on the side table.

"Take it slowly," his father said. "You'd better let us help."

"Just give me the porridge bowl in one hand and the spoon in my other. I will not be fed like a baby, and that's final."

However, at first, it proved to be more difficult than he'd anticipated, and he kept missing his mouth, spreading porridge on both of his cheeks. Twice his mother wiped his face, and then he had the hang of it.

But he had to concentrate, so talking was out of the question. However, the silence was deafening. He knew they were staring at him, and he didn't like the notion one bit.

"Tell me what happened *after* the explosion. And how is the house? Please keep talking, and I'll eat."

He listened to his father recount how two days earlier, the basement of their home at Grosvenor Square was destroyed and how the ceiling above had caved in, taking down their morning room, serving area, and some of the library. Christopher had been lucky. He'd been pushed by the blast to the front of the basement, between the butler's and the housekeeper's bedrooms. Moreover, the small fire that had started had gone out quickly, because the gas line had severed, and instead of feeding the fire, the gas began to dissipate into the street.

After the initial explosion, passers-by had almost immediately rescued Christopher and, because his father had insurance, the fire had been quickly contained by the London Fire Engine Establishment. Their house had been saved, yet it was, at that moment, deemed uninhabitable.

His father seemed to think it an opportunity to modernize further, whereas the Duchess of Westing could only look to the past, interjecting about the foolishness of gas every few moments.

Christopher tended to agree with her.

Then a knock at the door heralded a new visitor, who turned out to be their esteemed family physician.

CHAPTER SEVEN

Three days later, Jane was starting to feel a little ill. She was anchorless, had lost all joy to her step, and was unable to focus on the simplest of tasks. In a word, she was *doubtful.* It was a terribly distracting emotion she'd not ever experienced before.

Could she have misread the situation entirely?

Was Christopher Westing a cad?

Both of those notions seemed ridiculous. *So, where was he?*

During their parting at the Mulberry's at one in the morning, he'd practically promised he would see her the next day.

It had been nearly four days. Another ball was looming, and she'd hoped never to attend another, at least not as an unattached female.

Without Christopher coming to speak to her father and mother about courting her, without some tangible sign of interest, she could not gainsay her mother about attending the upcoming ball. It was vexing—and frightening. After all, she had put herself in a terribly compromising position with the marquess, and news of it could still become public.

She could only hope he would be at the ball and she would be brave enough to ask him his true intentions. All her future happiness now depended on the next words from his mouth. His wonderful warm and firm mouth.

Where was he?

Then, as if answering her prayers, their butler, Mr. Barnes, came into the drawing room to say she had a visitor.

Jumping to her feet, Jane nearly tripped in excitement, her heartbeat already drumming out a fast tattoo. Not waiting for him to reach her, she met the butler in the center of the room and took the calling card off the silver tray.

Jane's smile died. Lord Richard Fowler. *Who on earth was Lord Fowler?*

Still hoping this had something to do with Christopher, she told Mr. Barnes to show him in, and, of course, to send in one of the housemaids since her mother was not at home.

When she saw the man, she recognized him as a partner from the Linwalds' ball. There had been no cards and, thus, no names. He may have told it to her when he led her to the parquet dancefloor, but she'd been so focused on Christopher, she hadn't caught the names of other dance partners.

In any case, she and Lord Fowler had never had a conversation. Tall, sandy blond hair, green eyes, he dressed well. *What could he possibly be doing in her home?*

Letting him bow before she curtsied, Jane was relieved to see the door open again and one of the maids hurry in, promptly taking a seat at the far end of the room on a chair by the potted fern.

At that point, Jane sat on the sofa and gestured for him to take a seat opposite with the safety of a low table between them.

"To what do I owe this pleasure, my lord?"

"A courtesy call, my lady. I will get to the point. I am soon to take a wife."

Jane nodded. "My sincere congratulations. Would you like some tea?"

"No, thank you. I won't take up your time. I wish only to discuss my future marriage."

"Do I know your fiancée?"

He smiled. "I'm sorry, you misunderstand me. I am still in the seeking stage. What I should say is I desire to take a wife soon. I am of the age when I feel it is time. My parents wish it. My sister looks forward to welcoming someone into our family. And, of course, it is time to produce an heir."

"I see." *Did she? What was he rambling on about? Did he know Christopher? Could she simply ask him outright without seeming too forward?*

Before she could decide how to bring Lord Westing into their conversation, the viscount continued, "I am wondering if you would allow me to include you as someone who might be interested in becoming my wife."

She nearly said, *yes, of course*, before her brain caught up with his words. *Become his wife?*

"I'm sorry, Lord Fowler, if I seem slow, but I was not expecting any such offer from you, especially since we do not know each other at all. Are you asking for my hand?"

He shook his head. "No. That is, perhaps. Not yet, of course. I simply wish to know if you are willing to be courted, if you are desirous of becoming a wife—my wife—before I waste time."

She rolled her eyes, and gave him what she hoped was advice he would take to heart.

"Never, ever tell a woman she may be a waste of time."

He flushed. "Of course, my sincere apology. Let me start again. I am asking if you are at all interested so I may include you."

"Include me where?" This strange conversation was actually becoming interesting.

"On my list of potential wives."

Jane couldn't help laughing. There was no way to hide it behind her gloved hand as a cough, so she simply laughed while the man's eyebrows shot upward.

"I am not certain I understand what is amusing you," the viscount said, "but I sincerely hope I didn't offend you."

Poor man! He would never get a spouse with such a terrible way of speaking to women. *Included on a list, indeed!* She chuckled again.

"May I ask how many others are included on your list?"

He frowned. "Actually, none."

"Am I the first to whom you've offered this . . . honor?"

His cheeks flushed slightly. "Why, no. I have been turned down by two others."

"Are you saying there is no one on your list?"

Lord Fowler's face grew another shade ruddier. "That is true. My paper is blank."

Jane sat up straighter, leaning forward. "Dear God in Heaven! Is there an actual piece of paper? I thought you spoke metaphorically of a list in your brain. Let me see it at once."

"Well, I—"

"Come along, show it to me, or I shall not believe it exists."

The man fished in the pocket of his coat and drew out a single folded sheet. He opened it and showed it to her, but he didn't hand it over. Sure enough, it was entirely blank except for a scrawl across the top, "Potential Wives."

Oh, dear!

"If I understand your situation, you want a wife despite your heart not being engaged with any particular female, and so you are going door-to-door, as it were. Do you have criteria?"

"Lady Chatley, if your answer is no, then I shall excuse myself from your presence. As I said, I don't wish to waste time, yours nor mine."

She should simply let him leave. *After all, what was it to her if the man remained a bachelor all his life?*

However, the Fowler family had a nice house in Mayfair, and she believed he had no brothers. At least the Chatleys had Bernard to inherit her father's title, although absolutely *without her* by his side.

What a pity if the man seated before her continued on in such a foolish fashion when he was good looking, *possibly* intelligent, and would undoubtedly make some lady a decent husband.

Hm. Unfortunately, she lacked female friends. She had not yet heard back from Angela Burdett-Coutts regarding helping at Urania Cottage, but those women would all be unsuitable for a viscount. On the other hand, Jane was not short of invitations to all the best parties. Moreover, ever since the triumph of her orphanage charitable event, she had been asked to help out with more than one cause. Organizing and getting things done came naturally to her.

Why not take on Lord Fowler as another of her causes?

"I believe you are wasting your time going about this as you are, my lord. Women do not like a pragmatic approach when it comes to matters of the heart and particularly something as important and sentimental as seeking a spouse."

He stood up, looking defeated.

"Please, do sit down again," Jane implored. "I think I can help you."

"You would like to be on my list after all?" His face lit with hope.

She sighed. "I don't think you should consider for another moment you will ever manage to have a list full of names or even any, for that matter. I think you should count yourself fortunate if you find one woman who suits you and who wishes to marry you—and *vice versa*. What did you hope to accomplish with having many choices? What if you came to care for more than one? Even worse, what if more than one cared for you and you had to hurt the lady when you chose her rival?"

He sat once more on the sofa. "You are right. I thought to set down the names of some willing females and then weigh their suitability. It seems such a chore to spend time searching for a suitable mate only to have that person snatched up right when one is about to offer for her, or, after deeming someone perfectly desirable, to find out she is utterly uninterested."

Jane had a feeling both of these situations had already happened to him. Thus, he had turned to a more logical but entirely inappropriate manner of finding a wife—ask first, then discern feelings after. *No, it wouldn't do at all.*

"While I am not a matchmaker, I do know many people. Perhaps I could help you find at least one suitable choice for a wife."

He frowned. "Why would you help me?"

She considered her own situation. Having waited years for the only man who caused her heart to quicken to finally pay attention to her, she knew the feeling of hopelessness. More so now that he'd disappeared.

Indeed, if she let her mind dwell on Christopher, she would lose her cheerful disposition entirely. Lord Fowler gave her a purpose and someone to think about outside of her own confusing situation. Moreover, since she understood how important it was to find that one person in a multitude, she would happily help him look.

She was excited at the prospect of her new mission, considering it far better than moping about the house at loose ends.

"I shall help you because I can. And why not? Why shouldn't you have assistance in this important task?"

He smiled tentatively. "Are you certain you're not interested in becoming my wife? You seem precisely the sort of person to help me run my estate."

"I am not, but if you will accept my friendship, we shall suit quite well. I am going to the ball at Barclay House. Will you be there?"

He nodded.

"Then I shall see you there, and we will begin the quest for your wife. Please, until then, no more lists."

She held out her hand, and he handed over the offending paper.

"YOU'RE BEING HORRID," AMANDA said, "and I'm only trying to help."

"Well, stop trying. In fact, just leave me alone." Christopher's sister came in every few hours to sit with him, and they were boring each other to tears. The only other steady visitor over the past few days was Burnley, and he was due later in the day.

"I cannot." She shook the newspaper on her lap in frustration.

"Why?" he asked.

"Because Mummy and Daddy ordered me to keep you company."

"That's terrible," he muttered. "I'm sorry for your plight. How difficult it must be for you to have to walk into this room without any difficulty, perfectly able to see where you are going, and then sit in a chair that you can easily find on your own, and then read words you can see on a page. And then, when you're thoroughly fed up of this torment, how awful for you to stand up and walk out into the light to do whatever the hell you want with your day."

"Chris, I—"

"No, really," he continued. "I almost feel sorry for your burden of sight. So much easier to simply sit here all day in the darkness. Really, it is."

"Chris, please."

"Get out. I cannot stand the pages you read anyway. My brain is literally oozing out of my ears at the nonsense, gossip, and fashion editorials."

"I'm sorry." Amanda sounded close to tears.

Good!

"Out," he insisted. "Out!"

He heard her stand up and open the door. "Shall I come back in a few?"

"No." Then he imagined her never returning and how long tomorrow would be. "Not today."

"Very well. Maybe you should take a nap." And she left.

He reached for something to throw at the door, or at least in the direction of the door, and found only a pillow.

Take a nap! He was a twenty-six-year-old man with energy to burn. He wanted to run, play tennis, ride a horse, go for a walk, not take a damn nap.

What could he do on his own? Tossing the covers aside, wearing drawers and a shirt, he felt around the headboard. His valet had draped his housecoat there, as he recalled. His hands touched the soft thick fabric, and he took hold of it.

Standing slowly, still leaning against the bed, Christopher struggled into the cotton garment only to realize the belt was on the inside and he had it on inside-out. Remedying this, which took many long minutes as he seemed to always have trouble with the sleeves, he eventually began to sweep around the floor with his toes, searching for his slippers.

Giving up, he decided to walk barefoot. In any case, he assumed most of Lord and Lady Forester's home was carpeted. Inching forward, shuffling along toward the door, he didn't encounter anything until his big toe hit the leg of the chair his sister had vacated.

"Dammit all!" *That bloody well hurt.*

Reaching out, he guided himself around the chair, managing to brush the papers off it by accident and then crunch them under his feet. In another few steps, his hand touched the wall, and he worked his way along it until he reached the door and the latch.

His heart was pounding as he swung open the door, swearing again as it caught the edge of his small toe. He was probably bleeding. The throbbing pain only fueled his anger. It kept him moving forward, knowing he was being rash, when he could as easily have crawled back to bed. Literally, crawled.

Outside his room, all was quiet. He vaguely remembered his aunt and uncle's home, but had rarely been on the third floor with the guest bedrooms. He imagined it was similar to every other townhouse in Mayfair's fashionable neighborhood around Berkley Square. A long hallway with doors on the right, which was opposite the main staircase coming up on the left, and he recalled a window at the back end overlooking the garden.

Thus, depending on which room he had been given, there might be doors to the left and right of him and a staircase railing directly in front. He shuffled forward slowly, hands out until he hit the railing. If he'd been moving any faster, he could have plunged over it and put himself out of his misery with a broken neck. He would save that option for when he could no longer bear the damnable darkness and boredom.

Keeping his left hand on the bannister, he walked along the upstairs until he reached the curved end of the polished wooden railing. He could take a left and go down the stairs—barefoot and in his dressing gown. *What if there were visitors?*

Thinking better of it, Christopher released the railing and kept walking along the hallway, toward the back of the house. He wasn't sure how much space was on either side of him, nor if he was passing doors.

What was he hoping to accomplish? He had no destination, but it was nice to be up and moving again.

Why did he feel so weak after all that time in bed? He couldn't fathom the reason, but he felt tired already. Still, he continued, believing it might be good for his legs to keep walking.

Finally, after what seemed like far too long for a hallway, as if he'd walked through a hundred homes, his outstretched hands touched the window panes, marking the back of the house.

Now what? He pressed his face against the window and stared out. Opening and closing his eyes. After a moment, he realized he could feel warmth on his face. So, it was a sunny day. Orienting himself toward the hottest direction, he opened his eyes again—unending blackness, darker than it used to be when he could see and merely closed his eyes.

It was very quiet, too, he noted. In fact, he hadn't heard anything coming from any of the rooms, but he supposed if it was the middle of the day, as Amanda had said, then everyone was either downstairs or out. There might be maids tidying up, but other than that, he was probably alone.

Supposing it would be good for his health to walk back and forth along the hall, perhaps a few times, Christopher turned around. He decided to move to his left and feel his way along, maybe count the doors until . . . *Dammit! How would he know when he got to his room?*

Then he remembered he'd left his door ajar. Relief washed over him, and he scoffed at his own momentary panic. It wasn't as if he would wander to India if he went too far. Eventually, he would find his room.

Beginning his trek, this time he let his hands glide along the wall, feeling the seam of the wallpaper strips where they joined. It gave him more confidence than shuffling along in the middle of the hallway. When he came to the first door and moved on, he began to think this moving around while blind was rather easy. Then abruptly, he crashed into something that hit him from shins to waist, startling a yelp out of him.

Reaching out, Christopher realized he'd collided with a piece of furniture. Exploring further, he found it had a vase upon its surface, luckily still intact.

He moved around it carefully, then went back to touching the wall, only to trip over a stool, not higher than his ankle, a few steps later. Instinctively putting his hands out, there was nothing to stop him tumbling over. He crashed down to the floor with the stool still between his feet.

Lying there, both a little scared and embarrassed, he rested his cheek against the carpet, swearing softly to himself. Then he slapped the floor in anger, imagining if a maid came upon him, he would look like a child having a temper tantrum.

Unfortunately, he heard footsteps coming up the main staircase.

"Chris!" exclaimed his mother, and he heard her running toward him.

"I'm fine," he said lifting his head. "Just resting." And with that, he pushed himself to his knees.

"Resting?" She sounded afraid. "Shall I get Abner?" His valet had very little to do these days as Christopher hardly ever dressed properly.

"No." Reaching for the wall, he found it and used it to guide himself to standing. "I wonder if you can tell me how many things are in my path between where I am now and my room?"

"Of course." Then he felt her hand on his shoulder. "I am impressed you made it this far."

"So am I, frankly. But getting back is proving more difficult."

"There are three more doors until yours, but unfortunately, there is a tall chest and marble stand with a plant on it between two of the doors."

"I would be better off in the middle of the hallway, except then I couldn't count the doors."

"And you might take a tumble down the staircase if you veer to the right," the duchess pointed out. "Anyway, for now, take my hand."

He did, and they began to walk.

"Do you want to go downstairs?" she asked.

"In my dressing gown? Definitely not."

"Abner can get you dressed," she reminded him.

"To what end? What possible reason is there for me to dress and go downstairs? I mean, what will I do when I am down there?"

She hesitated. "You can sit in the parlor and then I can chat with you, and as others come and go, they can speak with you, too."

His stomach hurt with the futility of it. *That was his future? Having people talk to him as they left or entered the house?*

"I think I'll take a nap," he told his mother as they turned into his bedroom.

"Here we are," she said unnecessarily.

"Perfect," he said, banging into the chair again. "Dammit!"

"I'm sorry," his mother said, although it wasn't her fault.

"No, I am sorry I swore like that. If you could tell people to keep the furniture out of my direct path, that would be helpful. Amanda should have put that against the wall when she left."

"True. She probably didn't know you were going to leave the room."

Because he was just blind Chris who could sit in his room for hours waiting for someone to come talk to him or read to him. If this truly was his future, he wanted no part of it.

"I came to ask if you want anything?" his mother asked.

"My sight back," he muttered.

At hearing his mother sigh, he added, "No, there is nothing I want."

Sitting down on the bed, he felt as if he'd returned to a sanctuary . . . or a prison.

"All right," she said. "I'll be back shortly. I'll bring something to read to you. And I will ask Lord Forester to have the furniture moved from the hallway so you can walk along unimpeded. Remember, four doors between your room and the window."

"I'll remember." At that moment, he had no desire to ever leave the room again. Then he thought of Jane.

"Have I had any missives or calling cards?"

"None I haven't read to you. While most have heard of the accident or read about it in the papers, many don't know where to find us as yet. Such a nuisance. And it will be weeks before we can return home. I'll be back shortly."

He listened to her leave. *Should he assume Jane didn't know, or could it be she knew and was staying away?*

He realized it didn't matter in either case. She could hardly come up to his room to visit with him, nor could he imagine greeting her in this condition.

He decided to spend some time doing what he did every day, praying. He asked the Almighty constantly to please give him back his eyesight.

Perhaps his vision would return soon, and then, he would welcome Jane back into his life. Until then, he had to put everything aside that was important to him, including Jane and Parliament.

CHAPTER EIGHT

Jane was on the hunt as soon as her slippered feet touched the marbled entrance of Barclay House, a lovely venue for a ball. Flowers, musicians, candles, a throng of London society's wealthiest and loveliest—she saw and ignored all of it, entirely focused on finding one man.

"Jane, will you please slow down?" her mother asked as Jane rushed from the coat check through the length of the ballroom, into the dining area where the buffet of food was already being set out, and then out onto the veranda. He wasn't there. No one was. It was cold and drizzling rain.

Eventually, heeding her mother's pleas, Jane let her mother find them a table.

"Lord Fowler will be joining our table tonight," she told the countess, trying not to sound as melancholy as she felt.

Her mother's mouth opened, even as her eyes began to widen.

"No, Mummy, do not suddenly behave like a lunatic, please! I am helping him with a certain endeavor. That is all." She'd been sworn to secrecy and would not break his confidence for the world, and thus would say no more. "I have not the least bit of romantic interest in him."

Her mother nodded. "Who said anything about *romance?* Is he in need of a wife, and are you willing to become said wife?"

"Yes, he is, and no, I'm not. And please do not embarrass him or me. Moreover, regardless of your sour notion of romance, Mummy, a strong romantic feeling is the only thing which will induce me ever to say yes to a man who asks for my hand."

If she told her mother about Lord Fowler's infernal list, her mother would either be appalled or demand Jane put her name at the top of it.

Lady Chatley frowned, then gestured for one of the servers, procuring them each a glass of champagne, then she grabbed a spare.

"You are impossible, Jane."

Her despondent mother downed the entire glass in one go and then reached for the other one.

"Mummy!" Jane took pity on her. She ought to give her some hope. "Do you recall Lord Westing?"

Her mother never looked at the gossip rags because of her own philandering husband. It was too painful to read about the Earl of Chatley's carousing in print. Still, Jane knew only too well her mother managed to keep up with the news of every single, eligible bachelor, including whether one had recently gone on or off the marriage market.

"Of course I remember him. Terrible about—"

She broke off as Lord Fowler appeared before them.

"Dear ladies," he began, and bowed first over her mother's hand.

"Good evening, Lady Chatley." And then he turned to Jane and did the same. Then, while shooting a wary glance toward her mother, he asked, "Are you still game to help me?"

"I am. What's more, I created a list of my own." She could say no more until they were alone.

"Mummy, perhaps you should go chat with Lady Carmichael because his lordship and I are going to make the rounds."

Her mother shook her head. "Normally, you don't wish to speak with anyone at these events."

Jane offered her mother a beatific smile. "True. But with Lord Fowler, I'm more than happy to do so."

Her mother shook her head. "You are such a strange girl. I will be right over there." She pointed to an empty chair next to the esteemed Lady Carmichael. "And you will not go out onto the veranda, neither alone nor with a man."

"Yes, Mummy."

"Unless he is an earl or a marquess," her mother added. "Meaning no disrespect to you, my lord," she said to Lord Fowler, who was merely a viscount.

"None taken, my lady."

Jane's mother pursed her lips and gave her a severe glare. "Is that clear?"

"Yes, Mummy." She stood and kissed her mother's cheek, and then she let Lord Fowler lead her away.

Still hopeful of discovering Christopher, perhaps arriving late, Jane knew circulating through the crowd was the best way to do so.

"I shall introduce you to some ladies whom I think suitable," Jane told Lord Fowler as soon as they were out of her mother's hearing. "And you can tell me afterward if any are to your liking. Of course, it would help if you told me what manner of appearance pleased you."

Within minutes, Jane had drawn Lord Fowler into a conversation with two perfectly acceptable viscounts' daughters. And as they moved away, he said he preferred the brown-haired female.

She smiled to herself. That narrowed the selection down at least a little. Despite what he said, if a perfectly appropriate blond female pronounced herself willing to become Lady Fowler, Jane was positive Lord Fowler could be persuaded to widen his preference.

In fact, this didn't seem such a difficult task and was quite enjoyable. They spoke to another young lady, who seemed not the least bit bothered to have Jane in the conversation after realizing she was there only to facilitate an introduction and make it acceptable for them to speak when they couldn't do so alone.

They carried on their quest for an hour, and Lord Fowler met six or seven ladies and very much liked *all* of them. Jane rolled her eyes. Maybe he really didn't care with whom he spent his life.

Perhaps she needed to remind him of more specific husbandly duties.

"When you think about kissing any of these women, are you equally interested in all of them?"

He shrugged. "I'm sure kissing would be similar with each. They all have two lips, don't they?"

"And a tongue," she murmured, thinking of her kisses with Christopher.

"A tongue?" Lord Fowler sounded shocked, and then, in an instant, it struck her. He had never been intimate with a woman, not even a kiss.

Stopping right where they stood on the edge of the dance floor, she stared at him. He was probably two years older than she was, maybe even more. And she thought she had lived a sheltered life, even for a woman. *But he was a man!* She'd assumed they all found women to kiss and to do a whole lot more with, as well.

Perhaps she needed to encourage him to start kissing a few of these women.

This would be easier if he were like Lord Burnley, Christopher's friend, who had a reputation among the *ton* as being quite the man about town, as well as for leaving a string of broken hearts. He must have kissed some of those women in order for their hearts to become entangled.

"Do you keep company with Lord Burnley?" she asked.

"No. We went to school together, and I see him at these events, but we don't dine together, if that's what you mean. He's not my chum."

Lord Fowler said the word *chum* as if trying it out, as if having a close friend were a foreign concept, one he'd never experienced before, rather like a kiss.

Goodness gracious! She'd met someone even less social than herself.

Then his gaze went past her, to someone just over her shoulder.

"She looks nice," the viscount said.

Jane's head whipped around to see Lady Matilda Brethens, pretty to look at, not pretty to know. The opposite of *nice*. She would eat Lord Fowler for dinner and pick her teeth with his bones. Moreover, Matilda was a cousin about a hundred times removed from the queen but spoke of Victoria as if they were sisters. Lady Brethrens expected the world and, thus, seemed perpetually disappointed.

Why, she hadn't even liked the otherwise universally enjoyed food at Jane and Lord Cambrey's charity banquet!

"Oh, you don't want her, Lord Fowler. She would become your Xanthippe."

When he frowned, she added, "A nagging wife."

"No," he said, looking alarmed. "I wouldn't like such a wife in the least."

In any case, Jane was certain he needed to try kissing some of the women to whom he'd already been introduced. Certainly, that would help him understand how one experienced people differently.

"Perhaps you could enlist Lord Burnley to your aid."

"For what purpose?"

How could she put this?

"Perhaps to enjoy a gentleman's club or other amusements which young men get up to."

He was still frowning at her.

"I believe Lord Burnley devotes a good deal of time to thinking about the fairer sex, as well as spending time with them, and probably discussing them, too."

Lord Fowler's forehead smoothed. "Oh, I see what you mean. I believe you are correct in that he does have deep and wide experience in such matters, although I believe he is no closer to gaining a wife than I am. Truly, who is to say if his ways are superior?"

She sighed. At least Lord Burnley wouldn't marry simply any woman who agreed, which is what she now feared Lord Fowler would do—to his regret. She was certain having a male friend would help him to secure a wife. What's more, if they found Lord Burnley, perhaps they would also find Christopher.

"In any case, shall we seek him out?" she offered. "Perhaps you could compare your thoughts on the matter."

"Oh, Burnley isn't here. I don't think he's been to any social event since the explosion."

"The explosion?" she asked, half her brain pondering the merits of introducing Lord Fowler to an experienced widow.

"Why, yes, Burnley is not socializing at this time. Understandably so as he and Lord Westing are the closest of friends."

She jumped at the sound of Christopher's name. *Owen Burnley wasn't socializing because of his friendship with Christopher?*

"I beg your pardon, my lord. I don't know what you are talking about."

"You haven't heard?"

"Heard what?" Jane's heartbeat was beginning to race at the tone of Lord Fowler's voice, low and dire.

"A gas explosion rendered the Duke of Westing's townhouse utterly unlivable. Unfortunately, the marquess was in the middle of it."

All the air left her lungs. In fact, the entire room seemed entirely still and silent. She was focused entirely on Lord Fowler's face and his serious expression.

"How . . . ?" She swallowed her fear and tried again. "How is he? Was the marquess injured?"

"He suffered a nasty blow when half the dwelling collapsed upon him."

She needed to sit down as all the blood rushed from her head. Recalling how she'd been thinking unkindly of Christopher and his abrupt disappearance, she wanted to weep right where she stood.

"Lady Jane, you have gone all over pale."

Grabbing for his arm, not caring if it were inappropriate, she said, "Please return me to my mother's table."

"At once," he agreed as he led her toward their chairs. "I can see this news has shocked you, and I apologize. It happened nearly a week ago and was in the newspapers. I assumed everyone had heard. Let me assure you, Westing suffered no broken bones, no disfigurement."

She took in this new information, letting a swell of relief begin to take hold.

"You said a nasty blow. To his head?"

"I believe so, yes," Lord Fowler agreed.

"Yet he was uninjured?" she persisted as they reached the table, where her mother had already returned and had been joined by another friend.

Together, the older ladies were chatting and barely noticing their daughters whom they were supposed to be chaperoning.

At Jane's approach, however, they fell silent. Her mother, taking in Jane's countenance, started to rise, her hand at her throat.

However, Jane stared at Lord Fowler, waiting for him to answer her question.

"Actually, I am sorry to say," he began, and those words caused the buzzing in her ears to grow louder and to make it as if he were speaking very softly from far away.

She sunk into the only vacant chair, knowing had it not been there, she would have dropped to the floor. Then, after hearing her mother exclaim at her pallor, at last, Lord Fowler's words drifted into her brain.

"Lord Westing was rendered absolutely blind."

CHRISTOPHER KNEW IT WAS Burnley by the sound of his knock, more of a loud rapping than a muted tap as the staff did, or a quick slap before pushing open the door like his sister. And his parents didn't knock at all, merely saying his name before entering the bedroom. He supposed he would allow that for a while longer and then tell them to stop.

"Hello, old chum," Burnley said as he entered.

Christopher nodded his welcome.

"What, you don't feel like speaking today?" Burnley took a seat in the chair nearby, first dragging it across the rug to be closer by the sound of it.

Christopher shrugged, then thought for a second.

"If *you* shrug, I won't know."

"True enough," Burnley said. "But I'm not shrugging. I'm leaning back in this uncomfortable chair, and I now have one leg over the other, with my right ankle resting on my left knee, if you can picture it."

"I can."

Burnley had been a good fellow, coming every day since Christopher awakened, sometimes staying an hour or two, sometimes all day, and eating with him. It gave Amanda and his mother a respite.

"Do you want to know what I'm wearing?" his friend asked.

That made Christopher chuckle, a rarity these days.

"Absolutely not. Tell me the weather instead."

Burnley laughed. "Same. It's London. There is intermittent rain and intermittent sun. There is blue sky and occasionally clouds and gray sky. There is smoky fog or foggy smoke, depending on how you think about it. In more interesting news, Sophia is returning soon from the Continent, and I'll be back on chaperoning duty."

Owen would be watching over his sister the way Christopher used to watch over Amanda, another of his duties he could no longer perform.

"I met a girl." Christopher surprised himself by such a disclosure, but it felt good to have finally told someone.

His friend hesitated, then asked, "Here? In your room?"

Christopher could picture Owen looking around as if she would appear.

"No, you simpleton! *Before* the explosion." He ran a hand through his hair. "Everything in my life, from now on, is going to be categorized as before the explosion or after, isn't it?"

"Not necessarily. Never mind that philosophical rubbish, tell me about the girl."

"At Marlborough House."

"That was three weeks ago, at least. Why didn't you tell me sooner?"

"I had rather hoped to have a conversation with her father and even with the lady herself before I started babbling to the likes of you."

"Based on one encounter?" Burnley sounded incredulous.

"No. We kept company at the Linwald ball, and then we were partnered at the Mulberry's last dinner party."

"Based on a couple dances and a dinner, you were ready to ask her father for permission? She must be extremely special, or very persuasive."

"Stop it. Actually, I've known her for years. And you have, too, most probably. I'm speaking of Lady Jane Chatley."

Silence, then merely a single sound from his friend, "*Hm.*"

"What do you mean by that?"

"By what?"

Burnley was plainly stalling.

"By your thoughtful, noncommittal hum."

"Oh, you heard that? I would say, dear friend, your hearing has improved since the explosion. One might think your ears would have been damaged rather than your eyes."

Christopher sighed. "I wish it had been the case. Come now, tell me. What do *you* think about Jane?"

Another hesitation, then Burnley began slowly, "She seems a little proper for you, perhaps even reserved. Not a lot of vigor."

"Precisely my previous impression. She is actually none of those things you say, and she has vigor in spades. Beautiful eyes, too."

"Really?"

Christopher didn't care for his friend's interested tone. What's more, her beautiful eyes were ones he could never look into again. He clenched his hands at the surge of anger, an emotion that was coming more often now. First mere frustration, now white-hot fury at the senseless way he'd lost his vision.

And yet, he still sat there in the dark, thinking of a girl whom he would never see again. *What an idiot!*

It took a moment, but he managed to let go of the anger as he pictured Jane.

"Do you recall the cricket banquet? Remember how lovely Jane looked when Cambrey introduced her as the hostess?"

"Yes, she did seem quite attractive that day," Burnley agreed. "But I've danced with her in the past, and she barely looked at me or kept up her side of the conversation."

Christopher grinned. "Obviously you bored her."

His friend laughed. "And you do not, I suppose."

Christopher's smile died. They'd definitely experienced some sort of connection, he and Jane, and he'd been fully ready to pursue her.

"Maybe it doesn't matter anymore."

"What doesn't matter? What do you mean?"

"In this time which I think of as *after the explosion*, perhaps what I felt before is of no consequence. I've been confined to this room for days—*good God, I actually don't know how long*—and no one knows what to do with me. Including myself."

"The doctor came again yesterday, didn't he? What did he say?"

"His best guess is damage to my optic nerves, whatever the hell those are. He said they attach to the 'bulb of my eye.' Sounded disgusting."

Burnley didn't immediately respond. "So, when your belfry was knocked around, these nerves were damaged. And did he say if they would heal?"

"He didn't know. He said only there wasn't anything wrong with the actual lenses of my eyes, useless as they now are."

"I'm terribly sorry, old chap."

Having Owen express his condolence made it worse. He didn't want there to be anything for anyone to be sorry about. He merely wanted his sight back. Or at the very least, for someone to say it might return.

However, along with everyone else, he was starting to believe this was permanent, although he couldn't actually accept it. He still prayed, after all, and he spent most of his time thinking about what he would do when his sight returned.

"What about your head?" Burnley asked. "Does it still hurt?"

"No, not really, and before you ask, nothing else is amiss, either. I have no reason to stay in bed, yet here I am."

He heard his friend stand. "Then let's get you up and out, shall we?"

Christopher tilted his head toward him. "For what purpose?"

"To stretch your legs, I suppose. Have you been downstairs yet?"

He shook his head. "I've been along the hallway, and can do it quite well now." All vases and stools and small tables had been removed.

Burnley sounded chipper. "It's a lovely home, nice garden, you should see—"

He broke off, then added, "Sorry."

"No matter," Christopher assured him. "I've seen it before. I'll come downstairs if you promise me no one is staring at me. I'll go through the house, stroll the back garden, and then come indoors."

Tossing the covers aside, he swung his legs over the side of the bed and stood, then promptly fell backward onto the mattress.

"Blazes!" he swore. "I feel light-headed."

"Proof you need to get up and walk around more, if you ask me. However, you must do it more slowly. Besides, you're in your nightgown, so first I have to find you some pants."

CHAPTER NINE

Jane's mother would not let her go alone, nor would she cease asking why her daughter wanted to go uninvited to Lord and Lady Forester's townhouse.

"Lady Tabitha Forester is aunt to a friend of mine who is injured."

Her mother frowned. "You're speaking of Lord Westing, are you not?" Then she looked at Jane until she stopped staring out the window of the carriage and returned her mother's regard.

"Yes, I am."

The countess made a tut-tutting sound. "When I caught you in the garden at Marlborough House, you said there was nothing between you."

"You didn't *catch* me, because I wasn't doing anything at which I could be caught. Moreover, if you recall, I refused to speak of Lord Westing because you immediately wanted to push us into marriage."

"Nevertheless, I demand you tell me, is there something between the two of you?"

Jane sighed, then asked a question that seemed an excellent evasion. "If there were, would I be the very last one to know about the terrible explosion?"

"You never cared for gossip, my girl."

"This is hardly gossip. However, I was so intent on other matters, I didn't ask for the weekly news at all."

"Other matters, such as your mysterious endeavor with Lord Fowler?"

"Among other things." Her mother didn't know about her wishing to help with Dickens's Urania Cottage for fallen women, and she would most definitely not approve of her daughter becoming involved with such. Nor did she know about Jane's wish to become involved with the RSPCA.

"Tell me, Jane, does Lord Fowler want to marry you?"

Jane almost said yes, simply to tease her mother. Instead, she said, "We have arrived."

"What do you hope to accomplish by barging in?"

Would a moment alone with Christopher be too much to hope for?

"I would like to visit with the marquess if possible, but barring that, I would at least like him to know I stopped by and offered my best wishes."

The butler showed them into the foyer and then into the drawing room while he went to tell Her Grace they had arrived.

"That's the Duchess of Westing, not Lady Forester," Jane's mother reminded the butler as if he might somehow bring in the wrong lady of the house.

No sooner had they been seated than a loud noise had them back on their feet. Jane glanced at her mother, then went to the open doorway.

Peering into the hall, she spied Christopher sprawled on the floor, with Lord Burnley looming over him, apparently trying to help him up.

She gasped, then clamped a hand over her mouth as both men's heads swiveled in her direction.

Lord Burnley's eyes widened, but Christopher's unseeing gaze passed over her. Obviously, what Lord Fowler said was true.

"Who's there?" he asked as his friend put a hand under his elbow and hauled him to standing.

Jane hadn't truly believed it until that moment. *Christopher was blind.*

"Owen, who is it?" he repeated.

"Lady Jane Chatley," Lord Burnley said, his voice sounding choked.

"Dammit all!" Christopher said as if because he couldn't see her, then she couldn't hear him.

Lord Burnley coughed. "*And* her mother, the Countess of Chatley."

Jane glanced to her side to see he was correct. Her mother had joined her to stare at the proceedings in the tiled foyer.

Suddenly, Jane realized how rash an idea it was to show up without warning. Regardless, she could not deny her spirits lifted at seeing Christopher in the flesh. However, he might not feel the same way.

For one thing, he was not even completely dressed, wearing an untucked shirt over pants and no jacket or cravat, and his hair was an utter disaster. It didn't matter to her, of course, but she had an inclination being seen in such a state would prick his pride.

She was right.

His next words were directed to his friend, "Get me upstairs, at once."

Without a word in her direction, he let Lord Burnley guide him to the stairs, and then with a hand on the railing, he climbed them slowly.

Her heart ached with every step he took away from her. Moreover, it pained her not to be able to approach him or even to speak with him.

Lord Burnley, at least, turned and nodded in her direction.

"We should go," she said, feeling thick-headed for coming and terribly indiscreet.

Her mother gasped. "We cannot. I gave the butler my calling card. We can't simply disappear."

They retreated to the drawing room and waited until, a few minutes later, the Duchess of Westing arrived.

"I'm sorry to keep you waiting."

Jane and her mother stood hurriedly.

"No, not at all," Lady Chatley intoned. "We apologize for our unexpected appearance. We were passing by and stopped only to offer our sympathies and to inquire about your son's health."

Jane heaved a sigh of relief. In a pinch, her mother knew the right thing to say, the quintessential woman of polite manners.

However, the duchess looked a little wary. "After our family became displaced and our short visit to my in-law's home became so much longer, I haven't thought to entertain here. I didn't want to overstep my welcome as a guest of Lord and Lady Forester. Otherwise, Emily, you know I would have invited you to tea."

Jane's mother took the other woman's hands in hers. "You'll be back in your own home soon enough, I'm sure."

"We'll see," Helen Westing said distractedly, then she finally turned her attention to Jane. "I didn't know you were acquainted with my son. However, I can tell you what I've told the others—he is *not* accepting visitors of the fairer sex, nor does he need anyone to tend him or read to him."

Jane realized then that other young ladies had stopped by, hoping to get to the marquess under the guise of sympathy. Calling in as she and her mother had done clearly seemed to his mother to be mercenary at the very least since Jane had never visited the Westings before. The duchess was simply behaving as a protective mother.

Jane would have to disclose more information, which even her own mother didn't know, in order to save face somewhat.

"I assure you I had not intended to offer any such personal ministrations. Your son and I were partnered at a dinner at Lord and Lady Mulberry's only days before the terrible explosion at your home. Naturally, I, that is, we," she gestured to include her mother, "were concerned when learning of his condition. We shall take our leave now, as you must have much to do trying to get your home repaired while also preparing for your art exhibit."

The Duchess of Westing looked startled, her hand fluttering to her lace fichu.

"How did you know about that?"

Jane hoped she'd hadn't spoken out of turn. Christopher hadn't said anything about it being a secret.

"I apologize if I said too much. Your son mentioned it to me over dinner. He is very proud of you. Again, we apologize for intruding, and we'll leave you to your day."

Her own mother had grown quiet upon hearing the news of an unknown partnering over dinner, but then she sprung to life again.

"It is truly good to see you, Helen. If our daughters were closer in age, I'm certain we would have sat through many balls together while they danced. In any case, why don't you and Lady Amanda come to our home next week? Let me know what afternoon works for both of you for tea."

It was always tea, and only tea. Jane's father's boorishness precluded anything more formal involving both husbands and wives. Mayfair's many dinner parties, for instance, excluded the Chatleys because the earl might go missing at the last minute. Lady Chatley couldn't go alone to a couple's dinner, for there would be a gap at the table, considered most unseemly. Similarly, she never invited other couples to the Chatleys' townhouse for the same reason.

Not for the first time, Jane felt a twinge of pity for her mother whose social life had suffered for her choice of a husband. Moreover, her mother was correct about the age difference in daughters. Jane had already had a few Seasons before Amanda Westing came out that year, and thus, Lady Chatley sat with mothers whose daughters were from Jane's first Season, while the Duchess sat with mothers of the debutantes, if she attended at all. Jane recalled Christopher saying he was acting as his sister's chaperone during the Linwald ball.

Christopher's mother's expression softened.

"Thank you. Amanda and I would like to come, and then when—" she broke off and looked a little lost. "When my family has returned to our own home, I can properly entertain you in return," she finished.

"Don't give it another thought," Jane's mother said. "We will leave you to your busy day."

Soon, they were in their carriage.

"Jane," her mother said as soon as the horses got underway. "You have been keeping secrets."

But Jane didn't answer, her mind was fixed on Christopher who hadn't wished to even speak with her.

"Of all the people to be in the front hall," Christopher bemoaned for the hundredth time, lying on his bed wishing he could stare at the ceiling. "How humiliating!"

"It wasn't," Burnley insisted.

"You weren't the one on the floor like an animal."

"Jane Chatley didn't look the least bit offended."

"Tell me exactly how she did look, then. Was her face awash in delight to see me?" He couldn't hide the sarcasm or irritation from his voice.

"Of course not. She looked like a woman concerned, and, of course, she looked a little surprised. I doubt she expected to see you."

Christopher groaned again.

"Tell me what she looked like."

"I just did!" Owen sounded exasperated.

"No! I mean what was she wearing? How was her hair done?"

"For Christ's sake!" his friend exclaimed. "I can't remember. I think she had on a blue gown. She had hair, that is certain. And a hat, I think. Wait, maybe her mother was in blue, and she was in gray."

"Never mind," Christopher said. "It doesn't matter."

"You're right," Burnley agreed, seemingly relieved. "If I were you, I would picture her without clothing at all."

If he could see him, Christopher would punch him in the jaw and wipe off the wolfish expression he knew Owen wore.

"I don't suppose you would put your chin at the end of my fist, would you?"

His friend laughed heartily.

"I think I'm ready for you to leave," Christopher told him.

"Come now. Don't be angry with me. The next time we see her, I'll take note of everything, I promise."

"How will there be a next time? There won't, I tell you. At least, not for me. You can look at her anytime you like." The anger returned in a flash. If the veil of darkness would simply part, just on the other side was the world to which he longed to return—with light and faces and people whom he loved.

Groaning, he fisted his hands in the bedclothing and thought for certain he would go insane.

"Why not see her again?" Owen asked. "Invite her to tea in a few days and you can entertain her properly. It's not as if you need to play cards or take her hunting, for God's sake. Sit with her, drink tea, and eat biscuits. You can do that, surely."

Christopher considered. *Could he?*

"Perhaps," he allowed. "Do you think I should get dark spectacles as I've seen the blind wearing?"

"I don't know. Why do they even wear them?"

"God, we're so ill-informed!" Christopher bemoaned. "I'll ask my mother. Anyway, I expect I would need you to be there."

Silence.

"What now? Don't tell me you won't help me to visit with Jane?"

"I will get you downstairs and into the drawing room—with your hair combed this time."

Christopher groaned as he raised hands to his hair and fingered the mess Jane had just witnessed.

"While your talented Abner will do a better job of preparing you, I'm certain. In any case, even if I delivered you directly to the sofa, I would leave you the moment she arrived," Owen insisted. "I don't want to be in the middle of your conversation, catching her glances meant for you. Besides, only think on it. No one will criticize you for being *alone* with her."

Christopher did think about it. Burnley might be right. As a blind man, he couldn't make unwanted or inappropriate advances, at least, not without the lady's assistance. And he certainly couldn't attempt to jump on her without missing his quarry. She would be perfectly safe and could escape at any moment.

"I hope society views it that way," he mused, "for that would be the *only* benefit of this damnable blindness." He stopped running his fingers through his hair and looked to where he thought Burnley was sitting.

"Owen, will you write to her for me? This very moment? I'll dictate if you find pen and paper."

"I certainly will, old chum."

Thus, in a short while, Christopher began his letter to her.

"Keep it short, I think," his friend counseled, rattling the paper around in front of him. "Plus, I'm not a clerk, so speak slowly."

Dear Lady Jane,

I feel as though I should, and could, call you simply Jane.

"What are you saying?" Owen mused. "Are you really going to have me write that? *Should* and *could?*"

"Never mind. Start over." Christopher considered again.

Dear Lady Jane,
Let me start by apologizing for the ridiculous scene you witnessed in the foyer of Lord and Lady Forester's home.

"I wouldn't bring attention to it," Owen advised. "She saw it, and we all handled it with tact and grace. Why embarrass her by mentioning it? That's not very gentlemanly of you."

"But *I'm* the one who was embarrassed, not her."

"Of course she was! She didn't want to be caught standing in the doorway at that moment. She likes you, don't you think?"

"Yes," Christopher answered softly. At least, he thought she had.

"Then she certainly didn't want you to feel humiliated or even to know she was witnessing it. So that made her embarrassed to be caught."

Christopher considered it. "Oh, I see."

Then, realizing the word he'd used, he chuckled a moment and began again.

Dear Lady Jane,
It has been a number of days since I last saw you, and to my regret, I will never actually see you again.

"No!" Owen dragged out the word like a moan. "That's terrible. Too depressing, and it sounds as if you are all doom and gloom."

"Well, I am," Christopher reminded him sharply.

"She won't want to come then."

"All right. This is the last attempt," he told his friend, "or I shall give up entirely. And I don't want you to comment."

Dear Lady Jane,
Obviously, as you are aware, much has happened since the last time we were together. I would be very pleased if you would come to tea at my aunt Lady Tabitha Forester's townhouse in two days' time.
Yours sincerely,
Christopher Westing
P.S. You may come alone as I will not be a threat to your person. My sister can always sit with us if need be.

"Will that suffice?" he asked into the silence broken only by the sound of a pen scratching on paper.

"Yes. It is satisfactory. I'm folding it, and I'll give it to the butler when I leave." Burnley paused. "Now, tell me, old chum. Have you kissed her?"

CHAPTER TEN

Jane had the hand-written letter tucked into her reticule when she arrived once again at the Foresters' townhouse. She carried it with her in case the Duchess of Westing appeared and believed her once more trying to take advantage of her injured son.

At the mere notion of speaking with Christopher again, Jane's heart was thumping hard and fast in her chest, and she only hoped no one could hear it.

Her relief at receiving something from him after her disastrous appearance at Berkley Square was profound. All was not ruined! He still wanted her company.

What's more, when Jane was shown into the parlor, Christopher was already there, seated on a sofa, looking tidy and exactly like his former self. Except, of course, for his eyes, which were closed. He looked as if he were sleeping.

"Lady Jane Chatley," the butler announced, and she watched Christopher open his eyes before he stood.

Those beautiful blue eyes—they still looked perfect to her.

"I should take a step and greet you properly," he said by way of greeting, "but then I might trip. While falling at your feet sounds romantic, I fear it would only appear clumsy. And you've already seen me like that."

Jane stepped forward at once, compelled to put him at ease with her words and her actions.

"I shall make it as easy as possible for us to greet one another properly, as you say, although I contend even warm words from across the room are more than welcome. Unsatisfactory, as mere words are, however, I hope you don't mind if I grasp your hand instead."

Thus, saying her intention while closing the distance between them, Jane reached for one of his hands and clasped it between both of her gloved ones.

Immediately, he put his other hand on hers, and they remained that way, with all four hands melded.

"You look well," she told him, and it was the truth. Yet, as his eyes fluttered open and closed, it was a trifle disconcerting.

"I wish I could say the same about you."

She laughed, glad he had his good humor. "I do, in fact, look well," Jane assured him.

"Are we alone?" he asked.

She glanced around, even behind the ever-popular potted ferns in the corner.

"Yes. I didn't even bring a maid with me."

"And your mother let you come by yourself." He frowned slightly.

"Yes."

"It's strange, isn't it? I'm considered perfectly harmless now I'm blind, but we are already touching each other."

She heard a tone of annoyance in his voice, which puzzled her.

"Shall we sit?" he offered.

"Yes," she said again. She wondered when he would release her hands. He hadn't yet, and so they sat close, side by side.

"Tell me what you're wearing."

"Really?" She had never described her clothing before.

"Yes. In my mind, you look as I last saw you at the Mulberry's party, but you can't possibly be in a green evening gown."

"No. Definitely not. If you must know, I'm wearing mostly gray both my jacket and skirt, with pink trim and a pink shirt, perhaps too pale for my age and better suited to a debutante, but I rather like the color. It's a shade that reminds me of a certain rose in my mother's garden."

"I can imagine you now perfectly."

She smiled to herself, but then his next words shocked her.

"I wonder if we could remove your gloves so I can touch your hands."

"I don't think that's a good idea, Lord Westing."

"And that's the other thing. May we dispense with the titles and the formality. I think of you as Jane. May I call you such? And, in return, will you call me Chris?"

"I think of you in my head as Christopher," she acknowledged. "Do you prefer Chris?"

"As long as you don't say 'my lord' or 'Lord Westing,' I don't mind what you call me."

"Fair enough. But I won't remove my gloves. If I did, I know for certain someone would enter, and I would be barred from returning."

"All right. We'll take it slowly, Jane." He said her name with obvious satisfaction. "Are you smiling?"

"Yes. Thank you for inviting me to tea. I'm sorry I barged in the other day. I had only found out the night before about the gas explosion and felt like a ninny. The entire city knew about what had happened except me. Sometimes being a little removed from the network of society doesn't serve me well."

"I'm sorry you encountered me on the floor when you came."

She shook her head, then remembered he couldn't see her.

"Think nothing of it. I can understand how difficult this is. Or actually, I suppose I cannot. I can guess, though. Tell me your prognosis."

"Meaning, will I be blind for the rest of my life? Probably."

A wave of sadness washed over her, and she was glad he couldn't see her expression. It seemed silly to offer condolences, and far better to think about ways to help.

"I assume you have a good physician."

"I believe so. My parents tend to hire the best, and as you can guess, the foremost doctors want the patronage of a duke and his family."

"Yes, I can imagine," she said. "If it is to be a permanent condition, then you will need special training as well as some accommodations in your home."

He stiffened. "I'm not ready to think on any of that."

She hoped she hadn't offended him.

"Of course. Besides, you're not even in your own home at present. It must be more disconcerting being here."

A tap on the door heralded the entrance of a maid with the tea service. Immediately, she told him so before he had to ask.

"Thank you," he said. "This will also be my first attempt to eat or drink anything in front of someone who is not family. I confess, I'm a little nervous."

"Please, Christopher," she said, trying out his name and receiving a smile in return. "Don't be nervous around me. Treat me no differently than Lord Burnley."

He burst out laughing. "That will be impossible, but I do feel comfortable with you, all the same. The nervousness is more from taking a first step down an unfamiliar path, one I don't even want to be on. But let's get started nevertheless. I suppose you will have to pour the tea and hand me my saucer."

"How sweet do you like it?" she asked, thinking pouring tea for Christopher was one of the most pleasurable things she'd ever done.

"One teaspoon, if you please, and plenty of milk. And a dash of brandy."

She knew he was teasing.

"It appears the maid forgot the brandy but there are some jam biscuits."

"Very well. And leave the spoon on the saucer. I shall try stirring the tea myself."

He started to reach out, and she knew he would knock things aside.

"I think it best if you stay still, hands at the ready, and let me place the saucer into them."

"Good idea."

Jane did as she said and carefully gave him the pretty flowered china set to hold.

"Fine," he said, perhaps speaking to himself. "First, the spoon."

Jane had left a goodly space in the cup, pouring less tea than she normally would, but still, he seemed to hold it sideways, and she bit her lip as the cup tipped dangerously. She held her tongue. After all, he needed to practice.

Fumbling, nearly spilling the tea and knocking off the spoon, Christopher managed to get hold of the silverware and haphazardly stir.

"Perhaps a little less vigor," she advised, as tea went flying onto his trousers and her skirt.

"Sorry," he mumbled.

In another moment, he had placed the spoon back on the saucer.

"Perfect," she encouraged.

Again, he nearly sent the delicate cup flying as he attempted to locate the handle, but he succeeded. He even got the cup to his lips on the first try by going slowly.

"I could die of thirst at this rate," he joked. However, he did, at last, sip his tea and declare it perfectly sweetened. "Just the way I like it."

After another sip, he said, "And I do love the jam biscuits. But I suppose holding this and a treat will be too much." Then he lowered the cup to the table too quickly, the side of the saucer clanked against the silver tray, and the cup tipped over, spilling the rest of the tea onto the saucer and a little on the tray.

"I spilled it, didn't I?"

"That's what saucers are for," Jane pointed out.

"Is it? I thought it was for holding a spoon and for giving the cup better balance."

"Some people pour their tea into the saucer to let it cool, and then drink from it," she reminded him.

"Sounds disgusting," he said.

"Perhaps you should ask your family for a sturdy mug to drink from."

He paused, his head turned toward her, eyelids opening and closing.

"Jane, are you being cruel?" But he didn't sound insulted. He seemed amused.

"No, just practical. May I hand you a biscuit?"

"Please."

And thus, they went on, sipping tea as best he could and munching on biscuits, and chatting like old friends. Until someone entered without tapping, a woman who looked vaguely familiar but with whom Jane wasn't acquainted.

"Who is it?" Christopher asked.

"I'm not sure." Jane stood up as she spoke.

"I'm Christopher's Aunt Tabitha. I'm so sorry to intrude. I didn't realize he was entertaining company."

Christopher remained seated. "I apologize, Auntie. I mentioned it to your butler and to Uncle Cyrus, but I guess the news didn't reach you."

"No matter. I was looking for my needlepoint and knew I'd left it somewhere. Sometimes I'm so scatterbrained."

"I'm Jane Chatley," Jane told the woman because Christopher had fallen silent.

"I apologize," he said again, and this time, he stood. "How stupid of me. Without seeing the situation, it's as if I have to remind myself what is supposed to happen next.

Lady Jane, this is Lady Forester, my father's sister, who has taken us all in due to the folly of a modern gas stove. Auntie, Lady Jane is a friend of mine."

"Oh, good. I'm glad you have someone besides Lord Burnley to keep you company. He's such a rogue. *Ah,* there's my basket of needlepoint by the window. I'll leave you to your tea."

Before she could go, however, Christopher's mother appeared.

"I didn't realize you were having a tea party," the duchess intoned, her glance taking in Jane and her son.

"No, Helen, we're not," Lady Forester told her. "I've barged in on these lovely young people, and now I'm barging out again. I suggest you do the same."

"Please," Jane began, "you don't have to leave on my account, not either of you."

"It looks like someone ought to stay," the duchess said, sounding disapproving. "Only look at the state of you, Chris. Tea and crumbs everywhere. I'm so sorry, Tabitha, if anything is stained, we shall make reparations, of course."

In the awkward silence, Christopher sat back down. "I apologize, Auntie. I didn't realize."

Jane normally felt only respect for her elders and had liked the Duchess of Westing at their last encounter when she'd been protective of Christopher. At that moment, though, seeing his crestfallen expression, she felt a surge of annoyance, even downright anger, toward his mother.

"Nonsense," Lady Forester said, with a sideways glance at her sister-in-law. "Chris, your mother is being overly fussy. I assure you, there is no more mess than my own husband makes every time he takes his tea. Carry on, you two. Helen, a word, if you please." And she sailed out of the room in a rustle of satin skirts and starched crinoline, holding her needle-work basket, leaving Christopher's mother to follow.

"I'll be back in a few minutes," the Duchess of Westing promised.

"Oh, joy," Christopher muttered, and Jane thought his mother had heard him plainly for she was still in the doorway when he said it.

"Are they both gone?" he asked.

"Yes."

"Am I a ridiculous mess, covered in tea and biscuit crumbs?"

"No, not at all. There's a little tea spilled on the tray, and perhaps a splash on each of us." She felt the urge to giggle and tried hard to contain it. But she couldn't.

In fact, as she spoke, her laughter interrupted her words. "And there is a bit of strawberry jam on your jacket." She laughed some more. "And a little on the corner of your mouth."

Fortunately, he began to chortle as well, for she would have been mortified if he had been insulted. As they shared a laugh, all the tension left the room.

"And how," she giggled, "how did you get a piece of biscuit in your hair?"

"For pity' s sake, Jane, tidy me up at once."

She grabbed a napkin from the tray and dabbed his lap, despite realizing the utter inappropriateness of touching his thigh, even with her gloved hand and a cloth napkin. Then she slipped a hand into his jacket so she could hold the fabric firmly while she rubbed at the jam with the napkin. She could feel the heat of him through her thin cotton gloves.

By the time she began to wipe the corner of his mouth, she no longer felt any urge to laugh.

Apparently, neither did he. "Are we still alone?"

"Yes," she promised, rubbing her gloved thumb at the edge of his mouth, all pretense of cleaning him up gone as he caught hold of her hand.

His arms went around her, and she was thrilled he had no trouble finding her mouth with his own. They even both tilted their heads in opposite ways so their noses didn't bump.

He tasted of strawberry jam, and she delighted in the sweet kiss.

"I won't mess up your hair," he promised against her lips, and then she sighed and opened her mouth to his tongue's gentle ravishing.

For her part, she didn't have to worry about his hair, so she anchored her gloved hands at the back of his head and held him to her.

Eventually, they both needed to breathe and drew back.

"That was the only time in days it felt natural to have my eyes closed," he said.

"That was the only time in days I've felt content," she confessed.

"I am most certainly not content," he confessed. "I want more of you."

"I can hardly come here every day without tongues wagging in a terribly discomfiting way."

"Dear Jane," he said, then stopped.

"What?"

"It is only that on the other side of normalcy, with something huge and terrifying having happened to me, I no longer care a fig about gossips. I can't imagine anything much discomfiting me, as you say. But for your sake, I'll try to 'see' things your way."

"My way?"

"I mean in the land of the sighted where appearances matter above all else and reputations can be ruined by a couple sitting too closely."

Jane realized she was still crushed against him and drew from his arms and even scooted a few inches away on the sofa.

"Mother's intrusion has given me a plan for having you return often and become indispensable to others in my family as you already are to me."

Even while she was still considering his words—*her? indispensable to him?*—his mother reentered the drawing room.

"It is I," the duchess said before Jane could tell him who it was. "I'm sorry if I said anything to upset you, Chris. Your aunt was correct. I was being fussy, but only because I am acutely aware we are intruders in her home, and I fear using up all her hospitality. All for that ridiculous stove! It makes me want to strangle your father. Of course, your injury is the most important thing, but then the house being half-destroyed and the upcoming art show. I can't remember feeling so out of kilter."

After a pause, Christopher said, "It's all right. I will learn to be more adept as it seems I am to remain blind."

His saying the word put a pall over the room, and Jane's heart ached for the entire family.

He continued, "I was thinking how busy you are, Mother, and remembered how well Jane ran the charity event, raising all that money for an orphanage."

"Actually, the Earl of Cambrey and I raised enough to open two orphanages," Jane thought she should point out.

"Two!" he exclaimed. "Mother, weren't you saying how you feel as if you need another pair of hands? I'm fairly certain Jane has a pair."

"Oh!" Jane exclaimed, only then realizing what he was up to. He was foisting her onto his mother so she would have reason to haunt the Foresters' house. It would be wonderful to feel useful and to be near Christopher, too.

The Duchess of Westing gave her an appraising stare, and Jane found herself offering her a smile, which she hoped looked genuine and confident, despite her feeling a little terrified of the woman.

"Didn't you say, Mother, *if* you had a daughter, you would make sure she was trained to be organized and then enlist her in assisting you?" Christopher asked.

Jane was utterly confused by his question since Amanda Westing obviously existed. However, when both mother and son broke into peals of laughter, she realized it was a joke between them.

"Luckily, Jane is already an organized person," Christopher finished, "unlike our Amanda."

"You know, dear boy," his mother began, "I had no idea you listened to me so carefully."

She turned to Jane. "I do need help. My husband is overseeing the reconstruction and the workers, but soon, we'll be at the decorating stage. I believe in making the best of a bad situation. Since we have to paint and wallpaper and put down new flooring and carpets, as well as buy furnishings, we may as well do so in the latest style. Figuring what that is can be difficult enough. Getting the house redone before the current style is *passé* is another task altogether. Thus, we must go for the utmost *à la mode* in our design and ornamentation while appearing to remain timeless. Nothing less will do," she declared.

Goodness! It sounded like a Herculean task, indeed, and Jane felt a thrill of excitement.

"I would love to help you, Your Grace, in any way I can. But what of your daughter?"

"Amanda is young for her age, and her tastes are not yet mature. Moreover, she is one of the most disorganized people I know. She came home the other day and said she'd been in the wrong house for half an hour before realizing it wasn't her aunt and uncle's. She has far too many flittering thoughts going on, exactly like her father."

Jane didn't know what to say, as agreement would be tantamount to insult, and she was not close enough to the family for that.

"I can see you have good taste," his mother said.

Jane assumed by the woman's arched brow she meant because of Jane's interest in Christopher more than because she wore a stylish day gown.

"I hope I do, Your Grace."

"And don't forget the art exhibit, Mother," Christopher added.

His mother gave a large sigh. "I cannot believe it's only a month away."

"Congratulations," Jane told her. "The marquess has told me your medium is watercolor."

"Yes, the lesser-valued sister to oil."

Jane considered the watercolor book illustrations she loved no less than many paintings in museums. On the other hand, the exalted artists did seem to work in oil.

"Is it really less esteemed?" she asked.

Christopher answered for his mother. "It is. Watercolorists haven't yet received the respect of the art community, even though it is less forgiving and harder to fix mistakes. Isn't that right, Mother?"

The duchess raised an eyebrow. "True, therefore, I do not make mistakes."

Jane wondered if the woman was speaking in jest, but neither mother nor son cracked a smile, so she assumed it was the truth.

"Where is the exhibit?"

"At the Egyptian Hall in Piccadilly." His mother's cheeks turned a pleasing shade of pink, obviously excited by the upcoming event. "But the paintings are all at my studio. Would you like to see them?"

"Why, yes, of course."

"Tomorrow, Chris and I shall pick you up at your home and take you."

"NO," CHRISTOPHER SAID AFTER he recovered his voice from the shock. "*We* most certainly will not. Mother will take you by herself."

The idea he would go out into the world when he had barely made it into the drawing room without running into the door jamb and couldn't take tea without looking like a messy savage was ridiculous. *And terrifying!*

"I don't see why you won't go," his mother said.

"I cannot *see*, which is precisely why I won't go."

He heard her sigh, although Jane remained silent. He wondered what she was thinking. *Was she staring at him? Was she disappointed?*

"We will wait until you are ready to accompany us," his mother said as if coming to a decision. "Of course, it was too soon for me to suggest such a thing. Anyway, it gives me time to create a comprehensive list of what you can help me with."

Christopher realized his mother was speaking to Jane.

"There are easily a thousand details and tedious tasks. So good of you! Meanwhile, I'll leave you two to finish your visit. Good day, Lady Jane."

With that, she left.

"What on earth did you just do?" Jane asked him, while unable to keep all amusement from her tone. "A list with thousands of details and tasks?"

"*Tedious* tasks," he pointed out. "Soon, you'll be indispensable to her and, thus, forced to come every day."

"Maybe not *every* day."

He reached for her, fumbling, feeling every bit the clumsy oaf, but she helped him, taking hold of his grasping hands.

"Are we alone?" he asked.

"We are. Your mother looked disappointed, by the way."

He made a noise of sheer frustration, and it sounded to his ears like a wild beast snorting.

"Are you still there, Jane?"

"Yes, of course." She squeezed his hands in hers.

"What are you thinking?" he asked.

There was a long pause, making his insides clench uncomfortably with unease.

CHAPTER ELEVEN

"You may not like what I'm thinking," Jane said, and Christopher knew at once he would not.

"I think your mother gave in to you too easily. After all, she wasn't asking you to wander alone through the streets of the city, merely to ride in a carriage with us and go to her studio."

"You're right," he said.

"Am I?" she sounded cautiously delighted.

He thought he was getting quite good at understanding people's emotions by the tone of their voice.

"Yes, I do not like what you're thinking. Not one bit." He removed his hands from hers. "You have positively no idea the obstacles facing me for such a banal endeavor. It is not worth it."

"That's ridiculous."

Christopher was stunned by her callous response. "I beg your pardon?"

"I mean if you don't begin to overcome these obstacles for the simplest of excursions, then how will you get back to living a normal life?"

Was she serious? She sounded entirely so, not even a hint of irony at the mention of a "normal" life. As if he could ever have one again.

"Being blind has taken all my independence. Better I should be stone deaf. Why couldn't the explosion have deafened me?"

"Then how would you hear the members of Parliament and argue with them when they need your sound advice, especially after you become the next prime minister?"

"Parliament?" He wouldn't even be sitting in the back row, never mind ever becoming the leader.

"Yes, isn't that your duty and your destiny, like the queen's eldest son and the throne?"

"No longer." He knew he was speaking curtly. In fact, he was speaking to her the way he took the liberty of speaking to Amanda or Burnley. And he couldn't seem to stop himself, for he felt the writhing snake of anger twisting through him again.

"I see," she said.

Her words made his rage blossom, and he swore softly.

"I'm sorry," she said immediately. "A very poor choice. I mean, I *understand* your current point of view, but I sincerely hope it will change."

"If only I were deaf instead," he repeated, something he'd said to himself many times. "I could have read the other MPs' words, at least. I could have studied the acts they were voting on, perhaps put forth my own bill."

"A loss of any one of your senses would be a terrible blow. I know that."

He felt her comforting touch, rubbing the back of his hand.

"But to me, being able to converse with you is a blessing," she added.

She thought speaking with him a blessing? He took in her words and breathed deeply, holding his sharp tongue until he could let go of the anger again and speak courteously.

"I would rather *see* you," he insisted.

"I know. But let your hands be your eyes. Touch my face. It is the same face."

She lifted his hand from where it rested on his thigh and placed it against her cheek, then she did the same with his other one.

At first, he didn't move, feeling foolish, and then, he let his hands wander over her cheeks and chin. After a few moments, he recalled the few times he'd held her face in his hands. He could imagine her looking up at him, her deep-blue eyes sparkling, her beautiful bow-shaped mouth upturned. He should have looked longer. He would never have turned away had he known he wouldn't be able to look upon her ever again or into her lovely eyes.

Their whole wonderful lives had been ahead of them. Now . . . he didn't know what lay ahead. Running a thumb over each of her eyebrows, remembering the salty way she arched one to make a point, then he took hold of her cheeks again.

"Thank you for not flinching." Then he concentrated. "I wish I could slip my fingers into your hair and pull you closer for a kiss."

She gasped slightly.

"I cannot *feel* your smile," he added.

"That's because you surprised it off my face for a moment." She laughed a little. "It's hard to speak when you are squishing my cheeks."

He laughed, too, despite not really feeling happy, and then he did, indeed, give her face a gentle squeeze.

"*Ah-ha*, now I feel it," he said. "Your cheeks are bulging, and that must be a smile."

"True."

They stayed that way a moment, and he ran a thumb over her lips, memorizing the shape. Finally, he released her, hearing her sigh. He supposed she'd wanted him to kiss her. However, thinking of what he'd lost left him feeling passionless, lifeless. Even with Jane.

How was he supposed to be a man and feel virile when he didn't even know the color of his own cravat?

Dammit! He thought of something terribly depraved, and when he did, the anger and frustration returned, quickly.

She sensed it or saw it on his face. "What's wrong?"

"I cannot say." It was absolutely wrong of him to wonder what he was wondering, but the notion he would never know was eating at him.

"Tell me," she demanded. "You mustn't hide behind your blindness, and in return, I will be honest with everything I tell you."

Hide behind his blindness? What a thing to say!

He wanted to gouge his own useless eyes out, but he was supposed to remain polite in a civilized society. Inside, he didn't feel polite at all, not with the boiling fury that kept returning in an instant with no outlet.

"What color are your nipples?" he blurted.

He couldn't see her shocked face, so why the hell not ask what was on his mind? After all, he would never see her breasts. She could parade herself naked in front of him and he would not have the joy of her. The question would burn in his brain forever.

After a pause, he felt her withdraw. Jane pulled away so no part of their bodies touched.

"That's inappropriate," she murmured.

Imagining her entirely bare and what he would miss, he felt barbaric. She would never marry him now, and, even if she would, he wouldn't ruin her life by asking her for her hand. *Why not ask the questions he could not learn on his own?*

"I wish to know. You said conversing with me was a blessing. You said you would always speak honestly. Since that's all we have now, words, why don't you give me a description. Are your nipples pink or tawny colored? Also, your woman's curls on your mound."

She gasped, but he continued. The snake of anger had wound its way through him and found his tongue.

"Are they pale brown as the hair on your head or a darker shade?"

She stood up. "You are being lewd for no purpose other than to irritate me."

He had won. He had destroyed her silly notion she could describe to him everything he could not see, and he couldn't help but smirk at his own cleverness.

"It was *your* idea," he pointed out, rising to his feet. "Why don't we try using my hands to see instead? Come along, Jane. Remove your clothes and let me run my fingers over your body, just as you suggested. Then you won't have to use words to tell me anything."

"I'm leaving," she said, her tone one of sheer annoyance. "But as clearly as you are trying to drive me away, I will not let you. Today, I have other obligations," she added. "Hopefully, when I return, you'll have regained your manners."

"An obligation, am I? With *other* ones being more pressing than a pathetic blind man making lascivious comments."

"Stop it. You are *not* an obligation. You are my . . . friend. I know the real Christopher Westing is a charming gentleman, so I won't hold this against you. But I am leaving now."

He heard her footsteps as she crossed the room toward the door. Then they halted. Jane returned to where he stood in front of the sofa and, surprising him, she grabbed his face in her gloved hands and kissed him.

She did everything perfectly, tilting her head, fitting her lips to his, running her tongue along the seam of his lips. Instead of demanding entrance to his mouth, however, she opened her own, surrendering, leaving herself vulnerable.

Christopher grabbed hold of her, sinking his hands into her hair, aware but not caring about the mess he might make to her coiffure. Taking what she offered, he plundered her mouth with his tongue.

With his eyes closed, everything felt exactly the same as their other kisses. Exactly. And for a moment, he believed they could carry on as before, with their relationship growing stronger the more they were together. He had been close to asking for her hand after only a few hours of conversation and dancing, a single dinner party, and a handful of kisses.

As she drew away, and his hands slid from her, however, nothing was the same as before. He opened his eyes to blackness. And while she was going to leave, he was trapped.

However, her unexpected words reached him before she exited the room.

"I will *not* let you drive me away," she promised, and then he heard her leave.

Lifting his hand to his face, he smelled her floral fragrance on his fingers. In his head, the scent evoked her face, and it was as if he could see her.

"Maybe," he said aloud to the empty room. *Maybe something could still be possible for them.*

JANE WAS SHAKING WHEN she got into her carriage. How could she help Christopher? She couldn't manage or organize away his problems. He was a strong man who'd been dealt a terrible setback. She understood his anger, even accepted him taking it out on her.

Yet her feelings for him hadn't wavered. In her heart, she still preferred him above all others and hoped he felt the same about her. Unfortunately, instead of coming to her home to speak to her parents, he was refusing to even step outdoors.

Thus, what had felt like a fast-moving whirlwind since that night on the terrace at Marlborough House, now had dwindled to a gentle gust, which she doubted would propel them along toward a marital union.

Understandably, he had retreated and wanted to hide. She could not begin to guess how long it would be, if left to his own devices, before Christopher was ready to start living again.

What if this senseless tragedy caused him to give up entirely, not only on a good life but on their burgeoning relationship?

Deciding she wouldn't let him, she rapped on the ceiling of the family's carriage until the driver stopped. Lowering the window and poking her head out, Jane gave him a new destination.

"Take me to the London Society for Teaching the Blind to Read." She'd already determined its whereabouts. "One Avenue Road, please."

WHEN JANE SHOWED UP uninvited at the Foresters' home the following day, she fervently hoped Christopher would visit with her. She had brought him a present.

"His lordship will be down shortly," the butler told her without enthusiasm, and she wondered if Christopher had railed and raged before agreeing to descend from the upper floor.

It took a quarter of an hour by the clock on the mantle in the Foresters' parlor. Jane didn't mind the wait. He was worth it.

When he entered on the arm of a man she'd never seen, she approached them.

"I'm here," she said when only a few feet separated them.

Christopher nodded toward the man. "That will be all. I'll ring when I'm ready."

Jane hoped he wouldn't need to.

"Who was that?" she asked after the silent man had closed the door behind him.

"My valet, Abner. Did he do a satisfactory job in a short amount of time?"

"Yes, very," she promised. "You look incredibly handsome."

"Thank you. Shall we sit?"

She'd thought he might apologize immediately for his crude boorishness of the day before. She'd been all set to grant her forgiveness. Apparently, it was not going to be requested.

"No. I would rather stand," she told him. "Too much sitting is bad for one's health."

Christopher cocked his head, his glance darting across the floor as if considering.

"Then I am probably declining on a rapid basis." His tone was grim and humorless. "Mostly what I do is sit. If not that, then I am lying on my bed."

"I thought so," she said. "Lack of movement is not only bad for your constitution but also for your mental and spiritual condition."

"Some say frequent enemas or purging with fig syrup are necessary to maintain one's health, but I prefer to pass on those as well."

Enemas! He was going to start being crass again, but she intended to continue on her chosen path.

"I think it is time to reclaim some of your independence. Let us go for a walk."

He visibly recoiled. "No."

"What do you mean no? I'm not asking you to climb a mountain or voyage through a forest. A simple stroll is all."

"No," he repeated.

She couldn't help sighing. "You are simply being contrary. At some point, you must go outside."

"Must I?"

She wished he had a smile upon his face or in some way appeared to be joking, but she feared he was serious.

"Yes. What about going to Parliament? To go, you must leave the house," she insisted.

"Stop speaking of Parliament," he said, this time his tone was harsh. "That is no longer a possibility for me, and it is cruel for you to bring it up."

His words shocked her to her core. *Cruel?* No one in her entire life had ever accused her of being such. *Poor Christopher!* He must be distraught indeed. *Had he given up on all his dreams?*

"There is no reason for you to say that. You can go into the House of Lords and take part in the proceedings as well as any man."

"Why did you come, Jane?"

Oh dear! He didn't even want to visit with her anymore.

"I brought you a present." Yet suddenly, she felt a little nervous about presenting it to him.

However, his expression lightened, and he looked less severe and perhaps even a little interested.

"Did you really?"

"Yes, hold out your hands."

He did as he was told, and she placed a new walking cane across his palms. The director at the School for the Blind told her most blind men and women used a cane when walking as it gave them a sense of security knowing whether something was in their path.

She wondered why no one had thought to give him one.

He said nothing.

"I know a gentleman like you has many canes for different occasions," she began.

"Yes," he agreed, his tone flat. "I even have one with a sword in it."

Did he?

"But this one is extra-long for holding out in front of you without your needing to stoop over or be uncomfortable, and you will be able to detect anything a couple feet before you."

His hands ran up and down the long cane with the arched handle, and then he held it in his right hand and thrust it out in front. She had to dodge out of the way, scrambling to the side.

He heard her, for he turned his head in her direction. "My apologies. I'm liable to take someone's eye out, aren't I?"

And she had the distinct notion he'd done it on purpose to alarm her. Moving around the back of him and coming up on his left side, she took hold of his arm without warning and without asking.

"You can hold it out but angled downward without being a danger to anyone. Try it," she insisted, leaning across him to push the cane down toward the Persian rug.

"I know how a blind man's cane works. It also looks like the tool of a beggar."

"That's unfair. Why do people assume someone with an injury is a beggar?"

"Because when such an injury befalls the lower classes, they don't have the reserves of the wealthy to keep them safely in their homes, sitting on the sofa or lying in their bed, as I fully intend to do. They have to parade down the street with their canes and sometimes being dragged along by a flea-bitten dog. As they can no longer work, they have to beg. Luckily, even though I can no longer do anything useful, I don't have to beg for my supper, nor do I have to look like a beggar."

He wrenched his arm out of her grasp and tossed the cane onto the floor.

"Goodness!" she exclaimed. "You are trying my patience, Christopher Westing." She had raised her voice to him but couldn't help herself. "I want you to stop all this defeating pity at once. Only think what you are saying. A beggar, even a blind one, gets out in the world. Why, then, cannot you do the same?"

She had her hands on her hips, but it was futile since he couldn't see how he had annoyed her. "What's more, a beggar doesn't have me with whom to walk, and you do!"

He said nothing for a moment, and she hoped he might give in. He turned his head in her direction and pursed his mouth, looking as annoyed as she felt.

"I didn't invite you here today," he pointed out.

"I know."

"Why did you come?" he asked. "And don't say to give me a gift. Why are you here?"

Say it, she told herself. *Tell him.*

"Because I care for you. A great deal, in fact. And everything was going along so swimmingly." She paused and took a deep breath, then finished, "I don't want to lose you."

After a moment, he lowered his head. "I cannot believe you are worried about losing me. I am utterly unworthy of you, Jane. I cannot be a good choice for you. Don't you understand that?"

"No, I don't." She felt tears pricking her eyes. "I have had a fondness for you for years." Her voice had gone all soft and bleary, and she hated herself for it.

He lifted his head. "Have you?"

"Yes. You never noticed me, did you?"

He said nothing for a moment. "Of course, I noticed you. You are the fabulously capable Lady Jane Chatley."

"As I said, you never noticed me."

"I didn't look hard enough, it's true."

She shrugged, feeling sorry for herself. "You can say that now, but I was invisible to you. And I kept it that way because I would never throw myself at someone, push my way where I wasn't wanted. But then, suddenly, like a blessed miracle, you seemed to truly see me."

He made a sound.

"No," she said, cutting off whatever he might have been about to say. "You are not the only one who gets to be angry and bitter over this. You finally saw me as someone worthy of your attention. For a few hours over a few days, I was blissfully happy."

She began to pace because she couldn't keep still while saying so many intimate things.

"And now you cannot see and you have withdrawn your regard for me. It is too cruel." When she stepped on the cane, it snapped under her foot with a satisfying crack.

She would have to leave London to escape the heartbreak of losing Christopher. At least she would escape her cousin as well.

Just when happiness was within her grasp, it had all evaporated along with the gas in the Westings' godforsaken oven!

She stared at his handsome face, turned away from her. It was easy to believe there were fickle gods playing tricks on mere mortals, exactly as the Greeks and Romans surmised.

"I have not withdrawn my regard," he said quietly.

She held her breath, even as her body started to tremble.

"But, truthfully, for your own sake," he continued, "I believe you should forsake me. This is all I will ever be, a blind man—terrified, angry, trapped, useless."

A sob welled up in her. He was wrong but didn't know it.

"Jane, come here," he said.

And she did. Not caring who might walk in, she walked into his outstretched arms, wrapping hers around his waist, feeling his close around her.

"You are a saint," he murmured against her hair, and she laughed through her tears.

"No," she said, her voice muffled against his jacket. "I am simply a woman who is feeling sorry for herself and a little lost."

"That makes two of us, except for the woman part, of course."

That almost sounded like the humor of her Christopher from before. She drew back and looked at him.

"If you have not withdrawn your regard for me, nor I for you, then why don't we stop feeling sad and help each other?"

"How can I possibly help you?"

She couldn't say the first words that popped into her mind. *By loving me!*

"If you could try to think a little about your future, perhaps one with me, then I will be patient as Job."

"I cannot imagine my future anymore," Christopher confessed, "but I would like to have you in it, in some capacity. Never doubt that, although I am certain I will try to push you away again."

She reached up and stroked his cheek. "And I still will not let you."

Tugging his head down closer, she let him claim her mouth. Their kiss started out as gentle, compassionate, and comforting, flaring to passion in the span of a heartbeat. His hands drew her against him, one of his thighs slid between hers, trapping her skirts tightly. Her lips opened, and when his tongue touched hers, the heat pooled between her legs.

"Mm," she moaned against his mouth, and heard his answering groan.

This kissing, which used to be a delight, was becoming more torturous each time as her body clamored for something more. Desire, raw and fierce, laid hold of her whenever he held her in his arms, and she longed for him to slake his need upon her, for she could feel his firm arousal.

Moreover, she ached for him to bring her the sweet release she'd only read about in *Aristotle's Masterpiece* and in her English translation of Nicholas Venette's *Conjugal Love*.

In any case, whenever he touched her, she felt hopeful. When her skin got goosebumps and her insides melted, she knew he was meant for her.

"Will you walk with me?" she asked him, while their bodies were still touching and his breath and hers were blended.

"No," he said.

She bit her lip, defeated.

"Not *today*, Jane."

She blinked. Perhaps he was bending a little "When?"

He released her and took a step back. Standing with his legs slightly apart, looking strong, masculine, healthy, she felt her heart expand with love for him.

Love!

"I suppose I need to get another one of those canes you broke so thoughtlessly," he said, and she opened her mouth in surprise while his handsome face twisted into a wry grin.

"Yes," she agreed. "I suppose you should."

CHAPTER TWELVE

When Jane left the Foresters' drawing room after taking tea with Christopher, she asked the butler for the whereabouts of the Duke of Westing. Luckily, he was in the house, using the table in his sister's library for a desk.

With nerves fluttering in her stomach at approaching the duke, Jane tapped on the door.

"Come," he said.

She pushed the door open, and he rose to his feet.

"Your Grace, may I speak with you?"

"Of course." But his tone was puzzled. "I'm afraid, dear lady, I have no idea who you are, but I am happy to speak with you all the same."

"My apologies, my lord. I am Jane Chatley, Lord and Lady Charles Chatley's daughter."

His brows drew together. She hoped it wasn't a reaction to her father's dreadful reputation. So far, the earl's tarnish had not rubbed off on either her or her mother. Jane had never been excluded from genteel society, and no one snubbed her mother, except for the lack of couples' invitations. Jane very much hoped the duke was no different.

"Forgive me for staring, Lady Jane. Your appearance is surprising, that's all. Rather like suddenly finding a hedgehog in one's soup bowl."

Jane couldn't help the short laugh that escaped her lips, although on second thought, she supposed the duke could have chosen a fairer creature than a garden hedgehog to compare her.

"I am a friend of your son's," she clarified, thinking how incomplete the word *friend* was in this case. "I was visiting with him in the parlor."

"*Ah,* I see." His expression turned instantly somber. "Is anything amiss? Besides the obvious, of course."

Jane's heart twinged with regret. *The poor man!* Everyone knew it was his love of technological progress that had caused the explosion, and she could see he was laden with guilt. The Duke of Westing was sinking a small fortune into helping with the upcoming Great Exhibition at the nearly completed Crystal Palace to showcase all sorts of advancements in science, but he was helpless in the face of Christopher's injury. No amount of money could solve that problem.

However, she also knew the man she loved—*a relief to admit those words if only in her head*—adored his father, and Jane felt certain the duke's guidance and support would help Christopher to regain some measure of his former ambition.

"I greatly fear your son is slipping into the doldrums." She stood in the center of the room, wringing her hands like a ninny. "I don't know how to help him, but I am hopeful *you* can."

"Will you take a seat?" he offered.

"No, thank you, Your Grace. I won't take up your time. Your son needs some motivation." Her words came tumbling out as she felt close to tears but refused to cry before this important nobleman, a stranger.

"Lord Westing says he cannot—*will not*—return to Parliament. Yet I *know* it is his passion. Surely, there must be other men who have been members with various afflictions. Will you speak with him? I think he sorely needs encouraging."

To her relief, he nodded. "I will try. He is difficult to talk to nowadays. So bitter. He sees no one, except Lord Burnley." Then he looked thoughtful. "I suppose that is incorrect if you have just come from a visit with him."

He paused, glancing down at the thick volume on the table.

"I was reading about an old law, concerning property rights, and normally, my son and I would be discussing it, occasionally even arguing over our positions."

"You can still do that, surely."

A long, drawn out sigh from the duke worried her.

"As you say, he is despondent. Each time I try to speak with him about anything beyond the weather, he tells me to stop."

"Then you must not stop," she insisted. "Rather, you must tell him how blindness will not close the doors of government to him. It won't, will it?"

He frowned. "I see no reason why it should, but I don't know if he is ready to hear it."

Again, Jane's heart went out to him. Watching his smart, promising son lose hope must be wrenching to a father. Hopefully, he would find the words to help him. But Christopher undoubtedly needed more than mere words.

"I know you are on the committee for the Great Exhibition. I saw a list of some of the wonders which will be exhibited in the Crystal Palace. One of them may help your son. It's a machine to print raised letters in a new alphabet. Lord Westing could use it to make letters which are legible to both the sighted—because they look like our regular alphabet—and to the blind—because the letters are raised. He can touch the raised dots, ten per line, to read them. Most importantly, he can still write his thoughts easily."

"That's marvelous. When it comes to London, I shall go directly to the exhibit, even before it opens and seek out this machine."

CHRISTOPHER MISSED JANE THE moment she left. If his fate was to sit in the relentless darkness for the rest of his godforsaken life, he might find it bearable only were she to sit with him.

On the one hand, they had agreed they had mutual feelings, and she had pleaded with him to keep her in his life. *How could he turn down her sweet offer when she was the only brightness left to him?*

On the other hand, he could hardly ask that of her, to sacrifice her future to play nursemaid and companion.

"Hello," he said, listening for an answer. When none came, knowing himself alone, he let loose a yell. He was sure it rivalled any barbarian's war cry or Celtic clan's *sluaghghairm*, as they were called.

It felt damned good to let out the thick and dark emotions brewing inside him.

Not that he was a warrior. Not that he could even fight his way out of a ring of children at this point.

The door to the drawing room slammed open.

"Chris," came his father's voice. "Are you all right?"

He could hear the panic in the duke's voice and felt momentarily remorseful. However, it wasn't as if he could ride into the country and scream in private.

What could he say? "No, I am not all right. I'm blind."

Silence, and he could picture his father's disappointed face.

"There is nothing new ailing me, however, if that's what you are asking. I simply felt like yelling. I still do."

Then he sighed and slumped back onto the sofa, glad he hadn't misjudged the distance and ended up on the floor.

"I don't know what to do."

Still unspeaking, his father walked over and sat beside him. He felt the duke's large hand on his knee.

"You can still do most anything you want to do."

Christopher sighed. "That is utter shit, and you know it. Everything has changed. I can't walk out of this house and down the street. I can't hail a hansom cab by myself. Or perhaps I can, but I won't know if the driver really drops me where I want to go, will I? I can't play chess or cards."

"You hate chess," his father pointed out.

"I don't hate it. I just hate losing to you. At least, I don't have to do that anymore."

He tried to make light of it, but at that moment, he would gladly lose if he could see a blasted chessboard.

"What's this I hear about you not wanting to go to Parliament?"

What the devil! They'd been talking about him. Specifically, Jane had gone running to his father. He would have to speak to her about that. It most assuredly did not sit well. In fact, it made him want to yell again.

"There have been ministers with limited sight," his father continued, "and certainly many with limited hearing. And some have been brought into Parliament in a pushchair. There is no reason on earth you cannot come to Westminster with me and then, eventually, take my seat."

Christopher considered these words.

He simply couldn't imagine how to get out of the house, let alone go to Parliament. Leaving his aunt's home seemed insurmountable.

"Maybe you're right," he hedged, "but I will wait a little longer."

"For what?" His father's tone was impatient.

"I don't know. I'm simply not ready." He feared he never would be.

What would happen to the family seat in the House of Lords if he never got off the sofa again? He pondered this a moment. Maybe Amanda could be the first female member of Parliament.

Knowing her, she could singlehandedly destroy the government in a week.

If he didn't feel so sick inside, he would mention it, at least in jest.

"I'd like you to leave me alone, please, Father. And can you summon Abner?"

"To take you upstairs? I'll do that."

"No!" The idea of his brilliant, independent father helping him to find the stairs only increased his sense of pathetic helplessness. *How would he ever make his father proud again?*

"I would prefer Abner, if you please."

Without another word, his father left the room.

THE NEXT DAY, CHRISTOPHER was summoned by his mother mid-morning just when he was about to eat breakfast. When Abner helped him find her in the drawing room, he discovered she had a brand-new cane. *Jane!*

He had a feeling his mother was going to dragoon him by any means possible into going on an outing. A frisson of alarm raced down his spine. He had barely managed to successfully take tea in the parlor, after all.

"I don't know about this, Mother."

"It will be good for you," she insisted. "We go directly to my studio in Chelsea. Nothing could be simpler."

He was trying to tamp down the terror of venturing out into the unknown.

"Surely, with my assistance," his mother persisted, "and a footman, it won't be too difficult a venture."

Perhaps not for her! For him, however, the notion of going out into the world in absolute darkness terrified him. His pulse was racing at the mere thought.

"I am donning my gloves now, which means I am ready. You look ready, so we shall leave at once. If you have trepidations when we get underway, we can always turn around. Lady Jane won't mind."

"Lady Jane! Is she here?" Christopher suddenly wondered if she were even then in the room and had remained silent. If she had, he didn't think he would ever forgive her. Certainly, she would see abject terror in his expression, and he didn't want her to witness his cowardice.

"No, of course not. We will pick her up at her home on the way."

"You said we were going directly to Chelsea."

He heard her walk to the door.

"Yes, directly *after* picking up your friend."

His mother had said he appeared ready, but how did he know?

"How do I look?"

Silence. *Had his valet mismatched his tie and shirt?*

"Mother, I can't see you, remember?"

"Oh yes, sorry. I smiled and nodded my approval. You look dashing as usual, positively splendid, and I very much like what Abner has done with your hair. Speaking of whom, are you accompanying us, Abner?" she addressed his valet, whom Christopher had entirely forgotten.

"I don't believe so, Your Grace. Am I, my lord?"

"No. I think a driver and footman will be enough should I need assistance."

The next few moments were among the most frightening of his life. Hearing the front door close behind him, smelling the thick London air on a gentle breeze, walking down the steps with his new cane pointed out before him like a knight's lance, and feeling pavement under his foot instead of carpet or tile—*what an unwelcome adventure!*

After one misstep getting into the carriage when, somehow, his left foot missed the pull-down completely, swinging wildly in the air, they were on their way to Jane's house close by Hanover Square.

"Don't think I'm entirely gullible, Chris," his mother said when they were nearly there.

"I have never thought you so, Mother, but what are we talking about?"

"Thinking I don't know you are insinuating the lovely Jane Chatley into my life in order for her to be in yours, as well."

He smiled broadly for the first time in days. "And you don't mind?"

"Not if she can truly assist me. If she is a nuisance or a ninny, then I shall dismiss her at once," the duchess said.

"Mother! You can't *dismiss* her as if she were staff," he pointed out, suddenly worried she would offend Jane. Then it would be awkward as hell.

However, she made a humming sound, as their carriage came to a stop.

"I suppose you're right, especially if you like this girl. We must hope we never have to cross that bridge."

They didn't get out of their carriage. Instead, their footman went to the Chatleys' door, and Jane came out a minute later. When she climbed in, Christopher felt the gaping emptiness close around him again at not being able to look upon her. He was trapped in a bubble of darkness, knowing the world and all its light was carrying on without him.

After Jane greeted his mother, he tipped his hat, hoping it was toward her.

"How are you today, Lord Westing?" Jane asked, sounding chipper, and he knew by her tone she was delighted to see him out of his aunt and uncle's house.

"I am well, thank you. I apologize for not being the one to come to your door and collect you, nor for assisting you into the carriage. It goes against the grain of everything I've been taught to remain seated."

"I am sorry it pains you, but I am not at all slighted. I know you to be a gentleman," she insisted.

He recalled his obscene questions and felt his cheeks redden with shame.

"Are you well today?" he asked, hoping to redeem his earlier behavior.

"I am, thank you."

Then the three of them were on their way to the riverside and his mother's little studio in a house on Cheyne Walk.

Christopher realized Jane wore a light floral perfume, which he hadn't noticed until her last visit and which now made him feel the throb of desire, evoking their kisses in his aunt's parlor. He would ask her in private what it was. He also wished he could inquire as to what she was wearing and wondered if the blind were allowed to simply ask people to tell them about their clothing and colors.

That seemed inappropriate, however, so he sat quietly while the ladies continued their niceties.

His mother became more talkative as they neared the place of her passion.

"Of course, I had space in our home—before the explosion, I mean—but I like being amongst other artists in Chelsea. You may find my studio and even the street it is on to be very *Bohemian*. Do you know the word?"

"No," Jane admitted. "I do not."

"It is one of those words everyone is bandying about nowadays, particularly the art community, to mean *unconventional* in a favorable sense. Like Gypsies, except not as filthy transients and thieves, and now, everyone wants to pretend to be one."

"A gypsy?" Christopher asked.

"No," his mother said, "An exotically *Bohemian* artist!"

"I didn't realize," Jane said, sounding genuinely surprised.

"Neither did I," Christopher had a clear image in his head, and it made him laugh. "Are you saying you intend to wear a turban and leave us for life in a caravan?"

"Don't be absurd," his mother responded. "I merely want you both to be prepared for anything. Colored glass windows and flowers everywhere, and people in robes, and music, and all that."

"No!" Christopher exclaimed, hearing Jane make a sound like muffled laughter. "Not flowers and robes, Mother. The horror! Say it isn't so."

"Stop it, you naughty boy. You're making fun of me. Anyway, we're here."

And now the difficult part would begin. His first foray to somewhere he had never been before. His mother had only recently taken the studio, renting a room from a married couple who were themselves painters and who needed the money.

The footman would be there to assist him, so he tried to feel confident as he exited the carriage. Pavement underfoot, then the footman took his arm, and he had his cane in his other hand, eyes firmly closed. With the clank of a cast iron gate and a couple more steps, as directed, Christopher found himself indoors in a place predominantly smelling of turpentine.

"My studio is upstairs with a view of the river." His mother hesitated. "Well, that won't do you any good, of course," and he realized she was addressing him. "But across the street is a tiny strip of greenery, and then the Thames is floating by, nearly outside the window."

"Yes, Mother, I'm aware of the location of both Chelsea and the Thames."

He climbed the stairs slowly, feeling disoriented and as if he let go of the railing, he might topple backward.

"Jane, what do you think so far?" he asked, simply needing to hear her reassuring voice.

"The house is small but clean," she said from higher up the stairs. "I can see why your mother wants to spend time here. This may be Bohemian, but it is not vulgar."

"Vulgar!" his mother practically shrieked. "Why, of course not, dear girl. As if I would be involved in something unsavory. Here we are, top of the stairs, across the landing, first room on the left."

The footman escorted him through the doorway, then, to his consternation, his mother dismissed the man with a simple, "You may wait below."

As soon as the man released him, Christopher froze. He couldn't take a step. He might as well be at the edge of an abyss.

"There are rugs down, Chris, so don't trip."

"Mother!" he said irritably, as if her brief advice would help. Then he felt Jane's soft hands on his arm.

"Hold the cane out and take another couple of steps and you'll be in the center of the room. It isn't large, but it's filled with light, painted all white, and it has a very high ceiling."

"Just so," his mother said unhelpfully.

"Don't let go," he muttered.

Jane squeezed his arm reassuringly.

"There is a table in front of you with many tins—"

"Those are what we call moist colors, easy to use outside. Winsor & Newton, naturally."

"And there are cups with many paintbrushes, bowls of water," Jane continued, "next to trays with colored blocks in different blues and greens and lots of oranges, yellows and reds."

"Those are called cakes, and I mix them with water," his mother interrupted again, sounding thrilled to be sharing her art with them. "Those are all being used, but see, my new cakes are here."

Christopher already knew what they looked like and didn't mind being left out, hearing his mother's excitement as she showed Jane the rectangular watercolor blocks with the embossed stamps of the makers, such as George Rowney & Co or Newman's.

"It makes me want to try to paint," Jane admitted.

"And so you shall," his mother gushed. "After my show, you must come here, and I'll teach you how to get started. Then, if inspiration strikes, you will be on your way."

"Perhaps," Jane agreed, and Christopher wondered if she really would try.

If she did, what would she paint? He would never get to see it, and a wave of sadness crashed against him. Then Jane touched his arm again.

"Your mother's artwork is displayed on easels as well as framed pieces that are stacked around the room. Oh, Duchess, such lovely colors and the way you have captured the light. Chris . . . Lord Westing," Jane amended quickly, "some appear to shimmer and some are translucent and some are exact copies of their subject down to the smallest detail."

"I have seen her paintings, and I agree, they are wonderful. Mother, it seems you have a new admirer."

"Thank you," the duchess said, and he could tell by her tone she was beaming with happiness. "I very much like being in the studio, but I admit I also enjoy going outside to sketch and sometimes even to paint. As it turns out, I can paint quite quickly and capture the sunlight on a subject before the light changes. It's harder to do it properly later from a sketch or, worse, from memory. Spontaneity is my muse," she added.

"Does Father know you work outside? Where do you paint? Is it safe? This Bohemian area, as you call it, cannot be entirely without danger."

"Dear boy!" his mother said. "I am perfectly at ease here. There are so many others doing what I'm doing, mostly men, but sometimes women, and the men have wives who are also models. There are very talented people painting around me, like the one I waved to on the way in."

"Mother," Christopher said testily.

"I'm sorry. I forgot you didn't see him. William Hunt is his name. And there's another William around the corner, a Scot with the surname of Dyce. Fascinating to speak with. He's been painting frescoes in the new Houses of Parliament, Christopher, only imagine. They will be there forever. Massive things, they are, too. And guess who else is here, on this very street."

"We wouldn't know." Moreover, he could not imagine the frescoes, as she so blithely told him to do, and would have to rely on someone to describe them to him.

"Another William! The brilliant Mr. Turner. I know he uses his initials professionally, J.M.W., but he goes by William. Except here in Chelsea, where he goes by Mr. Booth for anonymity. He lives alone with his housekeeper, but any of us painters know him for who he is. And he is my inspiration—not for his unsavory lifestyle, of course, but for his landscapes."

"I thought *spontaneity* was your inspiration," Christopher reminded her.

His mother laughed, and Jane joined in.

"Spontaneity is her muse," Jane reminded him.

"Mr. Turner believes in it, too," the duchess said.

"So, you model yourself on this unsavory, brilliant man and go outside and paint."

"Well, he has painted all over the world, and I don't paint much beyond Hyde Park, but still."

"You have made Hyde Park look like the world, Mother." He wanted her to understand it was her style as much as her subjects that appealed to people.

"Thank you, dear. Often, I only go to St. James's Park, but I do like to sketch by the Serpentine. Perfectly safe in either place, I promise." Then she sighed heavily. "Although, we thought we were safe in our own home, and then look what happened to you."

Christopher felt her words like an arrow. If only he *could* look, but he knew what she meant. At any time, any moment, something could happen, such as with Jane's friend Lord Cambrey, hit and injured terribly by a reckless carriage driver.

Luckily, with only broken bones, the earl had recovered. But, in his own case, no one knew how to mend damaged optic nerves, if that was even the true cause of his blindness. Jane squeezed his arm again, and it heartened him.

After all, he wasn't dead. He was out on a beautiful day, by all accounts, with his mother and Jane. He could hardly ask for more.

"They must be oil painters," he said. "The couple who own the house."

"Yes," his mother said. "How did you know?"

"The turpentine smell was so strong downstairs. Up here, it's not nearly as bad. I'm glad you don't muck about with that stuff."

"You're correct. Their studio is on the ground floor, but I don't even smell it anymore. One becomes quite used to it. So, Lady Jane—"

"Please, call me Jane."

"Thank you, I will. I could certainly use your assistance to label all my paintings and to make sure any completed work that isn't framed becomes framed before the exhibit. Of course, we need to make arrangements for the transportation of my art to the Egyptian Hall. We'll be able to do that the day before, when they take down whatever is currently in the gallery."

"Very well," Jane said, sounding undaunted so far. "At the exhibit, to accentuate your paintings, do you think fresh flowers would be good?"

"Yes," his mother said emphatically. "I very much like that idea. We can arrange them on pedestals. It will show my realism as well as bring nature inside to augment the natural world of my paintings."

"Then we should go to Covent Garden a few days before and choose the very best," Jane said. "Do you have enough vases?"

"I'll give you a spending allowance, and leave that up to you," his mother said. "If you could choose the right vase and flowers for each painting—"

"*Hm,*" Jane interjected.

"What, dear girl?"

Christopher liked their familiarity in conversing. It boded well.

"Perhaps one for each painting is too much," Jane wondered. "Perhaps if we group the paintings to tell a story, whatever you were thinking when you painted, of course, then one pretty vase with appropriate flowers nearby would be enough, rather than one for each."

"Fine, yes, I'll leave that up to you."

Those very same words he heard numerous times from his mother during the next few minutes while they discussed a good typesetter for the tags, putting an advertisement in the *London Times*, and the all-important gallery lighting. She wanted to copy the diffused lighting of Turner's gallery by stretching herring nets across the ceiling skylights of the Egyptian Hall.

And then Jane started to look through the artwork, some leaning in stacks against the walls. She couldn't help exclaiming over those she particularly liked, describing her favorites for his ears.

"And refreshments?" she asked suddenly.

"I, for one, am starved," Christopher admitted, having skipped breakfast when he'd been abducted on this journey. He was glad of it, too, in case he'd made a mess of his clothing before they'd gone out.

"Actually, Lord Westing," Jane said, trying to remain formal with him in front of his mother, "I meant *during* the exhibit. Since it is not a museum, won't those attending expect something in the way of food and drink?"

"Yes, you are right, Jane," his mother said. "I'll leave that to you."

He hoped Jane wasn't losing her enthusiasm. He also hoped they would leave soon and go home to eat.

"I brought a swatch of silk I think would be lovely draped behind that large painting," his mother said, and Jane murmured something noncommittal.

"Oh, bother! I left it in the carriage. Chris, do be a dear and—" the duchess broke off realizing she couldn't send him scurrying back downstairs on a whim.

He froze, feeling the now-familiar uselessness.

"I'll go, Your Grace," Jane offered, and his sense of futility grew worse.

"Nonsense," said his mother. "I know where I tucked it. I'll be right back. You two carry on." And he heard her footsteps cross the studio and exit the room.

"You look annoyed," Jane said.

"I'm not annoyed," he bit out. "I'm furious!"

CHAPTER THIRTEEN

Jane was stunned. The day had been going so well.

"Why?"

"My mother just walked out and left us alone together."

She considered. "Yes. And?"

"Your reputation!" Christopher exclaimed. "We are alone, upstairs in a strange house in Chelsea, and she didn't even blink an eye. Or I assume she didn't. My mother has been lecturing me as sternly as an Oxford professor since the moment my voice deepened and I grew my first downy whiskers. And always the same lecture: Do not find yourself in a compromising situation with a female."

He rapped his cane on the floor for emphasis.

"Knowing *your* mother, I'm sure you've been told the same for an equally long time and just as forcefully," he added.

Jane couldn't help laughing slightly. "Unless the male was a marquess or an earl, but definitely not with a mere viscount or baron. Thus, in this situation, she would wholeheartedly approve, as long as I shouted it from the rooftop."

Christopher visibly relaxed. "Oh, I see. The husband trap."

"Precisely." She began to wander the room again.

"And will you?" His serious tone stopped her.

"Will I what?"

"Shout it from the rooftop and . . . trap me?"

She took a deep breath, knowing this was more than light banter.

"Would you be terribly angry with me if I did?"

"No," he said instantly. "If you wanted to trap me, I'd be honored but baffled. Unfortunately, I am certain you would come to regret it."

Jane was about to argue but heard his mother on the stairs and knew Christopher could, too, although neither could know if their voices had carried, or whether she had heard them.

"Regret what?" the Duchess of Westing asked.

Apparently, she had. *What to say?*

"Regret not eating breakfast," Christopher quipped before Jane could respond. "Your only son is starving, Mother. Shall we finish up for today?"

"Yes, as soon as I show Jane this silk swatch. I'll drape it on the frame. Just so. At the exhibit, of course, I'll have an entire curtain of it behind the painting. I want this one to be the focus."

"Which painting is it?" Christopher asked.

"It's one of Hyde Park with the little bridge and fountain, just two people, a very blue sky."

"And the buildings in the distance look so real," Jane said. "Your mother has chosen a russet red silk for the background that makes the entire painting stand out."

"It nearly matches the color of the walls in Mr. Turner's gallery," the duchess insisted. "I've been there a number of times. It's right on the side of his house on Queen Anne Street. Anyway, what do you think?"

"I think it looks lovely," Jane confirmed.

"Shall I retrieve the footman or can you make it downstairs?" the duchess asked.

"I believe I can make it down on my own," Christopher said. "I don't know whether to ask one of you to go in front of me and risk your life if I fall upon you, or keep you both behind me to pick up my bruised body if I do take a tumble."

"You hold the railing, and I'll take your arm," his mother said. "Jane can go behind. I'm sure we shall not encounter difficulty."

IF CHRISTOPHER BELIEVED BY her helping his mother, they would be able to spend time together, Jane feared he had made a grave error. For the Duchess of Westing heaped task after task upon her over the next few days, and Jane barely arrived at Berkley Square before being sent out into the world again.

On a rare afternoon at home, she suddenly had an unexpected visit from Lord Fowler for whom she had barely spared a thought.

"I fear your interest in our quest has lagged," he said, his face a picture of sadness.

Guilt took ahold of her. She had promised to help him find a wife, and she meant to keep her promise. After all, the man's future happiness was at stake, certainly as important as an art show.

"Not at all, my lord." And she recalled an invitation she'd received only the day before and set aside. "Are you intending to go to the zoo to see the hippopotamus? Did you know the Zoological Society is turning its unveiling into a gala next to Regent's Park?"

"Yes," he said, "there is a private party, too, at Lord Burton's home on the Cumberland Terrace. Don't you think the ladies will all be very scientific-minded and only interested in zoology and dry bones with a fondness for dreadfully dead, stuffed creatures?"

She started to laugh. "No, my lord. I think many, like me, will be interested in the hippopotamus from Egypt and even more interested in the quality of Thomas Burton's champagne and hors d'oeuvres. It will give you a chance to speak with some new ladies as well as some of the same ones, and not to worry about dancing."

"Oh, I never worry about dancing," he said.

She bit her tongue, for he ought to. Lord Fowler was not the smoothest dancer in the *ton*. However, she didn't want to suddenly become a dance instructor on top of everything else, so she let it go.

"What I mean is, it is nice to meet people in various venues, such as plays and the ballet, and even the zoological gardens. You'll have a chance to discuss various topics and your likes and dislikes. You will gain insight as to whether you wish to spend your days with a particular young lady. Imagine conversing over your morning tea or coffee for the rest of your life, with her being the last person you see at the end of each day."

"Yes, I understand. Every day is certainly not like a ball or dinner party."

"Exactly. In the upcoming weeks, we'll try to go to a museum and—" Then she had another idea. "And an art show. Are you interested in art?"

"Isn't everyone to some degree?"

"That's a very good answer," Jane praised him, "and perhaps true. There is a watercolor display coming up."

"Watercolor?" he repeated, sounding disappointed.

Christopher and his mother were right about people under-valuing the medium.

"I assure you the artist is quite skilled. You won't be disappointed by the lack of oil paint. Never mind that now. For the viewing of the hippopotamus, I shall meet you there."

"Alone?" he asked. "Perhaps I should collect you in my carriage."

"Most assuredly not," Jane said.

She wouldn't dare let her association with Lord Fowler in any way besmirch her reputation, not while she and Christopher were at the beginning of something that might prove to be extraordinary. Even then, while they talked, her maid sat in the corner, dozing off, at the same time representing the watchful eye of propriety and morals.

"I shall be with my mother. She will have many friends with whom to keep herself occupied. And you and I will speak with many interesting ladies at the party."

"I'm so pleased you haven't given up on me, Lady Chatley."

"I don't give up on anyone," she promised.

"FATHER, IS THAT YOU?" Christopher had been waiting in the library for his father for an hour, ever since Burnley had left.

He and Owen no longer held their visits in Christopher's room. Abner always had him ready and downstairs in the drawing room when his friend arrived. Sometimes, if the weather was fair, they sat in the back in Lady Forester's garden, and Owen read the papers to him, as many as they could get through.

And though his friend had asked him, Christopher hadn't yet acquiesced to a stroll outside the house. While the excursion the week before to Chelsea had gone smoothly, the notion of walking along with Burnley, perhaps needing to grab hold of his arm or requiring his assistance if he tripped, made him queasy. He wasn't ready for such vulnerability out in public, nor did he wish to embarrass his friend.

However, an outing with his father was another matter. After their last conversation, Christopher couldn't help thinking, daily, in fact, about Parliament and how much he missed it.

Despite what he'd told the duke before, he couldn't tamp down his innate interest in their government. Moreover, Christopher still couldn't dredge up enthusiasm for a life that didn't involve helping to run Britain in some capacity. In fact, despite thinking he faced insurmountable barriers, he didn't want to do anything else except benefit the British people by crafting and sponsoring new acts.

Although grateful to hear the news through Owen, he knew it was filtered for the papers. He most wanted to hear about what was truly going on in their nation's heart, in the chambers of the lawmakers, and for that, he needed the Duke of Westing. He craved returning to the echoing hall of the House of Lords, yearned to hear the ministers speak their minds, and desperately wanted to discuss Parliament's latest happenings with the man he most respected—his own father.

Thus, he waited in the library. It was a ridiculous place for a blind man, and Christopher could do nothing but sit amidst the books he could not see and let his thoughts run amok.

Sometimes, he contemplated the fateful morning when he'd gone downstairs to their old kitchen. Trying, in his memory, to stop himself from going there or urging his former self to leave more quickly—the futile endeavor always put him in a foul mood, but he found it hard to stop his wayward musings. In his brain, he continued to try to change the unchangeable.

Sometimes, he mulled over his first kiss with Jane, and it was now easy to recall her floral scent and the feel of her lips. Knowing she continued to let him kiss her, and kissed him back with equal ardor even *after* the explosion, always cheered him.

Little else caused him joy lately, and thus, he was ready at least to discuss the possibility of somehow fitting into his father's world once more. Unfortunately, except for their brief conversation when Christopher had well and truly shunned him, almost since that day, the duke had kept his distance. Or been incredibly busy.

Upon finally hearing footsteps that were certainly a man's and not those of the Foresters' butler, and even more unlikely to be a footman's or a coachman's indoors, Christopher had called out when they had passed by the open door.

Had his father seen him sitting there and kept on walking?

He heard the owner of the booted feet stop and retrace his steps slowly, unwillingly.

"Chris," Lord Westing said, his tone overly jovial, blatantly false. "Here you are."

"Yes," he replied, puzzled at his father's strange behavior of late. "Here I am. I have been in this house, lurking in one room or another for weeks. But you have been absent, at least whenever I am searching for you."

"Nonsense."

Christopher hated it when someone said that word, particularly when it was a cover for the truth.

"All right," he began again, "perhaps I mistakenly believed you weren't here because I couldn't see you. I assure you, Father, I was searching."

Silence. However, it spoke volumes. His father seemed intensely uncomfortable around him. *Was he ashamed of him?*

Christopher considered standing up and physically reaching out to him, but didn't want to embarrass the duke.

For a moment, unable to see the older man's face, he was at a loss how to proceed.

"I'm so terribly sorry." His father's agonized words came out of the darkness, shocking him.

The depth of feeling was clear in his father's voice, sounding thick with emotion.

"Everything that has happened is all my fault. I, who am head of this family. I, who am supposed to care for you and guide you—I've caused this."

Christopher sat stunned by his father's admission. His mother had said as much, yet her tone of exasperation, saying she wanted to strangle her husband, had seemed more in jest.

His father, on the other hand, sounded desperately serious, as if he carried a heavy burden indeed.

Did he blame his father? Christopher had spent more time wondering why he had gone foraging for something as silly as a biscuit to dunk in a nonexistent cup of tea, when he as easily could have gone out to a pub for fried fish and ale or to a club for a proper meal.

His father took a step farther into the room. "Say something. I can hardly bear what I've done."

Christopher swallowed, searching his own heart. "I don't blame you."

It was the truth. "If the workmen had done their jobs properly," he continued, "they would be alive, and I would be able to see. That wasn't your fault."

He felt his father's hand on his arm. "If I'd been content with our kitchen as it was, though."

Christopher shrugged. "Wanting to embrace progress, Father, it's the British way, isn't it? Look at our industry and manufacturing, our colonization, our railways."

He felt his father squeeze his shoulder but knew the man still needed reassuring.

"Anyway, the bathrooms were a good addition, we have—or, at least, we had—the best plumbing on the street."

"We will again," the duke insisted. "I've hired top-notch men. I was looking through the designs at the patent office—"

"Dangerous thing for you to do, Father!"

"What? Oh, a joke. I see. *Haha.* That's what your mother always says, too." And the duke laughed briefly, the heavy, sentimental moment having passed. "I found an amazing invention, a shower bath. We're definitely going to have one of those. Water spraying at you from all sides. Glorious!"

"Is it though?" Not wishing to dampen his father's enthusiasm, but the only thing Christopher could raise to the level of glory would be light, and lots of it. That, and holding Jane in his arms again. It had been too long.

"It *will be* glorious, Chris, I promise. In any case, your mother has enlisted help with her areas of expertise to get the house back up to snuff as soon as the builders have finished."

"Lady Jane Chatley," Christopher informed him.

"Is that the girl? Pretty with light brown hair?" Then he paused. "Oh, damn it all, Chris. I keep forgetting you cannot see her."

Christopher had a flash of gratitude. He could call up Jane's looks easily into his mind's eye.

"It's all right, Father. I've seen what she looks like. And I agree, she is beautiful."

"I said pretty." His father's tone was now one of interest.

Christopher shrugged. He knew what he'd seen.

"And has she taken a fancy to you in return?" the duke asked.

Christopher couldn't help smiling. He had never said he'd taken a fancy to her, but it must have been apparent in his voice and his expression. It was fine at home among family or friends, but it would put him at a distinct disadvantage out in the world, if others could see his emotions upon his face, while he couldn't see theirs. He supposed dark spectacles would help.

"We'll see," he said noncommittally.

"I can certainly put in a good word for you, my boy."

Dear God, no!

"Father, don't. Lady Jane and I are finding our way fine on our own. I know she came to speak to you about me, and I want you to understand, I'm not keen on being discussed behind my back. Please, say nothing more to her."

"I believe it answers my question, nonetheless, as to whether she's taken a fancy to you." Then the duke sighed and sat down in the other chair at the table. "I need to do something for you, son. I cannot let go of my culpability. It pains me to see you."

"Then you *have* been avoiding me?"

"A little, I suppose. What can I do? Set me a task and I shall do it?"

"I would like some spectacles, shaded ones, so I can open my eyes without wondering if people are staring at them because they're crossed."

"I shall obtain them at once. Also, I saw at the patent office someone is developing a dress hat with vents in it so the hot air can escape. Would you like one?"

"A ventilated top hat?" Christopher could only imagine the ridicule. "No, thank you."

"I may get one for myself at any rate."

His father fell silent, undoubtedly musing on the newfangled inventions that had always delighted him.

"Was there anything else interesting?" Christopher asked, for even talking about ridiculous patents was better than sitting in silence.

"Artificial leeches," his father said abruptly, "but we probably shouldn't use them without supervision."

Christopher shuddered. "No, but I imagine if one needed a leech, an artificial one that can't crawl away might be preferable."

"That's what I thought, particularly when needed around the mouth area. I've got one here in my pocket. Would you like to hold it?"

Before Christopher answered, his father grabbed his hand and placed an object a mere few inches long onto his palm. As he closed his fingers around it, he realized it was squishy in the middle and pointy at one end. He squeezed it a few times, imagining it filling with blood as it regained its shape.

"Thank you," he said because he couldn't think of anything else to say and handed it back.

"Never mind that, dear boy, besides the spectacles, is there anything else I can do?"

"I am considering . . . that is, I think I would like to return to Parliament, just to come and listen." Finally, he had said it, and he felt good about doing so. Then he added, "Despite the bash to my head, my mind seems to be as clear as ever, for what that's worth."

"I didn't want to push you, but I am very glad you've come to it on your own. No sense in your languishing, not with your fine brain. There are many blind men who've done fabulous things."

"Really?" Christopher couldn't readily think of anyone.

"Of course." Silence.

"Father? Are you going to tell me of some?"

After another moment's hesitation, the duke said, "Well, there was Mr. Braille, of course."

Christopher couldn't help making a sound of exasperation. "You only know him because the teacher at the blind school talked about him. He blinded himself by accident, didn't he? Before inventing a system, about which everyone, both here and on the Continent, is still arguing as to its usefulness. Hardly someone who fits into ordinary society as I wish to do."

Another pause. "Then how about Homer? He was said to be blind."

"No one is even certain he was a real person, Father. Even the ancients thought him an amalgamation of other storytellers. Next."

"Mr. Galilei," the duke tried again. "You can't say he didn't do important things or that he wasn't a real man."

"Of course not, but he did his great work *before* he became blind. He could hardly look through a telescope *after* he lost his sight, could he?"

His father cleared his throat with a little coughing. "Shall we go have tea, or shall I have it brought in here?"

"Neither." Christopher felt a prickle of panic. "Are you saying you actually cannot think of anyone who accomplished something important *after* becoming blind? Something good for all humanity?"

"I'm no expert. So, coffee, then?"

"I'm beginning to feel worried. Before I believed I would adapt and then have a normal life, except for being sightless. Now, however, I'm truly wondering if I'll become a useless lump, a potato."

"A *potato*? You're heir to the dukedom."

"How on earth can I be a duke?"

"There's no question of that, dear boy." And his father gave a short chuckle. "When I die, you will be."

"Thus, I will not accomplish anything except inheriting by stepping over your dead body, which I'll undoubtedly trip over."

"Come now, don't be gruesome. Let me think. *Ah-ha.* Horatio Nelson!"

"What of him? He wasn't blind."

"In one eye, and that happened *before* he trounced the French at Trafalgar. And he only had one arm."

"All right," Chris agreed. "He seems legitimately to have carried on despite impediments."

"And our great civil servant and poet, John Milton."

"Father, have you read his later books in which he complains bitterly about how miserable his blindness made him?"

"No, I suppose I haven't," the duke said.

"And he, at least, had forty-three years before it happened," Christopher reminded him.

"Chris, you are being unreasonable. The man wrote *Paradise Lost* after he became blind."

"I rest my case."

They both laughed.

"I suppose tea would be welcome," he told his father. "I need to practice eating and drinking and doing it without making a mess."

"I will help." The duke rang the bell for a servant. "And I've thought of someone else of whom you might not have heard."

"Yes?" If it was a juggler or a cobbler, he was going to throttle his father.

"John Stanley went blind very early and still became a great composer and organist. A good friend of Handel's."

"You may stop now, Father. It is unlikely I will write like Milton or compose like this Mr. Stanley. And if you suggest I take up the harp, as the celebrated blind harper, Mr. Humphrey of Denbigh, I may do violence to either you, me, or that damned artificial leech. Still, I hope I can go to Parliament and listen both to great men and to idiots, and know the difference."

Moreover, he hoped Jane could accept a man whose future had been severely curtailed.

CHAPTER FOURTEEN

"Yes, Your Grace." Jane said those words so much, she said them even in her sleep, awakening in the middle of an anxious dream in which she told Christopher's mother, yes, she would make sure the hippopotamus made an appearance at the Egyptian Hall during the art show.

That morning, however, she was going to spend time with Christopher. She'd done research on a few things she thought he would find interesting.

When she arrived, he was in the drawing room as before. The tea was still steaming form the pot's spout and must have just been brought in.

"I'm here," she told him.

"I know," he offered her a broad smile.

"How?"

"Your footsteps are different from any of the members of this household."

She sighed. "You're brilliant."

"And even if you'd crept in silently, when you sat close, I would know you by your perfume."

"Then I hope you like it."

"I do," he promised. "It is quintessentially Jane. And what is this alluring fragrance which clings to you so delicately?"

She'd been with him only a minute, and already, he had made her blush and feel happy. "Petals of pinks and a little bergamot oil."

"Come closer so I can enjoy it better."

Laughing, she took a seat beside him. "May I pour the tea?"

"Yes, I've been practicing, but I'm not up to pouring yet, and certainly not over Aunt Tabitha's rug."

Jane poured them each a cup. "No mug, either, I see."

"No, I'm determined to keep to my manners. I'm not a farmer!"

"Very well. One teaspoon of sugar and plenty of milk. Here is yours." She placed the saucer into his outstretched hands.

Easily, he balanced it in one hand, spilling not a drop as he picked up the spoon and stirred.

"You *have* been practicing." Now she hoped she could get him to practice something else, living a normal life again. "What do you want to do today?"

His expression was one of perplexity. "Do?"

"Yes, together." They hadn't had an outing since the visit to his mother's studio, and she was determined to get him out of doors. "I finally have an afternoon free."

"From my demanding mother, you mean."

"I wouldn't say that. I like being busy, and the duchess and I get along splendidly."

"As long as you say yes to her," he pointed out.

"True, but so far, I haven't needed to say no. Shall we go to Hyde Park and walk by the Serpentine?"

He froze. "I thought we would simply stay here and talk."

"It is a beautiful sunny day. Wouldn't you like to get some fresh air?"

"The air is quite fresh in here," he protested. "It's not like we'd be going to the country."

"Please, Chris. I long for grass and trees, and the path by the Serpentine is very smooth. Or don't you want to be seen with me?"

He laughed. "You know it's not that. I . . . I haven't been for a stroll outside since it happened."

"But you have been out. With me. And then your mother told me you went with your father to Parliament the other day. I'm so pleased for you."

"Yes, but it was startling. The same as always in how it smelled and felt, yet everything seemed different. And it was extraordinarily loud, and without seeing who stood up to take the floor, it was hard to figure out who was speaking. And so many people came over to wish me well."

"Is that a bad thing?" She sipped her tea.

"I didn't know who any of them were at first. They seemed to forget that. Moreover, they seemed to expect I would identify each speaker immediately even in a cacophony of voices. When my father had to remind them to identify themselves, a couple MPs got huffy."

"Those same fools would have been huffy no matter what," Jane guessed. "And their pride was pricked when you hadn't already memorized their voices. Don't let that worry you."

He shrugged without comment. She was going to have to push him a little.

Watching him sip his tea like a perfect gentleman, she marveled at his poise. And when she offered him a biscuit, he even dunked it and brought it to his lips without fault.

"Don't let any single experience stop you from progressing. Each time you've taken tea with me, you've done it more smoothly. If someone came in right now, they wouldn't know you were blind, and I bet we can even figure out how you can pour successfully."

"Oh, such aspirations," he said, sounding cynical. "To think, I have to work my way up to pouring tea!

"Going to the park will be easier than to Parliament, don't you think?" Jane continued to press her case, ignoring his sarcasm. "Certainly, there will be less stairs. Just the two of us strolling. I'll tell you where we are going and who is approaching if anyone does. Plus, I have some interesting information to tell you."

"Tell me now," he demanded.

She laughed. "No. If you walk with me, then, and only then, I'll tell you."

He hesitated a long time, and she assumed he would say no. Then he cocked his head. "Are we alone?"

"Yes." Immediately, her heartbeat sped up.

"If you insist on my going out, I will make a fool of myself in front of everyone for a kiss."

She caught her breath. "Your boon from me is a kiss?"

"Not any kiss. Not a peck on the cheek. One of *our* kisses." Leaning forward, expertly judging the distance and height of the table, he set his saucer and teacup down without incident.

"Give me yours," he ordered, and she placed her saucer and cup in his hands. After he set those down as well, he turned to her and held his hands out.

The anticipation of kissing him took hold of her. Her body was purring even as she placed her hands in his.

"Much as I want to press you back against this sofa and ravish you, someone may walk in, and thus, we had best remain seated primly."

"You will settle for a mere kiss with me?"

He leaned forward. "*Settle* is the wrong word, as is *mere*. I am honored to kiss you."

Still holding both her hands in his, he pulled her the rest of the way toward him, and then lowered his head and kissed her.

Thorough, unhurried, perfect but never enough.

When he drew back, she sighed. "How is it we are able to do that so effortlessly? You cannot see, and I always close my eyes, and yet . . . ," she trailed off.

"I agree, it is effortless. Our mouths seem to find each other, like magnets."

The notion of their mouths drawn by some unseen force made her giggle.

As if he could see, Christopher reached over and retrieved her saucer, handing it to her.

"Finish your tea, and we shall go. But you know how I feel about your reputation. If you won't guard it, I will. It cannot be *only* the two of us. We will have to take Amanda."

In half an hour, the three of them were alighting from his carriage at the northeast side of Hyde Park. If the Westings had been in their own home on Grosvenor Square, they could have walked the distance in ten minutes.

Instructing the driver to come back in an hour, they entered through the Cumberland Gate.

Giving only the merest hint of apology, Amanda ran off almost instantly after seeing two of her friends in the distance. "I'm sure you'd rather be alone anyway," she called too loudly over her shoulder.

"I wondered why she agreed to come so easily," he said.

"Now what?" Jane asked. His sister was vexing and immature, and Jane could never remember displaying either of those traits.

Christopher shrugged. "I suppose you are allowed to take the arm of a blind man without a chaperone. It's not the same as being alone together indoors. In any case, I can't be accused of trying to look down your décolletage. Though I certainly would if I could."

Jane wished he could, too. The notion of his gaze upon her skin made her tingle nearly as much as his hands upon her. Moreover, she still found herself dressing nicely for him despite him not being able to see her.

"I believe most will not even notice your condition," she told him, although his eyes were firmly closed. "But we shall walk and accept any reckoning which may occur."

"Wait," he said as Jane tried to take his arm.

He tucked his cane under his arm and drew from his pocket a leather case. Opening it, he unfolded a pair of metal spectacles with dark, gray lenses and placed them on his face without comment.

His new appearance momentarily startled her. Instead of disguising his condition, at least to her, they marked him as blind. For the first time, Jane accepted Lord Christopher Westing, heir to a dukedom and the man whom she loved without reservation, was truly sightless.

"I'm ready," he said into the silence, "but if you don't take my arm and direct me, we shall stand here all day."

Quickly, she took hold of him, turned in a southerly direction, and began to walk.

"I'll tell you if there is an obstacle, and you can tell me if I'm going too quickly."

They headed down the footpath, eschewing the nearby busier bridle path. Even so, with the weather being good, there were a number of walkers enjoying the park. She let people go around them who wished to move faster, and she nodded in greeting to those who came toward them.

All the while, she kept his free arm firmly wrapped in her own, and with his other, he held the cane.

"We are strolling," Christopher pointed out. "Now, will you tell me?"

"You sound tense," Jane said. "Are you well?"

"Frankly, I am frightened as I am practically every moment when not indoors, but if I hear your voice, it helps, so proceed."

Her heart sank a little. "I don't want you to be scared."

"That's unavoidable at present. I am out with a beautiful woman, and I don't want to fall flat on my face and humiliate either one of us, nor do I want to get hurt. It's possible a pebble or uneven pavement could send me flying, and I'll end up with a broken arm next, like your Lord Cambrey."

"He was never *my* Lord Cambrey. And we won't move quickly enough for you to go flying. That would be foolish, and neither of us is a fool. By the way, people are nodding and smiling and looking friendly, but I haven't seen anyone yet whom I know personally."

"Splendid!" he said without enthusiasm. "Jane, tell me what is your interesting information."

She nearly blurted, *I think I love you*, before realizing he meant the information to which she'd referred over tea.

"I met with the director of the London Society for Teaching the Blind to Read. Even though they house children and not adults, they could provide you with instruction. It's just north of Regent's Park."

Suddenly, it was like trying to drag a dead horse.

"Why have you stopped?" she asked.

CHRISTOPHER COULDN'T ADEQUATELY EXPRESS the immediate fury that boiled in him at learning Jane had spoken to someone outside his family about his condition.

"I've stopped because it's the only protest I can make to your inappropriate action."

Silence, although he sensed she was surprised.

"I cannot storm off," he continued, "nor look you in the eyes and express my annoyance. All I can do is stop and try to calm myself. But I can ask you to release my arm for a moment."

He felt her touch drop away as if he were a hot coal.

And then the terror rushed back. He was standing alone in the endless blackness. If Jane abandoned him, he would be stranded there forever, unable to complete the previously simple task of getting home. He would have to ask for help from a stranger.

Instantly, he felt sweat break out in the small of his back and under his arms. Fisting his hands, he took a deep breath to calm the burgeoning panic.

This was precisely the reason he had wanted to stay home. He shouldn't have listened to her. This was madness!

"Lord Westing, good day," came a disembodied male voice from close by, and he swung his head in the direction from whence it came.

During the long moment of silence, he wondered if Jane was still there, but he hadn't heard her move away. Moreover, he could still smell her perfume.

Then she spoke, and she was much closer than he'd imagined, right at his side.

"Good day, my lord. I'm sorry, I do not know your name."

"Can you not speak and introduce us, man?" the stranger still apparently addressed him. "Have you forgotten your manners along with losing your sight?"

Jane gasped, and Christopher finally recognized him as an acquaintance from the club. Not a friend, merely someone who occasionally sat with him, Burnley, and Whitely, and espoused on politics and other things about which he knew very little.

"Don't be an inconsiderate ass, Pomerson. I can't *see* who you are to introduce you. I only know it is you by the idiotic sentence you just uttered. Move along. You are not worth introducing to my lady-friend."

"Well, I never." And he heard footsteps crunching away on the gravel.

The day was becoming worse and worse.

"Jane," he said, so he could orient himself.

"Yes," her voice sounded unsure.

He'd insulted her, then insulted Pomerson, but the lingering irritation prevented him from apologizing.

"Explain how my sitting amongst the youngsters, looking like a great, stupid dullard while learning to read some form of alphabet for the blind, would have helped me in that last situation. Would it help me get home this very moment?"

"It wouldn't," she said after a pause. "However, once you were home, you could read instead of sitting doing nothing except drinking tea."

He felt as if she'd slapped him. Jane was clearly disappointed in him.

"If you want me to keep myself busy, then you should have seen the director of the blind school at St. George's Fields. It's only five minutes away. We could trace back our steps and go there even now. I'm sure I would enjoy the classes in basket weaving and worsted rugs. Why, I can even learn to make shoes!"

He clapped his hands in sarcastic glee, relieved when he didn't miss palm hitting palm, which would have made his gesture lose its effect entirely.

Unfortunately, his cane slipped from his grasp and clattered to the ground.

Jane remained silent, although after a pause, he heard her retrieve it for him.

The devil! Having her stoop and pick it up, possibly getting her gloves soiled while he stood there unmoving, confirmed he'd lost his status as a gentleman.

How could he escort a lady anywhere while she had to do the tasks which should be his?

"Is it after two?" he continued. "The *inmates*, as they call those unfortunate enough to be housed there, may be seen at work between two and five in the afternoon. Shall we go look at them, rather like specimens at the zoo? I am sure I could do my father proud because I understand I can make seven shillings a week producing doormats."

He was aware he'd raised his voice but couldn't seem to stop himself.

"You see, I, too, have done some research as to my options. And while St. George's Fields accepts people up to thirty years old, I am supposed to be indigent, not a bloody wealthy nobleman."

"I see," she said tightly.

After a moment, Jane added, "I know they also teach using Alston's raised letters. Thus, either school would assist you, of course. Yet, if you don't wish to be a drain on the funds of the poor, then I suggest you go to the blind school at One Avenue Road, as I first suggested."

He didn't know what to say. He wasn't angry at *himself* for doing research, nor for sending his valet out to learn what he could about the resources available. *Only at her.*

Why? Because he wanted Jane not to give a damn about his sight, and plainly, she did.

Perhaps, he would learn the cursed bumpy alphabet, but he doubted it would do him much good since there were hardly any texts to read anyway. Far more promising was the Braille system he'd discussed with his father. Although bigger on the Continent than in Britain, unlike Alston's embossed letters, he would have to learn an entirely new alphabet made up of six dots.

Wasn't he too old for that?

"I'm sorry I overstepped," came her soft voice unexpectedly. "I only wanted to help you to feel more comfortable."

He considered himself an ass of epic proportions. If she were in some dire situation, he would fervently do whatever he could to help her. He should be thrilled she was doing the same for him.

"I'm sorry," he muttered, knowing it was an entirely inadequate apology.

She took hold of his arm almost at once. "I guess you don't want to know about the schools for the blind in Scotland either? There are two. Or Mr. Dickens's recounting of the very impressive Perkins School in Massachusetts in his *American Notes.*"

She squeezed his arm. She was teasing him, and she didn't sound bothered at all. What's more, she had spent a lot of time gathering information. *For him!* And he had been an ungrateful churl.

He took a deep breath and tried again. "My sincere apologies. You are kind and helpful, and I have behaved boorishly."

Now, he desperately wanted to pull her into his arms and wondered if she would ever let him do so again. After all, in her opinion, he'd been sitting at home doing nothing. And when she tried to help him out of his trance-like lethargy, he'd yelled at her. In public.

"Maybe a little boorish," she agreed.

"Shall we walk farther?"

"Yes, we've barely begun. I intend to see the Serpentine and describe anything interesting to you in detail."

"Splendid." He felt her give him a gentle tug in the right direction.

"Where did you get those spectacles?" she asked after a moment.

"My father. What do you think?"

"You look rather mysterious and dashing in them. You're turning the head of many a young lady."

Surprised, Christopher barked out a laugh.

"I don't know if you're serious or not, but I appreciate the esteem-bolstering, nonetheless."

"I'm very serious, and you do look dashing."

Thank God! He'd been worried he looked like a fool from head to toe, but he also knew Jane would tell him the truth.

"I wish I could kiss you this very instant." Again, her hand squeezed his arm, as a sign of agreement. He hoped, anyway.

"I'm sure we can arrange for that again soon," she said, as if speaking about getting his boots polished or some other mundane task.

Knowing what they were secretly discussing caused a jolt of desire to rush through him, and without being able to glance down, he could only hope the evidence wasn't on display.

In about fifteen minutes, they'd reached the eastern most point of the Serpentine, and then, turning right, began to stroll its northern path.

"We should be glad it isn't Sunday," Jane said. "It is busy enough in any case. Women and children having picnics, there's a boy with a boat, more picnics. A few rowboats. Of course, some man is showing off and liable to tip his lady out of their boat. Oh, hello!"

She pulled her hand away, and he felt her crouch beside him.

"Someone's friendly dog," she told him, her voice coming from a few feet down. "Stick your hand out," she added, and trustingly, Christopher did.

"Lower," she added, and he stooped, still holding his hand in front of him, until he felt silky fur and then a warm tongue.

"You're a good dog, aren't you? Where's your family?" Jane spoke to it.

And then someone called out, "Hero," and the dog dashed away.

"I've been slobbered upon," Christopher said.

"As have I. It was a lovely creature, brown fur, white spots."

"Softest fur I've ever felt," he added. "Did it have a long tale or a short one?"

"Long, with a pretty plume."

"That's what I would have guessed."

She had taken hold of him once more and they were walking again.

"There is a wonderful book called *Textbook for Instruction of the Blind* on training dogs to help guide you. It's by a man named Johann Wilhelm Klein. So far, I haven't found it in English. Only in German."

"I've no doubt you'll learn Bavarian in time to train an adequate dog for me by week's end. Where has that Hero got to? Maybe we should abscond with him."

She laughed. "I'm glad you're not angry anymore."

"I had no right to be."

They were friends again. He could tell her something else bothering him without fear of looking weak.

"I'm having trouble judging distance. We could have already walked the length of Hyde Park and all the way to Kensington Gardens for all I can tell. Will you tell me when we are level with the receiving house? Do you know where I mean?"

"Yes," Jane said, "and I will. Probably a five-minute walk if we don't dally."

After a few minutes, with Jane telling him everything she saw—"another boy with a stick, another picnic, another boy"—until they were both laughing, suddenly, she paused and fell silent. Someone had stopped in front of them.

CHAPTER FIFTEEN

"Lady Chatley, Lord Westing, how good to see you both on this fine day."

"Thank you, Lord Fowler," Jane said at once, giving Christopher's arm another squeeze, as she made sure he knew who was before them. "It is very fine, indeed."

"And how is my favorite lady today?" came Fowler's next utterance, causing Jane to jump and her entire body seemingly to turn to marble.

At least, that was Christopher's impression as she froze beside him.

What was this all about?

"Fowler, is it?" Christopher said, easily picturing the affable man. "How goes it?"

The man was more oft to be found at a Tory club than at the Reformer's Club, and some considered him a dunce, but Christopher thought him harmless enough, rather bland, like a spotted dick pudding without the raisins.

"It goes well, my lord,' Fowler replied. "I was terribly sorry to hear about the explosion. I think I was the one who told Lady Chatley about it."

"Were you?" Christopher asked, feeling a prickling of unease. "I didn't know you two were acquaintances."

"Oh, yes," Fowler continued. "Well, more like conspirators, aren't we?"

Jane startled again. "Hardly that." And in an uncharacteristically rude way, she added, "We must get going. Good day, Lord Fowler."

Christopher felt her tugging at his arm, eager to get away.

"Good day to you both," said Fowler, not sounding the least bit slighted.

How strange!

Christopher wasn't sure he had the right to ask her anything. He hadn't made any declaration of love, nor did they have an agreement regarding the future.

Moreover, what if she and Fowler had passed some sort of message using their expressions and their eyes, some covert signal he couldn't see? Why else would the man not have cared at the brevity of their discourse? Especially if he were soon going to see Jane again.

This self-doubt was an unwelcome emotion. He would ask her—

"We are directly even with the receiving house," she said.

Then Christopher knew to his right was a building that looked like a small Greek temple with a portico and pediment supported by columns at the entrance. If anyone got into distress in the Serpentine, either by swimming in the summer or even skating in the winter, they could go into the Humane Society's Receiving House, equipped with male and female wards, and even hot baths to aid resuscitation.

"Good to know if you release my arm and I wander into the water, I am close to assistance."

She laughed. "I won't let you go," she promised, and he let his silly musings over Fowler evaporate.

A little farther up from the Serpentine was the small brick lodge belonging to the park ranger, with a tidy slate roof over its single story. He'd always thought the cottage looked as if it should be in a small country village, certainly not in the center of London.

Now, in his mind's eye, he considered it the perfect size for a blind man and his wife.

"Shall we continue?" she asked.

At least she didn't seem eager to get away from him. Since she wasn't going to say more regarding Lord Fowler, he could hardly make insinuations as to an association of theirs by bringing up the man's name again.

"Yes. To the end of this path, and then we'll go toward Victoria Gate."

"That will be busier than the footpath," she reminded him.

"I trust you," he told her.

"Thank you," she said.

In another ten minutes of companionable silence, dodging both people and carriages on the route, they'd reached the northernmost path of the park again, this time at its west end.

"Are you all right?" she asked, as another small tilbury carriage dashed by.

"Yes. It is probably more worrisome to you since you can see them. I feel perfectly safe."

As they took another right in the final leg of their circuitous stroll and traversed the top edge of Hyde Park, he was well aware of the crowded Uxbridge thoroughfare to his left. And when they finally approached the gate at which they'd entered, a few yards before reaching it, he heard singing.

"What is that? Who is singing?" he asked her, enjoying the pleasant sound.

Where previously she answered each of his pestiferous questions immediately, now she hesitated, making his smile vanish.

"Tell me," he urged.

"It's the children from the St. George's Fields School for the Indigent Blind." Her tone was stilted.

"Oh yes," he said. "The *inmates*. Do they look as though I might fit in?"

"Stop it, Chris. They're no different than you. The same hopes and dreams. They're simply poor and extraordinarily lucky that Mr. Day created his Blind Man's Fund. I managed to get some blind orphans out of the East End gutters and into St. George's Fields *only* because of the generosity of those who view them as worthwhile. And now, they sing as if they're the happiest people in the world."

The more she spoke, the more he hung his head.

"All right," he said, "you are a saint, they are all blessedly fortunate, and I am an ungrateful clod who has too much money and would trade it all for a working pair of eyes. And how do I know I'm not another of your charitable cases?"

He felt her arm on his.

"Because we kissed *before* you became blind. You felt what I felt, didn't you?"

That certainly put him in his place. They took another few steps.

"Yes," he answered as his emotions wavered from the familiar anger to resignation to hopelessness and back again. Underlying all of these was a tenderness for this remarkable woman beside him.

"Don't judge me, Jane," he added. "It is too soon for me to think of my condition dispassionately or to count up my other blessings."

"I understand," she said, her tone softened. "I was too harsh. Most of the people at St. George's Fields never had what you had to lose, so I imagine it might be easier for them. I'm sorry."

Having her apologize made him feel even worse. Like an absolute pig head. This outing had been ruined by his own terrible mood swings and discourteous behavior.

"Are we almost there?" he asked testily.

"Yes. I even see your coach and driver. What's more, Amanda is up ahead waiting."

"Good. Normally, this wouldn't tire me at all, but having to worry each step I take will send me head over heels has made me feel quite fatigued."

Again, she said softly, "I understand."

Christopher didn't think she could, for he barely understood how he could go from elation at walking with her, as if they were a normal couple, to feeling the depths of despair within minutes. He didn't like experiencing doubt about himself. He didn't like not being able to see Fowler, wondering if the man was making eyes at Jane.

He felt weary indeed.

He didn't even protest when she didn't come inside the Foresters' home. She simply made sure he and Amanda entered the front door at Berkley Square, as if they were children, before she got into her carriage and rode away.

He felt emasculated on top of everything else. Heading straight upstairs, able to find his room easily now with a hand along the wall, he let his valet help him to bed for an early evening nap.

Like a bloody invalid.

Christopher wanted to throw something at the wall after Abner departed, but he was mindful of it being Aunt Tabitha's home—as well as the fact he wouldn't have the satisfaction of seeing the object smash into bits.

And then he realized when they returned to Grosvenor Square, their house would have been redecorated and nothing would be familiar. He would no longer know what his family's home looked like.

For some reason, that thought alone made hot tears prick his eyes. As he turned his face into his pillow, he let himself have a good, pitying cry.

JANE SAT ALONE IN her parents' parlor, drinking a bracing cup of strong, sweet, milky tea and contemplated the man she loved. What an unsettling day!

Of course, Christopher was frightened. She did understand. And maybe it was simply too soon. Eventually, though, she was sure he would want to read whatever texts were available, and more would become so every year. Additionally, he would want to write, and therefore, she'd also started looking into writing machines, such as the Raphigraph, to assist him. Regardless, she knew it was not the time to tell him of her discovery.

He would be stubborn and cling to the notion if he couldn't do things as he had done them before, then he wouldn't do them at all.

She wished she had a close friend with whom to discuss her warring feelings—for, in truth, she felt at battle with herself between doing nothing to help, which Christopher seemed to prefer, and moving mountains for him to obtain whatever services she hoped might assist him.

All at once, she thought of Lady Margaret Angsley, the Countess of Cambrey. They'd struck up an understanding if not exactly a friendship, when they were both visiting John Angsley, the Earl of Cambrey at his country estate two years earlier. The earl had been feared permanently disabled due to a carriage accident, which had broken his arm and, more severely, his leg, leaving him in a pushchair for months of convalescence. Jane was well aware of all Margaret and John had managed to overcome in terms of his terrible injuries.

She was certain the Cambreys would be in London this time of year, and quickly penned the countess a note asking if she could visit her. Then Jane sent it off before she could change her mind. What better woman with whom to strike up a friendship than one already happily married, who wouldn't see Jane as a rival, and who had experience with an injured man?

The next day, she received a return note inviting her to tea the following afternoon. And then she spent the rest of her time working on tasks for the duchess, only running into Christopher when she was about to leave his aunt's home.

Jane had been sequestered in the library with the duchess, who had taken over the room from her husband. Instead of important-looking papers regarding parliamentary acts, there were now swatches of drapery fabrics and wallpaper, as well as fashion magazines from France. His mother even had some of her watercolors with her to consider what colors they would put on the walls.

As Jane was leaving, Christopher descended the main stairs. By himself, hair combed, dressed impeccably, moving rather quickly with his right hand skimming the bannister, he had his eyes closed and was whistling. He sounded . . . happy!

Without thinking, she began to whistle along with him. It was a familiar parlor song, and she'd heard it played on the pianoforte dozens of times.

Christopher stopped with his foot on the last stair, his head turned to her.

"Lord Westing," she said, not feeling comfortable using his given name when she could be overheard by his family. "It is I, Lady Jane."

He chuckled, seeming in good humor. "I am quite familiar with your voice, my lady. And now I know what your musical tone sounds like as well. Again," he commanded, "start from the first notes."

She took a deep breath and whistled the tune along with him, losing her breath after a minute.

"You are a far superior whistler," she praised, "but I do not get to practice as my mother forbids such unladylike behavior in her company."

"If you were my wife, I would let you whistle whenever you wished. Your pitch is quite perfect."

If she were his wife? Goodness gracious! If only he would ask.

"Are you only now arriving, as I hope, or are you going to break my heart and leave?"

Jane felt a twinge of regret. She would give anything to say she had just arrived and could remain for hours in his company. Wickedly, she hoped there might soon be a way to let him ravish her on the sofa, as he'd mentioned before. Surely, she could lock both the doors to the room and feign ignorance should someone rattle at them to enter.

"I have to leave," she confessed, letting her gaze feast on his handsome face.

"Is it late? I've lost track, I'm afraid." He took the last few yards and stood before her, not too close, not too far. Uncanny how he was now able to do that.

"If it's nearly dinner," he added, "perhaps you could stay and join my family for our evening meal."

If only she could. Instead, she was going to meet Lord Fowler at the opening of the hippopotamus exhibit at the zoo. She had an inkling her plans were going to bother Christopher, although it had seemed harmless enough at the time she'd invited Lord Fowler.

Suddenly, it felt like betrayal, especially as she hadn't mentioned it. Now, it was too late to do so. Christopher would ask all sorts of questions. In any case, she was certain he wouldn't want to go to a viewing. And since there would be no awkward, unexpected encounter, she saw no need to tell him now.

Dear God! She was debating herself again!

"Any other evening, I would be very pleased to join you," she promised, "but my mother is expecting me in short order. We have plans."

"I understand. Another evening, then."

"In all likelihood, I will be back here within a day, although I think I am next meeting your mother in Chelsea where we will match up the newly printed tags to her paintings. I do hope I didn't get anything wrong."

"Like tagging a sailboat painting as a horse in a meadow?" he mused.

"Exactly," she said.

"I wish I could help, but for obvious reasons, I cannot." Christopher shrugged, but his unhappiness at not being able to assist in such a simple task was palpable.

Her heart clenched in sympathy for him. His moods altered more quickly than most, as he went from something he could still do, such as whistling, to facing something he couldn't.

If only there weren't servants around, Jane would hug him. Or if she had time to sequester them both in the drawing room, she would do more than that. Instead, all she could do was take a step closer and grasp his hand in hers.

Keeping her voice low so only he could hear, she whispered, "When next I come, I hope you will offer me the invitation to dine once again, as well as some private time."

His attractive mouth turned up on one side, a half smile. Then he nodded and squeezed her hand.

She found it difficult to leave him there, but as she approached the door, the butler appeared with her coat, which he helped her into before opening the door and hailing her carriage driver.

"Good day, Lord Westing."

"Good day, Lady Jane," Christopher returned, looking to her like a man at loose ends who needed to figure out a new purpose. He was too young to sit idly by, and plainly, it was eating at him.

She nearly opened her mouth to say something but thought better of it.

CHAPTER SIXTEEN

When Jane entered her family's home, her mother was waiting, a large smile upon her face and a missive in her hand, which she was waving around like a victory flag.

To Jane's utter dismay, Lord Fowler had sent word he would be picking them up at their home. Naturally, her mother had intercepted it and read it as he had addressed it to both of them.

"The zoo will have a crush of people at the opening, and I might never find you otherwise," he'd written. "We must go as a party."

Jane supposed he was correct, however, now she had to deal with her mother's raised eyebrow and insinuations of romantic attachment.

When Lord Fowler came to collect them an hour later, Jane hadn't shaken the melancholia of seeing Christopher in distress. Still, she had promised the awkward viscount a wife, and a wife she would find him.

"I'm pleased you two are spending more time together," her mother said on the way to Regent's Park and its spectacular zoo, addressing Lord Fowler. "It can only make the heart grow fonder."

"Mother!" Jane admonished, but short of telling her she was helping Lord Fowler find a wife, a task of which Lady Chatley would definitely not approve, she couldn't dissuade her mother from the opinion the viscount was courting her.

"I am already very fond of your daughter," Lord Fowler confessed, which Jane didn't think helped matters.

She gave him a discreet shake of her head, which, of course, her mother saw.

"Young people," Lady Chatley said, rolling her eyes. "Completely illogical."

Lord Fowler leaned forward in a way Jane had learned to identify as his debating stance, even while sitting in a carriage.

"In any case, Lady Chatley," he said, "according to the famed song, it is *absence*, not *time*, that makes the heart grow fonder."

Jane's mother pursed her lips. "I am familiar with the song and with the chronic absence of a loved one. I can assure you, it doesn't do a whit for fondness but rather resentment grows by leaps and bounds."

Lord Fowler sent an alarmed glance to Jane, perhaps realizing he'd crossed into dangerous territory. The long absences of the Earl of Chatley had plagued her mother's existence and curbed her social pleasures, but Lord Fowler could not have known.

All Jane could do was shrug and let him get himself out of it.

"I will defer to your advanced—"

Jane gasped to cut him off. *Was he going to refer to her mother's age?*

"Advanced wisdom," he completed after a deep frown at Jane.

Inwardly, Jane sighed with relief. Her mother had, in fact, been testier than usual. Lord Chatley had stayed home barely a week before announcing his attention to go to the Continent for a month. As far as Jane knew, her mother hadn't even spoken to him before he'd left.

She'd assumed the tension in their house would dissipate at her father's departure, but her mother was still unusually irritable. Jane hoped this evening's diversion would help.

The hippopotamus enclosure was mobbed with fascinated Londoners. Although Jane caught a glimpse of the beast and tried to appreciate how far it had traveled, not to mention how unusual its appearance, she wanted to get on with her evening's task. Moreover, it was nearly impossible to encourage Lord Fowler to engage in conversation with eligible single ladies while everyone was cheering each time the animal took a step. The zoo was loud, crowded, and smelly.

She knew they would have better luck once they got to the private party on Cumberland Terrace, and thus, as soon as they could, she urged her mother and Lord Fowler to begin the short stroll to the edge of Regent's Park and to Lord Burton's home.

"I wonder if he can smell the animals on a hot day." Lord Fowler said. "It seems not only the odor of their excrement but also their food, rotting in the sun, would find its way here."

Lady Emily Chatley shot him such a look of disgust; Jane wondered Lord Fowler didn't drop on the spot.

"Perhaps, when we get there," Jane said, "you might stick to pleasantries about the hippopotamus and the other animals, too, but not mention *excrement* or *odor*."

"Yes, of course," Lord Fowler said.

Jane couldn't believe she had to counsel him on that in mixed company. If he would say such in front of her mother, what wouldn't he say to people at the party?

As it turned out, not much. Despite her advice, he mentioned the close proximity to the zoo twice and wondered loudly, even calling out to their host, as to whether the scents of the animals infiltrated his townhouse and yard.

This drew a withering glance from Lord Burton. After that, Jane stuck closer to Lord Fowler and attempted to steer him into a conversation with Lady Adelia Smythe, who predictably was standing quietly by herself looking for all the world as if she were examining the wallpaper.

After a painfully short and awkward discourse on the merits of eating chicken versus partridge with the latter coming out as the favorite, Jane dragged Lord Fowler away from the lady, who seemed to be trying to escape by actually blending into the wallpaper.

"Really, Lord Fowler! Do try to ask a sensible question of a lady and then allow her to speak. Don't ask something silly and then talk over her answer."

"But I could barely hear her, and I wasn't certain she actually *was* speaking."

"Yes, Lady Smythe is a soft-spoken one." Jane scanned the room. "Let's try Miss Swintree. Do you know her?"

And off they went to bother another young woman.

When Lord Fowler finally dropped Jane and her mother home at midnight, Jane was exhausted, but pleased at how their list was shaping up. Two ladies actually seemed to like the viscount, and that was a vast improvement over utter disinterest. Moreover, he had shown an apparent interest in return.

After she laid down in her bed that night, she wondered if she should suggest he change his hair or the way he let his valet tie his cravat. However, as she began to yawn, she switched her thoughts over to Christopher and his soft, thick hair with its hint of curls at the nape of his neck.

Recalling how she enjoyed running her fingers through it while he kissed her, she drifted off to sleep.

"MOTHER, YOU DON'T NEED her this afternoon. You'll have her all day tomorrow."

Christopher had his arms crossed and was blocking his mother from leaving the parlor to send a message to Jane. At least, he *thought* he was blocking her.

"I suppose next you'll tell me I'm working her too hard," the duchess huffed.

He sighed. "I might, but Lady Jane would take me to task if you treated her any differently, for she loves to be busy."

"Jane is a sharp girl. I'm very fond of her," his mother said, "and I'll leave her alone this afternoon and tonight, as you requested. Everything is ahead of schedule for my show, but we still have oodles of work to do renovating the house if we ever hope to move home again. Do you *know* what your father is up to?"

He grimaced. "Are you referring to the shower bath?"

"The what?" his mother practically roared.

Dammit! "Um . . . ," Christopher stalled.

"Never mind," the duchess snapped. "I do not want to know. I meant the fire-escape apparatus."

It was the first he'd heard of it. "It's probably a good idea and only meant for our safety."

His mother gave a long-suffering sigh. "I'm going to my studio, Chris. Do you need anything before I go?"

Only Jane, he mused. *Or maybe a desire to learn basket-weaving.*

"Why don't you hop in the carriage and go to the Reform Club? Your father is there."

She might as well have told him to travel to the moon.

"We'll see."

His mother made a clucking sound. "You always say that when you dismiss my suggestions. Oh good, Lord Burnley is here. He'll take you."

"Take him where?" Owen asked from behind him. "Good day, Duchess. You look scrumptious, as usual."

"Utterly inappropriate," she muttered, but Christopher would bet his mother was blushing. "Will you take Chris to the Reform Club? Eat there, enjoy some other company, get him out of this house."

"Yes, Your Grace. I am ready to do your every command."

"No," Christopher said, "he isn't. Don't I have a say in this?"

"If you can stroll all over Hyde Park with Lady Jane, you can certainly go to the club with Lord Burnley."

Christopher opened his mouth to protest, and then thought, *Yes, I probably can. And why not?* What was he afraid of anyway?

Everything! Tripping. Making a fool of himself. People staring.

On the other hand, if Jane didn't witness any of his humiliation, he should stop caring. She was the only one in whose good graces and high esteem he wished to remain. Moreover, he couldn't *see* people staring, so he could be blissfully unaware as long as Owen didn't tell him.

"All right. Let's go at once," he said, turning toward his friend. "Before I change my mind."

"I'm over here," Burnley said, his voice coming from the other side of the room.

Merriment boiled up in Christopher, and he let it out in a hearty laugh, with Owen and his mother joining in.

"Off you go," his mother said, as if sending schoolboys out to play.

However, before they could go anywhere, a new set of footsteps indicated his sister had arrived.

"You all missed the most amazing spectacle yesterday," Amanda said. "I won't make you ask, I'll tell you—the Egyptian hippopotamus. What a creature!"

"I bet it was an absolute mob," his mother said.

"My sister is recently back from the Continent and tried to bully me into taking her," Burnley said. "I told Sophia we shall go when the throng has died down."

"Lady Jane was there," Amanda added, and Christopher could hear the mischief in her voice. "Did she *tell* you she was going?"

He nearly didn't answer but had the feeling all eyes were upon him. Even his mother had undoubtedly deduced he had a *tendre* for Jane.

"Lady Jane doesn't have to tell me anything," he pointed out, feeling defensive. "However, she did, in fact, mention yesterday she had plans."

Why hadn't she told him about the zoo? The answer was obvious—because he was blind, and it was pointless to invite a blind man to an exhibit. She would rather go with her mother.

IN A VERY SHORT while, Christopher found himself at the Reform Club, chosen over White's for its better food and for its discourse in the political sphere rather than gossip and gambling.

Thankfully, it felt, smelled, and sounded entirely familiar—all male voices, distinct aromas of cigars, pipes, hair pomade, and Chef Soyer's delicious concoctions.

Christopher had decided to use his cane and wear his glasses so there could be no doubt as to his condition. Also, he had learned with his cane how easily he could tell for himself what was in front of him and where the next step was located. Jane had been correct, and thus, he didn't need to hang onto Burnley like a clinging rose bush.

As at Parliament, many voices interrupted his forward progress, suddenly coming out of nowhere, wishing him well. A few men even unexpectedly slapped him on the back, which would have sent him flying if Owen hadn't been there to steady him.

"Table," he said to his friend the second time it happened. "And wine. Now."

When they were seated, he asked, "Is my father here?"

"I haven't seen him yet." And Owen ordered for both of them.

"Anyone else interesting?"

Burnley hesitated. "Is there someone in particular you're asking about?"

In truth, he'd had Fowler on his mind since his walk with Jane, although the man was unlikely to be there.

"I haven't seen Whitely in ages," Christopher said, then laughed at his own words. "Obviously, I haven't *seen* anyone in ages, but I haven't spoken with him, either. Are my friends avoiding me?"

"Don't be absurd. I'll call him over if I see him. I'm sure there are many old chums who'll stop by the table. Most of them didn't feel comfortable invading Lord and Lady Forester's residence. It would have been different if you'd been in your own home."

"My own home, as you put it, will be nothing like it was by the time my father and mother get finished putting it back together."

"With Lady Jane's help."

Christopher nodded. "So, you know about that."

"Everyone does. Lady Jane's been running around like your mother's parlor maid. I'm grinning if you want to know."

Christopher had a prickling of unease. "Why?"

Their food arrived, and while he could easily handle a glass of wine by himself, he realized he was going to need assistance for the prime rib and baked potato.

"I hate to ask, but can you tell me where my food is."

"All right, picture your plate like a sun dial with north at the top. I'll butter your potato, which is at the east. No, sorry, that's my east, your west. And the meat is more like southeast for you."

"What's in the north?"

"Peas, of course, with a little mint sauce."

In a few minutes, with Burnley's patient cues, Christopher was cutting his prime rib as if he could see, but it took all his concentration and careful prodding with knife and fork to eat his meal and clear most of his plate, so he did so in silence.

"Dammit all!" He exclaimed when he dropped his peas again and put an empty fork into his mouth.

"Here," Burnley said, and Christopher felt something tap the back of his hand. "A spoon for the peas."

"I'm not a savage," he declared and dropped his silverware onto his plate. "In any case, I'm full."

At last, he could get back to their conversation. "Why does the notion of Lady Jane helping my mother make you smile?"

"What?" Burnley sounded startled. "You're like a dog with a bone remembering that snippet of conversation from half an hour ago. It's only that she never showed an interest before, so, naturally, people are talking."

"And what are they saying?"

"That Lady Jane is after you through your mother."

"That's ridiculous!" If he could have pushed his chair out and stood up in a huff, he would have.

"Calm down, old chum. I'll call over the waiter for more wine, shall I? And here's Whitely, as requested. I didn't even have to gesture to him, he saw us."

Christopher turned his head in the general direction from which he expected George Whitely to approach, and sure enough, he received a clap on the shoulder, making him jump.

"Good to see you, Westing."

"I would say the same, but I cannot."

"Oh, right. Sorry, old boy."

"Don't mind him," Burnley said. "He gets testy like a badger around any words to do with sight. You'll get used to his cranky ways. Have a seat. We were about to order more wine."

"Make it brandy, and I will."

"*Pay* for the brandy, and we will," Christopher quipped. And they all laughed, the tension gone.

"Is it true that Lady Jane Chatley has set her cap for you?" Whitely asked immediately.

And just like that, the tension was back.

"Bodswell's ballocks!" Burnley exclaimed. "You shouldn't have said that."

"Why?" Whitely asked. "Is it a secret between you two hens, acting like old women drinking a pot of gossip water?"

"No," Christopher said. "That's what you're doing by bringing it up—as if I would talk about the lady with you two dunderpates."

"And that's why you shouldn't mention Lady Jane," Burnley clarified. "Annoys him, even more than using words to do with seeing. I believe our boy Christopher here is smitten."

Damn them. He was awfully glad he had on his dark glasses. If they could see his eyes, they'd know for certain.

"That's not your business," he said.

The other two laughed.

"Anyway," Burnley continued, "you already told me how you liked her since the Mulberry's dinner party."

"What!" Whitely exclaimed, and Christopher knew they wouldn't drop it now.

"Indeed," Burnley confirmed to George. "And now, by her keeping company with the Duchess of Westing, everyone thinks Lady Jane wants our boy here."

Christopher considered the ramifications. *Was Jane's reputation being terribly damaged?* He'd only wanted to provide a logical reason for having her nearby. He hadn't considered how others would view her as being manipulative. It was balderdash! She could certainly have a husband without going to any great lengths.

"Anyway," Owen continued, "I fail to see the problem. If you wish to stop the *ton* talking about her as if she were a she-wolf hunting injured prey, as if the only way boring Jane could get a husband were to . . . ."

Christopher started to rise from his chair. He was determined to escape this nonsense.

"Now don't do that," his friend beseeched him, and he felt a hand on his shoulder. It must have been Whitely, for Burnley was on the other side of the table. "I'm only telling you the truth. If you want to stop them from talking, then you must declare for her. Let your intentions be known."

Whitely made a coughing sound. Then Burnley fell silent, and Christopher had the distinct notion they were signaling each other.

"I may be blind, but I'm not stupid. What's more, even unable to see, I think I can bang your two heads together. I would appreciate it if you stated clearly whatever is passing between you."

"Brandy," Owen called across the room to a server. Then he muttered, "I think we'll need it."

They waited in silence with Christopher feeling a little ill. *What news did Whitely have regarding Jane?*

As soon as they each had a glass in hand, Christopher said, "Out with it."

George Whitely sighed, although everyone knew he loved being the center of attention.

"If it were me, I would not declare for her. She's been a quiet, reserved girl for ages, but suddenly, she's behaving like the proverbial gadfly, and always with one man."

"Fowler." Christopher knew it at once and downed his brandy in a gulp.

"That milksop?" Burnley asked, his tone surprised.

"I saw them myself," Whitely confirmed. "Last night, at the opening of the hippopotamus exhibit and then at Burton's party afterward. They weren't hiding their association. Also, at a couple balls I've been to lately. Thick as thieves as they make the rounds."

Jane was Fowler's *favorite* lady, as he, himself, had proclaimed. And then she had dismissed his words and quickly taken Christopher away from the viscount.

She had lied to him, or at least, she'd withheld the truth. She'd said she had to get ready to go out with her mother.

If it had been simply an evening with Lady Chatley, Jane might even have invited him to go along.

It had been an evening with Fowler.

"I thought she went to the zoo with her mother."

"Her mother!' Whitely exclaimed, then snorted. "The countess might have been there somewhere in the crowd, but Jane was undoubtedly accompanied by Lord Fowler."

Fowler! Christopher wished he was alone as he had to school himself to maintain a semblance of placidity. Inside, he boiled. If he'd been standing, he would have dropped into his chair.

Frankly, he was surprised by this turn of events. Jane seemed open and trustworthy. True, he was now blind and, thus, had restrictions, but she had willingly become more deeply involved in his life. *Or had she?*

She had accepted the task of helping his mother, but it hadn't really resulted in their becoming any closer. They certainly hadn't viewed any wild beasts together.

Because he could no longer *view* anything.

Was it possible she was interested in him as a husband but in someone like Fowler as a companion?

If he'd been able to see the looks that had passed between her and Fowler, he would have known at once what their relationship was.

"They might simply be friends," Christopher pointed out, hearing a snort from Whitely.

"Why is that hard to believe?" he persisted.

It was Burnley who answered. "Has she mentioned this friendship to you? I've never noticed their keeping close friendly company, not like you and, for instance, Maggie Blackwood, a few years back."

"That's Countess Cambrey to you," Christopher pointed out. "Her husband would thrash you if he heard anyone other than family call her Maggie."

"Owen is shrugging at your words," Whitely informed him. "I don't think our Burnley is worried about being thrashed."

Footsteps heralded the arrival of another, and then Christopher heard his father's voice.

"Wonderful to see you out and about, my boy. I just had lunch with an old chum. I'm off to hear a new bill in the afternoon session. Will you come with me?"

"Yes," Christopher pushed his chair out and reached for the cane he'd leant against the table when he'd first sat down.

"Are you angry with us?" This came from Burnley.

Envious of their vision, even resentful of their freedom, perhaps, but not angry at them.

"Of course not," Christopher said. "I appreciate our conversation, and I'll consider it."

"Shall the two of us have another cup of gossip water and see what else we can find out from anyone here?"

The idea of Burnley and Whitely asking questions about Jane didn't sit right. He would simply ask her himself.

"No, that's quite all right." He hoped they respected his wishes. Having his own friends talking about Jane would raise even more excitement among the *ton*, and, if found out, it would certainly embarrass her.

Christopher turned toward where he thought his father stood. Suddenly, it felt a little awkward.

"May I take your arm?" the duke asked before Christopher could ask him.

"Yes, thank you, Father."

"Good day, Your Grace," each of his friends said politely. Everyone liked his father.

"Good day, gentlemen," the duke said, and led him from the table.

It took a few minutes to get out of the club as more goodbyes had to be said, more promises by his father to support this or that bill when it was presented in the House of Lords. Eventually, they were getting into their carriage.

"I've been thinking," his father interrupted his thoughts, "how we might want to take a visit to one of the schools for the blind and see what they can offer you."

Christopher sighed, but strangely, it didn't make him angry when his father brought it up. With Jane, unfortunately, her suggestion had made him feel lacking. In either case, however, he wasn't keen to go back to school.

"I probably should learn the raised alphabet, but I don't believe there is anything else I need from a blind school. And I'm sure we can find a teacher who will come to me. Moreover, I've decided you're correct, Father. There isn't any reason I cannot expect eventually to take your seat in Parliament. I hope you will support me in this."

The duke clapped him on the knee. "So glad to hear it. I will support you, and why not? Maybe you'll even be the first blind prime minister."

Christopher felt a modicum of hope. Perhaps his life hadn't been totally destroyed. Some of his future might continue as planned.

"I think we should get you a proper secretary, too. I know your sister has let you down with reading the papers, and she would be hopeless at taking dictation."

"Agreed." Christopher much preferred Burnley's version of reading events, but Owen only had so much time on his hands.

"If it were acceptable for you to have a woman as your assistant," the duke said, "I would suggest you ask Lady Jane."

Christopher jumped slightly. *Did all conversations include mention of Jane?*

"A most capable young lady. Of course, you couldn't have her until *after* your mother's art show and *after* our house has been decorated. Your mother has been singing the girl's praises loudly. I think she's hoping her usefulness will rub off on Amanda."

His father chuckled at his own words.

"More's the pity, but you absolutely must have a male clerk. Unless you married Lady Jane, of course. Then you would still be next in line *after* your mother. Ha!"

His father seemed quite pleased with his own little jokes. Christopher wished he knew what Jane's feelings would be on the matter.

Another thing to add to his list of questions, right after the one regarding her association with Fowler.

❧

CHAPTER SEVENTEEN

"I'm so glad you came by," the Countess of Cambrey said, her tone warm and friendly. "We had fun, didn't we, at Turvey House?"

Jane and her mother had visited the Earl of Cambrey's country residence in Bedfordshire on the River Great Ouse when he was convalescing from an accident that took the life of the other driver. It had occurred soon after she and Lord Cambrey had hosted the charity banquet together. At the time, Jane's mother had been pushing her to tell the man she loved him.

But she hadn't and so she didn't. What's more, Margaret Blackwood had and did, and thus, John Angsley, the Earl of Cambrey, had become engaged while Jane was visiting, much to her mother's annoyance. The Countess of Chatley felt as if he'd been stolen out from under her nose.

Now, John and Margaret were married and had a child, a little girl, named Rosie.

"At the time, your earl was not having much fun, as I recall, and you were rather betwixt and between," Jane reminded her.

"You helped us," Margaret recalled. "I was ready to give up on him."

Jane couldn't help but smile. "I'm so glad it worked out. The tea is delicious, by the way, as are the cakes."

"I shall pass on your compliments to our cook." The countess tossed her glossy curls over one shoulder, looking resplendent in a sapphire blue gown. "But you didn't come here for those delicious little sponge and cream cakes, even though they are my husband's favorite."

"No, I came because of our conversation at Turvey House."

Margaret frowned. "I'm sorry. I don't feel as sharp as I was even a couple months ago. I've been told by my older sister it's *baby brain*." She laughed. "I think she must be right, for ever since I had our Rosie, I've been more forgetful, sometimes downright wool-headed."

"I didn't really expect you to recall any particular conversation," Jane assured her. "Only that we talked as friends. In fact, there is one evening's discussion I barely recall at all."

"*Ah,*" Margaret nodded knowingly. "I think you had too much wine, and it didn't agree with you."

"Unfortunately, too much for me is usually a sip over one glass," Jane admitted ruefully. She had a vague notion she'd been sick in the Cambreys' parlor and, thankfully, only Margaret had been witness to it. But what she'd said beforehand, she couldn't recall, nor wanted to.

"In any case, I am not too proud to tell you, I do not have many female friends."

The countess clapped her hands. "Nor I. Really only my sisters, and they don't count, and my one childhood friend, Ada Kathryn, who isn't presently in Town. But why?" Margaret barely hesitated. "Never mind, I know why. It's because you always seem too perfect. Other women are intimidated."

"Oh." Jane thought a moment. "I have always assumed it was because I'm an earl's daughter, and thus, deemed extremely strong competition with my hefty dowry and familial connections. I cannot imagine anyone thinking I'm perfect."

"For me, it was because of my looks." The countess said it so matter-of-factly, Jane could not consider her boastful or vain.

It was true, after all. Margaret Angsley was a cut above most women, radiating beauty and a vivacity that attracted men and, as Jane was now finding out, apparently repelled women, at least those who were too insecure to befriend the countess.

"I am so glad I don't have to worry about the Season anymore," Margaret added, "or my appearance." Then she brushed her fingers over her own flawless cheek and patted her perfectly coiffed hair.

Jane smiled. Obviously, the countess didn't have to worry about her appearance as she knew it was impeccable.

"That was thoughtless of me," Margaret suddenly said, sitting forward. "You are not yet married and are still tied to the social event calendar."

"That's quite all right," Jane said. "I would be happy to retire from the marriage market if my mother would only let me."

"Do you not wish to marry, then?" Lady Cambrey looked befuddled by such a notion.

"I have never feared *not* marrying," Jane said, choosing her words carefully. "Would you have married without love?"

Margaret smiled. "I see what you're asking. And as a matter of fact, I was prepared to do that very thing. A woman in my position, the middle daughter of a disgraced baron, I couldn't be too choosy, nor did I have anything to entice a man except my looks. Thus, time was not on my side."

She paused and picked up her plate with one of the small moist cakes upon it.

"If it hadn't worked out with John, whom I love beyond anything, then I would have married a man with whom I had a friendship and shared mutual respect. Someone with whom I could have enjoyed a life, even if it would have been without passion. Someone like my friend Lord Westing."

Jane knew she had jumped, for she rattled the teacup she had just picked up, even as the countess popped the cake into her mouth.

Her lovely eyes widened at Jane's reaction.

Surely, Lady Cambrey's mention of Christopher was more than a fortunate coincidence. It was the perfect opening.

"Strangely, I have come here to speak to you about Lord Westing."

Margaret shook her head. "The poor man! I couldn't believe it. Actually, I could, of course. Terrible accidents obviously occur every day. I know that as well as anyone. I sent a basket of fruit and some of these little sponge cakes to the Foresters' home when I learned he was there. But I didn't know you were friends."

"I hope we are," Jane said, feeling her cheeks heat. After all, they had kept company, and had kissed. Moreover, in many ways, they did seem to be kindred spirits. "We may be more than that, too." At least on her part, she already loved him fiercely.

Margaret smiled, and it was, indeed, a dazzling one.

Jane, who usually felt secure in herself, experienced a pang of envy and wondered why Christopher had let this beauty get away. He truly must not have felt anything for her or her for him. Still, it was disconcerting to hear Lady Cambrey, while still Miss Blackwood, had been on the brink of snatching him up as her consolation when her romance with John Angsley was not going smoothly.

Moreover, knowing Christopher's gallantry and his sense of gentlemanly duty, he undoubtedly would have married Margaret if he'd thought he could ease her suffering.

Jane would have had to watch it unfold, entirely unnoticed, and her affection for Christopher would have, by necessity, been forever kept hidden.

"I would be exceedingly glad to learn you and Lord Westing had formed a match," the countess declared. "I know you are both smart and kind."

She clapped her hands, sending cake crumbs flying. "Why, the more I think on it, the more I love the idea. Matchmaking is such fun."

Considering Lady Cambrey had done nothing to make the match, Jane hid a smile. If the countess were to experience the difficulty of finding a wife for one such as Lord Fowler, she might not think it such a joy.

"You know Lord Westing, maybe better than I do," Jane said, although she knew his lips and his tongue better. Of that, she was confident. "I want to help him, but I don't know how, nor do I think my assistance is particularly welcome."

"Men have such pride," Margaret said.

"I'm sure that's true," Jane agreed. "Each time I spend time in Lord Westing's company, I attempt to steer him toward something I think will be helpful in his new state of blindness, and it ends up angering him."

"Maybe you're trying too hard."

That made tears prick Jane's eyes. "It is simply the way I am. I like to do things to get something accomplished. And I've fallen in love with a man who could certainly use my help, if only he would let me."

There, at last, she'd confessed her love out loud.

The countess nodded. "Oh, how very brave of you to tell me. How can I help?"

Jane sniffed and retrieved her handkerchief from her reticule. She'd been terribly inconsiderate to become teary upon her first visit!

Would the countess really want to be her friend if she offered no more to their relationship than sniveling and drama?

"I'm dreadfully sorry," Jane offered. "Somehow, saying the words of what is in my heart has made me feel quite emotional. I do not want you to do anything, nor did I come here thinking you could help. Merely being able to speak to you has certainly taken a weight from me."

She gave Margaret a watery smile and added, "There are so many other factors, such as not knowing precisely Lord Westing's feelings at this time, as well as the fact other ladies are using his blindness to try to approach him."

She fiddled with the gloves in her lap. "I know it means nothing to him, but others are lumping me into that group since our friendship was newly formed *before* the explosion and no one had yet marked it." Jane shrugged. "Then there is the matter of my father wanting to marry me off to my cousin to keep his title close and his money closer."

Margaret had stayed quiet as Jane listed her woes until this last statement, which made her frown.

"And you have no feelings for your cousin?"

"None that are pleasant, no," Jane admitted.

"We had a similar situation in which our cousin wanted to marry my older sister. They were not suited at all. Luckily, it came to naught for Jenny quickly gained the affection of the Earl of Lindsey, as you are undoubtedly aware."

Jane nodded. Everyone knew of the deep love of Simon and Jenny Devere.

"I believe my father will make life extremely difficult for me if I don't go along with his plans. But still, I won't."

"How will you resist?" Margaret asked.

"I will leave London if pushed. I will not be entirely destitute, nor do I fear whatever might come next."

"You see, Jane, that is why you are intimidating to other women. You stand your ground and you are, in fact, perfect."

Jane smiled, feeling a little better already. Except when she left this sanctuary of a room in this magnificent townhouse with this charming lady, she would be in exactly the same situation.

"Then why does my life feel as if it is unraveling?"

The countess looked thoughtful. "Because your heart is engaged. I know the feeling well. Besides listening, is there anything I can do? Shall I speak with Christopher the way you once spoke to John on my behalf?"

"Oh, no," Jane protested. "I already knew Lord Cambrey's feelings about you, so it was a simple matter to remind him to tell you. In my case, I have an inkling Lord Westing likes me, but the injury is making him rethink many things in his life. I fear I may be one of them."

"I'M WEARING MY FAVORITE riding habit," Jane announced when Christopher found her waiting in the parlor.

"Why?" he asked. He was ready to discuss Fowler and the future, and wasn't expecting any detours or distractions.

"Because we are going riding!"

Her enthusiasm was not contagious. It was ridiculous.

"We most certainly are not."

He heard her move around the room, her heavy apron gown swishing over the bifurcated skirts underneath it. He tried not to think of what was under those.

"There is no reason on earth why we cannot," she insisted. "I enjoy it. I've seen you riding, and I know you enjoy it. We both have well-behaved mounts. I'm not asking you to jump any fences, simply to ride with me. I'm shocked you haven't done so already with one of your friends or with your father."

"Because no one else is trying to kill me," Christopher explained. *What was wrong with her?*

"What is wrong with you?" she asked, strangely echoing his thoughts.

"I beg your pardon." It seems she had arrived hoping to antagonize him and draw him out in a fight.

"I mean, I understand you cannot see. I accept it. You must accept it and—"

"And?" he prompted when she hesitated.

"And move on."

The familiar fury began to kindle. How dare *she* accept it, as if his blindness impacted her life.

"What has got into you?" he asked, crossing his arms.

Where was the placating, practical helpful Jane? This one was decidedly prickly.

"You will be on a horse as you've been on since you were a child. You will ride on a bridal path and find out how easy it is. Easier than strolling the way we did before because the horse will most assuredly not walk into a tree or into another horse, for that matter. You won't even need your cane."

Christopher opened his mouth to protest, but, truthfully, her words had merit and he couldn't think of a good excuse not to try. He hadn't considered riding a horse because, if he thought of it at all, he'd imagined he would be alone. With Jane by his side, however, it seemed suddenly possible.

All at once, he decided to agree. "All right."

"Honestly, Christopher!" she exclaimed, sounding exasperated. "You are not namby-pamby. I would bet my life on it. So why are you persisting in behaving as if—"

"I said, all right."

"What?" Her tone was flustered, confused.

"I will go riding with you," he declared. "Only give me a few minutes to change."

"Oh. Very well, then," she sounded surprised but pleased. "I assumed you wouldn't, and I was prepared for a long argument."

"You are a stubborn woman," he mused. "I wouldn't have had the energy to argue all day. I'll return shortly. And we must take a footman. If something were to spook my horse and it ran away with me, I wouldn't want you to risk your own safety trying to chase me down or attempting to bring my horse under control."

"Agreed," she said at once. "Also, for my reputation," she reminded him, and he could hear the amusement in her voice.

"Precisely," he said and left her.

"CHRIS, ARE YOU—?" BEGAN Amanda Westing's voice as she rounded the doorway into the parlor where Jane waited. "Oh, it's you," she finished, neither particularly friendly, nor unfriendly.

Jane was standing by the fireplace. "Good day, Lady Amanda."

"You may call me Amanda. We're not too formal around here. Have you seen my brother?"

"Yes, he went upstairs to change. We're going riding."

"Really?" The girl's eyebrows rose up practically into her hairline. "Is that wise?"

"I believe it will be fine."

"Are you *interested* in my brother?"

Jane successfully stifled a gasp. Amanda knew it was inappropriate to ask such a thing, and thus had done it purposefully to get a rise out of her. She would not give evidence it had worked.

"That is *not* your business," Jane said as politely as possible, and even maintained a kind expression. She hoped it was, anyway.

"Is that all you will say on the matter? I don't recall you and my brother ever going riding before, nor were you ever at my mother's beck and call the way you are now. Yet ever since Chris's accident, you are here in our home almost as much as I am."

"This isn't *your* home," Jane said flatly, feeling defensive. Moreover, she was only there at the Forestors' townhouse so often because, when she wasn't trying to help

Christopher out of his apathy, she was doing the Duchess of Westing's every bidding

"And if your mother needs *my* help, perhaps it is because her own daughter lacks a certain usefulness."

What on earth had gotten into her? Jane nearly clamped a hand over her mouth at her own uncharacteristic rudeness. Instead, she clenched one hand around her riding crop and the other in her skirts.

Amanda, however, only twisted her mouth in a slight smirk.

"It's true. I find menial tasks, such as picking out curtains, to be drudgery of the most tedious kind."

The girl was shameless in her unwillingness to help.

"What kind of drudgery is *not* tedious?" Jane asked, blinking her eyes wide.

This time, Christopher's sister frowned, considering her words.

"None, I suppose. In any case, as a duke's daughter, I wouldn't consider spending a moment running around after this and that, creating labels for paintings, and ordering flowers, and such."

So, Amanda knew what Jane was doing for the duchess. Rather precisely, too. Perhaps the girl had asked her mother about the various responsibilities. And maybe she was even a little hurt at not being included. Jane wondered if she could forge a friendship with Christopher's sister after all.

"Are you too busy to assist me with any of the final preparations before the show? I'm certain your mother would appreciate your involvement, and I would welcome your help."

Amanda narrowed her eyes. "I just told you, I don't like to do those kinds of tasks."

Was it pride over being asked by Jane, or was Amanda really saying no?

"Still," Jane persisted, "to help your mother, we could work together."

"I thought that was what *you* were for." Amanda set her hands on her hips. "After all, how else will you worm your way into the position of becoming my brother's marchioness? I applaud you, in fact. I didn't think you had it in you. You always seem so cool and removed from the mere mortals in the world, disinterested in everyone when in the ballroom. Suddenly, you're so helpful when it suits you, when Chris cannot see to defend himself, when my mother is all helter-skelter and distracted. But I see what you're doing."

Jane tapped her crop against her skirt, feeling irritated. Young and immature was one thing. However, Amanda Westing was simply bad-mannered, not to mention presumptuous.

Yet she was being protective of her family, particularly her older brother, so Jane couldn't be too angry with the girl. And certainly not hurt, for Amanda knew nothing of what Jane and Christopher had already shared.

"You know not of what you speak," she said, trying to be patient.

"I do. I saw you with Lord Fowler at the zoo," Amanda blurted. "I've seen you with him more than once this Season. If you like him, then you should leave my brother alone. Clearly, you want to be a marquess's wife because anything else will set you down a peg, but you want to find your amusement with someone else at the same time."

Amanda was delving into territory she had absolutely no right to go. People could get hurt by such gossip.

"In any case," his sister added, "you are not the *only* female visitor Chris has had."

She was undoubtedly speaking of the young ladies who came directly after the accident, trying to be the soothing comfort he most definitely didn't want. Or need, as far as Jane was concerned—women who would wrap him in a cocoon and smother him. What he needed was a good swift kick. She tapped her crop again because she intended to be the one to give it to him.

"That is not only not *your* business, as I said before. Neither is it *mine*," Jane said firmly. "If your brother wishes to have visitors of either sex, it is not my concern, nor should it be yours. He is a grown man."

"Are my ears burning?" It was Christopher. "Am I the grown man of whom you ladies speak?"

"I was just leaving," Amanda said. "If you are really going for a ride, please be careful, brother dear." And she kissed him on the cheek as she passed. "Lovely to speak with you," she tossed back to Jane when she reached the threshold. "Lady Jane, do give my regards to Lord Fowler when next you speak."

Vixen! Jane thought, among other unkinder words.

"Are you ready, my lord?" she asked, hearing the overly bright tone to her own voice and already knowing Christopher was going to ask questions.

"Shall we discuss my sister's remark first or while on horseback?" he asked.

Jane sighed. Although she loved Christopher, she would not embarrass Lord Fowler on a whim, simply because of Amanda Westing's spitefulness. For all she knew, the girl was listening at the door and would instantly spread word of Jane's assistance in finding the viscount a wife. That wouldn't do.

For one thing, Lord Fowler would end up with many social climbers going after him for all the wrong reasons, and for another, she would be breaking a solemn promise.

"I am not sure there is anything to discuss, but if there is, I believe we should refrain from doing so until we are riding."

She approached him and then walked past him in the narrow space of the doorframe. He turned at that moment toward her, and they were only inches apart.

If Amanda weren't close by, Jane could imagine leaning into him, stealing a kiss or at least sniffing the scent of him, manly, with a touch of essence of citron and vanilla, but mainly the refreshing scent of Pears soap.

Before she had slipped past him entirely, his hand shot up and grasped her arm, uncanny in his ability to find her whenever he reached for her. Or kissed her.

"No," she said, without thinking of anything except Amanda lurking and perhaps returning at precisely the wrong moment.

CHAPTER EIGHTEEN

Christopher snatched his hand back, feeling like a naughty child reaching for a sweet treat.

"I apologize," he said at once. He was, above all, a gentleman. Lately, with Jane especially, he had started to use his blindness as an excuse to behave in a less-than appropriate manner.

"No," she repeated. "I mean, there is *nothing* to apologize for, but we are standing in a doorway." Suddenly, he felt her lean closer, and then she whispered into his left ear, "Your sister may still be close by."

"*Ah,* yes. I understand." That was certainly a better reason than the myriad others going through his head, particularly how Jane no longer wanted his touch or Fowler usurping him in her affections.

"Our horses await us and a footman should already be outside, as well."

In a very few moments, he found himself in the saddle of Feldspar, a chestnut gelding, whom he'd ridden for the past two years.

Jane was to his left, and the footman's horse clopped along a short distance behind.

"Tell me about your riding outfit," he said. "Color, style?"

She laughed. "I thought you would be more interested in my horse, for she is good horseflesh, I assure you."

"We can get to that in a minute."

"Very well. I have on a faun-colored habit. Silk, of course, because my mother said it would be warm today."

"Very smart of her, and of you."

"Thank you. My topper is black with—"

"Feathers?" he interrupted, picturing Jane's hat with feathers streaming out behind.

"No, just a matching tan veil around it."

He mentally changed his image of her. "Chin strap?"

"No, I'm being rather devil-may-care. If my hat falls off, so be it."

"As long as you don't fall off with it."

"I have never fallen off a horse, my lord, and I do hope today will not be the first time."

"For either of us," he quipped. *God willing!* "And I would wager you have one of those knitted bracelets for your crop handle."

"Not knitted. They are usually crocheted, and yes, I am wearing one. They are prettier than a simple wrist strap in my opinion. And, in answer—if you were going to ask—I have dropped my crop a few times, so the bracelet is useful as well as attractive. And it seems a little strange to me you should even have noticed one before. You must have quite a keen eye trained upon lady riders."

He laughed at that. Whenever he had kept company with a woman, he often suggested they go riding. In truth, he considered the figure of a woman upon a saddle to be a truly attractive one, and if her gown was tucked correctly, then it gave a man an unparalleled view of her bottom.

He wished he could see Jane's figure right then.

"I can easily picture you upon your . . . what color mount?"

"A peat-brown pony, and she is a little on the heavy side. Jess, I call her."

"She's not an Exmoor is she, by any chance?"

"She is, in fact."

"Fabulous! Then I've seen you in the distance, in this very outfit on that very horse. Early in the Season, right after Ascot, I'll warrant it was."

"You're correct. Jess and I ride quite often, and this is my favorite habit. Of course, I have seen you, as well, my lord."

"Four hundred acres at Hyde Park, and yet it always feels as if one sees everyone on the bridal path."

Or, at least, he used to see them.

"True," she agreed. "At least you will now be spared the continuous nodding in greeting right, then left, then right, bobbing one's head. It gives one a neck ache."

She was making a little jest about a benefit of being blind. He smiled to himself. What's more, it didn't offend him, nor did he feel fury brewing. *Strange.* He hoped he'd passed through the worst of his bitterness for the little good it had done him.

"What is your horse's name?" she asked as they approached the park from the north.

"Feldspar."

"An unusual name," she noted.

"The horse is solid as rock."

She laughed. "And thus, Jess should be called Gelatin or Aspic."

The mirth bubbled up inside him, thinking of Jane on a horse named Aspic.

"Good day," he heard her call out. "My mother's good friend," she added after a moment. She is very hard of hearing. Mostly, I am merely nodding. How do you feel?"

"Perfectly at ease. My neck is not straining with tedious nodding. My horse is obeying me as usual, and no one has crashed into me yet. You were right. Are you *always* so right?"

Silence.

"Well?" He hoped he hadn't offended her.

"I don't know how to answer that, my lord." She sounded amused. "Of course I am not always right. There was that time . . . *Hm*, well, once I . . . ."

He heard her giggle softly.

"Actually, I can't think of any terrible instance of wrong-headedness at the moment."

His laugh burst from him, and it felt good. Everything felt good, riding his favorite Town mount with his favorite lady and her sense of humor and fat pony.

"Here he is, out and about."

It was Whitely's voice. "Good day, Lady Jane. Westing."

"Good day, Whitely," Christopher answered after Jane murmured her greeting. "How is your father's gout?"

It was a joke between them. George's father was the picture of health, but every hint of ailment was declared to be the onset of gout, even a headache.

"Oh, dear," Jane exclaimed, even as Whitely laughed.

"Not to worry, dear lady. Your escort is playing the buffoon. My father is well, as he always is."

"Are you alone?" Christopher asked him.

"Burnley isn't here, if that's your question. Or he might be, but if he is, he's with his latest conq—" he broke off and coughed. "He is with some young miss. No offense," he added, undoubtedly directed at Jane.

"None taken," she assured him

Christopher decided he would ask later for her opinion of a man whose lady-friends were considered conquests. Or, on second thought, maybe he wouldn't. But he certainly would like to.

In fact, he wished to discuss everything with her and hear her views. It was a novel wish. He had a notion she would even give a reasonable opinion on parliamentary acts. How wonderful to have a mate with whom one could talk government. His mother and father loved each other, but their worlds of interest were entirely divergent.

"I'm off," Whitely announced. "I'll be at the club later if you're considering another outing. At White's."

"Not the Reform?" Christopher wondered.

"No. Had a falling out with a fellow there. Going to keep my distance for a bit as he goes weekly to Paddington."

The pugilist club in Paddington was renowned. Although boxing wasn't Christopher's idea of amusement, he'd given it a try. However, the Paddington club's pugilists were serious and brutal. Still, Whitely's remarks sounded like cowardice, which didn't sit well.

"Do you need a second?" he asked, then realized the stupidity of such an offering. "I mean, Burnley is a good man to have at your side."

"Won't come to that, I hope," George said.

"I cannot believe my ears," Jane vowed. "Are you two speaking of a duel?"

Whitely laughed, and Christopher joined in.

"No, Lady Jane," Whitely promised. "While it was a noble practice—"

"A pigheaded, dangerous one," she interrupted, and Christopher could well imagine her outrage. She probably looked even more alluring when her dander was raised.

"While it was a pigheaded practice," Whitely began again, "we have had to let it go into the mists of history. Regardless, if someone were to greatly insult my honor or a family member's, I can imagine calling him out at dawn, pistols at the ready."

Christopher rolled his eyes. He had better explain. "We were not discussing pistols at present, only pugilism. Boxing, if you will."

"I see." She didn't sound impressed.

"I don't believe I'll need a second, old chum, but I'd rather have you in your state than Burnley with both eyes."

Laughing at his own poor joke, Whitely wished them both a good day and trotted off.

"Your friend is in good humor," Jane remarked as they started forward again, their horses clopping along at a mere walk.

"Yes, he can amuse himself to no end, which is why he ends up having these falling outs. He doesn't know when to keep his mouth closed." Which reminded Christopher of George having said he wouldn't declare for Jane because of Fowler.

How should he approach the subject of the viscount and ask Jane her feelings for the man? It was entirely beyond the pale to simply bring him up, yet he couldn't think how Fowler could possibly arise in casual conversation. Except . . .

"Tell me about the hippopotamus."

"Oh, it was splendid. Have you seen one in a book?" she asked.

"I have seen a sketch." It looked as fantastical as a giraffe or a rhinoceros. Such strange creatures, especially to have on English soil.

"If your sketch showed a beast proving God has a sense of humor as great as Lord Whitely's, then the drawing was accurate. The hippopotamus is a large animal especially in its girth, looking like a sausage whose skin might burst at any moment. It had the most ridiculously short legs, rather like a pig. In fact, it reminded me of a very large boar without bristles, and friendlier looking, almost with a dog's nose—a bulldog, not a terrier. When it lay down, it looked a bit like a walrus. It had tiny, silly ears, which kept flicking in movement. I vow, it almost smiled and appeared pleasant, then it opened its great jaws, and I've never seen such massive teeth—great tusks curling up from the bottom and down from the top. I don't know how it closed its mouth, frankly."

"Thank you," he said when she'd finished. "Your description was excellent. I can practically see it. What sound did it make?"

"We should go together so you can hear it. It grunted and sneezed and even sounded like it was laughing sometimes."

"Like Whitely?" he asked.

"A little louder and more like a bark, otherwise," Jane teased, "yes, *exactly* like him."

Before she could move on to another subject, Christopher added, "I would, indeed, like to go and hear the hippopotamus, if you wouldn't be bored seeing it again. I cannot promise you a party afterward, such as Lord Burton threw, nor the scintillating company of Lord Fowler."

Jane said nothing at first, and Christopher would have given a lot to be able to see her expression.

Finally, she commented, "I am happy in your company, my lord, and I don't need a party."

She hadn't mentioned Fowler. *Now what?* He supposed he had to be blunt.

"You are in Lord Fowler's company frequently, I'm told."

"It is easy to get hold of the wrong end of the walking stick if one listens to gossip," Jane advised and said nothing more.

Bloody hell. She was as tight lipped as a clamshell. Plus, she was being unreasonable since listening was the only way he could gather information.

"When more than one person hands you the same stick," Christopher began, thinking to continue her quaint phraseology, "then it behooves one to grasp it."

For the second time in a few minutes, he rolled his eyes.

What on earth was he even babbling about? Grasping at sticks. More like clutching at straws.

"Be that as it may," Jane began, but in the back of his mind, he could hear a clattering sound in the distance and coming closer.

"While I will not break a confidence, I can tell you—"

"What is that?" he interrupted her. "Do you hear it?"

"No, I . . . yes, I do." He heard her saddle creaking as she turned. "Oh, dear God!"

"Jane, what is it?" For she had gone silent.

At the same time, he could hear screams now and the thundering sound of hooves and the odd clattering noise, which Christopher was now certain was a broken hitch being dragged behind horses, obviously loose horses without anyone at the reins.

"Runaway horses!" his footman called out.

Pushing aside the terrible jolt of fear pulsing through him, Christopher reached over toward her, thinking to grab her horse's bridal and keep it calm as they moved to safety. However, she must have turned her mount to look at what was bearing down upon them because instead of her pony's bridal, his fingers brushed its haunches behind her saddle.

"Jane, quickly," he urged. "We must get to the side."

"They're dragging someone," she said, ignoring him. "No, they must've run over someone and she got caught—oh, dear God!"

"My lord," Cyrus exclaimed, alarmed. "We must move."

"Jane," Christopher insisted. "They will sweep through here and—"

Her horse, which must have been facing the oncoming disaster, reared up by the sound of it, and she screamed.

"Cyrus, grab the lady's bridal if you can. Is she still seated?"

"Yes, my lord," Cyrus said.

At the same time, Jane apparently recovered her wits and responded, "I am. Ride to your right, quickly."

Christopher could only hope the way was clear as he urged Feldspar with his bootheels, tugging the reins to his right. His horse seemed only too glad to move in that direction, and Christopher had to trust the animal wasn't taking him into trouble or running over a picnicking family.

The runaway horses and all the sounds accompanying them ran by close behind him an instant later.

"Jane!"

"They have passed us now," Jane said to him quietly.

He pulled on the reins and came to a stop, beginning to reach for her.

"I'm here," she said from his left.

"Are you hurt?" he asked at once, wishing he could take her into his arms.

"No, it was awful, though. A terrible sight."

Her voice was shaking, and appropriate or not, he reached out his hand and commanded her, "Take hold."

Immediately, he felt her gloved fingers grasp his.

"There is a lady, bleeding upon the path," she told him, and he wished he could spare her having to describe it. "I think . . . she is dead. People have encircled her and someone has draped a cloak over her. Oh, Chris!" she wailed.

He circled his pommel with the reins to keep his horse steady, then leaning sideways, he pulled Jane toward him and into his embrace. It was awkward and uncomfortable but the best he could do.

"I'm so sorry," she said, her wavering tone not sounding at all like the capable Jane Chatley he knew and had come to adore.

"Whatever for?" he asked.

"For panicking and for not moving. I nearly got us both killed by dawdling, and your footman, too. I was as still as a statue watching the horses approaching."

"If I'd seen it, I might have been the same," he said. "In the end, *you* saved us."

"I didn't," she said tearfully.

"You did. I couldn't determine which way to go. I could have gone left thinking I was close to the edge of the path and gone in front of them. If you hadn't told me to go right, then I would have remained where I was." He rubbed his hands up and down her back, trying to calm her.

"Cyrus," he called out. "Are you here?"

"Yes, my lord."

"Is there anything we can do for the injured?"

"I think not, my lord," and his tone made it clear nothing could be done for the woman who'd been hit and run over.

"What about the carriage the horses broke away from?"

"Far down the path. Others have gone down to see the state of them."

"Then let's get Lady Chatley home. I wish I had a carriage in which to take you," he told her. "Can you still ride?"

Jane sniffed. "Yes." But he felt her hand squeeze his, so he remained unmoving another minute. Then, she pushed away from him, the brim of her jaunty hat knocking off his spectacles as she did.

"I'm fine," she promised, as he fumbled to catch them before they slipped from the saddle and were lost forever.

He snapped the armpiece as he clasped the spectacles against the pommel of his saddle.

"Blazes!"

"What is it?" Jane asked, sounding anxious, an unfamiliar nervousness in her tone.

He didn't like the sound. It reminded him too much of his own voice for the first few weeks after the explosion.

"Nothing, merely my own clumsiness." And he put the broken spectacles in his jacket pocket. "Cyrus, you can lead the way," he told the footman.

"Yes, my lord. Follow me."

And their little party moved slowly along the grass, eventually returning to the bridal path far past the dead woman from what Christopher could tell by the distant sounds behind them.

After a few minutes of silence, Jane said, "Only think, she was simply out for a stroll a few minutes ago. And then, just like that." She said nothing more, and he didn't know what to say to console her.

He was already resigned to a new awareness of the fragility of life and the swiftness with which one's condition could change. He wouldn't be brutally frank with Jane, who'd witnessed death today, but this cruel twist of fate was his reality ever since the explosion. The difficulty was not in conceiving how someone out for a stroll could now be dead. The struggle was in not caving in to the fear of the unknown, which he faced each moment in his sightless world.

Most fervently, he hoped this didn't change Jane.

Starting back in the direction they'd come, they eventually passed by the vehicle whose hitch had broken, setting off the tragic chain of events.

"It looks like no one from the carriage was hurt," Jane said softly, and without thinking, Christopher opened his eyes, glancing around.

It was an exceedingly bright day, he thought and then stifled a gasp.

A bright day!

For a moment, he believed he saw the play of shadows, which would mean his eyes had detected light. He thought he'd seen movement, like a tree branch swaying across his vision, darker than its surroundings.

He blinked and stared. Now, it all seemed simply the same shade of black, but it might actually be a paler darkness than before. Or was it simply because he wasn't wearing the spectacles?

Had he imagined it? he wondered. *What a disconcerting day!*

They were lucky to be returning as a group, unscathed. Jane's horse could have collided with the runaways. Or she could have been thrown from her pony's back.

Moreover, he would have been helpless to stop anything bad befalling her.

Another man, even Fowler, could have seen the danger, grabbed her horse's reins if Jane were paralyzed with fear, and pulled her to safety. Christopher, on the other hand, had to wait for *her* to direct *him*, and it had nearly been too late.

He was a fool. Each time they had been out, he'd worried over whether he would trip and embarrass her.

He'd fretted over her reputation. The entire time, he should have been considering her wellbeing.

Just because he accepted the fickle nature of fortune didn't mean he had to like it. Nor did it mean he had to accept the added danger in which he put those around him.

A grim realization settled over him, but he could think of no alternative.

He would have to let her go entirely.

CHAPTER NINETEEN

Catching herself gripping the handrail on her way down the stairs at her Hanover Square home, Jane admonished herself once again for being irrational. Ultimately, nothing had happened two days earlier to change her life. She was fine. Christopher was fine, too.

However, she had been unable to completely let go of the anxious feelings plaguing her.

It was not only having stupidly remained frozen in the line of danger, moved to action only by Christopher's voice urging her to safety. It was also the haunting vision of the woman lying in the path. Lifeless.

Jane thought of that woman's day, waking up and going about her toilette, then dressing. Maybe she was a mother or a young bride. In mere moments, her life had ended, and she would never go home again. What if she'd been about to do something important? What if those who loved her never recovered from their sorrow?

"Stop it!" she said aloud as she entered the parlor, only to come face-to-face with her cousin seated on the sofa.

"Stop what?" he asked, standing. "What a strange way of greeting."

"Bernard!" she exclaimed. *Why had no one told her of his visit? And where was her mother?*

"Jane, you look well."

"Where is my mother? You do know my father is away."

"He is expected back any day, and I inadvertently beat him here."

It was all news to her. Unwelcome news, too. This could only be about one thing.

"I'm checking on my inheritance," he announced unashamedly. "And weighing my options."

His gaze flicked over her. Undoubtedly, he considered her to be an option.

"I hope you were not brought here on false pretenses," she began.

Was there any way on God's green earth she could see herself marrying Bernard Lowther? He was not ugly. He was simply Bernard. She'd encountered him at least a dozen times in her life, and he'd never made more than the tiniest of ripples in the lake of her existence. Not like Christopher, who caused waves to crash on her shore simply by being near her.

"I don't believe I know what you mean. When your father dies, I will become the next Earl of Chatley. Is there any doubt to that?"

Why couldn't Parliament enact a law that passed property and titles down to daughters? She would ask Christopher when next they met about this possibility. She doubted even if it happened, it would occur in time to save her from being used as a pawn between uncle and nephew.

Regardless of Bernard's wishes and her father's, she would not give up her legal existence into this man's care. He might be a saint, for all she knew, but he was a man whom she didn't love or value. It would be foolish of her, and she hoped she was not a fool.

"There is no doubt you will inherit," she confirmed. "But I do not believe my father is in imminent risk of dying."

As she said it, the dead woman's face flashed before her eyes.

Dear God! She was a fool after all. Imminent death was upon any one of them at any moment.

"Are you well?" he asked. "You have gone quite pale."

Just then, as Jane sank into the nearest chair, her mother entered.

"Lady Chatley, good day. I fear your daughter is unwell."

"What!" the countess exclaimed and rushed to her side, picking up her hand, even as she put her palm to Jane's forehead. "You are a little clammy and pale."

Bernard said her father was delayed coming from the Continent. Even then, he might be dead at the bottom of the English Channel, victim of a storm that shattered his ship, or lying on a roadway having been thrown from his horse.

Come to think of it, he would never be upon horseback on such a journey, but rather in a carriage. Still, his carriage might have broken down or been robbed at gunpoint. He would refuse to give up his purse and the highwaymen would shoot him. Or he could as easily have been killed falling down the stairs at an inn on the way home.

Her mother and she would have to move out immediately as Bernard would take over. They weren't prepared. No one was *prepared* for disaster, or it wouldn't be called a disaster. Christopher hadn't known he was seeing his last sight any more than the woman in Hyde Park had known she was breathing her last breath.

"Jane," her mother said, drawing her from her reverie. "What is happening?"

She could not explain to her mother, especially not in front of Bernard, how she was having a crisis—something in her brain had been overcome with fear. She wanted to speak to Christopher. He would understand. Of that, she was certain.

She had been so quick to demand he push himself to do things he considered impossible. And she'd expected it of him and not given him enough acclaim.

How had he done it with such grace?

Ashamed of how Christopher had been the one comforting her after the park incident, Jane shook her head to think he had experienced the entire thing in darkness.

How did one live with such fear?

Jumping up, causing her mother to gasp, she said only, "I'll see you later, Mummy." At the door, she recalled her cousin and turned.

"Good day, Bernard. I hope you enjoy your visit." She nearly added something about removing her from his list of options but decided against it. Her erratic behavior was probably cause enough for him to think twice.

Summoning the family's carriage, she went directly to Berkley Square. Giving the Foresters' butler her name, even though he well knew it by then, she asked for Lord Christopher Westing, *not* the duchess.

"Please tell him it is of utmost importance."

As she paced the attractive room, it seemed an eternity before Christopher appeared. When she turned at the door's opening and saw him, the flux of emotions she experienced took her breath away.

"Where are you?" he asked.

"I'm here," but instead of staying put by the fireplace, she walked toward him. Then she passed by him and closed the door. It had no lock, but it was the best she could do. She wanted to be alone, safe, with the man she loved.

"What's going on?" he asked her.

NEARLY AS SOON AS Christopher asked the question, he felt Jane's arms go around him. They didn't encircle his waist for a friendly hug, either. Her hands crept up his chest and behind his neck, until he felt her fingers entwine in his hair.

The delicate floral scent of her filled his head, and he breathed deeply.

Before he could say another word, however, he felt her body rise, as if she were going up on her toes, and then, her lips were firmly upon his.

He groaned. The past few times they'd been together, there had been no opportunity for them to share an intimate moment. And despite having made up his mind she would be better off without him, he could not turn down her offer. Not when she was his heart and his body's one desire.

He dropped his cane and pressed his palms to her back, drawing her closer. And although Jane was doing an admirable job of kissing him with her soft, warm lips, he needed more.

Slanting his head, he licked the seam of her mouth until she opened it, and then he was inside her, sucking her hot tongue, tasting peppermint—*she'd eaten a mint sweet, perhaps?*—and pulling her hips against his.

When she moaned in response, the sound sent a surge of lust into his loins.

Their kiss was long, drawn out. *Aggravating, frustrating, perfect.*

Knowing where he was and how many steps it would take, he backed her against the door she'd just closed. Then he could entirely flatten his body against hers. When it wasn't enough, when he felt her hands running up and down his back wildly tugging at him before clasping into his hair once again, he fisted his hand in her skirts and began to draw them up.

"Yes," she hissed against his mouth, encouraging him to further decadence.

Using both hands, he lifted her gown and its many layers of petticoats to her waist, pinning them between their bodies, so his fingers were free to discover what lay underneath. *Silk drawers.*

Of course, Jane who was perfect beyond measure would have the lightest, softest silk drawers. He wanted to tear them off her.

Restraining himself, instead, he slid one of his hands into the opening between her thighs. The drawers, separate short pantlegs tied at the waist, gave easy access to her body, to her most sensitive place, to the soft curls over her mound, and—

"Ohh," she cried against his mouth when he touched her core.

It was wet, warm, slippery, glorious. He didn't need to see her. He could feel she was resting her head back against the painted wood behind her. He knew her eyes were closed and her mouth, open. He could hear her panting.

It was a sound that fueled his desire. His shaft was throbbing with need despite his brain knowing he couldn't do anything about that now. At the very least, Christopher could pleasure her—*quickly!*—mindful of the fact it was broad daylight despite the darkness enshrouding him, and they were in the fastidious parlor of the Foresters' home.

"Jane, Jane, Jane," he murmured, his lips against the soft skin of her neck as he touched her swollen womanhood, slipping his fingers inside.

Her body responded at the gentlest touch. He stroked her intimate place, again and again, quickening the speed as he felt her stiffen, was amazed at the dewy moisture against his palm. He brought his free hand up and cupped her breast through her gown and corset, and pressing gently with his thumb, he could feel her pert nipple.

As he caressed her, continuing his ministrations between her spread legs, she found her release.

Never had a woman come for him like that. With so light a touch and so swiftly. With the long dearth of physical pleasure, he knew he could do the same, just as easily. Unlike Jane, though, still shuddering in his arms, his release would be a messy business, better left to the privacy of his room when he would imagine her slender fingers encircling his shaft.

If he kept thinking like that, he wouldn't be able to wait.

Jane suddenly sighed, and he pictured her eyes opening and her lips in a beautiful "oh" of amazement at what had occurred so naturally.

Easing his hand from beneath her legs and letting her skirts fall, Christopher claimed her mouth again, that beautiful mouth with its splendidly shaped lips.

"*Mmm*," she murmured against him. "That was . . . ," she trailed off.

"I'm glad," he said.

Then, to his surprise, she giggled. "I'm standing in Lord and Lady Forester's parlor."

"As am I." He reached down and adjusted his painful pole to ease the discomfort.

"Are you all right?" she asked, sounding curious, and he knew her gaze must be on his movements.

"I am. Not to worry. My body became excited at your pleasure."

"It was wonderful," she told him. "I should feel embarrassed, but I don't. Not with you."

Because I can't see? he wondered.

Immediately, he realized that was the newly insecure man in him thinking wrongly. Jane hadn't meant such a thing.

"Because we are so comfortable together?" he surmised.

"Precisely," she said, still inches from him. "It's why I came today."

His expression must have displayed his shock, for she quickly amended her words.

"I don't mean I came here to do . . . what we . . . what you just did with me. I meant, I came to see you because I was thinking strange and discomforting thoughts after the other day, after what happened in the park. I wanted to tell you about them because I can tell you anything. I also came to apologize."

"Apologize?"

"Yes, for insisting so adamantly that you go on outings with me."

Didn't she want to go out with him anymore?

He took a few steps back and heard the crack as he stepped on his cane and broke it. He also could hear her adjusting her gown, probably smoothing it with her hands.

"What are you wearing?" he asked without thinking.

"You are changing the topic." Then she added, "A cream-colored gown and jacket. Both have black piping."

"It sounds *au courant*," he said.

"Yes," she agreed, sounding distracted.

"All right, tell me why you want to apologize."

"Because the world is a terrifying place," she said hurriedly. "I was not sympathetic enough. I brought you the cane and made you go walking and riding."

Without her pushing him, he would probably still be afraid to go outside.

"You were right to insist," he said. "Daily life was not going to get any easier by my hiding indoors. This *is* my life now." He tapped his broken cane with the toe of his shoe.

Moreover, he'd seen no more phantom shadows, despite spending time in the garden without his spectacles, hoping to see some quality of light and darkness.

"And the sooner I accept it and learn to live with it, the better."

"You're right," she said, "but . . . ."

"But what?" he prompted into the silence.

"At any moment, anything can happen."

He sighed. "I know. And it *will* happen whether one wastes time worrying or not."

After a moment, he felt her hand on his cheek. Before he could appreciate her tender gesture and cover her hand with his, the door handle rattled and he felt Jane spring back, putting some distance between them.

"What's going on in here?" It was his father.

"Good day, Your Grace," Jane said, sounding completely normal.

"Good day, Lady Jane. It looks as though some mischief is afoot."

Christopher felt a shard of alarm. *Had his father seen something? Was Jane's dress in disarray?*

"A misstep is all," came her calm voice. "Lord Westing dropped it and stepped on it before I could retrieve it."

The cane!

"That's the second one in a month, isn't it?"

Christopher recalled how Jane snapped the other one on purpose but said nothing.

"Then there were your spectacles. That's why I came to find you. I am going to Parliament and would like you to accompany me. We can go to the oculist on Tothill Street and get another pair, and I suppose there is some place nearby we can get another long cane. Maybe we'll buy two of each."

"I was just leaving," Jane said.

Had she been? They had been discussing the ephemeral quality of life.

"I didn't mean to interrupt you young people," his father pointed out, but he didn't leave the room.

"Not at all, Your Grace," Jane assured him. "It sounds as if you have important business to which you must attend."

"Before you go, dear girl, if you would be so good as to ask my wife if there is anything she needs. She's in the library."

"Of course, Your Grace. Good day."

"And to you, Lady Jane," the duke returned.

"Good day, my lord," she repeated, and Christopher could hear she'd taken a step closer to speak to him.

"And to you," he returned. He wanted to ask her when they could next meet, as all his previous chivalric notions of keeping his distance and ordering her to go out with other more capable men had dissolved as soon as he'd got close to her again.

He was weak when it came to Jane. Yet, she also made him stronger. It was a paradox.

He listened to her footsteps as she left the parlor. *Good God! To think what had occurred a few minutes earlier.*

"Nice girl," his father said. "I like the stuff she's made of. So glad your mother has her help."

Christopher considered how lucky he was to have her, too. *But what would she get out of it? A life of describing everything in detail and . . .*

"Are you ready, my boy?"

"Always, Father," he said, something he used to say to him all the time and hadn't felt like saying since the explosion, but pleasuring Jane as he had, having her melt in his arms, had certainly given him a newfound sense of assuredness.

JANE REALIZED HER HEART was still beating quickly. It had been hardly any time from when Christopher had done such wonderful things to her body to when his father had entered the room. As she knocked on the library door, she was counting herself lucky she hadn't still been rearranging her skirts when the Duke of Westing had entered.

What a debacle that would have been!

"Jane, dear. How did you know I needed you desperately?" the Duchess of Westing asked, and she had to push all thoughts of Christopher and what their moment of intimacy meant, if anything.

"Did you know we've had calling cards from three young ladies this week, all wanting to come visit my son?"

Jane frowned. *Why was the duchess telling her this? Moreover, why hadn't Christopher told her?* "No, I didn't, but then, how could I?"

"I only mention it because I would like your opinion on them. I know you and Chris are friends. If you can give your opinion on the merits of these young ladies, it would be most helpful. I understand you are nearly engaged, yourself. Surprising to me, as I had a notion you and my son might have been heading toward an understanding, but that was my baseless assumption. The heart goes where it will, as they say."

Jane had stopped listening after the word *engaged*.

"Your Grace, I am not 'nearly engaged.'" How could she know of Bernard's arrival in London when she'd learned of it a short while ago? "I don't know where you heard such a thing."

"Oh, dear me! Then it wouldn't be right for me to discuss the other ladies with you, as you may consider them rivals. I don't know how I got it all cockeyed. I thought Amanda said you were expecting a proposal from Lord Fowler any day."

Jane pursed her lips to suppress the sigh of frustration. Christopher's sister needed to find something to occupy herself besides her brother's affairs.

"Speaking of Lady Amanda, she told me in confidence she wished very much to help with the house decorating and the fabric choices, the paint colors and even the carpet runners."

"Preposterous!" the duchess exclaimed. "She has never shown an interest."

"She said you would say such a thing. She is extremely intimidated because you are an artist with such a vast knowledge of color. She doesn't think you will value her input or consider it useful. She said she would even protest greatly if you asked her, so as not to embarrass herself or disappoint you. Yet she truly wished you would take her under your wing and put her to work. She wishes to learn and to help."

Jane sat at the table and picked up a few magazines. "Unless you don't want your daughter to be involved."

"No, I do," the duchess said. "I simply assumed she would refuse."

Jane tried to look wise. "Then you must order her to help so she cannot say no."

"Jane!" the duchess exclaimed, and Jane thought she'd gone too far, until Her Grace's next words. "You are absolutely correct. What a dear and thoughtful girl you are. I only hope it will not upset our own arrangement, which has been proceeding so nicely."

"How do you mean?"

"I don't want you to think I am playing favorites by giving my daughter the lion's share of the work or asking her opinion over yours."

Jane smiled, and her joy was genuine down to her toes. "Not at all. I cannot imagine anything that would make me happier than to see you and Amanda working together."

Should she ask about the other ladies? She decided against it, after what Christopher had just done with her, she felt confident she was first in his regard. Still, her curiosity demanded she ask him privately about their identities.

"I believe Amanda is upstairs," the duchess added. "I have a mind to send for her now."

Jane nodded. "It would be best if I made myself scarce when you do. If she thinks I had a hand in it, it would only add to her sense of insecurity. Let the idea of her working with you come directly and entirely from you. Don't you think?"

Jane was shocked at herself, but she was in too deep to change her course. She blinked her eyes guilelessly and let the duchess decide what she would do.

"I believe you are correct. Will you go purchase the netting for the lights, then?" she handed Jane a piece of paper. "Here is the address."

With her new task, Jane set out feeling measurably better than when she arrived, feeling afraid of her own shadow. Christopher had been correct. There was no sense worrying when whatever would happen would happen anyway.

And then she remembered Bernard Lowther was waiting at home—not a vague fear over some possible future catastrophe, but a very real cousin who saw her as an option.

CHAPTER TWENTY

The day of the Duchess of Westing's art exhibit dawned clear and sunny.

One hurdle out of the way, Jane thought. No one would be kept away by massive downpours or, worse, enter Egypt Hall shaking their drenched umbrellas onto Christopher's mother's watercolor paintings.

The show would open at two o'clock and continue into the evening. Her own mother was going to come regardless of the unknown whereabouts of Jane's father. Unfortunately, she would be accompanied by Bernard Lowther. Jane had managed to avoid him thus far by extreme and uncharacteristic rudeness.

In fact, within the confines of the Chatley townhouse, she'd seen him only twice, each time *before* he saw her, and so had escaped his company, except for the evening meal. She knew he wouldn't be so crass as to bring up the topic of marriage at the table, especially with her father still absent.

Jane had purposefully never again mentioned the art show to Lord Fowler, knowing Christopher was going to attend to support his mother. She simply didn't want one man encountering the other. Lord Fowler was bound to say something that would force Jane to reveal her collaboration with him, which she had promised not to do. She had no wish to humiliate the viscount.

All men had pride, as Lady Cambrey and she had discussed, whether feeling damaged from an accidental injury entirely out of his control, or trying to find a woman with whom to spend his life. She hoped the latter's quest would soon be over, as Jane found being overly social both tiring and a nuisance.

At twelve sharp, Jane passed between the Egyptian Hall's pillars, which themselves stood under life-sized mystical statues of ancient people high above the street. She felt as if she were entering another world, styled as an Egyptian tomb. However, inside, because of a large central skylight, it was bright and airy, the opposite of what Jane thought a tomb would be like.

The day before, she'd directed workmen to hang the netting to diffuse the light, according to the duchess's exacting standards, copying Mr. Turner's own studio.

Also, within the past twenty-four hours, Jane had helped the hall's owner to hang the duchess's paintings from wires all around the main room. Each had its cream-colored name card, neatly printed, attached to the bottom of the frame. The perfect accompanying flowers were even then being delivered. Jane had the vases ready and would spend the next hour arranging them and setting them on pedestals near the appropriate artwork. Chef Soyer, personally, would bring the refreshments at any moment to set upon a table tucked away at one end.

The crowning touch would be a string quartet playing in the middle of the room, and Jane hoped they would show up half an hour before the event.

Before she knew it, Her Grace had arrived, as had the chef. Soon, a beautiful tablecloth was draped over the refreshments table, and Soyer, a diminutive man, was walking around admiring the artwork while his staff set down platter after platter of hor d'oeuvres. The musicians, only three of the four, were in place, with no one knowing if the fourth would make an appearance as he had last been seen staggering from a pub the night before.

Exactly how the music would sound played by a trio, Jane had no idea. And while she and the duchess were still deciding on whether to change the musical selection, the owner of the hall opened the doors to admit the public.

At the head of the crowd were the Westings and the Foresters.

"Play whatever you wish," Christopher's mother exclaimed and rushed to greet those entering.

Jane took a deep breath and nodded reassuringly at the only violinist, who had an anxious look on his face.

"Just go through the list I gave you," she told them. And they began with Mozart's light second movement of his *Divertimento*.

Plastering a smile on her face, Jane took a few steps backward, toward the surrounding pillars that lined the room, and watched the reaction of those who entered.

How she wished she and Christopher could exchange a look of camaraderie, particularly after what had last occurred between them.

Without going up to him in public, speaking with him, or touching him on the arm, she could not even share an acknowledgment that he had brought her into this satisfying association with his mother. At some point, she would thank him.

In a few minutes, she'd helped herself to a cheese-filled puff pastry and was drinking a glass of wine when she spotted Lord Fowler enter the hall.

Drat! Moreover, he was moving toward her as directly as the crow flies. Frantically, she did two things—notice the whereabouts of Christopher on the other side of the room, deep in conversation with Lord Whitely as they stood in front of a painting of horses, and secondly, scan for some young lady whom Jane thought Lord Fowler might like and be liked by in return.

No one was readily apparent. There was the awfully shrewish Lady Matilda Brethens, from whom Jane had already warned the viscount to keep away, and a handful of silly girls, all Amanda Westing's friends, who'd undoubtedly come in the hopes of encountering the blind marquess and tasting Chef Soyer's marvelous creations.

"Lady Jane," Lord Fowler greeted, bowing to her and attempting to take her hand in his even though she was holding a glass.

If he kept tugging, he would end up with her wine on his trousers.

Thankfully, he gave up and bowed again.

"You look lovely."

"Thank you," she gave a slight incline of her head in return. "We are here today to look at the art, however, not me."

"You are prettier than any painting."

Unwanted compliments didn't give her any joy. If Jane could only spy the right woman for him to bestow such smooth praises, she was sure he would have success. Luckily, Lord Burnley's sister had just arrived with him. Jane had never met her, a pretty girl who'd been living in France. Perhaps the viscount would take a fancy to her, and vice versa.

"Do you see over there?" she directed Lord Fowler's gaze toward the Burnleys. "Lady Sophia is just back from the Continent. I hear she is most amusing." In truth, Jane had actually heard nothing about her at all.

Later, she could ask Christopher, she supposed, and determine if the girl might be a match for Lord Fowler. For the time being, however, the viscount could test the waters by himself.

"I'm not sure it would do for me to leave you by yourself," he said. "Not very gentlemanly of me. Besides, if we are close, we can speak frankly."

Jane sipped her wine, wondering how to escape. She could check on the food, make sure the musicians were happy—look for a cricket bat with which she could smack Lord Fowler over the head—but everything was running smoothly. There was nothing for which she needed to be pulled away from his cloying attention. She would simply have to lie.

"I must check in with the musicians, as we are one short." She curtsied quickly and turned away.

Unfortunately, he followed her and kept on following her like a stray dog hoping for scraps. No matter what she did, perfectly centering a vase on a pedestal, adjusting a frame, even picking a crumb off the carpet, he was at her elbow.

Finally, when she could think of no other pretend tasks and ran the risk of shrieking in frustration, Jane dragged him around the back of a pillar, and then into one of the Egyptian Hall's many nooks.

"Speak frankly," she prompted him.

"We must stop the quest."

Jane gasped. She had failed him. "No, don't give up hope, Lord Fowler."

"I haven't," he promised and sent her a happy smile. "I have found someone I like above all others. Shall I tell her immediately?"

"Do you think she feels the same?"

"I'm not sure, but I'm willing to risk ridicule."

"I do not think you will be ridiculed. Any woman would be lucky to have you. You have a straight posture, a fair amount of hair, a good mind, and an even better fortune."

"Ha, Jane you are amusing."

She had been entirely serious, and not trying to be amusing at all.

"Is she here?" she asked.

"Yes." He sounded happy. "Quite close."

"Is she someone I've introduced you to?"

"Not exactly." He sent her an odd look.

"Really?" Had he been socializing on his own? "Don't keep me in suspense."

"Jane!" came a screech that could only be the Duchess of Westing.

"I'm so sorry, Lord Fowler, we shall have to continue this another time. Just like a watch, this exhibit has many moving parts."

In fact, rather like life, Jane thought. *And sometimes, she found it difficult to keep them all running smoothly.*

"Can I help?" he offered kindly.

"I don't know what Her Grace needs, but if you'll check the refreshment area, please let me know if anything is amiss. And do help yourself to the most delicious hors d'oeuvres, all from Chef Soyer, a friend of the Duke of Westing."

"Jane!" the duchess's tone sounded more urgent.

"I must go."

She stepped back into view and felt the eyes of half the attendees upon her, causing her cheeks to warm. *What on earth could make the duchess behave in such an indecorous manner?*

And then, like an unthinking dullard, Lord Fowler appeared directly behind her. She knew this because she heard a small collective intake of breath from those looking in her direction and also because he ran into the back of her, causing her to jump forward.

Dear God!

Even the string trio, as she now thought of them, missed a few notes of Schubert's dramatic *Rosamunde*, which— already lacking their second violinist—sounded eccentric to her ears.

Scanning the room for reactions, Jane saw a few ladies whispering behind their fans and gloves and realized a few gentlemen were laughing, no doubt, at Lord Fowler's indiscretion.

Even worse, there was Lord Burnley standing with Christopher, and he wasn't laughing. He was scowling at her, and then—*no!*—Lord Burnley was leaning over to say something discreetly to his best friend.

She couldn't watch. Knowing the next thing she saw would be disappointment or anger on Christopher's face, she turned away, practically running toward his mother, standing in the midst of admirers.

"Your Grace, what is the matter?" Jane tried to keep the exasperation from her voice and failed.

Christopher's mother was beaming broadly and holding an empty glass of wine.

"My first sale! Lady Mulberry wants the sailboats, *both* paintings. And I didn't think about how to wrap them. I didn't really think about sales at all. No parcel paper, no string, no bags. We're not prepared!"

Jane wanted to clamp her hand over the duchess's mouth. For one, the duchess had drunk too much, perhaps due to nervousness, and thus, she was speaking extremely loudly. Everyone was staring.

And for another thing, they weren't selling the paintings off the wall and wrapping them up in paper as if they were legs of lamb at a butcher's shop.

"Calm yourself, Your Grace. We are simply taking the names of those who wish to purchase and will deliver the paintings over the next few days. We're not pulling them down now, elsewise others could not enjoy them throughout the show. I have cards with the word *sold* already printed for precisely this occurrence."

And she pulled them out of the side pocket of her fitted jacket where she normally kept such things as theatre tickets and a few coins. From another pocket, she withdrew a small sharpened pencil.

"I'll write Lady Mulberry's name on the back and tuck one into the frame of both the sailboat paintings." Jane held the little white card up so the Duchess of Westing could see it. Christopher's mother snatched it and practically giggled.

"Sold!" she exclaimed, reading the block print type. "Jane, you are marvelous. But write her name on the *front* so everyone can see."

Just like that, the crisis was averted. "Have you seen my husband, dear girl? I want to share the news with His Grace."

"I'll look for the duke, I promise, and perhaps you should go to the refreshments table and try some of the food. I promise you, it's scrumptious."

"My stomach is too aflutter with nerves to eat. Maybe I'll just get a little glass of wine."

"You are already holding one, Your Grace."

"Why, yes I am! But it's empty," she pointed out. "I'll see you later, Jane." And she wandered toward the server who was refilling wine glasses.

"Duchess," she called after her, stopping the woman momentarily. "Please do not sell the same painting twice and don't forget to tell the interested party to see me so I know who is buying which one."

"Yes, yes, of course, Jane. I'm not a ninny. Where did you say His Grace was?"

Jane hadn't, but she scanned the room, her glance resting on Christopher looking grim and Burnley still right by his side, glaring at her in his stead.

Being glared at by proxy was nearly as bad as by the person who was angry.

Then she spotted the Duke of Westing with Lady Amanda on the far side of the room.

"He is over there," she pointed him out, "and your daughter, too."

"Marvelous," the duchess repeated. "I'll see you later."

As soon as she disappeared into the throng, Jane was torn. Should she speak with Christopher immediately, in the middle of the crowded exhibit? Or wait until it was all over?

She wasn't going to be given a choice, for the two gentlemen were heading directly toward her.

Even as they reached her, so did her mother and her cousin. All parties converged at precisely the same moment.

"Jane, dear, you have done a superb job. Hasn't she, my lords?" Lady Chatley included them. "Can you believe the food and the flowers? Of course, it's all your mother's artwork that makes the exhibit so fine," she added, looking at Christopher, who politely turned in her direction, knowing he was being addressed.

"I have seen many of my mother's paintings before, Lady Chatley, but I shall not have the pleasure of seeing the flowers." His tone was polite but not warm.

"Nor have we yet to taste the food," added Lord Burnley, looking sourly at Jane.

"Well, you simply must. The pork tartelettes are divine," her mother gushed. "Jane didn't cook the food 0f course. Chef Soyer did, but she was closeted with him for ages deciding on the selections. And I think her choices are superb."

Jane could tell Christopher was seething, even without being able to see his eyes behind the smoky gray lenses of his new spectacles. His body was rigid, and his face was a mask of annoyance. No amount of hors d'oeuvres was going to make up for her having let her reputation be tarnished by a secretive *tête-à-tête* with Lord Fowler in the dark recesses of the Egyptian Hall.

Not when everyone saw it.

"I wasn't *closeted* with Chef Soyer, Mummy. He came to Lady Forester's home, where I discussed the food with him in their parlor. With plenty of light. And the door was open. And a maid was present."

Realizing she sounded defensive, she stopped talking, especially because her mother was frowning and Bernard sent her a look of perplexity.

"Yes, of course, Jane. I didn't mean to imply otherwise." Lady Chatley glanced at Lords Burnley and Westing. "Jane has always had a flawless reputation."

That pronouncement only made it worse. Apparently, her mother and her cousin had missed the earlier *faux pas*, but by the way Christopher's mouth twisted, it would seem he'd had an earful from Lord Burnley on how very flawed she was in that regard.

And then to add fuel to the flame, Lord Fowler appeared and greeted everyone in turn. He didn't seem to notice the frosty reception from Christopher and his friend. Instead, he turned to Jane with a ready smile.

"As you requested, my lady, I checked the refreshment table. There is nothing amiss. Guests are loving the food, particularly the salmon and soft cheese puffs and the sliced pear and sharp cheddar on crackers."

"Divine," her mother commented.

"My favorite are angels on horseback," Lord Fowler added. "May I get you some?"

His tone was warm and *too* familiar, and she'd already lost her appetite, even for oysters wrapped in bacon.

"No, thank you, Lord Fowler." Maybe it was precisely the right time for another glass of wine however. Before she could ask him to fetch her one, and thereby remove him from the group, he said the unthinkable.

"May I steal you away a moment to continue our . . . ?" he trailed off, and Jane wanted to sink into the floor and disappear.

Even her mother gasped softly at his unfortunate suggestion of secret intimacy, and Bernard showed him the first measure of interest.

Completely out of character, Christopher swore aloud, causing Jane's mother to gasp again.

He quickly apologized, while Burnley took a step toward Lord Fowler, perhaps to threaten him on his friend's behalf.

Jane knew her eyes were as large as dinner plates. In the space of a moment, fisticuffs were about to break out at the Duchess of Westing's art show. And it would be all her fault. Moreover, Lord Fowler seemed utterly clueless as to the mayhem he was causing.

Somehow, knowing where his friend was, Christopher raised a hand and managed to lay it on Lord Burnley's arm, halting him.

"I don't believe *now* is the time, Lord Fowler," Jane said quickly. "I need to focus on the duchess's art show and her guests."

"Of course. It was only that I was so excited by the topic of our recent discussion," he said, and she wondered if he could possibly speak without saying the wrong thing.

She stared at him, unable even to think how to respond.

Luckily, her mother, who'd rescued her from chaos before, chose that moment to excuse herself along with Bernard, inviting Jane to go with them.

"There are many people here to whom we should introduce your cousin."

"Agreed," Jane declared, deciding her safest action was a quick escape with her family. Lord Fowler could fend for himself!

Dropping into a low curtsey to one and all, Jane hurried through her parting words, "My lords, if you'll excuse me."

At least Christopher could hear how her voice was coming from somewhere at his elbow, for with his title, the deepest respect went naturally to him.

He didn't respond except with a subtle inclination of his head. Lord Burnley uttered a curt "Good day," and Lord Fowler called after her, "We shall speak later."

He might as well have screamed her given name, too!

The rest of the exhibit passed without incident, except for the excited exclamations from the Duchess of Westing each time a painting sold. When Jane next searched for Christopher, he had departed.

That night, when she collapsed into bed, she decided she must, at the very least, explain there was nothing romantic between her and Richard Fowler. Perhaps it truly mattered to Christopher. *And if it did, what precisely did that mean?*

AFTER BREAKFAST, JANE DECLARED her intent to go to Hatchards book shop where she had ordered something special for Christopher weeks earlier, an English book in Raphigraphy type, which he could read without learning anything new. She'd been sent word it had arrived, and it had cost her, or rather her father, a pretty penny.

Considering what had happened the evening before, she thought she ought to have a peace offering the next time she encountered the seemingly rankled marquess.

"I'll go, too," her mother said surprisingly. Book shops were not usually to the countess's liking, but this famed shop at 187 Piccadilly had the most exquisite stationery, and Lady Chatley loved penning letters.

Jane had made her purchase, aware out of the corner of her eye that her mother was speaking with someone. Turning, she saw the back side of Lady Mulberry strolling out the door, and Lady Chatley standing, mouth open, staring at her from the first opening in the shelving. Jane could see by her expression her mother had been told something quite distasteful.

Hurrying over, Jane began at once. "Mummy, it was not what it looked like."

"It looked as though you had been secluded in the shadows with Lord Fowler. That's what I was just informed."

"Oh." She'd assumed Lady Mulberry had mentioned her and Christopher's disappearance during the dinner dance.

"Oh, indeed! Now you tell me at once, Jane, are you and the viscount romantically involved?"

She grabbed her mother's arm and dragged her farther into the bookstore.

CHRISTOPHER HAD BEEN LEFT to his own devices when his father hurried off with the store clerk to obtain a book on the French Revolution, a political upheaval which fascinated the duke. This meant he could do nothing but stand and try to look inconspicuous—as inconspicuous as a blind man could be surrounded by books.

Then he heard Jane's voice, crystal clear from the next row over.

"No, Mummy, I swear, there is nothing romantic between us. There is nothing between us at all. It is not like that."

Christopher stood frozen, barely breathing. *Was Jane speaking of their association?*

"Then why do you spend so much time with him? Don't you know what people are starting to say?"

"I am simply helping him. He is an unfortunate soul, who cannot find his way in this world without help. I have taken it upon myself to offer that help."

What had she called him? An unfortunate soul?

"His future looked utterly bleak, but now, with my help, it has improved."

"Then you are not falling for him?" her mother sounded disappointed.

"Absolutely not."

Jane sounded appalled. In fact, she sounded so convincing Christopher believed her.

"I promise you," she continued, "he is nothing more than a special mission, an undertaking of mercy, if you will, and thankfully, it is coming to an end."

"You won't be spending time with him anymore?" Lady Chatley asked.

"No, with my main task coming to an end, there'll be no reason for me to meet him. Frankly, I'm relieved. Helping him started as a lark, but, as time has gone on, being with him has become increasingly tedious, and I had to hide that fact so as not to insult him."

The devil take her! Christopher felt ill. She certainly hadn't feigned tedium when she'd climaxed in his arms.

He wished they would move away, or at least stop talking. He also hoped his father didn't choose that moment to return since, if discovered, Jane might know he'd overheard her cruel words. His humiliation would be complete.

His luck, as usual, ran out.

"Chris!" boomed his father's voice. "Where are you?" Then he lowered his tone slightly. "Lady Chatley, Lady Jane, good day."

"Good day, Your Grace," came Lady Chatley's voice. "How do you fare?"

"Quite well, except I've lost my son hereabouts. Chris," the duke called again.

He had to speak now, or be found out as an eavesdropper.

"Here I am," Christopher said, quietly, hoping to sound farther away. Then he shuffled his feet in place, and finally took real steps to come upon the group.

"Have I found you?" He might as well pretend he didn't even know the ladies were present. "Did you get what you were looking for, Father."

"Yes, I've got it. Lady Chatley and Lady Jane are here."

"Are they?" Christopher said, trying to keep his tone neutral. "Good day, ladies."

"Good day, my lord," each said in turn, and his feeling of betrayal grew at Jane's familiar friendly voice.

"Shall we go?" he asked his father. "We don't want to be late for the proposal."

They were listening to a speech by Lord Brougham that morning on his proposed Interpretation Act."

"What is the act on the floor today?" Jane asked.

Christopher heard his father clear his throat, and knew the duke was going to launch into a long-winded explanation of the act ironically designed to shorten the language used in parliamentary acts.

"You wouldn't be interested," Christopher said quickly. "Tedious to a woman's mind. You ladies continue with your book browsing and shopping. Good day."

And so there could be no delay, he turned and with the help of his cane—Jane's blasted idea, of course—he easily made his way out of the shop, knowing his father would follow.

He supposed that answered all his doubts about whether Jane saw him as a task. She certainly had said that clearly enough.

Capable, skilled, helpful Jane Chatley. He hoped never to speak with her again.

✦

CHAPTER TWENTY-ONE

"My brother is out," Lady Amanda was only too glad to inform Jane when she appeared at the Foresters' home the next morning, clutching the precious book and asking for Christopher.

Jane tried to escape before the girl could say any more. She failed.

"And do not think for an instant I don't know *you* are behind my mother's sudden wish to have me involved in her plans for remodeling and refurnishing our home on Grosvenor Square."

Jane decided neither to confirm nor deny it.

"Are you being helpful?" she asked her. *And more importantly, keeping busy and out of Christopher's affairs?*

Amanda's mouth twisted into a grimace, and she crossed her slender arms over her well-endowed chest.

"She gave me no choice."

Jane tried again, remaining placid. "Do you hate it so very much? Being with your mother, doing something which brings her so much joy?"

That gave the girl pause. Frowning, Amanda chewed her bottom lip.

"Actually, I don't hate it. I bet you wish I did." And she stormed off.

God help the man who married her!

Jane only got as far as the foyer when Christopher arrived home, cane in hand, wearing a light jacket and hat. Alone.

She shook her head in wonder at the change in him. Without a misstep, he removed his gloves and set them down on the hallstand, slipped his cane into the holder, and hung his hat.

At that point, she realized she was being terribly rude by not making her presence known to him.

"Lord Westing," she said, and his head turned toward her. His expression wasn't friendly, however. That pained her. "Will you come speak with me in the parlor?"

He hesitated. *Would he turn her down?*

Then, without his cane, he walked steadily toward her, gesturing for her to proceed him into the room. He closed the door firmly behind them.

"Shall I call a maid to chaperone?" He asked belatedly, already sounding irritated.

"I trust no one in this household will gossip about me as being disreputable, and I won't stay long," Jane said.

"Very well. What can I do for you today? Or what can you do for me? Something further to ease my misfortune and alleviate the bleakness?"

She didn't care for his cynical tone. *Be brave,* she counseled herself.

"I came to speak to you about Lord Fowler."

His expression froze over.

"You wish to tell me of your engagement," he said. "Completely understandable. I was going to advise you I thought him a good choice."

Her mouth dropped open, and it took her a moment to regain her thoughts.

He was going to advise her?

"Absolutely not."

"Absolutely not what?" he asked, his words clipped.

"Absolutely, I'm not engaged."

He pursed his lips, his jaw muscle tightening visibly, displaying his annoyance as plainly as if she could see his eyes flashing.

"After the display you and Fowler put on at the Egyptian Hall, you ought to become engaged immediately. Everyone already assumes he is your paramour."

She felt like swearing in an unladylike manner.

"Lord Fowler is *not* my paramour," Jane ground out. Christopher ought to believe her. After all, they had shared kisses . . . and more. *Did he think she did the same with every man?*

"Truthfully, I no longer care," he said. "I am weary of hearing about you and the wretched viscount. Always 'Lady Jane and Lord Fowler' comes floating to my ears, and then there you were—*behind* a column—at Egyptian Hall, disgracing yourself."

Jane felt her ire rise. "Disgraceful, was it? Yet when you grab me and take liberties with my person, that is fine, is it?"

She stomped her foot with frustration. "You have no right to insult me with insinuations, nor should you be commenting on my behavior with Lord Fowler, not after what we have done. Wouldn't you agree?"

He expelled a frustrated sound, perhaps a muttered oath.

"Come closer," he ordered.

Surprised by his demand, Jane found herself walking toward him.

"Are you closer?" Christopher demanded.

"Yes." As soon as she spoke, disclosing her proximity, he grabbed hold of her, yanking her body to his and causing her to drop her package.

Gasping, her lips were open when he took them. It was a fierce kiss, not tantalizingly gentle as their kisses usually began. Moreover, one of his hands was soon at the back of her head, messing up her hair, knocking her small jaunty hat askew despite the hatpins anchoring it. He held her in place and ground his mouth against hers. It was wickedly tormenting.

Jane lifted her hands to his chest, not sure whether she wanted to hold onto him or push him away. She settled them on either side of his cravat, as her annoyance began to dissipate.

Christopher could simply declare for her, then all this ridiculous confusion would go away. What's more, this kissing was becoming too often a comfort for *his* wounds. If he were not blind, she would not put up with being used thusly. *Would she?*

Having at last made her decision, she pushed firmly at his chest, and after the briefest tightening of his grip, Christopher released her.

Would he apologize?

"You should leave," he said flatly.

She hadn't expected that, especially not after he'd kissed her.

Opening her mouth to protest, she stopped herself. *Were they really having this argument over Fowler? Surely not.*

"You're correct," she returned, trying to sound calm, even as she snatched up her gift and stomped across the Persian rug, hoping he could hear her displeasure.

Jane was at the door before she stopped. Christopher could go only by what those around him told him. His ears had been filled with tales of her and the viscount, attending balls, having an intimate chat behind the column, going to the zoo.

Both Amanda Westing and Owen Burnley were only looking out for Christopher because they loved him. But she loved him, too.

Jane sighed, turned, and rested her back against the door. She was not being a good friend by leaving his head stuffed with images of what was most definitely not happening. She would have to break her promise.

"I am assisting him," she said quietly.

"Assisting him how?" Christopher shot back at once, proving his senses were keenly trained on her still. "The way you assist me by bringing me canes? Or the way you assist me by moving into my open arms and parting your lips?"

"I am insulted you would ask." And she was. "I am helping Lord Fowler find a wife."

His sightless gaze which had been directed to the rug lifted toward her, a slight furrowing to his brow.

"I beg your pardon?"

"I take him around to speak to young ladies, and then we discuss their attributes and how well-suited they are. You are aware how difficult it is to speak privately to ladies. I facilitate it on his behalf."

He considered this for a long while.

"And you remain close by to chaperone their conversation, if you will?"

She released the breath she hadn't realized she was holding. Plainly, he understood.

"I do, but I have a way of becoming inconsequential and unnoticed."

"That's impossible," he asserted.

She shrugged, even though he couldn't see it. "It has worked for me for three Seasons, I assure you. It even worked around you."

She saw a flush appear on his cheeks.

"It was stupid of me not to notice you."

Jane could not fault him. For her part, she had never tried to attract him.

"I did it for a reason. Not to be a wallflower, but so I could observe without being bothered. And I admit during my first Season or two, I was hoping a man might catch my fancy."

None had interested her like Christopher. When he had shown no interest, however, she'd become an expert in being aloof.

"And then I decided to keep myself as inconspicuous as possible to avoid the drama of unwanted attention or, worse, unwelcome marriage proposals until such time as my mother allows me to leave the marriage market. I have hopes it will be after this Season."

One way or the other, by fall, she would be finished with the social grappling and manipulations of the *bon ton*. Of that, Jane was determined. She'd already checked on the cost of passage to France. And if she changed her mind about fleeing to the Continent, she had received a letter from Mrs. Burdett-Coutts inviting her to be a part of the anti-cruelty toward animals movement and its related vegetarian society. There was a place for her to learn more at Northwood Villa, a hospital dedicated to vegetarians, in Ramsgate, Kent.

Jane was fairly certain she would miss eating roasted chicken, although she could certainly leave behind English beef, no matter how fine and tasty. She much preferred to see a cow in the field, batting its long eyelashes and making its distinctive lowing sound, than to see a slab of it hanging in the butcher's window.

In either case, she would have preferred working with wayward girls, but Mr. Dickens had said no to a young lady such as herself being anywhere near them, and certainly forbid her from living with them and counselling them in Shepherd's Bush.

That was undoubtedly for the best since she'd discovered only recently how hot and eager her own passions could flare. *How could she possibly advise a girl to keep her skirts down when she'd let Christopher raise hers so readily?*

Indeed, simply recalling it made her heart beat faster and her insides grow tingly. Moreover, she wanted him to do it again and wanted to do the same for him in turn, whatever precisely that entailed.

"So, Fowler means nothing to you?" Christopher persisted.

He must have been convinced she was in a relationship with the viscount, for clearly, he was having trouble accepting the plain truth.

"Correct," she promised.

"And I have been behaving like an ass where he is concerned?"

She smiled to herself. "A little, but please don't let on to anyone what I've disclosed. There is no reason to humiliate the man who simply needed help. Besides, at your mother's show, he started to tell me how he'd found someone at last. He didn't have a chance to tell me who it is."

"That's why you were behind the pillar?"

"Yes."

"That was foolish of you," he reprimanded.

"I am aware." She thought bitterly of the contrast between how she might be viewed by those who saw her emerge from the shadows compared to how Lord Fowler would be utterly unscathed.

"Your reputation is your most valuable asset," Christopher continued. "That's what my mother tells Amanda, and it was drilled into me how my ruining a lady's character would be akin to stealing from her or evenly perpetrating a grave assault. I understand now. Hearing Burnley cast aspersions upon you at the art show was painful."

"It's not fair," she said.

He uttered a sound of pure frustration. "Fair or not, it is the truth."

"Do you think I don't know that? I have always been the epitome of discretion."

"Until lately," he pointed out. "What has changed?"

Truthfully, she simply no longer cared. That was why she ended up on the terrace at Marlborough House when Christopher discovered her. It was why she'd let herself be alone with him on more than one occasion at parties and balls. As far as she was concerned, she was nearly at the end of the ridiculous spectacle of being on display during the Season. She considered herself almost free of the marriage market, and it was by her own choice.

Moreover, Christopher had every opportunity to give her some hope she would not have to face the future alone. Yet, all he could say was he considered Lord Fowler *a good choice* for her.

She might as well ask him. She had nothing to lose.

"Why don't *you* offer for me and save my tattered reputation?"

He didn't respond. In fact, he hesitated for too long, and she was glad he could not see her flaming cheeks.

CHRISTOPHER COULDN'T BELIEVE HIS ears. If he didn't know Jane to be an intelligent, well-bred lady, he would think she had no sense of decorum at all. She must be feeling terribly conflicted to ask him such a thing.

He, for one, certainly felt confused. He was most definitely *not* interested in asking for her hand to save her reputation. A paltry, weak reason for binding two lives together, one he'd always loathed and had thus spent his years of adulthood avoiding.

However, he could easily imagine dropping to his knees and offering her his name and his body simply because he was finding it increasingly difficult to conceive of a life without her.

At least, that was how he felt until yesterday in Hatchards. He certainly didn't want to be her undertaking of mercy for the rest of their lives.

Unless he had it all wrong. He ran his hand over his face and smelled her perfume on his palm, making his body stir again. Without even asking, he knew she'd been speaking of Fowler and not himself. The kiss this morning proved it. His night of torment had been for nothing. She plainly didn't find him to be tedious.

Despite the strides he had made, however, he could not relinquish the concern any woman saddled with him would be sacrificing a full, rich future.

Did Jane want to travel abroad? He couldn't conceive of leaving England ever again. Surely, she would grow weary of a husband who couldn't take her dancing, to museums, and to the theatre. He was still bitterly aware she hadn't gone with him to the zoo, even though he could have heard—and smelled!—the hippopotamus.

The top layer of cream on the miserable trifle of his life was sour, not sweet—it was the knowledge he would be a terrible companion, more a burden than a husband, someone to whom Jane would have to spend her life describing their surroundings. He would be her onerous task, until the sweet release of widowhood set her free from him.

Long before that time, she would come to resent him.

He would spare her the disappointment and spare himself the disgrace.

She was still standing there. He could hear her breathing, waiting for a response to her bold and unfortunate question.

"I am content with our current relationship as friends. Anything else is not possible."

That should be the end of it. Instead, her voice came back strong and clear, "When we kiss, are we *merely* friends?"

He sighed. He was not a rake by any means. No one would ever label him such. Yet he had made love to a few women, and had gone much further with them than he had with Jane. Of course, like most men his age and with his status, he had also paid the exorbitant price of an experienced Cyprian to enjoy evenings of absolute ecstasy under skilled hands and mouths. Not often, but he had done so, using his worn copy of *The Swell's Night Guide*.

Those were the encounters he replayed in his mind when he pleasured himself.

Or used to—before every woman in his dreams was replaced by Jane and her perfect lips smiling at him, while her pretty eyes flashed intelligently. Once he'd felt her curves under his fingertips, it was easy to imagine her when he took himself in hand.

What's more, he'd never before felt the tender emotion she evoked in his heart—the warm feelings when he eagerly anticipated being in her company and wanted to put her needs above his own, the feelings he was starting to realize were love.

"Yes," he said firmly. "Merely friends."

He loved Jane Chatley, her voice and scent and taste and her wonderful brain and sense of humor. *So how could he condemn her to being his nursemaid?* Someone like her could go far in London's glittering society. She could do anything she wanted, oversee a salon of literary giants or artists, and she should marry the most powerful man in Britain, beneath the prince consort.

Why on earth would she want a blind man?

"I'm leaving now," she said. "I simply wanted to set your mind at ease about Lord Fowler." Her tone resonated with hurt, and he felt a sudden surge of panic he would never see her again.

Would Jane simply disappear from his life?

She had been in their home almost daily for so many weeks, helping his mother. The art show was behind them, and surely, their house decorating plans must also soon come to an end.

"Will you return?"

"I have to. I promised your mother. At least for another week."

He heard the latch under her fingers as she opened it.

"Jane, don't be angry."

She laughed, humorlessly, bitterly. "Of course not. I value our *friendship*. Good day, Lord Westing."

He wasn't an idiot. He knew very well she wanted to take him on as a lifelong charge and would do so if he asked her. Jane was generous and kind. But he would be a responsibility, an obligation. It made him sick to think of being such, recalling how he felt when he thought she spoke of him the day before. She deserved so much more.

Her footsteps moved quickly across the marble foyer.

CHAPTER TWENTY-TWO

"Jane, dear, I knew you wouldn't let me down."

If her sister or his mother didn't guess something had happened between them, Cam would eat his hat. Or perhaps Eleanor was too young to think of what might have occurred, and his mother . . . Well, she wasn't too old. No, that was certain. Luckily, she was preoccupied with her in-laws' arrival.

The Duchess of Westing's voice stopped her in the front hall. She had just placed her gift for Christopher on the small table where stray gloves were scattered. His name was not on the brown paper packaging, but it would be obvious whom it was for when opened.

The duchess's words reminded Jane she was supposed to begin taking Her Grace's paintings to those who had purchased them. Instead, she had hoped to flee the Foresters' townhouse, go home, and soothe her hurt feelings with some early afternoon sherry.

Turning slowly, she encountered Christopher's mother, with fabric folded over one arm and the leg of a chair in the other.

"It was a great success, was it not?" Jane murmured, wondering what the duchess would do with a single chair leg.

"What was, dear?"

"Your art show."

Her Grace made a clucking sound. "Mustn't live in the past, dear girl. That's all behind us now. Except for getting the paintings to the right people. And that's why you're here. You'll do that, of course, won't you?"

The duchess had the knack of ordering her before asking, but it was fine. Jane had intended to do so anyway. Her talk with Christopher had simply sent her intention scurrying from her brain.

"I came in a little cabriolet today, I'm afraid. I didn't bring a large enough carriage."

The duchess smiled. "That's fine, dear."

And Jane relaxed. She was being given a reprieve for the day. Then Her Grace called out, "Christopher!"

Dear God! Now what was the woman doing?

The parlor door opened, and he appeared.

"I'm here, Mother. I didn't hear the front door. Is Lady Jane still here?"

"Yes," Jane said, and her voice cracked. She coughed and tried again. "Yes, I'm still here."

"Jane is taking my paintings to their new homes today. I'm sending her in the landau, and I want you to go with her."

Jane gasped. She hoped Christopher didn't think she had devised this plan.

"Your Grace, I can come back another day with my father's carriage. Lord Westing needn't bother himself with this."

"Of course, my son will find it no bother." The duchess laughed and juggled the fabric and the chair leg from one arm to the other. "I insist. We can't keep my public waiting. Besides, you are here and Christopher is here. It will get him out and seeing other people. I mean, meeting them, of course, interacting, if you take my meaning."

"Mother," he said with irritation dripping from his tongue. "We take your meaning."

"So that's settled then," she added. "You know how much I appreciate your help."

Jane considered what had transpired in the drawing room only minutes earlier.

"We could take Lady Amanda along as a chaperone." Although in truth, having his younger sister along made the entire trip even less appealing. *Perhaps the girl could be persuaded to sit up with the driver,* Jane thought wickedly. *Get a little sooty London air into her nostrils.*

The duchess paused. "Amanda? Hardly necessary as far as I'm concerned, but that's up to you. I don't think anyone will fear for your reputation when you're with Christopher."

"And why is that, Mother?" His tone was like the edge of a knife.

Oh, dear! That was the wrong thing for the duchess to say. Jane hoped she hadn't meant it because it had certainly sounded condescending and emasculating.

"Why?" he asked again. "Because a blind man can't possibly be a threat to a woman?"

Jane watched him clenching his hands at his sides.

"What on earth are you saying?" his mother asked, walking toward the sparkling clean side windows of the huge front door and examining her fabric in the daylight.

He sighed. "I'm saying Jane's reputation would be as threatened by being with me alone in a carriage as it would if she were to—oh, I don't know—lurk in the shadows with the likes of Lord Fowler."

Jane swallowed. He was not going to let her transgression go easily.

The Duchess of Westing's head snapped up as she comprehended his words.

"I didn't mean to cast aspersions on your ability to ruin young women," she said, sounding put out. "I'm quite sure you're able to ruin a young lady, as well as any man in existence. Normally, however, I try not to consider my son debasing women," she added, frowning at Christopher. "Nor was I referring to your blindness, but rather your impeccable character and Jane's, as well."

The duchess sent Jane a placid smile. "I certainly didn't think anyone would mind if you two were out delivering my paintings. With a footman and a driver!"

"It would be inappropriate, Mother, just as it was wrong for you to leave us alone in your studio."

The man had a memory like the proverbial Greek camel!

The duchess simply shrugged.

"Mother, I cannot believe I am the one having to remind you of these simple rules."

Jane hoped they would end their hostile conversation, or at least, wait until she was no longer within hearing. They were certainly treating her like one of the family.

"A blind man is still a man!" Christopher added, his tone sharp.

The duchess sniffed. "I never thought otherwise. You are being overly sensitive and harsh with me. However, you may take Amanda, if you think she will be helpful. But why would anyone lurk in the shadows? And who is Lord Fowler?"

She looked at Jane, who, after a brief pause, decided she had to answer.

"He was at your exhibit. He bought the horse in the meadow with the pretty cottage in the distance."

"How sweet. I do like that painting. Strange to think they will now be in other people's possessions and I won't see them again. Ever."

Christopher's mother started to look genuinely upset.

"Only think of the joy they will bring," Jane reminded her, "and now your studio has so much more room for you to paint many more."

"Very true. Thank you, Jane. You are a helpful girl and always know what to say."

How she wished that were the case.

"Obviously, you can't go over cushion fabrics with me *and* deliver my paintings, so I'll have to muddle on without you, I suppose. But on second thought, you simply cannot take Amanda. I need her. You shall have to take one of the maids."

"Is that agreeable, Lady Jane?" Christopher asked. "It seems my mother is taking over your day."

Jane considered. He was giving her a way to bow out if she wanted. Yet her earlier temper and even hurt feelings were somewhat abated. She knew perfectly well he desired her. The more time they spent together, the more likely he would confess to feeling more than friendship.

"Yes, it is agreeable, my lord."

The duchess made a sound of exasperation. "Don't you two think you should progress to Jane and Christopher by now." Then she wandered down the hallway. "After all, Jane has become like family, like another one of my children." She disappeared behind the Foresters' library door, which currently housed all of the duchess's samples and ideas for decorating.

"I wish you could see me standing here, feeling awkward."

"Why?" he asked, his manner still not approachable the way it used to be.

"Because then maybe you would soften again, and we could start over. Friends, as you suggested."

She watched him clench his jaw, then take a deep breath.

"Better I treat you as my friend than as my sister, as Mother believes," he said at last, then he flashed her his familiar grin.

She chuckled. "I admit, I don't think of you as my brother."

"Good. Friends then, and we shall grab a willing housemaid to accompany us."

"I suppose it would be prudent," Jane agreed. "You don't want to get caught in a sticky situation like on the terrace at Marlborough House. My mother nearly had us measured and married within the hour."

She thought he would laugh. He didn't.

"Would that have been so bad?" he asked.

How could he ask that now after turning her down?

"I only meant . . . no one wants to be pushed into marriage," she reminded him. "Or trapped. We talked about it that night and at your mother's studio."

In a few minutes, Jane found herself in the Westings' luxurious five-glass landau, surrounded by as many paintings as would fit with her and Christopher. The maid had been sent to sit with the driver, completely negating her purpose as far as Jane was concerned. If she wanted, she could lean over, past the frames tucked at their feet, and kiss him. Not that she would. Humiliating herself once today by asking him to marry her and being turned down was enough.

Thus, their cheerless party departed from Berkley Square to begin the deliveries. Most of the purchases were within a two-mile radius where the wealthiest of the *ton* lived. Some were the duchess's friends. Others wanted to make sure to be included in the latest fashionable *objet d'art*, in this case, a fellow aristocrat's watercolor paintings, and a woman artist, at that.

Unfortunately, she and Christopher barely spoke. Jane started to describe where they were until he held up his hand and asked her to refrain from sounding like a guide.

She snapped her mouth closed.

Except for Lady Mulberry's house, where Jane refused to get out of the carriage, at each stop, she accompanied the footman to the door, while Christopher stood in plain sight on the pavement. Many buyers had signed banknotes already, which Jane slipped into a leather pouch. Some had simply written and signed their intents to pay.

When she got back into the carriage after the fourth stop, she laughed aloud.

"What is it?" Christopher asked, closing the door behind him.

"Having butlers and housekeepers handing me large sums, the whole process is peculiar."

"I suppose you are like a tradeswoman now."

"I cannot imagine there is anything I could do or sell that would engender such large amounts of money to change hands. I may try painting as your mother suggested."

"You should," he said, still sounding flat. "You will excel at it, I have no doubt. Speaking of success, I believe the decorators are finally starting at our old house next week."

"Yes, your mother told me."

"Will you still be involved?"

"I think your mother and Lady Amanda can make all the final decisions."

"Amanda?" His tone was incredulous.

"Yes, she's been helping."

He paused. "*Helping?* I am trying to fathom how that could be."

Jane hummed softly to herself. *Would he approve of his family being manipulated by her?* She wasn't sure now that they were on shaky terms.

"How noble of you," Christopher muttered, "fixing one Westing after another."

Crossing his arms, he leaned back, and she understood all too well what he meant. He still thought himself a task she'd set for herself.

"I'VE CAUGHT UP WITH you at last."

Jane looked wildly around, hoping to see an escape. Stupidly, she'd come downstairs and entered the library before lunch, thinking she could return safely to her room after snagging a book on French translation. However, Bernard had breached her sanctuary and cornered her.

"I was just leaving," she said, trying to push past him.

He sighed. "Are you simply rude or a terrible coward?"

His accusation meant nothing to her. Let him think of her what he wished, so long as she didn't have to discuss marriage with him.

"I am heading out to deliver the last of the Duchess of Westing's paintings." She did intend to do so at some point, and perhaps now was the time.

"Perhaps I can be of assistance."

She stared at him. She had no intention of being in the close confines of the carriage with her cousin.

"I believe Lord Westing will accompany me."

Jane didn't really know that. In fact, she doubted it. When they had finished the day before, Christopher bid her good day and disappeared into the recesses of the Foresters' home. It seemed as if, even their friendship had come to an untimely end.

Bernard raised an eyebrow. "I knew you spent a great deal of time with the Westings, but I didn't realize you kept company with the marquess. Do you have an agreement with him?"

She nearly laughed. It wasn't for want of trying, practically begging Christopher to declare.

"No," she said. "We do not." She supposed lying might have been a good option to get rid of Bernard, but she didn't doubt it would get back to the Westings and cause her extreme mortification. Imagining Amanda's smirk and worse, recalling Christopher's silence before turning her down—if she pretended to an arrangement, she would be publicly denounced.

"That's good, then. Let's speak frankly. After all, I came a long way to London."

"Your home is but an hour hence," she pointed out.

"It could be *your* home, too," he said.

And so it began. Apparently, they were going to have this conversation about joining in a matrimonial union.

"After all," he added "this house will be mine as well someday."

What a heartless bastard!

"Maybe an Act of Parliament will change matters," Jane snapped, merely to be contrary.

He blinked. "I don't know what you mean."

Of course he didn't. "Never mind. Just wishful thinking," she said, and took a seat so he could as well. "Very well, let us talk, cousin."

"Your father agrees it would be good for the family if we married."

"My father is not here," she pointed out.

"Actually, he is. He returned sometime late yesterday."

"Oh." No wonder her mother had been absent in the morning. She often removed herself from the house to visit with her friends when the earl was in residence.

"In any case, he's already told me he agrees on the efficacy of such an arrangement."

Her first reaction was to twist out of the noose that was being slipped over her head.

"If you marry me, my father will most certainly not want to give up anything until he dies. You will be a resident in *his* home if you choose to live here. Wouldn't you find that intolerable?"

"He said he would gift us the country house in Chipping Ongar."

Her father never liked the country, so that was no surprise.

"Don't worry. We wouldn't be social outcasts," Bernard added. "We could still come to London for the height of the Season."

He had it all worked out apparently.

"Do you truly wish to marry me?" she asked bluntly, staring at him.

He looked like a Chatley, with brown hair and eyes, and the small nose and high cheekbones of her father. There was nothing inherently unpleasant about him, except . . . she recalled her mother's words about cruelty.

Could one see such a trait? Was it in the rather tight way he held his lips perhaps?

Those lips drew into a thin smile. "You are as acceptable a wife as any other female."

She waited, but nothing else came forth. Fiddling with the book on the table before her, she asked, "So, you are not interested in love?"

His eyes widened. "Are you a romantic, then?"

She supposed she was, with a good dose of caution.

When she didn't respond, Bernard cocked his head and took his measure of her.

"Why wouldn't I want to marry you? You are attractive, you can carry on a conversation without stuttering, and you bring a hefty dowry. I would be a fool to look elsewhere. As long as you don't turn out to be barren, you are positively the ideal spouse for me."

His mentioning the word *barren* brought the image of them attempting to reproduce into the forefront of her brain. Her stomach squeezed uncomfortably. The notion of getting undressed before Bernard and having him touch her was frightening, not exciting. And something else, repulsive. She was frankly surprised by her visceral, severe reaction.

Before Christopher, she had certainly been kissed and not been repulsed, merely unmoved. Now, thinking of how he had made her body react, she couldn't imagine tolerating anything less. Quite frankly, she couldn't imagine any other man putting his lips or hands on her.

Again, she would rather go without a man entirely.

"You make a very good case, cousin, at least to the advantages you would enjoy. The benefits are all on one side, however. Why would I want to marry you?"

Let him think on that a moment. But he didn't. Bernard looked instantly and utterly surprised.

"Why wouldn't you?" he shot back. "You have had no offers apparently, and you've had three Seasons."

"Not quite three," she protested, as they were still in the heart of her third.

"Still," he said, giving her a disparaging look. "The alternative is ending up a spinster."

A word which frightened so many women, and would Jane, too, if she didn't have a little money put aside.

"So, the only thing you can say to recommend you is you are my only choice?"

He frowned. "Of course not. You will also get to remain in your home."

"Yet it will never truly be *my* home, just as it is not my mother's, despite how she has lived here many years and run it as well as any countess could."

"Yes, *your* mother." He contemplated a moment. "Do you love her and care about her?"

"Of course."

"Then perhaps she is the best reason for you to marry me. Otherwise, where will Lady Chatley live?"

Again, a heartless bastard!

"Naturally, if you said you didn't want her here after we take ownership," he continued, "then out she would go. Only think how for the first time, you will be in control."

He had just displayed how very little control she would actually ever have. Moreover, she thought her father would leave Jane's mother enough money to set up her own residence.

Wouldn't he?

"Are we in agreement?" Bernard asked, looking confident.

Jane looked down at the book of French and knew the path she wished to take. But her mother's welfare was certainly a new wrinkle in her plan. In any case, the less said to the likes of her cousin, the better.

"Your points are valid. That is certain," she said diplomatically.

He smiled, and she wondered if her mother might be correct about the cruelty lurking behind his Chatley eyes.

Moreover, just as this conversation determining her wishes was entirely a sham since her father and Bernard could make any decision they wanted, her agreement, or disagreement, was as binding as her own ability to make a contract in the eyes of the law—in other words, not at all.

CHAPTER TWENTY-THREE

Amanda dumped something onto his lap, and Christopher felt like throttling her.

"Please warn me, sis, before you send boulders raining down on me. I nearly shed my mortal coil."

Amanda only laughed. "It's just a book."

"*You* were reading a book?" He picked it up. It was large both in height and girth. "And a big one, at that!"

"Of course not," she scoffed. "I found it in the front hall. It was thoughtlessly wrapped in brown paper with no form of address at all. I hoped it was something exciting, but, alas, it's just a book."

"Probably something Father ordered while at Hatchards the other day." That awful day when he thought Jane despised every moment she'd spent with him. "Why would you give it to me? I'm blind, if you recall. Are you being cruel?"

"Chris, no! Have I been such a terrible sister?" She sat beside him. "The book must be for you because it is all bumpy. Feel it for yourself."

Instantly, his heart sped up at the possibility. If Amanda was right . . .

Opening the cover, he ran his hand down the right-hand page and his heartbeat doubled. *Dear God!* At first, he made no sense of it, then slowed down and traced the first line again. He realized it was not a strange, unfamiliar alphabet, it was simply English, but embossed with raised points so he could feel each letter.

"Guy Fawkes," he read after a moment, and Amanda gasped in delight. He read the next line, "Printed in Raphigraphy Type." Honestly, if he'd been alone, he might have wept.

"What is Raphigraphy?" his sister asked, having caught his excitement.

"It's the name for a special typeface called Decapoint when it has been condensed. The teacher at the blind school near Regent's Park said it was invented by a Frenchman named Braille. Can you see the letters?"

"Yes," Amanda said. "They are fainter than regular print but I can easily read them. Turn the page," she urged.

He did as she asked and felt the left page, which was blank, and the right, which was the next title page, "*Guy Fawkes or The Gunpowder Treason: An Historical Romance* by William Harrison Ainsworth." Then lower, it said, "Published 1841."

Amanda sighed. "What a pity! It's not a gothic novel. Just some dry old history."

Ignoring her, he began to read a letter to Mrs. Hughes, obviously Ainsworth's patron. And then, he reached the preface and read aloud, "The tyrannical measures adopted against the Roman Catholics in the early part of the reign of James the First, when the severe penal enactments against recusants were revived—"

"Stop!" Amanda pleaded. "Or I shall scream. I'm leaving." With that, she rose from the sofa.

"All right," he said, barely listening as he kept his fingers on the embossed letters.

"Only tell me, dear brother, are you happy?"

"Ecstatic," he said.

She kissed him on the forehead and was nearly out of the room before he called after her, "Ask Father and Mother which one bought this for me."

"When I see them," she said, and her steps went out the door.

A book about the unsuccessful attempt to blow up the Houses of Parliament in 1605, a story full of politics and history—Christopher would bet it was from the duke.

"I WANT TO SHAKE my father," Jane railed the next day when she found her mother in the dining room going over the day's post. An invitation had arrived for the Chatley family from the Foresters to dine along with another few couples during one of the Westings last evenings before they moved home to Grosvenor Square.

Sadly, her mother had to decline.

"Your father was here a few moments ago and said he would be busy. I hadn't even told him the date of the dinner party. When I mentioned that, he repeated *he would be busy*, regardless of the date."

The countess stopped talking as the maid brought in their tea. When Jane wasn't out and about, she and her mother tried to take afternoon tea together daily. The maid poured and left.

Her mother picked up a teaspoon and idly stirred in her sugar, looking down at the pretty lace tablecloth and the invitation resting upon it.

"I can tell by the extra bounce to his step he has a new mistress." Then Lady Chatley gasped and dropped her spoon. "I cannot believe I said that to you. I must be entering my dotage to be so careless."

Jane could hardly stomach her mother's worry over propriety.

"I am not a child. What's more, I've been aware of my father's depraved ways for a long time. Depraved and cruel. Why would he waste his life and yours? Instead of a union of minds and hearts, you are two people who did nothing more together than create me."

Her mother sighed. "That was not my choice, but I have come to accept how things are."

How things are! "Your husband is a sad individual who doesn't deserve you or the estate, or even me."

Her mother smiled. "You are my feisty Jane, and you are right. I would certainly be better off a widow."

Jane could not be shocked, for she had thought the same thing many times on her mother's behalf. However, she was surprised her mother voiced it.

"Mummy, I am so sorry."

Lady Chatley shrugged. "I have had a comfortable life. There is nothing to be sorry about. However, I have not yet fulfilled my duty to get you happily married. I know you don't like it when I have upon occasion pushed you toward one man or another."

Jane rolled her eyes. "More than occasionally, I would say."

"But only toward men whom I could see were upstanding. Lord Cambrey, for one. The way he worked with us for the benefit of the orphans, I could tell he was caring and thoughtful. Same with Lord Westing, or even Lord Fowler. These are not men who would play you for a fool as your father has with me."

"You are correct on all three counts."

"And can you not love either Fowler or Westing?"

Jane sighed, but there was no point in confessing her love for Christopher.

"It is not as if they have nothing to say in the matter. Choosing a husband is not like choosing from among a container of sweet treats where the treat has no choice. The men do have a say in the matter."

Her mother's mouth twisted as if she disagreed. "If you wanted to marry a man, even if he were hesitant, I believe you could have him. You are Jane Emily Chatley, the most capable girl I could ever imagine raising."

They smiled at each other, and Jane finally sipped her tea.

"I am grateful you aren't forcing me into a match with Bernard. I was afraid you would, simply to benefit the family."

Her mother lowered her head. "I fear Bernard is too similar to your father. You mustn't marry a man who isn't worthy of you, for he will spend his life proving you correct."

Jane's heart clenched again. Before she could offer comfort, her mother continued.

"I had a young man interested in me once." Her tone lightened as she spoke. "A viscount's son, a true gentleman. The prettiest blue eyes I ever saw on a man."

The countess sighed. "For some reason, Charles Chatley decided he wanted me, too. Unfortunately, as soon as my father caught wind of an earl wanting his daughter, I had no choice."

Jane could easily see why her father had chosen her mother.

Lady Chatley drained her cup and poured another one.

"I would never force you as I was forced. Thus, you have choices I did not, but I still want to see you well settled."

"What happened to your young man?" Jane realized her own voice was thick with emotion, picturing her lovely mother as a hopeful debutante.

"I broke his heart. He moved to the Continent. I have wondered if your father ever encounters him when he's there."

A shocking notion. It made Jane sad to think of her mother contemplating her faithless husband coming across her blue-eyed man with the broken heart.

"He never married?" Jane asked

"No." She paused. "He has written to me upon occasion."

Jane's pulse sped up thinking of the man perhaps still waiting for her mother after all these years.

"Did you answer?"

"No," her mother said quickly. Perhaps too quickly. "Do you know how easy it is for a man to divorce his wife on grounds of adultery?"

Jane's mouth dropped open.

"You don't think Father—"

Her mother fixed her with a piercing stare. "I couldn't take that chance. I have never given him the slightest cause to doubt me, not a hint of scandal, not a whiff of interest in another man. As soon as you were born, I fell absolutely in love with you. You have my heart, Jane dear. If I had tried to escape unhappiness with my husband, I would have lost everything. A wife has no legal existence, as you know. If I'd left him, I could take nothing, not even you. And you are the *only* thing I would not give up. A little unhappiness over a husband is nothing compared to the love for a child. Certainly, I couldn't lose you to him in a divorce."

Her mother sipped her second cup of tea. "Then I would have had to make myself a widow to keep you."

Jane caught her breath, because she was quite sure her mother meant it.

"The good news in our present state of existence by English law, and I believe it is the *only* good news, is I cannot be blamed for practically anything because Charles and I are considered one. If I set our house on fire, as it is really *his* house and we are the same legal entity, then I cannot be blamed. The law looks at it as if he had burned his own house down. Not that I would, of course. I am simply pointing out the ridiculous extremes to which the current law takes us. I cannot be convicted of stealing from him either as we are one body under the law, and he cannot steal from himself."

Her mother picked up the invitation from the Foresters.

"Very strange isn't it. If I were a bad woman, an arsonist or a thief, then I am protected entirely. If I am simply a good mother whose husband is an unloving, cruel adulterer, there is nothing I can do."

Jane reached over and touched her mother's hand.

"No, don't be sad for me, Jane dear. I should have demanded a marriage settlement, or, at the very least, my father should have. Naturally, we shall have one in place for you when the time comes."

Jane felt a wave of guilt wash over her. All the times she'd felt restricted or pressured by her protective, sometimes over-bearing mother! And all that time, her mother could have up and left her to the careless keeping of her father. Instead, she had stayed with Charles Chatley, a gin-drinking profligate, for Jane's sake.

JANE TOOK HER OWN maid with her to the Foresters' townhome and retrieved the rest of the paintings. She saw no one as the Duchess of Westing and Lady Amanda were at their old home on Grosvenor Square, and Christopher was at Parliament with his father.

There were only a few watercolors left, one of them for Lord Fowler.

Luckily, he was at home when she stopped by, and soon found herself in his drawing room, her maid seated nearby, and Lord Fowler exclaiming over the beauty of the painting.

Jane thought it rather sweet how he considered where to hang it. When asked, she gave him her opinion, and they walked the length of his residence until he decided to put it in his dining room, which lacked any wall art currently except for a long horizontal mirror over the sideboard.

The pretty meadow with white wildflowers and a roan horse, along with a cottage in the distance, looked perfect on his pale gray wall.

"Gives the room a bit of life," he quipped. "Of course, if my future wife doesn't like it there, it can be moved at once."

Jane preceded him back into the drawing room. "I do apologize for being remiss in fulfilling my promise on that matter."

"Dear Lady Chatley, as I tried to tell you at the art show, I have made my choice."

When she sat down, he did as well.

"And has the lady agreed?"

"I haven't asked her yet," Lord Fowler confessed. "However, I think that will be merely a formality."

How could he think that? Unless, he already had spent a great deal of time with the lady in question.

"Do you have some indication she returns your feelings?"

He eyed her a long while. "I do."

His manner was strange, and the small seed of worry she'd had since the art show quickly blossomed. At Egyptian Hall, Lord Fowler's intensity and the way he'd crowed to her about finding a woman he liked "above all others" and his wanting to "tell her immediately" had unsettled her.

She swallowed. Jane didn't want to hurt him. Obviously, because of the amount of time they'd spent in each other's company and the overly familiar way they'd spoken, he had drawn a conclusion of regard she simply didn't feel.

"I am not certain you'll be pleased to hear my choice," he continued.

No, she wasn't, not if he'd fallen for her.

"I wish you had said something sooner." She would have reminded him she'd had no wish to be on his list of potential wives.

"You have been so busy, as you said, that I couldn't speak with you." He hung his head. "I know you tried to dissuade me, but my deepest sentimental emotions have become involved. I fear you will not be pleased."

Dear God, it was her he loved.

"I beg you to reconsider," Jane said.

He shook his head. "How can you be so certain it will not be a good match. My heart is engaged. I cannot foresee a life without my lady. I'm not sure of the way to put it decently. In short, I love—"

"No, Lord Fowler, do not declare it aloud." Jane wanted to tear her hair out. *How had she mucked up this simple task so wretchedly? Poor Richard Fowler was about to face a terrible disappointment.*

"Whyever not?" He had a bemused smile.

"If you do, then I will have to outright deny you. It will be a dreadful scene. You are not supposed to love me!"

She must nip it in the bud. She could no more imagine Lord Fowler lifting her skirts the way Christopher had, than Bernard.

"I do not," he said.

"No, don't say it," she continued. "The whole point of this exercise was . . . what did you say?"

"I do not love you, Lady Jane."

She frowned. "Yet you wish to marry me?"

He looked shocked. "Well, no, I do not."

Jane opened her mouth, then closed it. "I believe I have got the wrong end of the walking stick, have I not?"

"I hope you are not offended." Lord Fowler rose from his seat and inappropriately came to sit beside her.

She glanced toward her maid, whose eyes had grown large at the course of the conversation so far.

Lord Fowler patted her shoulder awkwardly.

"Dear Lady Jane, at first I had hoped you would come to care for me, but soon, I pushed you entirely out of any consideration. And you were right, there is room for only one lady in my heart, certainly not a list full of them."

She took a deep breath and relaxed. He didn't care for her. *How wonderful!*

"I am delighted for you and am absolutely not offended. Please, don't keep me in suspense another moment. Who is the fortunate female?"

"Lady Brethens." He announced the name breathlessly with almost a reverence usually reserved for discussing a saint.

Surprise reverberated through her, followed quickly by puzzlement. *Matilda Brethrens?*

"I know you do not approve," he began, "but she and I suit each other."

"It is not for me to approve or disapprove," Jane began, then recalled she had in fact warned him away from this very woman. "I am puzzled, however. When did you converse with Lady Brethrens to such an extent as to decide you love her?"

"Here and there," he said. "She was at practically every event you and I attended. At first, I gave her a wide berth, as you suggested. However, something about her drew me in. I suppose, at first, it was her perfect ringlets. Then I saw her dimples when she smiles."

He had a beatific look upon his face, and Jane felt her own heart soar. He truly seemed to be a man in love. *How rare and wonderful to witness!*

"When she didn't dismiss me out of hand, we found we had similar interests." Lord Fowler nodded to himself. "She is fastidious, to be sure, but I often agree with her opinions and even with her complaints. Although she certainly has a fair number of them, I will admit."

Jane smiled at his last phrase. Here was a man willing to take on a wife whom she had called a *nag*, and to do so because he loved the rest of the lady despite her flaws. Yet, she would bet her last hatpin the watercolor painting would be moved from the dining room if Matilada Brethrens took up residence.

"And not that I am one to kiss and tell, but she kisses very sweetly."

Jane clamped a hand to her mouth. He definitely shouldn't be disclosing such a thing. On the other hand, she was glad he had discovered that important fact.

"Lord Fowler, I am so pleased. I really am." Jane stood, and her maid jumped to her feet, as well. "I hope you will tell Lady Brethrens of your feelings at the earliest possible opportunity, and I fervently pray she reciprocates."

"I will send you a missive and tell you how it turns out," he promised. "Hopefully, you will read the announcement in the newspapers in any regard."

Her mood sunk a little. In all likelihood, she wouldn't be there to receive a note from him, nor could she tell him so. Secrecy was crucial, or her father would empty her account before she could withdraw her money. It would be risky anyway, and she must be certain to leave a large portion of her saved allowance behind or her father would be notified at once by the banking clerk.

In any case, she didn't have a forwarding address as she was still deciding between the position at Ramsgate with the vegetarians, and a place in the sunny south of France.

"Good day, Lord Fowler. I wish you well and may all good things come to you."

"And to you, Lady Jane. If you don't mind my saying so, it is your turn to find a spouse."

She tried to laugh lightly, but could give him little more than a brittle smile as she departed.

WITH BERNARD IN HER home thinking she was in agreement with his plans and her father having returned, alive and well, from his latest jaunt of philandering, Jane realized she had mere days to leave before an announcement was made. Each day, she sent a servant to the Bank of England with a bank cheque payable to herself and with strict instructions to hand it to a different clerk of funds.

Each day, she withdrew as much as she thought would not raise eyebrows.

The notion of never again seeing Christopher was agonizing but didn't change her mind about leaving. After all, she'd spent a few years suffering from unrequited love without him so much as smiling at her. Over the past few months, she'd happily shared intimate moments with him, confirming she had correctly placed her affections.

If her life was to be spent without a man, she was content to have found someone to love, and who, for a short while, seemed to feel something similar.

Content but certainly not happy.

Regardless, Jane could not let any of what had occurred since the Marlborough House terrace break her spirit. Nor would she let herself be shackled in London, forced to marry Bernard.

However, as she paused in the writing of a letter to the Countess of Cambrey, one thought tormented her—her mother! *How could she leave Emily Chatley to the terrible consequences that would surely occur in the wake of her escape?*

They had butted heads over the years, but their love was deep and true. Her mother had devoted years to raising Jane, chaperoning her, teaching her, and being her companion.

Without Jane, her mother would no longer have even the restricted social life of accompanying her to balls and parties, picnics, boating, and riding in the park. Her mother, already pitied for having a debauched husband, would be disgraced by the daughter who ran away. She might even be blamed for Jane's inability to fulfill her duty.

Basically, Lady Emily Chatley would become housebound as no respectable society matrons would invite her anywhere.

And then there was the future. When Bernard became earl and his wife eagerly claimed the title of Countess of Chatley, her mother would be cast aside. *Where would she go then?*

In a flash of stark comprehension, Jane knew the only way to truly repay her mother was by staying and marrying Bernard, thereby making sure Emily Chatley had both a home and the respect due her for the rest of her life. Jane owed her that much, and more.

She had run out of options. *Good God!* She should have snagged Lord Fowler when she had the chance. But even that wouldn't have kept her mother in her own home when the Earl of Chatley passed and Bernard took over. Most husbands wouldn't accept a mother-in-law under their roof, especially when newly married. And then there was her mother's pride.

Would the countess accept the position of resident in her daughter's home if it were elsewhere than the Chatley residence?

Even if Christopher suddenly set aside his stubbornness and his doubts, Jane couldn't leave her mother to Bernard's control.

Jane set down her cup, then picked it up again. It was empty. She hadn't noticed finishing it. Suddenly, she couldn't breathe.

It was clear what she should do—sacrifice the rest of her life and all her happiness to protect her mother.

CHAPTER TWENTY-FOUR

"Mother, where is Lady Jane these days?" Christopher had told himself he wouldn't go asking after her, drawing attention to his need for Jane. Then the moment he realized his mother was in the parlor, he had done that very thing.

"I'm sure I have no idea," the duchess returned. "I've seen less and less of her lately. Pity! I really like that girl. You would do well to . . . Never mind. I am not *that* type of mother. The heart goes where it will. If your heart wanted Jane, I'm sure you would have acted on it by now."

He felt the familiar surge of regret. It always started with a flash of memory, of going into the kitchens, talking with the now-dead Mr. Elms, and then awakening in the endless darkness.

Waking up in the mornings was no longer the great disappointment it had been for months. Quite used to opening his eyes and seeing nothing, Christopher faced each day thinking of the things he could still do.

Including reading once again. Thanks to Jane. The book had to have come from her, for no one else he knew claimed knowledge of it. He'd dictated a thank you note to Amanda, had his mother check it in case his sister was up to any mischief, and then sent it off. He'd heard nothing in reply.

Only occasionally, such as that moment when his mother mentioned his heart, did regret once again overcome him, followed by a wave of fury at his fate. Usually, he took a deep breath, let it crest, and then release its hold. The anger had lessened considerably over the weeks, particularly as "normal" life returned.

Even with the occasional taunting of a shadowy flicker in his vision, he had accepted his situation and was determined to have the best life possible.

However, each day without Jane felt lacking. When he thought how well she'd handled his accident and subsequent blindness, he knew there was no other woman like her.

"I do like her, too, Mother. And admiring her as I do, how selfish would it be of me to ask her to be my wife? Don't you think she could do far better?"

"Chris, I know this has been hard on you, and every day, I am amazed by the grace with which you're moving along with your life. And I am extremely biased because you are my extraordinary son and I am a proud mother. Yet, not once have I ever considered you selfish, nor do I think any young lady could do better than to have you as her husband."

"But the tedium of describing our surroundings," he pointed out.

"*Pish*. That is nothing. No woman minds talking about what she sees."

He ran a hand through his hair. "What about my being able to take her places?"

"What of it? You still can. You may need a footman at times, but surely, making small accommodations to your life is worth it to gain such a lady."

"But she could be the wife of any man, don't you think?" He wanted his mother to talk him out of pursuing Jane. Or maybe he wanted her to convince him to give in to the desire, one which he couldn't relinquish no matter how he tried.

He felt a hand on his forearm.

"I think Jane would, indeed, make a strong wife for any man, no matter how high up he were in social ranking or even in the government. Including you."

"Thank you, Mother. I'm going for a walk." Without thinking too much about it, he snatched up his cane from the stand next to the front door, slapped his hat onto his head, and left. First, a walk around the square to clear his head.

And then, if his thoughts hadn't changed, perhaps it would be time to take that long-promised visit to the Chatley residence at Hanover Square and declare his intentions to Jane's father.

"LORD WESTING TO SEE you, my lady," their butler announced.

Jane was in the back garden, her mother somewhere close at hand, probably consulting with the cook about dinner. Unfortunately, Bernard was also nearby, having just returned from riding. He popped out onto the terrace behind the butler.

"What does *he* want?" her cousin wondered aloud, his tone both rude and sour.

Jane sprang from her chair. She ignored him and addressed their butler.

"You may escort him through." Then she considered the slanted back step where the stone had sunk and which no one had bothered to fix.

"No," she called after him as he'd already turned heel. "On second thought, please show the marquess into the parlor and tell him I shall be right in. And order tea."

"Shall I come with you, cousin?" Bernard asked, blocking her entrance into the townhouse. "It is rather unseemly for you to be alone with Westing, especially when we have voiced an understanding between us."

"As you are very aware, it is absolutely inappropriate for us to be alone, as well. This very moment, you are in violation of every moral code with which I've been raised. Even if we'd already sent out the announcements, it would be against the rules of common decency for us to be closeted alone."

"We are not 'closeted,'" he reminded her. "We are outdoors."

"In a walled garden. Step aside," Jane ordered him, amazed at the hissing quality to her own voice. She felt positively ferocious in her desire to get to Christopher. "My mother will join me in the parlor with the marquess."

"Very well." Bernard moved around her, taking her seat in the garden. She glared at the back of his head. He had better stay put or she wouldn't be responsible if she flew into a rage and ripped off his overly long sideburns.

Taking a calming breath, she hurried along the passage to the foyer and then into the parlor. Her mother would be called for in due time. Not immediately, but soon.

"Lord Westing," Jane said to the broad-shouldered figure standing in the middle of the rug—loving him with all her heart even as she took in the familiar sight of him.

She remembered months ago, staring out the front window, dreaming of the moment he would arrive when she would no longer have to imagine a future without him.

Finally, there he was.

"Are we alone?"

"For now."

"Are we still . . . friends?"

"Of course."

"Come closer, so I can smell you better," he demanded.

She grinned. *What a sausage head!* And yet his words started her insides humming with excitement. She closed the space between them.

"Did you come closer?" he asked her.

She hesitated. As soon as she spoke, he would take her in his arms. *Wouldn't he?* The long moments of anticipation caused her body to tingle and a strange and fluid heaviness to pool between her hips.

She studied his handsome, slightly arrogant face. *How had she not noticed his arrogance before?* she wondered. It was incredibly attractive.

She sighed slightly, and his head tilted toward the sound.

"Jane?" he questioned, his voice low.

She swallowed. "Yes." Her voice came out on a whispered breath.

Instantly, his arms reached for her, yanking her forward, off her feet, until she collided with his hard body. His hands remained on the small of her back, holding her close. Unerringly, his mouth found hers.

Raising her arms around his neck, she held fast.

Hungry for him, with her heart thumping, Jane opened her lips and let him inside. His tongue swept into her mouth and tangled with her own, even as her fingers spread wide into his soft hair, tugging gently.

Liquid warmth pooled instantly between her legs, dampening the cotton of her drawers. She was on fire for this man. raising her hips toward him, she felt his answering thrust, and the pressure of his hard shaft just above her mound.

They seemed to groan in unison.

Then, there was a tap at the door. Jane had never moved so fast, springing back and nearly landing on her bottom. As it was, she was standing on the hem of her gown and trying to right herself when the maid came in carrying a tray with tea.

"It's the maid," she declared loudly. Too loudly. The girl set it down on the low table in front of the sofa.

"Shall I pour, my lady?"

"No, that's fine. I'll handle him. It! I mean, I'll handle *it*. The pouring. I will pour the tea," Jane corrected herself, before coughing to cover the nervous laughter welling up in her throat.

Thank goodness it hadn't been her mother or Bernard at the door.

The maid wasn't fooled, keeping her gaze lowered as she left, a smirk on her lips. The girl knew better than to say anything or even acknowledge the reason for her mistress's flustered state.

Jane's gaze went to the fall of Christopher's trousers. The bulge of his desire was evident. They had to calm themselves because the next person to enter would surely be her mother, as soon as she got wind of the marquess's presence.

She cleared her throat. "Shall we sit?"

"That may be painful," he muttered. "Give me a moment, and then I shall, but you will need to assist me."

"Of course." They stood in awkward silence while Jane stared at his male parts.

"You are staring at my trousers, aren't you?" he asked.

"No," she began, but then saw no reason to lie. "Actually, yes."

"Knowing that, makes it impossible for me to quell my desire."

She sighed. "How about knowing my mother may enter at any moment?"

He paused. "Yes, that will work." In another moment, he added, "I can sit now."

Immediately, she took his arm and led him to the sofa.

"Would you like some tea, my lord?"

He chuckled softly. "Probably a good idea to keep my hands busy and full so I don't take you in my arms again."

Jane was just pouring milk into both cups when her mother entered.

"Mother," Jane welcomed her, and Christopher stood and directed his bow toward the door.

"Good day, Lord Westing," her mother said, shooting a questioning glance toward Jane. "May I say you are looking well."

"Thank you. And you also, my lady."

"Thank you," she said, and a second later, Jane saw her mother frown as it dawned on her the absurdity of his statement, and then she smiled.

"You are joking with me, my lord. You scoundrel."

"Positively not," he said, sounding serious. "I am certain you look as lovely as you ever did. If you will only tell me when you have taken a seat, then I, too, may regain the sofa."

Jane's mother crossed the room and took her favorite wingback chair. "I am seated."

"Very good." And Christopher resumed his seat.

"What brings you here, my lord?" her mother asked.

"I wanted to thank your daughter for all she did for my mother and for our home. Her assistance was invaluable."

Jane smiled to herself. She had thoroughly enjoyed learning even a little about the art world.

"And I'm hoping my gratitude is not misplaced when I also thank you for the book." His face was turned to her. "It has brought me hours of joy as you knew it would."

She felt tears of happiness in her eyes. She had so hoped he would take the time to learn the Decapoint.

"I am very glad."

"If I may ask, my lord," Lady Chatley said, "how it is it possible you are reading?"

Between Jane and Christopher, they explained the embossed letters.

"That was thoughtful of you, Jane." Her mother gave her a curious look. "In truth, Lord Westing, with all you are doing, one could easily forget your affliction."

His affliction? Jane thought. *Like a farmer's sunburn or a case of the gout.* If only it were so simple. She'd learned being blinded had affected him not only physically but emotionally and mentally as well! He was not the same

Christopher Westing from prior to the explosion, but he was still the man she loved.

"Thank you." He cleared his throat. "I had also hoped to have a brief word with Lord Chatley."

"Oh," her mother said, and gestured to Jane, even flapping her hands about, clearly asking her what was going on. Unfortunately, the sleeves of her dress made noises as she did so.

Jane shook her head, hoping to make her stop moving.

Did Christopher mean what she thought he did? It would be too cruel! For she had only just come to terms with marrying Bernard, then returning to live in the family home as a married woman after her father departed—*God save his sorry soul.*

Everything pointed to her carrying out her familial duty and thereby making sure her mother had a roof over her head the rest of her life. She had pondered and examined her soul. She had prayed to God for guidance.

"Is there a problem?" Christopher asked into the heavy silence.

"My father isn't home at present," Jane told him. As far as she knew, that was the truth, although he might be passed out upstairs in all likelihood.

Besides, at this juncture, with the notion firmly in the earl's gin-sodden brain of saving the sizable dowry, keeping it in the Chatley coffers by marrying her to Bernard, she had a feeling he would refuse even a duke's son.

"When do you expect him?" Christopher persisted.

Jane fell silent. When she glanced at her mother who was attempting to suss out the situation and determine which way the wind was blowing, Jane could only shake her head. It was too complicated.

Her mother nodded. "I couldn't say, my lord. Lord Chatley is unpredictable, shall we say?"

Jane thought that was too kind word, almost a whimsical one, to describe a neglectful drunk.

"Perhaps, Lady Chatley, in his absence, I could speak with you then. In private," Christopher offered.

Oh dear. Was he really doing this now? Jane could still feel the press of his lips against hers. She would be deliriously happy to feel them again for the rest of her life. On the other hand, she couldn't enjoy a day of happiness knowing her mother suffered alone.

Again, she shook her head at her mother.

"While I may speak with you on certain matters," the countess began, her eyes widening as she looked at Jane, "meaning those in the female realm, so to speak, there are other issues which it is not my place to discuss. I fear you wish to speak on one of those."

Jane nodded approval at her mother. She certainly didn't want her mother speaking alone with Christopher. After all, the last thing she'd told Lady Chatley was of her disinterest in Lord Westing as a husband—comparing him to an unwilling sweet treat, if she recalled correctly.

"Very well. It was rash of me to show up uninvited and expect things to go my way. Do you think I might at least have a word with your daughter alone?"

"Oh, no," her mother said at once, "that will not do."

Jane waved her arms, nodded, and clasped her hands in prayer begging her mother to allow them that kindness.

"I mean, yes, of course," the countess corrected herself, sounding as if she didn't know her own mind.

Christopher frowned. "If you're certain."

Jane nodded again.

"Yes," her mother said. "I'll leave you two to speak. Won't I?" she looked to Jane again, making sure that was what she'd intended.

"Thank you, Mummy," Jane said, reassuring her with a smile.

Her mother rose, making gestures at Jane which she couldn't fathom.

Christopher rose, too.

"Good day, Lord Westing. I'm glad to see you looking so fit."

"Good day to you, Lady Chatley."

When the door closed behind her mother and her footsteps had died away, he sat down again, his thigh touching Jane's.

"That was odd," Christopher said. "I feel a bit topsy-turvy, to tell you the truth."

"I know, and I apologize. My mother was battling between her duty to protect my reputation versus her tolerance of my—"

He leaned over, took her by the shoulders, and drew her close.

"Are we alone?" he murmured, his mouth already close to hers.

He didn't wait for an answer before his lips claimed hers once again.

"*Mmm,*" she moaned against his mouth. The throbbing of her body's core was almost painful, but having his arms around her, smelling his clean scent, tasting him—it was all too delightful to stop simply because of the fervent and persistent longing pulsing between her legs.

His hand rose to her right breast, cupping it through her day gown, over her wildly beating heart, and she felt both her nipples pearl in response.

Desperately, she wanted to touch him and trailed her fingers along his thigh, heading for his—

He froze, pulled back, grabbed her hands from him, and scooted along the sofa.

"Christopher, what—?"

"Hush!" he commanded, and then the door swung open.

THAT WAS TOO CLOSE. Christopher heard the telltale footsteps only an instant before the door opened. Thank

God his hearing had become his most used sense, or they would have been caught *in flagrante delicto*, as the saying went.

And he knew by the step, the intruder was not her lenient mother.

"Jane!" came an unfamiliar voice, sounding a bit forward for his liking. Male, but too young to be her father.

He felt Jane stand slowly, without guilt. *Good girl!* He did the same, glad to know the tea set was still in front of them.

What could be more innocent than a cup of tea?

"Good day, cousin," she responded. "Lord Westing, my cousin, Mr. Lowther, has joined us. You may have already met each other at your mother's art show."

Christopher nodded, disliking the man on . . . hearing, if not on sight.

Jane, indeed! Her cousin shouldn't have addressed his unmarried cousin by her first name in a stranger's company, although Christopher wasn't really a stranger and had mere few seconds earlier been devouring Jane's mouth.

Still, her cousin didn't know that, and, thus, it was an unseemly breach of etiquette.

"Yes, of course," Lowther responded. "Your mother's paintings were quite the thing, up to snuff and beyond, I'd say. And do you paint?"

"If I did, I wouldn't be doing so any longer," Christopher reminded him.

"Oh, right, right! Sorry, old chap."

"Were you looking for me for some reason in particular?" Jane asked her cousin, sounding frosty.

"Not especially. I passed your mother in the hall and realized you were alone. With Lord Westing."

He paused, and Christopher could only imagine Jane and her cousin having a staring battle.

"And?" Jane prompted, sounding more than a little angry.

"And we wouldn't want any missteps at this stage, would we?" her cousin asked. "Not when we are close to making an announcement."

Christopher had grown very good at keeping his face passive, keenly aware of how others could be studying him without his knowledge. The spectacles added a layer of privacy he also greatly appreciated.

Still, he couldn't help tightening his jaw and feeling as if he could grind his molars to dust.

They were close to making an announcement!

"We were merely having tea," Jane explained. And now she did sound flustered. Clearly, it was on account of her cousin's statement.

How could she so passionately kiss him when she now had an intended?

There must be some misunderstanding.

"Your announcement is one of a wedding, I assume," Christopher said, surprised how very disinterested his tone remained when inside, he was in turmoil.

"Yes, of course." The cursed Lowther sounded very pleased with himself while Jane—*his Jane!*—remained tellingly silent.

"In fact, I was upstairs a minute ago speaking with her father about certain financial arrangements."

The misunderstanding had been entirely his. The Earl of Chatley was at home to certain gentlemen apparently. Christopher had better take his leave before he had no teeth left to gnash.

"I must be going," he said, turning toward Jane. "I thank you for the tea and conversation." And the extraordinary kisses that made his groin ache. *Dammit!*

"You're welcome." Her voice could not possibly sound smaller or sadder, but she had made her choice, with every opportunity to gainsay her cousin. Perhaps she needed one more chance, which he would gladly give.

"Was there anything else you wished to tell me?" he asked.

"No, my lord," she replied softly.

"And will you be working with my mother any further?"

There was a hesitation that unnerved him. *Was she exchanging a message with her soon-to-be betrothed?*

"Our task was nearly complete," she said. "However, I had planned on seeing your mother again soon."

A strange, noncommittal answer, but it was obviously the best she was going to provide.

He reached down for his cane where it had been resting against the sofa, but it had slipped away from him.

"Allow me," Lowther said, and a moment later, Christopher felt the handle of his cane pressed into his hand.

"And your hat," Jane said, and he remembered it being knocked from his head at some point while they were kissing.

If she'd tried to place it on his head, dressing him like a child, he vowed he would knock it aside, but she only touched the brim to the back of his free hand. He snatched it and put it on, used his cane to find a clear path around the table, and took his leave.

"Good day, Mr. Lowther, Lady Jane." And he left, feeling as if he could howl like the famed wild wolf of the middle ages. Hunted to extinction throughout the British Isles, it was the perfect animal to describe his feeling of having no place in this world anymore.

At least not in Jane's world.

CHAPTER TWENTY-FIVE

A *door had certainly been firmly shut,* Jane thought. *Never to be opened again.* And Christopher was on the other side of it. She'd felt the restrained contempt in every fiber of his being when he'd left.

"That was very wrong of you to be secluded with Lord Darkness," Bernard admonished her, as if he had any right.

"What did you call him?"

"Only what some in the *ton* are saying. He used to be the sunny, happy, blessed Marquess of Westing. Now look at him. Poor bastard! I almost feel sorry for him."

Jane was shocked into silence. *Feel sorry for him?* But he was Christopher Westing. Nothing had changed in regard to his greatness, as far as she was concerned. Bernard was a fool, as were the *ton* who underestimated what Christopher would do with his life.

"I suppose we ought not to be alone either, as you said in the garden. I don't want my future wife tainted in the smallest regard," her cousin added and strolled to the door. "But don't let an indiscretion like that happen again. If it does, I won't be pleased."

Jane's hand went to her mouth, recalling the pleasure of a few minutes earlier. She had let Christopher leave under the mistaken notion she didn't care for him.

No, that couldn't be right. How could he not know how she felt about him when her body came to life under his touch? Instantly, like a flame to lamp oil.

A moment later, the maid entered. "Your father wishes to see you, my lady."

Walking slowly into the front hall, Jane considered the events of the morning, then of the past Season, then of her life in general—each small and large step that had brought her to this moment. The times she'd held herself aloof when someone had shown an interest. The joy she'd felt working for a charitable cause. The support of her mother. The intense loneliness.

The man she loved beyond reason had just walked out. The man she didn't care about she would undoubtedly and dutifully marry. The man she had grown to despise awaited her upstairs.

Slowly, she climbed the stairs, hesitated at her father's private study, then passed it to her own room. Realizing she hadn't enjoyed a sip of the expensive tea downstairs, she rang for her maid, waited patiently, and ordered a fresh pot.

CHRISTOPHER SAT BACK IN the carriage, letting the familiar worn leather encompass him, and considered all that had taken place. In the course of four months, he had fallen in love, lost his sight, lost his will to live, finally regained some equilibrium of mind and purpose, and then lost Jane, his heart's desire.

Who the hell had he pissed off to deserve this living nightmare?

Still, he felt he could carry on. Because of her. She'd fought him tooth and fingernail to make sure he didn't give in to the darkness. He wasn't useless. He wasn't an invalid.

He was a blind man with a good mind, a loving family, a place in society, and a promising future in government.

Except he now felt entirely devoid of hope. He wanted a life filled with love. He wanted Jane.

JANE HEARD HER PARENTS fighting and realized her mother must have broached her father in his study. Perhaps it was on the very topic that was consuming her mind with fear and loathing. Then it went quiet.

Rising to her feet, she intended to check on her mother, although she had never feared violence from her father. In truth, the more he drank, the more harmless he seemed because he usually nodded off early in his chair.

At that moment, as if Jane's musings had summoned her, Lady Emily Chatley's familiar soft tap struck the door.

"Come in," Jane told her.

Her mother entered, along with her familiar scent of lilacs. She had the warm, loving smile she always projected to her only child. Jane could easily recall walking in the park with her mother when, without the countess's firm grip, Jane would have tumbled over onto her knees.

Of course, there was always a governess in the background, but her mother was an involved child-rearer, one who displayed her love for her daughter in every touch, every little gift, every word of praise, every tolerance.

It had not been perfect, certainly. There had been those times when Jane felt smothered, controlled, pushed, manipulated. If she'd had more female friends, she had no doubt she would have discovered their mothers were the same. The aim of every mother at every ball Jane had ever gone to seemed to be identical—show her daughter in the best light possible, with a gown suited to her coloring and figure, with hair that looked *au courant* and becoming, and with enough dance lessons that the girl wouldn't fall on her face in front of potential suitors.

And her mother had done the absolute best job at all of those tasks. Jane had always felt loved and capable, as well as intelligent and beautiful—because of Emily Chatley.

"Are you all right, my love?" Her mother kissed her cheek. Nodding to the pot on the small tabletop, she asked, "Didn't you just have a cup with Lord Westing? And why are you taking tea up here?"

"Honestly," Jane began, *and with whom else could she be so honest?* "I was keeping out of Bernard's way, and Father's."

"I see." A shadow of worry flashed across her mother's face. "That's actually why I wanted to speak with you."

When her mother didn't say anything more for a moment, Jane realized tears were filling the older woman's eyes. She took hold of the countess's hands.

"Mummy, what is it?" *Had her father injured her mother?*

Emily Chatley quite uncharacteristically bit her lower lip.

"I want to ask you a personal question."

How strangely formal of her mother!

"Of course. Anything."

"Is there possibly a relationship between you and the Marquess of Westing?"

Jane wished she could answer yes. With her entire being, she wished it so.

"No," she uttered.

Her mother's face crumpled, and the tears spilled over onto her soft, pale cheeks. In fact, she looked the embodiment of how Jane had felt since Christopher had left earlier.

Seeing her mother's distress, Jane dragged Lady Chatley to sit beside her on the small tufted divan where Jane normally read her books, pulling her down beside her.

Her mother pulled a handkerchief out of her sleeve and dabbed at her face.

"I'm sorry," she whispered. "I imagined I saw a spark of something between you. Then you wouldn't let me find your father or speak to Lord Westing myself on his behalf."

Should she tell her mother she'd been right about seeing something between her daughter and Christopher? It was pointless now, so Jane held her tongue.

"You didn't want him to offer for you, that was clear."

Perhaps Jane could have a career on the stage if her mother believed that.

"Mummy, it wouldn't be for the best were I to make a match with Lord Westing."

"I have been so hoping you were developing feelings for someone. How about Lord Burnley?"

Jane managed a grimacing smile at the notion. "Least of all him."

The fact her mother was still trying to get her to marry elsewhere than Bernard only reinforced her selfless love for her daughter. However, Jane could not possibly leave her behind to a life of uncertainty and eventual homelessness.

Her mother nodded. "Then what are we to do, my Jane girl?"

"I will marry cousin Bernard. It is best for all concerned."

Her mother's eyes widened, and she shook her head.

"I hoped when your cousin arrived, he would have ideas of his own as to whom he wanted to marry. However, instead of raising an objection, he is quite determined to have you."

Jane hung her head, trapped as expected.

"Just as I am determined he shall not," her mother continued.

"What?" Jane raised her head.

"When you were a girl, a parliamentary act determined married mothers, such as myself, as long as we had impeccable reputations, would be allowed to keep our young children, even if our husbands left us. Prior to that, a man could have actually given his child to one of his mistresses to look after, and there would have been nothing a mother could do."

Jane did know it, although she'd had no idea her mother had ever given the Custody of Infants Act a second thought.

"That law came too late anyway," the countess continued, "and it would only have allowed me to keep you until you turned seven. As you were already ten at the time, it did me no good. What mother could relinquish her child at such a tender age, practically the very time you started needing me the most?"

"It seems barbaric."

Her mother nodded. "We can thank Mrs. Norton for even that small progress. Poor lady, what she has endured." Emily Chatley looked out the window, clearly her thoughts far away.

Everyone had heard of Caroline Norton and the injustices she'd suffered at the hands of an abusive husband, who went so far as to beat her until she miscarried and then took from her their three remaining children before locking her out of his house. She fought back through the law. When her husband took her earnings from writing novels, she sent her bills to him since she didn't exist under the law, and he had no choice but to pay.

Mrs. Norton could not win a divorce against him, but that only increased her determination to evoke change. She devoted herself to changing both marriage and divorce laws for women, and was still fighting with the help of powerful friends.

"And still we wait for a way to divorce an intolerable husband, and more importantly, for a law that allows a mother to keep her child until maturity." She squeezed Jane's hand.

"Thus, I stayed with your father," her mother murmured.

"I know you stayed with him for me. I wish there had been another way."

Lady Chatley shrugged. "The only love in this home is betwixt you and I. It has always been empty of friends. Your father was either away or too far into his bottle of gin to be seen in public. My friends wouldn't come, and when I tried to strike up friendships for you with other young ladies, their parents wouldn't let them come here either. And you already know how my status as the humiliated cuckquean has not served me well in society."

Her mother had shocked her to the core, mentioning her father's infidelity and drinking. Foolishly, Jane had assumed his actions hadn't bothered her mother. *And why?* For the simple reason her mother had always seemed focused on her.

"May I?" Lady Chatley gestured to the pot of tea and the single empty cup.

"Of course." And Jane watched her mother delicately pour a splash of milk into the bottom of the cup before adding the still hot tea as she had seen her do hundreds of times before.

However, this time, it seemed as if her mother were performing a ceremony, girding her loins for what she was going to say or do next.

After stirring in exactly one level teaspoon of sugar, Lady Chatley lifted the cup to her lips, closed her eyes, and sipped.

"Perfect."

Jane said nothing, merely waiting, feeling a little in awe of the power steeping inside her own mother.

Finally, the Countess of Chatley turned to her daughter. "You will not and cannot marry Bernard Lowther. I forbid it."

Jane knew her eyes had widened, but then she considered again her mother's plight. "I was sitting here thinking how it might be my only choice."

"Don't you dare!" her mother exclaimed. "Don't you even think of marrying a Chatley."

The tight ball of tension that had settled in Jane's stomach from the moment Bernard had arrived dissolved instantly. If her mother were on her side and truly meant what she said, then all would be right.

"I had hoped over these past couple of years you would find a man you wanted to marry, one who would take you out from under your father's power. Now, I shall do it myself."

"But if I married, what would happen to you? Only think of the future after Bernard becomes the next earl."

"I was prepared for the indignity. Even before this whole farce with your cousin arose, if I had seen you happily married, I had thought to go to the Continent, if I could bear to be apart from you. Now, we shall leave together," her mother continued, "for there is no life for me here without you."

Without thinking, Jane tossed her arms around her mother, despite causing her to spill tea onto the rug. Of course her mother would have gone to the Continent, for wasn't that where her blue-eyed young man was? Perhaps all those times her mother had given her a little push toward Lord Cambrey, for instance, it was so Emily Chatley could be free to follow her viscount and her heart.

"I'm glad you approve," her mother said.

Instead of worried, her mother's expression was placid.

"I, for one, am so looking forward to a long trip," her mother added. "And some letter-writing."

Jane smiled. "I had only just come to the realization I couldn't leave you behind. I would have married Bernard for your sake. However, if I was going to leave, I had half a mind to go to Ramsgate."

Her mother giggled unexpectedly. "Ramsgate? In Kent? Whyever for?"

"For the sake of the anti-carnivores. Also known as vegetarians."

Emily Chatley's laughter filled the bedroom. "Jane, you are unique. But if you choose the English countryside, I shall not be able to go with you. It is too close, and your father will make things extremely unpleasant for me and, of course, refuse me a divorce as happened to Mrs. Norton."

"Then we shall go to the Continent, as you wish."

Her mother raised the teacup toward the window. "To the Continent."

She took a sip and handed the cup to Jane, handle-side first.

Jane lifted it high and echoed, "To the Continent" before taking a sip.

"Oh, Mummy. That *is* the perfect cup of tea!"

CHAPTER TWENTY-SIX

With her mother making her own surreptitious monetary withdrawals and discreetly overseeing the packing of their trunks, Jane drew on her gloves and left for a last visit to the Foresters' home.

She didn't ask the butler for the marquess, only for the Duchess of Westing. Their meeting was brief, with Jane promising to visit her at the Westing's newly restored townhouse in two days to begin the decorations in earnest. Jane hated to lie, but she had wanted to say goodbye in person.

"I won't keep you, Your Grace," Jane said. "I only wanted to let you know I won't be coming back here."

"Of course not," the duchess said. "I shall see you over there."

Jane ignored her comment. "I also wanted to tell you how much I've enjoyed working with you."

"Thank you, dear. And I, you. You are an asset, to be sure."

"And I greatly appreciate the set of watercolors you sent over. I shall try my hand at them soon." Jane had been thrilled when the package arrived, determined to reproduce some picturesque area in France with a crude attempt at painting.

The duchess smiled. "I cannot wait to see your endeavors."

How she would love to have Christopher's mother as a mentor. All Jane could do was nod as if she would, indeed, be able to show her efforts to the duchess.

And they parted company. Jane lingered a moment, unable to accept she was going to walk out the door and never see or speak with Christopher again. Hesitating in the foyer, footsteps drew her attention to the passageway leading to the back of the house. Her hopes raised as her heartbeat sped up, but then Lord Burnley appeared. He must have been visiting with Christopher.

"Lady Jane," he said, his tone dripping with disdain. Moreover, he came close—too close—hands behind his back and towering over her, scowling.

"Why are you so angry with me, Lord Burnley?" she asked outright, throwing politeness to the wind since she was leaving London. It was a very liberating feeling, knowing her freedom was merely a day away.

He made a sound of derision. "You behave like a strumpet."

She laughed. After all, his opinion didn't matter to her anymore, nor could it harm her where she was going. Still, she was curious just the same.

"But the thing is, I don't. I practically always behave more demurely than most any woman I know."

"Lord Fowler," he pointed out, scowling harder if possible.

"You are like an old woman with a bee in her bonnet. The viscount and I have never been alone together. Behind a pillar in a room full of people is hardly a hanging offense. Moreover, you and I have been in the same circles for years. You know my reputation is untarnished, and there has never been a hint of scandal attached to my name. So, tell me truthfully, why do you dislike me?"

He stared at her. In fact, he rather insolently looked her up and down.

"Truthfully," he confessed, "I do see what he sees in you. Or rather saw, when he could see. Strange how none of us saw what he saw in you before he did."

Obviously, he was speaking of Christopher and making a hash of his explanation.

"What Lord Westing saw in me before he lost his sight is not your business."

"It most certainly is. He is my best friend and has been through a horrendous ordeal. He's had quite enough disappointment for a lifetime."

Jane sighed. "And you think I may be his next disappointment."

"I am certain of it by his ill humor today."

Undoubtedly, Christopher had not taken the farce which had occurred in her parlor at all well. That was not surprising. However, they had both suffered.

"And you are angry with me because you think I have hurt him. It never occurred to you he has hurt me, has it?" She looked Lord Owen Burnley directly in the eyes, refusing to be cowed by his intimidating manner.

His forehead furrowed at her question.

"I thought not," she said. "Poor Christopher Westing. Blind and helpless, prey to the likes of evil Jane Chatley, who, in your opinion, inexplicably went from a reserved snoot-nose—yes, I know what people said—to an indecorous Jezebel. Pretending to like the company of a blind man while playing him for a fool, first with Lord Fowler, and then, if you dig deeply enough, even fielding a marriage proposal from my cousin, Bernard Lowther."

She watched his eyes widen.

"Oh, yes," she nodded. "There are even more machinations afoot."

She considered how blissfully happy she would have been if Christopher—blind, resentful, difficult, and angry as he was at times—had simply fallen in love with her and claimed her for his own. She was still convinced it was the path they'd been on before the damnable explosion.

"Men! You are as much a blind fool as your friend."

"A blind fool, am I?" Christopher asked from hallway. "Or are you referring to one of Burnley's other friends?"

Her heart instantly pounding, hard and fast, she felt her cheeks heat.

Drats! That was not well said of her.

Lord Burnley even sent her a triumphant glance. *Blast the man!*

She opened her mouth and nearly defended herself, then thought better of it. She was leaving, and nothing said here today would change that fact. Besides, she did think them both a couple of fools. Burnley was making things worse, bungling in where he didn't belong, and Christopher . . . well, he had tossed away her heart for reasons she couldn't fathom at the very moment she'd asked for his help.

By the time he'd come to his senses, it was too late. Now that Jane understood the truth, she had to protect her mother, as her mother had always done for her.

"Nothing more to add?" the marquess prompted as he came closer.

"No," she said. "I was just leaving. I came to speak with your mother, and I have done so. If I hadn't been waylaid by Lord Burnley, I wouldn't still be here."

"Waylaid? Why were you discussing me with Lady Jane?" Christopher asked his friend, his tone quietly furious. "Does this happen a lot, among my friends, talking behind my back?"

"No!" Lord Burnley said. "I was simply—"

"Simply what?" Christopher ground out as she looked between them.

It was her turn to make a face of triumph. She almost stuck her tongue out at Owen Burnley.

"I was reminding Lady Jane that you are in a somewhat delicate state."

"A what? Good God, man! If I could see your face, I would give it a pop. How dare you?"

"I am your friend," Lord Burnley insisted.

"Which doesn't give you the right to treat me like an invalid. Especially to Jane. She's the only one who has pushed me farther than I wanted to go. Anyway, what is your grievance with her?"

"I don't want you played for a fool!"

Christopher swore a blue oath. "Even if *she* calls me a blind fool, I don't want you treating me like one."

"What of Fowler?"

"The lady and I have already discussed him. How could it be *your* business?"

"That's what I said," Jane put in, before realizing she'd said she was leaving. Instead, she was watching the proceedings as if attending a pugilists' match. Both their heads swiveled in her direction. She swallowed.

Seeing Burnley's defensive manner and Christopher's anger, she recalled this was precisely the outcome she didn't want. Christopher needed his best friend, now more than ever.

"And what of her cousin?" Lord Burnley retorted, and Jane cursed her own loose tongue.

"I know about her cousin, too!" Christopher was practically shouting.

"There is nothing to know," she insisted, which was the truth. "I was simply taunting your friend who was being impertinent. It was wrong of me. Good day, gentlemen. I hope you recall your close friendship and resolve your differences at once. You are behaving like children."

Regardless, she still wanted to stick her tongue out at Owen Burnley.

With a last glance in Christopher's direction, drinking in the sight of him as best she could, Jane left. This had not been how she wished to last see him, nearly apoplectic and hurt by feeling betrayed. Luckily, she had plenty of other delicious memories of him, touching her, kissing her, which she could call upon in the lonely hours between sunset and sunrise.

THE FOLLOWING DAY, WITH Bernard and her father out somewhere together, which didn't bode well, Jane's mother instructed the butler to bring their trunks downstairs. They had hired a carriage to take them to the train at London Bridge Station, fearing the pandemonium of Waterloo and its many platforms.

In turn, a few hours later, depending on how long the train stopped for lunch, they would be deposited on the coast in Folkestone at the hotel belonging to the steamship line. After a night, they would cross the channel to Boulogne, France, early the next morning and begin a new life.

They had accepted the fact they would have to deal with pickpockets, thimble-riggers, and even men falsely dressed as clergy on the train. Yet together, they felt more excited than fearful. At the last moment, her mother decided to leave both their maids behind, as the young ladies had local sweethearts, and removing them to France seemed cruel.

Jane's mother was still upstairs, making sure she had everything she wanted to take.

"Surprisingly little," she'd told her daughter earlier. Jane stood watch at the front door, anxious to get under way. If Bernard or her father returned at that moment, it would be an ugly scene. Hearing a carriage arrive out front, she peered out the window. It was neither their carriage-for-hire nor the Chatleys' landau indicating her father's return. It was the Westings' landau, emblazoned with their emblem on the door.

Her heart sped up at once. *Christopher!*

She opened the front door as the carriage door also swung open. However, not Christopher but his sister disembarked. It was too late to close the door, so Jane waited while the young woman approached.

As if a disagreeable encounter with Burnley hadn't been enough, Amanda Westing was now on her doorstep.

Jane sighed, doubtful this was going to be pleasant. Mindful of the trunks in the hall behind her, she stepped outside and closed the door.

"Lady Amanda, to what do I owe the pleasure?" *Perhaps a tooth extraction, or was she there to kick Jane in the shin?*

"I am here to apologize."

Of all the possible things the girl could have said, Jane would never have guessed that.

"I don't understand." Jane said, wishing she could invite her inside. "For what?"

Amanda was twisting her gloved fingers in front of her. "I have not been terribly supportive of my brother's association with you."

Jane looked past her to where the carriage awaited. "Are you alone?"

"My mother is with me."

That made more sense. "She brought you here to speak with me?"

"Oh no, it's not like that. She told me you weren't coming to the Foresters' anymore, and I hoped it wasn't because of me. I know Christopher likes you ever so much."

Jane felt a warmth spread through her. Amanda was looking at her, bright-eyed and direct, without giggling, and without meanness.

"I finished what I was doing with your mother, and the next tasks will be back at your own home." Besides having the English Channel between her and Mayfair would preclude Jane's further involvement. "It wasn't to do with you, and I'm glad Lord Westing has such a devoted sister."

"I think you are sweet on him. Are you?"

Jane sighed. "That is neither here nor there."

"But it is. You see, I brought other ladies home to meet him. He barely spoke a word to any of them. You are the only one who brings him out of his dark brooding self, except for Lord Burnley and father, of course, when he takes Chris to Parliament."

'There you are, then. Your brother is coming along nicely, as best as can be expected. He has friends and family."

Lady Amanda looked her straight in the eyes. "But I believe he wants you."

Jane didn't know how to respond. It would be easy to dispel Amanda's silly notions, by explaining how she'd suggested he ask for her hand and been soundly turned down. However, that was between her and Christopher.

"I think your brother has a long path ahead of him and will find someone who makes him happy."

Amanda looked down at the doorstep, then back up into Jane's eyes.

"If you truly don't have a special feeling for him, then I guess it is all right."

"What is?" Jane asked with a shiver of trepidation.

"Lord Burnley is bringing his sister to dinner tonight. My mother says she would be an excellent match for my brother."

Jane felt the pain like a sword blade between her ribs. Undoubtedly, Owen Burnley would be pleased by such an arrangement. With Jane out of the way, not only would he have his best friend to himself again, he would gain Christopher as a brother.

"I understand Lady Sophia is recently back from France. Such an excursion puts the polish on a girl."

"I suppose you are right. Anyway, I must go." She glanced back toward the carriage. "We are on our way to Covent Gardens. Mother says I may choose the flowers for the table tonight, and I asked her to stop here on the way. Of course, my mother said stopping unannounced isn't done, but I had a feeling you wouldn't mind."

"And you were quite right," Jane assured her. *When had she developed a warm feeling for the spoiled Amanda?*

"Good day, then, Lady Jane."

"Good day."

Amanda turned away, then looked back at her. "The book was a wonderful gift for my brother. I wish you could have seen how thrilled it made him. And you were quite correct about my helping my mother." She shot her a grin that instantly reminded Jane of Christopher's smile. "I thank you for pushing me to do so."

Jane nodded. "I'm glad it worked out. And I do thank you for coming to speak to me. I am certain you will finish up your Season splendidly."

Amanda blushed prettily. "Perhaps I shall see you at the next ball."

Jane could have lied, but other words slipped out. "I think not. I'll be trying a little of the polish myself soon. Good day."

After she closed the door, Jane was annoyed with herself for mentioning she was leaving. And she would do well to get away before anyone could start speculating on where or why, as the *ton* loved to do.

CHRISTOPHER COULDN'T BELIEVE JANE had stayed away so long. Obviously they'd had cross words, but his mother was sorely missing her. *He* was missing her!

The Westings had moved from the Foresters' townhome back to their own on Grosvenor Square in the best section of Mayfair, and he'd found it easier than expected to make his way around. There had been a few furniture mishaps, and he'd bored his sister to death by asking her to tell him every detail of each room's appearance, what was new, and even what the shower bath looked like. Then, he'd proceeded to soak himself trying to figure out how it worked on his own.

He kept hoping he would run into Jane in the foyer or the parlor. He was determined to make her forget Bernard Lowther and marry him. After all, the extraordinary quality of their kisses proved what he knew deep inside—she was meant to be his and she loved him.

He'd even planned what he would say to woo her into agreeing to be his wife.

Thus, he'd haunted the front of their home, hoping she would return. Merely being in her company seemed a bounty of good fortune, of which he hadn't been appropriately grateful.

Finally, their butler—*not* the Foresters' but their own at last, back as it seemed from storage, although Christopher didn't really know where the man had been—told him a young lady was there who would identify herself only as *his friend.*

Jane! The warm feeling and the desire to see her rushed over him, even if "seeing" her meant listening to her sweet and smart voice, sniffing her delectable perfume, and maybe kissing her lips if he was very lucky. He had only to convince her that marrying a blind man was infinitely preferable to marrying a sighted weasel like her cousin.

Truthfully, Christopher didn't know the man at all, not even what he looked like. He might *not* be a weasel, but something didn't sit right with a man marrying his cousin—it intimated doing so for the wrong reason. In this case, he had no doubt it was financial.

Feeling downright desperate, wondering if any day, his mother would tell him she'd read the Chatleys' banns in the paper, finally, his waiting had paid off.

"Jane," he greeted her, as he entered the parlor. He knew it wasn't truly fit for company yet, at least not to his mother's exceedingly exacting standards, but Amanda said it was already gorgeous.

"Alas, no," came a familiar voice. It took him only a moment to place it.

"Margaret? I mean, Lady Cambrey." He stopped in his tracks and bowed. "This is a surprise."

"And a disappointment, it seems." She didn't seem upset, merely amused.

"No, not at all." Even he had to admit his voice didn't sound convincing. "Excuse me for not exclaiming upon your beauty, yet even without my sight, I know you are standing there, looking breathtaking."

"I am," she said. "How good of you to remark upon it."

The countess had a lovely laugh, different from Jane's, who didn't laugh often enough, but when she did, it stirred his blood.

"To what do I owe this pleasure?" he asked, hoping to display more enthusiasm.

"Actually, you owe the pleasure of my company to the very lady whose name was upon your lips a moment ago."

"Lady Jane?"

"Yes, precisely. Come sit with me," Margaret insisted, taking his hand and bringing him to the sofa, although he already knew how many steps it took to get there. "We shall chat about Jane and how perfect she is for you."

How did she know about his feelings for Jane?

"What's going on?" he asked, then recalled his manners. "Would you care for tea or coffee? I promise, I'm quite good at drinking in public now."

She laughed again. "I never doubted you."

"That sounds like something Lady Jane would say. She is very good at prodding me to be my best."

"So, you don't mind her helping you?"

"God, no. I would probably still be curled up in my bed if not for her persistence."

"She was under the impression her assistance was not welcome and, in fact, angered you."

Christopher shook his head. "Sometimes, I admit, I do get angry. I didn't expect this." He gestured at his own face. "This new life came as a shock.'

"Understandably so. I like your spectacles, by the way," Margaret told him.

"Thank you. Lady Jane does, too."

"Where is she?" the countess asked suddenly, sounding as if she believed he were hiding her, perhaps in a cupboard under the stairs.

"What do you mean?" he asked.

"She has left town, and no one knows whence she's gone. I am not happy about it." Margaret made an exasperated sound. "She and I were becoming friends."

His mind was swirling with questions, and he would swear his heart was suddenly beating more quickly as the full impact of Margaret's words hit him. *Jane was gone!*

"How do you know?" he demanded.

"She told me she wanted to be my friend. That's how."

"No. What I'm asking is how do you know she has left town?"

Margaret gave an audible sigh. "She sent me a short missive saying she wished we'd had more time to enjoy our new friendship and thanked me for listening. She apologized for going away without telling me where."

"I don't understand." Christopher considered his conversations with Jane. "She said nothing to me."

"Did you part on friendly terms when last you spoke?"

He thought back. The last time he and Jane spoke was when Owen was being a cad. *Is that what drove her away?*

"She had been working with my mother, first on her art show and then choosing the colors and fabrics for the renovation of our home."

"It looks lovely, by the way," Margaret said. "Has someone described it to you?"

He nodded. "Yes. My sister has learned a bit of patience and kindly told me in detail. I know this room now has a Persian rug in cream, red, gold, and green, with pale green and gold stamped wallpaper, and gold curtains. The chairs are solid cream and the sofa upon which we sit is a pattern that somehow doesn't clash with the rug. Did I get it right?"

"Perfectly correct. So, Jane did this, did she?"

"Yes." He frowned. "But since we've moved back, Jane has come not at all."

"I wonder if your mother or sister knows anything."

He had no idea but intended to find out.

"Did you part on good terms?"

It was the second time she'd asked. "What makes you wonder about that? What did she say to you? I didn't even know you were friends."

"We spent a little time together at my husband's country estate in Bedfordshire, before Lord Cambrey and I became engaged. Jane and her mother visited, and I was jealous of Jane's . . . perfection."

He couldn't help but laugh. "She does exude capability, charm, poise, correctness, while seeming humble. I suppose you're right. In a word, perfection."

"You didn't even mention her looks. Fresh yet polished, pretty yet understated."

"Looks have become less important to me, as you may well imagine," Christopher reminded her, "but I do know she is quite beautiful, radiant even."

"Yet you allowed her to leave. Simply to slip away."

"That's not fair." Christopher had spent days hoping she would return. "She didn't give me any notice. No chance to stop her."

"She never gave you a chance? I find that hard to believe." Margaret's tone was still light and friendly, but laced with a hard edge, as if she knew he'd pushed Jane away.

In his mind, he recalled the moment everything had changed. She had asked him to marry her, and he had turned her down. By the time he'd changed his mind, it had been too late.

"I see you recall something," the countess said. "Lady Jane told me—"

"Told you what?" Christopher urged her when she stopped abruptly.

"I cannot say too much because that is unfair to my new friend. Moreover, to disclose what is in her heart is for her to do, not me. However, if you have feelings for her, which I think you do, you should pursue them. And I can tell you this much—although I don't know where she is at present—she had to leave to escape an arranged marriage."

"What?" he roared, getting to his feet.

"I know! Shocking, isn't it? And with her heart elsewhere *engaged*, what could she do?"

"Elsewhere?" he asked, feeling all the fight go out of him.

"You are not so dense, are you, Christopher?" Margaret stood, too. "Lady Jane wasn't simply helping you in the same way she helped the orphans, or me, for that matter, once upon a time. It was something else entirely. Anyway, I hope you find her and bring her back. Clearly, it would be best for you and, I believe, best for her, as well."

He felt her gloved hands take his own for a warm grasp.

"Good day, dear friend. I'm glad to see you looking so well. My husband tells me you've been going to Parliament."

"I have." He walked her toward the door. "I thought that life was finished for me, but sitting in the House is still my destiny and my duty."

"Bravo!" Margaret exclaimed. He felt her kiss him on the cheek. "When next I visit, I hope you have put everything to rights."

CHAPTER TWENTY-SEVEN

"What can you tell me about Bernard Lowther?

"You told me, nay, you *yelled* at me that you knew all about him," Burnley replied at once. "Anyway, I don't know much. He is the oldest in line for the Chatley earldom. He came to Town a few weeks ago, maybe longer. Don't you recall he was at your mother's art show?"

Christopher considered for a moment. "No, I don't. I think I was in a red rage over Fowler."

"Oh, right. That muck up!"

Christopher heard Owen pour himself a drink. They sat in his friend's parlor on Gilbert Street, a short distance from the Westing townhouse in the northern portion of Mayfair. Burnley had purchased his own home a year prior, and Christopher thought all the man needed now was a wife. His friend, however, had shown no interest in settling down, and much preferred variety in his female acquaintances. More variety than might be good for a man.

Christopher had walked there directly after the Countess of Cambrey departed.

"Brandy? Or is it too early for you?"

"Luckily, I can't see a clock," Christopher said and held out his hand.

His friend pressed a glass into it.

"Did you know anything about Jane and this cousin?"

Silence was a telling answer. Then Owen confessed, "Your Lady Jane mentioned fielding a marriage proposal from him. That was right before she called us both blind fools."

"I see."

"What?" Owen spluttered. "Are you actually making a jest about your sight?"

"What? *No!* I mean, I understand now why she called me that. And to think, I left her with that blackguard. If I could have seen her face, I would have known she was miserable."

"And where is the old girl?" Burnley asked.

"The *old girl*, as you put it so cavalierly, has left London to get away from an arranged marriage with this cousin."

"Christ!"

"Exactly," Christopher said. "I could have spared her needing to flee."

"You wouldn't marry her to save her from her cousin, would you?" His friend's tone was one of utter incredulity.

"Of course not. I would marry her because I *love* her."

"Oh," Burnley said, and nothing more for a long minute. "I botched things up for you a bit, didn't I?"

"I managed to do that all by myself, but I need to ask your help."

His friend clinked his glass against his unexpectedly. "Anything."

"Help me find Jane."

"Mummy! Come quick." Jane was looking out of the window of the small, whitewashed cottage they had rented temporarily in Marseille. It had been a long journey from

Boulogne to Paris and then to the southern city on the Mediterranean. They had traveled for two weeks by train and by carriage. It had seemed endless, but at last, they had arrived.

"What is it, dear?"

"The view! It's splendid. The water is such a glorious color, and so many boats, too."

"Jane, dear, I am exhausted. I did glance at the sea before we came indoors." Her mother sighed loudly. "How could they tell us there was a Paris-to-Marseille railway when there were tracks that didn't connect? I will look at the view tomorrow. It will still be here."

Jane laughed. "All right, Mummy. We shall spend our days practicing our French and eating *pain au chocolat*. And tomorrow, I am going to sit by the sea and paint."

Her mother leaned her head back on the sofa. "I'm not sure this is the place for us. Even the canal for drinking water hasn't been finished."

"*Mm.*" Jane wasn't really listening. She was looking at the French translation book she'd bought during their few hours in Paris.

"This may be the place for us, Mummy. Who knows? In any case, it is far enough, we shall be safe."

"For a while," her mother agreed.

Her tone caused Jane to set down the book and go sit beside her.

"We are intrepid travelers, are we not? Remember when we went to Turvey House together?"

"And stayed with the Cambreys? Yes, that was a much easier journey, was it not?"

"But we've made it, Mummy. We're here."

"With the fishermen," her mother grumbled. "And that large hospital along the way. It gives me the shivers."

"There are also bakeries and delicious cafes. Little shops and the *Place de Lenche*. And we have to see the pretty pink stone of the court building. We shall find a maid to come help us tomorrow. Only think how brilliant it was of you to find this cottage at short notice."

"You're patronizing me, darling daughter. If you hadn't struck up a conversation with that woman on the train, we'd still be sitting at the last station this very moment."

"But *you* asked her about lodgings."

Emily Chatley closed her eyes. "We cannot hide here forever."

"Mummy, we've only just arrived. Let us at least stay as long as the journey took. Where would you like to go next?"

"If you are to have some semblance of a normal life, we must go back toward civilization." She opened her eyes and scrutinized her daughter.

"You mean Paris." Jane wrinkled her nose.

"Why are you doing that with your face, dear? Didn't you like it there? I know we were only passing through, but you must have seen the civility of it and the people."

In truth, it made her think of her father and the many times he'd left them for the Continent. She'd heard her parents fighting about the "doxies in Paris." And her father's retort as to how they were "preferable to a rigid English wife."

"Surely, you don't want to go there," Jane said.

"Why not?"

Her mother stared at her and Jane stared back. She would not bring up French doxies. In the end, she simply shrugged, and her mother rolled her eyes.

"Only think of the shops and the theatre," her mother continued. "It's not London certainly, but nothing ever will be. No, Jane. This Mediterranean lark was a whim to get us away from prying eyes and far from the English arm of the law. It's perfect for the moment, but I do not intend to stay in a fishing town for the rest of my years."

"Very well. Just let me paint a little here," Jane said, "and then you may pick the next place. If you truly don't mind Paris, then neither do I."

And they fell into an easy arrangement, just as if they were back in London on Berkley Square.

A WEEK LATER, JANE came home carrying her painting supplies in a basket. Their new maid, Bettine, who came only four days a week to clean and cook, was sweeping the front room. At least twice a week, she brought fresh pastries from the patisserie her family owned, and the aroma permeated the cottage.

Jane's mouth began to water at once.

"Bonjour, Bettine, comment ca va?"

"Bien, mademoiselle. Et vous?"

"Tres bien. Voyez." And Jane held out her art work for the young woman to look at. The thick paper, secured in a flat wooden frame, was still slightly damp.

"Oh, c'est belle. Vous etes une peintre?"

"No, mais I try *un peu. Vous comprenez* 'try'?"

"Oui." Bettine smiled at her.

"Où est ma mère?"

Bettine put a hand to her hip.

"Elle est allée poster une lettre. Je lui ai dit qu'il n'y a pas de poste aux lettres jusqu'à demain mais—"

Jane held up her hands. "I'm sorry, Bettine, but I don't understand you. *Je ne comprends pas.*"

"Your mama, she had a letter, mademoiselle," and the girl waved her hand around as if holding paper. "I told her no post until tomorrow, but she said she would mail it anyway."

Who was her mother writing to? Jane set her painting kit down and removed her gloves and hat. *Was her mother writing to someone back in England?* They had discussed doing so in a few months but not so soon.

And then she recalled her mother's young man who went to the Continent and who had written to her mother for all these years.

Would she? Could she?

Jane considered the situation. Given the circumstances, if their places were reversed, she would write to the man she'd loved twenty-three years earlier if she knew he were still unmarried and she was finally within traveling distance of him.

Yet, what of Charles Chatley? Jane didn't condone infidelity, but as she went back outside to sit on the front step and look at the sea, feeling daring without her gloves and hat, she knew it wasn't her place to pass judgment.

What was good for the goose, as they said, was good for the gander.

"SOMEONE MUST KNOW WHERE Jane has gone."

"Her mother knows," Owen said drolly, puffing on his cigar while he and Christopher's father sat in the Westings' new dining room after dinner. Burnley and his sister, Sophia, were guests, and Amanda, along with the Duchess, had taken Lady Sophia to the drawing room to sip port and wait for the men to come play cards.

Of course, Christopher would only be able to sit and listen to the fun, although his father was considering ways to make the cards "readable" to his son's fingers without the rest of the players being able to tell what the cards were.

"You are not amusing," Christopher pronounced. He had been shocked to learn Lady Emily Chatley had fled with her daughter to parts unknown. Shocked and pleased. In some regards, it made him a little less worried about Jane.

Yet, they might be anywhere from John O'Groats at the top of Scotland, to the toe of the Cornish coast. It had already been in the papers for a week how Lord Chatley had raged at the loss of his long-neglected wife, far more so than at the loss of his daughter for whom he now needn't fund a dowry.

Then there was the nephew, who the *ton* only just discovered had been thinking of marrying young Lady Jane Chatley. That made for mockery of epic proportions. Some cartoonist had drawn the two men, Chatley and Lowther, one larger, one smaller, wearing matching clothing, both staring out the front door of their home wondering where their women were.

Burnley assured Christopher it was more amusing than it sounded when he'd described it

When first hearing the news from Margaret, Christopher had experienced a moment's triumph—Jane had not wanted Bernard Lowther, after all. Then immediately afterward, he'd felt a fearful realization. He might never again be in Jane's company.

She'd done what she'd first told him she believed was for the best—shelving herself with a modicum of dignity.

Dammit! He didn't want her shelved, along with her vibrant laugh and quick mind. Not to mention her luscious body he'd only just begun to explore. He simply wanted *her*. All of her. For himself.

How could he find her when he couldn't see? He feared he really would have to rely on Owen.

When they entered the drawing room a few minutes later, the ladies were speaking French. Or Lady Sophia was speaking fluently, and Amanda and his mother were making a valiant attempt.

"Jane was right about the polish," Amanda said, and Christopher's ears perked up.

"What are you talking about?" he demanded.

Amanda frowned. "Do not snap at me, brother. I didn't drive Jane away. In fact, I went to her and thanked her. Did *you* ever thank her?"

He felt his face grow hot. He could have married her when she'd asked him and been living in absolute delight these past weeks instead of abject torment. But yes, he had thanked her.

"Do not berate your brother," his mother said. "At least, not in front of guests. No one here caused her to leave. Of that, I am certain."

"I know I was kind to her," his father said. "I even told her she was a welcome surprise, like a hedgehog."

Everyone exclaimed aloud again.

Why did his family always have to play out a scene from a Punch and Judy show instead of behaving normally?

"Just tell me what you meant about 'the polish,'" Christopher pleaded.

He knew Amanda was adjusting her skirts and looking around to make sure all eyes—except his, of course—were on her. She loved the attention.

"I stopped by the Chatley residence a few days before the ladies' mysterious disappearance," she began, as if this was going to be a long story for a winter's night. "Jane was ever so kind to me, and I wanted to give her my gratitude."

"Such a good girl," the duchess said, and Christopher was sure his sister was basking in their mother's admiration, however unwarranted.

"I mentioned how Lady Sophia was just back from France, I don't remember how you came up," she added quickly, obviously addressing Owen's sister, while making Christopher wonder exactly what Amanda had been up to. "And Jane said France puts polish on a young lady, or something to that affect. Does that help?"

"No," he said. "Not really."

"Maybe this will," his sister continued. "When I asked her if I would see her at the next ball, she said she would be trying a bit of the polish herself. So, there you go. Mystery solved."

"I believe she's right," his father said. "Why wouldn't our smart Lady Jane go to France?"

Why, indeed? Christopher thought. But France was easily two times as vast as Britain. If she was there, he could not imagine how he would locate her.

CHAPTER TWENTY-EIGHT

A month later, Jane found herself back on a train heading to Paris. Her mother longed to see the fashionable ladies, and Jane had a single-minded purpose—to find a blind inventor named Pierre François Victor Foucault.

They were determined to keep a modest existence while living in a nice apartment in one of the upscale quarters of an *arrondissement* on the north side of the Seine.

"In any case," her mother said, "even if our apartment is small, Parisians spend their time outdoors on the streets and in the busy cafes."

Jane smiled at her mother's knowledge gleaned from English newspapers. And then considered the mysterious letters from her long-ago love. They had definitely been corresponding in the past few weeks. Perhaps the blue-eyed man had told her more about Paris than she'd let on.

At the earliest possible opportunity, as soon as they'd settled into their second-floor apartment in a six-story building built around a courtyard, Jane dragged Lady Chatley to the Society for Encouraging National Industry. Jane had gleaned the name from the upcoming Great Exhibition's list of contributors for the Crystal Palace in

Hyde Park. The society, in turn, told her the whereabouts of Monsieur Foucault, a former student at the same school that Louis Braille later attended.

Monsieur Foucault was also a brilliant mechanic, as the exhibitor list described him. At Braille's request, he'd devised the Raphigraph machine she'd once mentioned to the Duke of Westing. It was still months before the Great Exhibition, but Jane was determined to procure a writing device for Christopher.

Finding the Frenchman's abode, with her mother at her side, Jane climbed the stairs with growing excitement. Soon, they had been served *café au lait* by his wife, Adélaïde, and had purchased one of his machines, which he called a piston board. It condensed the unwieldy Decapoint type—Braille's invention so sighted people and blind people could read the same text—into a smaller size so more words could fit on a page. It also allowed the blind to easily print letters.

Jane was beside herself with excitement. After arranging for it to be shipped directly to Grosvenor Square, London, she considered it a day well spent.

With it, Christopher would be able to create text legible to both the blind and the sighted. Moreover, he would be free of relying on someone to whom he had to dictate, thereby retrieving both his independence and his privacy, too. *He could even write love letters,* she thought before wondering why that nonsense filled her head. He would use it to write parliamentary acts.

She only wished she would be there when the device arrived. Just as she could only dream of ever being in the same room with him again.

Take heart, she admonished herself. *This was not the time to falter.*

A PACKAGE CAME FROM Paris, and Christopher was

practically jumping up and down like a child on Christmas Day, eager to have it opened!

Jane! It had to be from her as he knew no one else in France.

His father was reading the paper aloud to him in the library when their butler entered.

"This was just delivered for Lord Christopher, my lords. Postmarked *Paris, France*. Shall I open it?"

Even though he wouldn't be able to see whatever it was, Christopher's excitement doubled at the notion of her hands having touched whatever was inside. Maybe she had even made him something. At once, he was convinced it was a painting.

Of course, it could have no real bearing on his life, unless it were a case of brandy, and it was, indeed, big enough to be such. Or so his hands told him when he ran them over the wooden case the butler had placed on the table.

"How exciting," Lord Westing said. "Something from abroad for you, laddo."

"Yes, I heard, Father. Open it, please," Christopher struggled to keep his tone steady.

"We'll handle this, Reg," Lord Westing dismissed their butler.

In a moment, his father exclaimed in delight. "Why, I believe it is . . . yes, it is! There's a pamphlet all in French, created on the very machine itself, but it's clear what it is. How marvelous!"

"Father," Christopher was ready to explode. "What is it?"

"A writing machine for the blind. A Raphigraph."

Trying to imagine how the blind could write, Christopher couldn't concentrate for a moment on a strange machine he didn't understand. His thoughts kept wondering about Jane.

"Is there a note? Something from Lady Jane directly?"

He heard his father's hands rustling in the box. "No. I'm sorry."

Christopher set his disappointment aside. Jane had been thinking of him and had spent, no doubt, a great deal of money to procure this invention and send it across the Channel. The least he could do was appreciate it.

They spent the next hour playing with it. All Christopher had to do was use his right hand to depress the pistons, of which there were ten arranged in a fan shape, easily accessible. When he pushed them in different patterns, they produced the dots in the shape of letters. He wrote and handed the paper to his father who read it aloud.

Then his father tried it and wrote something, which he handed to Chris who ran his hands over the raised dots.

Tears sprung to his eyes as he silently read the words with his fingers:

You had better go find this young lady, bring her home, and marry her.

From your loving father.

Immediately, he wrote—*dear God, he could write again!*—to Owen Burnley telling him they would leave the next day for the Continent. If his friend couldn't go, he would go alone!

"BLASTED FRENCH," OWEN SAID too loudly as Christopher secured them a carriage from the port of Calais. Many cabriolets for hire awaited the ferry as it arrived from Dover, England, and they simply had to get in one without insulting the driver so terribly he dropped them off in Germany.

"Hush!" Christopher admonished, and not for the first time.

His friend spoke not a word of the Gallic tongue, carried a grudge about the Napoleonic Wars, and apparently suffered from a prolonged hangover as the trip had been so quickly proposed. He had groaned the entire time on the steamship, and was still groaning.

"No one will let us in their carriage if you look as though you are going to be sick on the upholstery."

"I'm breathing deeply, and I don't look sick," Owen assured him. "You are gesturing in the wrong direction," he added. "I'm waving down a driver now. This way."

Soon, they were traveling toward the residence of Monsieur Foucault, printed on the back of his explanatory pamphlet. *Had Jane made sure to include it on purpose? Or was it a lucky circumstance?*

Either way, after weeks of having no notion as to her whereabouts on the Continent and on the verge of hiring a private detective, Christopher was certain he would find her.

Monsieur Foucault turned out to be an interesting individual. Although his wife, a seamstress, was out, he was fully able to host Christopher and Owen, boiling water, preparing his coffee, and laying out some biscuits.

"You are completely blind, are you not, monsieur?" Christopher asked, when Owen explained what he was witnessing.

The man laughed. "Yes. Since the age of six. And you, monsieur, how long?"

Christopher tallied up the time. "Half a year." Six months since his world had changed, but slowly, he was getting some of it back.

They discussed things Foucault had learned at school, some things he'd discovered on his own. He gave Christopher sympathy and advice without pity.

"Your invention is amazing, monsieur. That's why I came. My friend sent it to me, and I need to find her to thank her."

"Mademoiselle Chatley was adamant I get the piston board to you as soon as I possibly could. You are pleased, yes?"

"Very," Christopher said. "It must have been expensive. If you tell me how much and how to find her, I can repay her."

"I see. I mean, I am blind, but some things I see as clearly as anyone. I am not sure it is for me to tell you the lady's location."

"Please, Monsieur Foucault. I beg you. I have been trying to find her for many weeks. I love her dearly and wish to marry her."

"Christ!" Owen exclaimed before adding, "We've been in France for barely a few hours and already you have picked up the emotional habits of the French."

Luckily, Foucault did not take offense. Instead, he laughed. "We are certainly a people ruled by our passions. There is nothing wrong with that. If my Adelaide were here, she would agree."

"Can you help me?" Christopher asked him. "For the sake of passion?"

After a brief hesitation, broken only by Owen muttering something under his breath, Foucault said, "The piston board was thirty-five francs. I know this lady must care for you deeply to spend such an amount."

"I have no idea how much that is in pound sterling," Owen protested.

"Hush!" Christopher waited for the information he needed.

"Your lady and her mother are staying in the fourth arrondissement. That's the right bank."

"That's all you know? Don't you have an address?" Christopher asked.

"They mentioned that in passing to my wife, conversing as women do. I did not ask because I was not delivering my machine to them. But I am fairly certain she said they are in the Quartier Saint-Germain. It is small. Not so hard to find two English ladies there."

"Thank you, monsieur."

A few minutes later when they were back in the hired carriage, Owen decided they had to find rooms for the night. They'd spent the previous evening at an inn in Dover and had already had a long day of travel.

Christopher, on the other hand, wanted to press on with their search.

"You do not know it, but it is already dusk, old chum," Owen said. "If you love me, you will let me eat and sleep. I promise, I will be up with the roosters and by your side."

"As my eyes," Christopher reminded him.

"As your eyes," Owen repeated, "and honored to be so. Tomorrow, we shall scour Paris's right bank and retrieve Lady Jane."

Christopher could hear the smile in his friend's voice.

"Very well. Find us two rooms."

"*Nice* rooms," Owen said, "On you. As well as a full dinner. Your treat."

"Anything else?" he asked, feeling better than he had in ages. He was in the same country as Jane at last.

"I would ask for a couple of those famous French courtesans, but I suppose the nature of this trip, and your newly pronounced love for Jane, preclude such amusements."

"Only for me. If you are determined to enjoy your night in such a manner, then for God's sake, ask a locale which brothels are safe. You don't want to bring the pox back home with you from some *maisons d'abattage*. Better yet, see if you can borrow another man's *lorette* for the night, a bit of a higher-class woman. You can ask the concierge at our inn."

"And you know this how?" Owen sounded a little in awe.

Christopher shrugged. "I'm not *Saint* Christopher, you know!"

Owen simply laughed.

JANE WENT OUT EARLY to the local boulangerie, as she did every morning. Each neighborhood had its own, as well as a patisserie and a bistro. She could imagine becoming large in her hips in the years to come because there was nothing like French baked goods in the morning.

Today, she'd also brought home some newspapers. It took them hours to decipher, and filled mostly with local news, but sometimes, there was a snippet of something international, particularly about English aristocracy or American political figures.

Truth be told, Jane wondered if she would ever learn anything about Christopher by reading the papers. Probably the only big news of an English marquess would be his marriage announcement, and that was something she didn't particularly want to read.

"I'm tired of coffee," her mother said when she came out of the bedroom in her dressing gown.

Seeing her mother in a state of déshabille, Jane was reminded of the Duchess of Westing's word *Bohemian*, which Her Grace had taught her and Christopher the first time she'd taken them to her studio. She couldn't imagine her mother ever leaving her bedroom in London in a state of undress, with her thick brown hair in a braid over her shoulder. Yet here, Lady Chatley thought nothing of lounging in her robe at all hours.

She supposed her mother deserved this respite from the constant vigilance of the *ton*. And nowhere was quite so relaxed as Paris, especially if one were a visiting foreigner.

"We can buy tea, Mummy. Why haven't we?"

Her mother sighed.

"What's wrong?" Jane asked her, setting still-warm croissants on a plate before brewing coffee.

"I hope we're doing the right thing," her mother confessed. "I mean, look at you, fetching food and making breakfast like a peasant."

Jane bit her lip to stop from laughing. They had already found a woman who would come nearly every day to prepare lunch and dinner and to help clean.

"I like doing for myself. You know that. Of course, we did the right thing. Aren't you happy, Mother?"

"I'm happy being with you. I just want the best for you. I always have. Will you marry a Frenchman?"

She said it with such distaste, Jane couldn't contain her laughter this time.

"Mummy, if I fell in love with a Frenchman, I would be happy to marry him. Then you would have grandchildren."

She set the table with creamy butter and preserves, along with fresh berries, and then poured them both coffee with cream. Next, Jane spread out the papers, keeping her translation book at hand.

She liked *Le Constitutionnel*, a paper of commerce and politics, but also literary interests and useful subjects, such as the train timetable. There were a few ads, which her mother would peruse. Mostly, Lady Chatley preferred the fashion magazines, of which there were many. She looked at the images and occasionally pointed to words, making Jane look them up.

However, when Jane opened *La Presse* to the page with news outside France, right before a large headline of "Californie," which seemed to be about a new territory granted statehood in America, Jane saw death notices of the notables. And her world spun.

Instantly light-headed, she thought the room was tilting under her chair, and she splayed her fingers on the tabletop to keep herself steady.

Dear God!

She stared at her mother.

After a moment, Lady Chatley glanced at her, and froze, her face paling with fear.

"Jane, dear, what is wrong?"

Should she tell her? Of course she must! It was irrational to think she wouldn't.

"It's father." She took a steadying breath. "He's dead."

CHAPTER TWENTY-NINE

Christopher climbed the stairs to the apartment of the "English women," and he felt as if he had traversed a massive desert, one of extreme longing for Jane Chatley, and, at long last, he had nearly reached her lush oasis.

Foucault had been correct. It had taken but a few queries in the quarter at the types of shops women would visit, and they'd been given an address. Jane and her mother certainly had no *hôtel privé*—the French equivalent of a mansion in the city—but they had a well-appointed apartment nonetheless, in a building with a respected concierge.

The apartment square had a large double, wooden door closing it off from the street. Through this, everyone must enter, and it was fiercely guarded by the concierge, a gatekeeper of sorts, who, along with a porter, oversaw everything and everyone in the apartments. She also collected and distributed mail, accepted deliveries, and kept out those who didn't belong.

In Jane's case, the concierge was a slightly suspicious woman, who nevertheless had her hand out as soon as she realized she had two English lords on her doorstep.

For a few francs, she told Christopher and Owen which door in the courtyard to enter and how many stairs to climb, and let them pass. *So much for security.*

Upon reaching Jane's apartment, Owen knocked and, in a few moments, Christopher heard footsteps approaching. They were Jane's, he was certain.

When the door opened, he heard her gasp and his heart nearly burst, especially as he could almost see a shadowy outline of her.

His vision had changed, although neither improving nor growing worse for months. Disclosing that fact was for another day. However, even with his glasses on, he could make out a shape. Jane's shape.

And then, she was in his arms. Exactly how it happened, he was unsure. He may have taken a step forward, but he was fairly certain she had launched herself at him, and he had caught her.

"You are here," she murmured against his jacket. "How can this be? How can you be here?"

He said nothing as he drew her close, then raised his hands to cradle her beloved face, and nearly poked her in the eye and in the nose before he settled his palms on her cheeks, holding her still and taking her mouth with his.

This proper English gentleman found himself kissing a proper English lady in the doorway of a Parisian apartment, and didn't give a damn who saw them.

Until he heard her mother exclaim loudly behind Jane, and then, belatedly, Owen, who must have been getting an eyeful, coughed to warn them.

Still, neither of them moved. He rested his forehead against Jane's and breathed in the familiar scent of her. Petals of pinks and a little bergamot oil. Light, beautiful, sensual, and warm—just like the lady, herself.

"I love you," he said.

"I love you, too," she said back.

Her mother shrieked. Next to him, Owen laughed, and finally, Jane pulled him inside.

Jane let Christopher hold her hand, even as they sat side-by-side and conversed in a group, with her mother seated on the other side of her and Lord Burnley in the spare chair. Their small sitting parlor was filled.

Her heart was still pounding, and she thought everyone else in the room could probably hear it.

He was here! He loved her!

She wanted to speak with him alone, but they had other matters to attend to first.

"We read only this morning that my father had passed away. We don't even know from what cause?"

"My condolences to both of you," Christopher said. "I didn't know."

"Condolences are unnecessary," her mother said surprisingly. "We wouldn't be here in Paris if not for him."

Jane wasn't sure what to say to that. She hadn't wished her father dead, but she could not pretend to feeling any sorrow, either. Thus, why should her mother, who had suffered far more by his odious behavior?

"My father made life somewhat difficult for both my mother and myself," Jane said, trying to be diplomatic so as not to shock these gentlemen who had better parental relations.

"You don't need to explain," Lord Burnley said. "No one who saw how the Earl of Chatley treated his family would blame you for not wanting to cover yourself in black and hang crepe upon every mirror."

"Still," Jane said, "in the interest of respect, we shall recognize a mourning period, won't we, Mummy?" Jane wasn't keen on wearing black for the next year, but would follow her mother's lead.

"As for the crepe, the house is no longer mine to worry about." The countess didn't sound the least bit unhappy over the prospect of having just lost her home.

"I wonder if cousin Bernard has moved into Father's suite yet."

"While you were away," Christopher remarked, "your cousin asked a young lady for her hand in marriage a few weeks ago. Miss Swintree, if I recall the name correctly."

"I hadn't heard," Jane said. "I suppose Bernard was not important enough to end up in the Parisian society pages when he was simply heir to his uncle's title. I believe I once introduced Lord Fowler to Miss Swintree. He didn't care for her."

"Speaking of your Lord Fowler," Christopher continued, "he has become engaged to—"

"Lady Brethrens!" Jane exclaimed and clapped her hands.

"Yes, just so," Lord Burnley confirmed.

"I am so happy for him," Jane said. She was exceedingly happy for herself, too, at that moment.

"Will you come back to England with us?" Christopher asked, giving her hand a surreptitious squeeze.

She hesitated only to glance at her mother, who had a pensive look upon her face.

"We had decided to live in France for years," Jane told him. "It is a shock to realize we can go back at once. Mummy, are there ramifications of our flight?"

"I don't believe so. With your father gone, there is no one to press charges against me for desertion, and, better yet, no one to force you into marriage with anyone whom you don't wish. If he left us anything in his will, then I expect we shall still be entitled to it. However, I am not returning to England just yet."

Jane felt Christopher squeeze her hand again, and then she exchanged a look with Lord Burnley. She wasn't sure what her mother intended.

"I have a letter to post," Lady Chatley further declared. "First, Jane, I need a word with you in private."

In a moment, after excusing themselves, Jane and her mother closeted themselves in her mother's bedroom.

"You love Lord Westing," her mother said bluntly.

"Yes."

"Why didn't you tell me? I asked you about your feelings for him before."

"I could see no point. If I pursued a marriage with him, you would have been left to the loneliness of a life with a terrible husband, followed by eviction from the new earl."

Jane's mother said nothing, only grasping her daughter tightly.

"I have written to my . . . friend. More than once since we arrived. His name is Daniel. He lives not far. Now that I am a widow, I intend to meet with him."

Jane felt a bubble of happiness. The pangs of guilt over having kept her mother anchored to her father for the past twenty-one years—guilt she hadn't even fully realized she carried—evaporated.

"I am so happy for you. May I meet with him, too?"

Her mother smiled, looking years younger. "Yes, I would like that. Do you think your marquess will delay his return trip? You do intend to go home with him, don't you? And marry him?"

"I suppose I'd better wait until he asks me." They laughed together.

"I will invite Lord Burnley to accompany me to the post office, and let you two speak privately."

"You will leave us alone? I'm not sure Lord Westing will approve of that. He's very proper, especially when it comes to my reputation."

"We'll see," her mother said. "Things are different in Paris."

Her mother was right, as usual.

In a few minutes, Jane found herself alone with Christopher. It had seemed an impossible dream only that morning. And now, it was an incredible gift.

"We must talk about the future," he said, "but I hate to waste time speaking when I can kiss you instead."

"Maybe we can talk quickly and still have time to kiss after."

His laughter, so husky and masculine, sent a shiver down her spine.

"Or we could start with a kiss and then talk," he offered. "Are we alone?"

In answer, she slid her hands behind his head and drew him down, letting him latch onto her lips, before she opened her mouth to him.

Instantly, her body was tingling, as if her blood were humming through her veins.

Without thinking, she drew back enough to speak. "Do I make you ache, the way you make me?"

Without answering, he reached up and pulled her hands loose, and then placed her palm on the front of his pants. Then he grasped her face with his hands and deepened the kiss.

Jane could feel the throbbing of his shaft against her fingers, and longed to touch his bare skin.

When he had ravished her mouth, he said, "This is torture."

"Agreed."

With her hand still on his male member, she let him run his fingers down the length of her neck and then slip them inside the front of her gown, touching her as best he could.

"I have ached for you every damn day since the first time we kissed," he confessed.

She nearly told him how she touched herself at night when she was alone in her bed, recalling the things he'd done to her body.

"I suppose we should talk," she said.

"Yes. Why didn't you tell me about your cousin?"

That was not the question she expected. Besides, it was difficult to carry on a rational discussion with the tips of his fingers on her breasts, and her hand cupped around his shaft, so she drew back.

"For what purpose?"

Christopher made a sound of exasperation. "So I could help you."

"How?" she persisted.

He tilted his head. "You are being obstinate. I would have married you had I known your father was forcing you to marry your cousin."

"I understand." She sighed. "You would have asked for my hand to rescue me from a bad marriage. I didn't want that. I wanted you to propose because you intended to ask anyway. Anything else would be a sad affair. There are others I could have married if I wanted simply to avoid my cousin."

Or there would have been if she'd cared to let them get close.

"Instead, I chose to take my own path. Do you know why?"

"Yes," he answered without hesitation. "Because you are a headstrong, willful woman who always has to do things her way, which may be the right way, but still. And without compromise."

She laughed. "Oh dear! I can't tell if you are insulting me. That sounds half complimentary but also critical."

"Because I nearly lost you. Would it truly have been better to do it your way than to let me help you so we were together for the rest of our lives?"

"I did ask you to marry me once," Jane reminded him. "You turned me down."

He remained silent, looking thoughtful.

"I suppose I wanted you to want me because you couldn't live without me. I certainly don't want to be your *mission*. I want to be your husband and take you for my wife for no other reason than we can't bear to be apart."

"Then I suppose we should marry," she told him. "For that is certainly how I feel about you."

He smiled. "I used to only trust what I could see. How limiting." He stroked her cheek. "Now I trust what I can hear in your voice."

"And what about what you can feel?" She placed his palm over her racing heart.

"Yes, I definitely trust what I can feel. I would marry you this instant in a Parisian mayoralty, but my mother would kill me if I don't let her attend our wedding."

"Agreed," Jane said. "My mother has dreamed of helping me pick out a dress and trousseau since I was in pigtails."

"Then you will come back with me tomorrow?"

Jane shook her head, even knowing he couldn't see her.

"For the past twenty-one years my mother has given over her life to caring for me. Finally, she has a chance for love, and I wish to support her. Will you wait for me?"

"Only if I can wait here in Paris. I am *not* going home without you."

BURNLEY LEFT A FEW days later, and Christopher remained in their inn, only a few streets away from Jane and her mother's apartment. He thought he might be frightened, a blind man in a foreign country, but he wasn't. He had come too far to let a little thing like the darkness of Paris stop him from enjoying himself with the woman he loved.

He spent his days with Jane, strolling in the Tuileries Garden, attending the Opéra-National, and dining at the famed Café Anglais on the corner of the Rue de Marivaux. She never seemed to grow tired of describing things when he asked, just as his mother had said, and sometimes, he could almost "see" as well with her words as he could with his eyes.

They were dining in perhaps the most expensive restaurant in the city, La Maison Dorée, famed for its food but more so for its design, its artwork, and the gilding both on the exterior and inside. Entering through the exclusive doorway on the Rue Laffite, they were seated in a private "cabinet."

Enthusiastically, Jane told him of the gold lacing on the balconies and balustrades, of the men and women dressed as if they were at the theatre. He smiled at her joyful descriptions, thinking himself a lucky man to have fallen for a woman with such a pleasant voice.

She'd just finished telling him what was on the menu—*poulet de grain à la broche* and *filet de boeuf bouquetiere*—and marveled over the eighty thousand bottles of wine beneath their feet in two floors of a wine cellar.

"I only want one bottle," he joked when a figure appeared at their table, and he turned toward it.

Jane gasped.

"What is it?" Christopher asked.

"You turned when the waiter arrived. Can you *see* him?"

He sighed. He didn't want to get her hopes up. His own had risen and crashed so many times, he understood how terribly disappointing it could be.

"I am aware of shadows," he told her. "At first, only in the brightest sunlight, then a couple months ago, I realized everything wasn't absolutely as black as it had been."

"Do you think your sight is coming back?"

He shook his head. "I no longer taunt myself with such notions. If it does, I will feel blessed, but if it doesn't, I am at peace with my situation."

He felt her hand rest on top of his. "You are the bravest man I know."

Lifting her hand to his lips, he kissed it. "I am the luckiest man I know."

CHAPTER THIRTY

Christopher smelled smoke, which wouldn't have been alarming in itself, except he was climbing the stairs to the Chatleys' apartment and had never smelled it strongly in the stairwell before.

It was an ordinary evening, and he had arrived early to take Jane to dinner when he caught the scent. Moreover, he realized he could hear screams somewhere close.

Reaching her landing at a run, he pounded on her door, at the same time jiggling the latch, but it was locked.

When there was no answer, he put his shoulder to it and broke it down. More smoke was in the apartment than in the hallway. He could tell by how his lungs burned each time he drew a breath. He began to cough.

"Jane," he called out, and then he heard her coughing.

Not as familiar with her apartment as his own room at the inn, still, it no longer bothered him to move quickly through places he couldn't see. He traversed the front room and entered the hallway to the private rooms behind.

"Jane," he yelled again, wondering if she had fainted.

"I'm here," she called out, coughing harshly. "I can't see. I was trying to pack a bag."

"Forget the bag! Where is the fire? And where is your mother?"

"The fire is coming from the courtyard, I think, but I believe someone's rooms have caught alight somewhere below us. I shut the windows at the back, but the smoke seems to be coming through the floor." She stopped to cough violently.

"My mother is with Daniel," she added. "She's safe."

They heard a loud pop, as if a timber or an entire floor had been compromised.

"We must get out of here. Now," he ordered.

She coughed again. "I can't see,' she repeated, sounding terrified. "I blew out the lamps in case they added to the fire danger, and the smoke is terribly thick."

By following her voice, and her coughing, he found her at last, realizing he was having trouble breathing, too.

"Grab some cloth, anything, and hold it to your face. Then reach out your hand to me."

She did as he asked, and he caught hold of her hand, then yanked her down to her knees.

"What are you doing?"

"The smoke rises. We can breathe better down here. If our hands lose contact, grab my sleeve, my pant leg, anything, just stay with me."

In a few minutes, even though he could feel the heat under his hands from the fire below them, they were at her door and out on the landing. Standing, he drew her up beside him, and they ran down the steps to hit a crowd of people outside.

He tightened his grip on her hand so as not to lose her.

"Get us to the street," he directed, and then let her lead them in the dusk through the throng to the wooden doors that guarded the courtyard.

"The fire brigade is here," Jane told him as they stood in the street and breathed deeply. The cool evening air was a welcome relief.

"We'll go back to my rooms and send word to your mother that you are safe."

JANE FOUND HERSELF IN Christopher's suite of two rooms, a living area and a bed chamber. And she started to shake.

"I'm so cold," she said.

"I put out the hearth fire thinking I would be out for the next few hours. Let me light it again." He set down his cane before efficiently lighting a new fire in the grate. Soon, the room was growing warmer.

"Where are you?" he asked as he stood up.

"Here," Jane said, still standing in the middle of the room, unable to move, watching him as he found his way to her.

His arms went around her.

"You're still shaking. I don't think it's from the cold. You had a nasty shock, and it's coming over you now. Come, sit by the fire. I've got some brandy."

Jane's normal instinct to do for herself and for others had evaporated. She let him lead her to a chair, still experiencing moments of sheer terror. Occasionally, she jumped thinking her mother would be worried, then recalling Christopher had already sent word through the concierge downstairs.

Their apartment might be gone, or it might have been saved. All their belongings would smell like smoke. But she was alive.

"You saved my life. I was stupidly packing bags, letting myself get overcome with smoke, and then I couldn't even think how to get out when I couldn't see."

"All perfectly natural," he assured her and then pressed a glass into her hand. "Take a sip. Or two. Drink it all down. I promise you'll feel warm inside and out, and it will calm your nerves."

He crouched down beside her, and she sipped, coughed, then drank it all down and handed him the glass.

"Do you feel better?"

"Yes." In fact, she did.

Jane kept reminding herself she was perfectly safe. She could see the small fire dancing merrily in the clean grate and knew nothing bad was happening. Moreover, Christopher was with her.

He stood and put her glass on the small sideboard. "I'll go downstairs and see if they have rooms for you and your mother."

"Wait," she said urgently and stood.

"Are you all right?"

"Yes. But don't leave." She touched his face. "Kiss me. Please."

He groaned. "That's all I've wanted to do since we closed the door, but, Jane, I don't want to take advantage of you right now. You are fragile."

She laughed. "No, I'm not. I'm alive. And we're alone. Kiss me."

He yanked off his spectacles and put them on the sideboard and then drew her close.

When his mouth claimed hers, she knew it wouldn't be enough. Tonight, she intended to give herself to the man she loved. After all, first an explosion nearly took him, then a fire almost killed her. The good Lord was practically shouting at them to hurry along.

Christopher clearly needed no second invitation. His hands were already in her hair, messing it up and feeling for the pins which held her coiled braids in place. As soon as he had the plaits down, he ran his fingers through them, undoing the skeins until her hair was completely loose around her shoulders and down her back.

"I've wanted to do that for ages," he confessed. "And this." He began the long process of undressing her, but after undoing the buttons at her cuffs and beginning on those down her back, he became impatient and started to kiss her again.

As their tongues danced and their hands roamed up and down each other's backs, Jane realized with every breath, she was breathing in the acrid scent of smoke.

Would their first lovemaking be tainted with that unpleasant aroma?

Pressing her hands against his chest, she pushed away slightly.

"Yes," he said, sounding wretched. "You must stop me or you will be utterly, irrevocably compromised."

Jane giggled nervously at the thought. "I'm *not* stopping you," she promised. "I intend to be fully compromised before this night is done. I was simply wondering if you could ask for a bath to be brought up."

She watched him swallow.

"Yes. An excellent idea."

Twenty minutes later, the porter's son carried in the last of the steaming water buckets in his bulging arms and left them alone with soap and towels.

"Your floor is going to get wet," she told him, "when we do my hair, but if I don't, the smoke will linger in it for days."

"Just tell me how I can help."

She let him continue undoing the buttons down her back, having worn an impractical gown, never thinking she would need to undress without her mother or her useful button hook.

Soon, Jane stood in her drawers and chemise, which she quickly stripped off before stepping into the hot water.

"It is unfair," he muttered. "I haven't keenly mourned my eyesight in weeks, not until this moment."

She laughed. "It has made it easier on me, I must say. Come closer."

He did. "Shall I kneel and tend you like a maid?"

"No," she said, picking up the washcloth and starting to bathe. "Why don't you tend me like Christopher, Marquess of Westing?"

To her amazement, he began to undress, removing his cravat, collar, and cuffs, then his shirt. He stood before her with his chest bare and let her look her fill.

Then he knelt down by the tub, stuck his arms in the water, and slid the cloth from her hands.

"Let me," he said, and she did.

It was heavenly. He skimmed the soapy cloth over her sensitive skin, lingering in her most intimate place.

Her head back, Jane moaned, causing him to abandon the cloth entirely and let his fingers discover her heat.

"I want to taste your nipples, but I might drown," Christopher pointed out. And she grinned.

"This is delightful, but difficult. Let me soap my hair and—good, there's one bucket of clean water left to rinse it. Then it's your turn."

"Capable Jane," he said, but he didn't look the least bothered when, in a few minutes, she switched places with him, and, after removing his pants and drawers, he stood in the bathtub, looking to her like Michelangelo's famed David.

"You're peeking at me, aren't you?" he asked.

"Yes, and you are magnificent." Her first look at a man's naked flesh, real, not in a book, nor a statue either, and she was not disappointed.

"You look more . . . powerful than any drawing I've ever seen."

He lowered himself into the cooling water with a satisfied grin on his handsome face.

"These towels smell like lavender," she said, "and now my hair does, too."

"My comb is in the bedroom on the vanity," he offered. "You can sit by the fire and start drying your hair."

"Yes, my lord."

"You're being saucy," Christopher said. "I like that."

And then he submerged himself, and she went to find his comb, marveling over the intimacy of bathing in the same room with him, as if they were already lovers. Oddly, she felt not the least bit awkward, only excited with anticipation of what would come next.

His bedroom was small but with nice furnishings, a four-poster bed and thick mattress, and a very soft carpet under foot. *Perfectly befitting a duke's son,* she supposed. It was worlds apart from her apartment.

She'd stopped thinking about the fire until that very moment, and she'd stopped shaking, too. Christopher had been the balm she needed.

"I'm getting out now," he informed her, and she hurried back into the sitting room to watch him emerge, like a male Venus from the water.

"You're peeking again, aren't you?"

"Isn't that why you called me in here?" Jane asked.

He chuckled. "Where are the towels?"

Handing one to him, she realized it was the first time he'd asked for help since he'd broken her door down.

"You are a wonder, my lord."

"Am I? Shall I take off my towel again?"

She laughed. "Oh, yes! In fact, I'll forget about the endless process of drying my hair by the fire. I'll just scrub it with my towel and then—"

"And then?" he prompted.

"I hope you will take me into your bedroom."

"Are we alone?" he asked, grinning broadly.

THEY FELL TOGETHER ONTO the counterpane. Christopher rolled her under him and raised himself upon his arms above her.

"Is it too cold in here?" he asked.

"Despite your wet hair dripping onto my shoulder, I am quite warm. Your body is like a blanket."

"I assure you, my body is *not* like a blanket, which is warm and soft." He nudged her with his erect shaft, until he nestled between her thighs. "I am more like coal, boiling hot and rock hard. Yet I will keep you from catching chill in any case."

She giggled. He loved that sound.

"You do smell like lavender," he said, kissing her shoulder, then her neck.

"As do you."

"I want to kiss all of you at once. I don't know where to start."

She pulled his head down until their lips met. Even as her mouth opened under his, her legs spread farther, and the tip of his shaft seemed to be drawn between her damp folds.

It was too soon. He didn't want her memory of their first time to be one of pain. It would take only a few minutes of restraint on his part to get her so ready, she would barely feel the initial twinge as he broke her virginal barrier.

"Begin with everything you've done to me before and then add the finale," she instructed.

He blinked. *Everything he'd done to her before? The finale?*

His cock throbbed at her words.

What a minx!

He kissed his way from her mouth to her chin and then lower. Her collarbone was delicate, he stopped to feather it with light kisses before nibbling down to her breasts. He paused with his head a breath from her left nipple.

"Christopher," she said exasperated, and he felt her lift herself off the bed, pushing her breast to his mouth.

"What color are your nipples?" he asked against her skin.

She answered immediately. "They are ruddy, but not pink, more of a blush color with an undertone of fawn. Can you picture them?"

His mouth went dry, and he licked his lips. "Perfectly."

Then he latched on, hearing her gasp as he settled down to worship her body. First one nipple, then he plucked at the other one, feeling her hips buck against the restraint of his body pressing down upon them.

"*Ohh,*" she sighed. "This is lovely."

Her words brought him out of his mindless stupor, and he slid one of his hands between them while continuing to tug and tease at her nipples with his mouth and teeth.

"Yes," she hissed as he slipped a finger between her moist curls and touched her.

"You are so wet," he intoned. All her passion, like sweet honey, awaited him.

Gently at first, he stroked in circles around her nubbin while pressing the heel of his hand to her mound as it rose to meet him.

"Yes," she said again, and he could hear how close she was to unraveling.

Continuing to stroke near her bud, he slid his finger into her slick passage, and in an instant, she was riding his hand and crying out her pleasure.

He could wait no longer. His shaft throbbed, his lower back ached, his ballocks pulsed. Guiding himself once more into position, while she was still wet and open to him, he slid inside her. Her legs encircled his hips, and her hand grasped hold of his shoulders.

"Please," she begged.

Lady Jane Chatley, the embodiment of his fantasies for half a year, was begging him.

Good God! He could barely breathe. And he was trying to go slowly so as not to cause her pain.

He hoped it wouldn't bring her pleasure to a screeching halt when he—

She sunk her fingers into his buttocks, and he surged into her, until he was seated as far as he could go.

"*Arr,*" he cried out with sheer elation.

"*Umm,*" she moaned in abject pleasure.

He drew back, and she hissed until he thrust forward again. Back and forth, feeling her hips rise each time to meet his.

Had there ever been anything so perfect as their coupling?

Her body was so tight, squeezing him until he was panting with the effort not to climax too soon, and then, there was no choice. He had to let go.

With another roar, he spent deep inside her, while her hands and her legs still wrapped around him.

He hoped they could go more slowly next time.

"That was exquisite," she said, her voice muffled underneath him, and he recalled his manners, rolling to the side, with one of his legs still across hers.

"I hope I didn't hurt you, or squash you," he added. "I'm sorry if I came too quickly."

"I don't understand," Jane said. "I felt a tremendous release and then you did, too."

"You would have felt it again if I'd been more patient."

She hesitated, and he stroked her shoulder and down along her arm, unable to keep from touching her smooth skin, even as he seemed to raise gooseflesh.

"Really?" She sounded doubtful. "I can have that feeling more than once during the same . . . session?"

"Yes. Next time, you'll see." Reaching down, he drew up the counterpane from where they'd kicked it to the bottom of the bed and covered her. With her wet hair and the fire untended in the other room, she might be getting chilled.

Then he stretched out again beside Jane. *He was lying beside Jane!* He would count his blessings except there were too many.

"You did agree to marry me, didn't you?"

She hesitated. "You didn't actually ask me."

Good Lord! He'd botched the most important question of his life. He had best rectify that at once.

He laced his fingers through hers. "Will you marry me?"

"Yes," she answered immediately.

"And you won't change your mind, my lady?"

"Why would I?" Jane squeezed his hand and yawned.

"Just say 'no, my lord.'"

"No, my lord."

She yawned again, and he followed suit, not realizing he was drifting off to sleep until the pounding on his sitting room door awakened him sometime later.

CHAPTER THIRTY-ONE

Five months after she'd first set foot in France, Jane was back on a steamboat, heading for Folkestone, England, this time with Christopher, her mother, and her mother's fiancé, the Viscount Daniel Graham. Lady Chatley and Lord Graham had decided to have a small registry wedding and then divide their time between London and Paris.

Her mother laughed a lot nowadays, smiled even more, and let the handsome man with the violet blue eyes hold her hand in public.

Jane liked the quiet, tall viscount who patiently taught them French words whenever they faltered in public and who spent the evenings conversing with Christopher about the current state of the French republican government under President Louis-Napoléon Bonaparte.

After being discovered in Christopher's bed, Jane's reputation was at long last destroyed. And her mother, of all people, seemed the happiest about finally catching her daughter with a man. And a marquess of all men!

Lady Chatley had taken one look at Jane wrapped in Christopher's dressing gown and clapped her hands, thrilled her daughter was going to be a marchioness and, some day, a duchess. Lord Graham's cheeks had gone bright red, and he'd retreated to the hallway of the inn.

Christopher dictated a letter to his parents informing them of his engagement to Jane. That had been a week past, and now, they were all returning home.

She and her mother would take lodgings in a Mayfair apartment and then send a missive to the new Earl of Chatley and determine the lay of the land.

Watching the channel pass swiftly under the hull of the boat, with her fiancé at her elbow, Jane smiled each time she recalled losing her innocence to Christopher.

Would they truly wait for the wedding night to experience such intimacy again?

"Are you pleased to be returning to England?" he asked her.

"She is smiling quite broadly," her mother answered for her. "I think we are both happy."

Jane blushed, as her thoughts were definitely not about England.

AFTER AN ENGAGEMENT OF four months, not too long as to drive the happy couple to distraction, and not too short as to raise eyebrows, Jane and Christopher were married in St. George's Church, a stone's throw from where she grew up on Hanover Square.

Christopher liked the fact he knew what it looked like already from worshiping there and attending other weddings in the old church, which held its first service in 1725.

"It's plain but elegant," her mother said when they first discussed the possibility.

"Christopher said it puts the focus on God and on the bride on her wedding day," Jane reminded her when she was alone with her mother. What's more, there was plenty of room in the spacious aisle, side galleries, and pew boxes for all the Westing and Chatley wedding guests.

"Plus, the stained glass makes up for any lack of ornamentation, don't you think?" Jane asked.

"Now that you have your marriage settlement in place," her mother declared, referring to the contract she'd insisted be drawn up allowing Jane to keep her own money, "I am entirely content."

Christopher had been not only willing but insistent she have a settlement contract, making Jane entirely certain of their future happiness.

And since, against all expectation, her father had left both his wife and daughter enough to live happily if frugally, neither Lady Chatley nor Jane need worry about the fickle hand of fate.

In the interim before Jane's wedding, her mother threw all decorum to the wind and married her viscount within a month of returning to England, and no one in the *ton* could blame her. Of course, she had a marriage settlement drawn up for herself as well, although it seemed to Jane that Viscount Graham was going to cherish his new bride for every possible moment of each day. They were adorable.

Jane lived with them until her own wedding day, where upon she moved into her new home on Arlington Street. The Duke and Duchess of Westing gifted their son the spacious townhouse nestled in a corner between Green Park and St. James's Park.

The duchess seemed particularly pleased at its location between her home and her Chelsea studio, and Christopher warned his new bride their favorite watercolorist would undoubtedly be dropping in at every opportunity.

"I don't mind. I love your mother," Jane assured him.

On a cold, rainy March evening, Christopher and Jane hosted a party a week after they married when she was truly settled in. The best part about their home was its short distance to Marlborough House where their romance began.

"We can creep onto the lawn," Christopher said, "if it ever stops raining, and re-enact the moment I first knew you were the one for me."

She squeezed his arm. "That is a bald-faced lie, my lord."

He drew her close, even as party guests were entering their parlor. "Do you remember that moment when you stepped toward me on the terrace? Everything changed for me in that instant."

"I remember," she whispered. "It was the first time you truly 'saw' me."

"And I loved what I saw. I still do."

He bent low and kissed her to the cheers of those already present and witnessing the happy newlyweds.

"I have something for you," the duke told Jane, holding out a large box.

"After everything you've already given us," she said, smiling at her new father-in-law, "you shouldn't have."

"He tried to give it to me," Amanda said, tossing her curls over her shoulder as she passed by to take a seat in the parlor.

"No, no," said the duke, turning slightly red. "Not the *same* one. Another one."

The Duchess of Westing scolded her daughter. "Amanda, don't embarrass your father."

"Now, I am dying of curiosity," Christopher said, as Jane opened the lid.

"A parasol, and it's lovely, too! It will keep the sun off perfectly in the summer." The colors were muted and tasteful, and Jane couldn't see why her new sister-in-law would scoff at the gift.

"Open it," Amanda said.

Jane moved into the center of the room and opened it. Then she burst out laughing.

The duchess and Amanda joined in.

"Tell me," Christopher pleaded.

"Well, it is most unusual," Jane began. "It has peepholes made of glass sewn into it."

"Clever, don't you think?" the duke asked. "I don't know what's funny about it. You can see where you're going. As soon as I spied it in the patent office, I ordered one. I mean two, one for each of my girls."

Jane's heart filled to bursting. Even if the man was fibbing and had presented the same parasol twice, he had publicly stated she was like a daughter to him.

"Thank you, Your Grace. I shall use it every day," she promised.

"And the sunlight will go right through the glass holes and burn your skin to a crisp," Amanda said.

"The glass might even magnify the sun's effects," Christopher pointed out.

"What?" the duke exclaimed, pausing to examine the parasol. "I didn't think of that."

"Oh, Father," Amanda said, and they all laughed again.

"It may not be the most practical thing," Jane said, "but it was very considerate."

"I have something else for you, but it will take longer to give you. I have workmen coming tomorrow."

"Father," Christopher warned, and Jane couldn't help but think of the gas stove incident. It was probably on all their minds even though the Marquess of Westing could more clearly see shapes than he had before, yet still no colors.

"Like *chiaroscuro* all the time," he'd told her when describing it.

"This time," the Duchess of Westing declared, "my husband actually has a good idea."

"Then why wouldn't you let me install it in our house?" the duke complained.

"While they argue, will you serve wine or champagne?" Amanda wanted to know.

Jane rang for wine before dinner, and then described to Christopher the plans his father had brought with him.

"The diagram says it is a fire-escape. There are numerous ropes and pulleys that will hang on the outside of our home . . . at *every* window," Jane added, feeling a little less than enthusiastic. "And a basket for lowering us and . . . our . . . children to the street."

Her cheeks warmed. She hadn't thought about having a baby yet, but there were two drawn into the illustration.

"Another brilliant invention from the patent office," Christopher surmised. "I believe I recall you mentioning it, Father."

"After what you went through in Paris," the duke said, "I knew you'd like to have peace of mind."

"Christopher was magnificent in the fire," Jane reminded them. "Completely calm while leading me to safety."

"You are too little to remember when Parliament burned, first the House of Lords, and then the Commons. Within hours, we all realized there was no stopping it. People were mesmerized by the size of the fire," the duke recalled. "Some watched from boats and the rest of us by the bridge. We could do nothing but stare at the conflagration as it took the Palace of Westminster."

"Father, I was eight," Christopher reminded him. "I remember it well, although Jane might not. The smoke and the smells hung over the city for days."

"Weeks, my boy. All the historical relevance and artifacts gone because of careless workmen burning tally sticks. Tally sticks! It was a terrible sight to see. For a short while, they thought it might have been from a gas explosion, too, or even careless servants at Howard's Coffee House. Wonderful little place, right inside the palace. They had the most delicious fruitcake. *Hmm.*" His Grace fell silent a moment, perhaps contemplating the moistness and delicacy of the cake.

"Father, your point?"

"That fire was sixteen years ago, and still, the Commons Chamber won't be finished for another year or so. But look, we've rebuilt our home in half a year, better than ever. Everything good as new."

Not quite everything, Jane mused, despite how well Christopher had adapted to his situation, better than anyone could have hoped when recalling the angry, withdrawn man of a year earlier. No one would think to call him *Lord Darkness* ever again.

EPILOGUE

In December, the Duchess of Westing exclaimed from the doorway late one afternoon while they were visiting his parents, "Turner is dead," before she ran into the room and collapsed on the sofa.

"I saw men at the entrance to his home when I was returning from sketching, and I inquired as to the hullabaloo."

She put her head back, eyes closed, and placed her arm over her head in dramatic repose.

"I hoped he was unveiling a new work or announced a new show, so I went over to ask."

"'He's left us, Your Grace,' one of the men told me. Then he added, 'Wretched cholera.'"

Jane gasped.

"Naturally, I backed away and covered my face with my sleeve," the duchess continued. "But nothing can be done for that great man. I am terribly saddened."

It was Christopher who found the bright spot, reminding his mother of what Turner had left behind for all of the world to enjoy.

"His paintings are his legacy, and we are fortunate he was so prolific. He has made English art an international success. And you shall add to that legacy."

Jane thought he was laying it on a bit thick, but the duchess perked up and asked what they were having for dinner.

When they retired to their own home that night, Jane marveled at her husband's laughter as he recalled something his father said or at the way his sister had half a dozen suitors on a string.

"You are a joyful man, Lord Westing."

"Thank you, Lady Westing. You give me no reason to be otherwise."

And as he often did, Christopher started to undress her. His hands skimmed over her body as he unfastened her fichu and touched the swell of her breasts before he unclipped her belt and encircled her waist with his broad hands to hold her close a moment, and then patiently, he undid her buttons before sliding her gown down her shoulders.

With this evening ritual, Christopher awakened her passions, which she knew he would dutifully satisfy.

Tonight, however, he paused, cupping her breasts in his hands before sliding his fingers over her bare stomach and thighs.

After a brief, poignant hesitation, he asked her, "Do you have something to tell me?"

Her heartbeat sped up, and she hesitated.

In the next moment, he swept her off her feet, holding her naked in his arms.

"Wife, have you been hiding something?"

She giggled as he carried her to the bed.

"I don't need to see you clearly to know your body has changed." He placed her gently on their big, soft mattress, and she scooted back to the headboard. He climbed on after her, grabbing hold of her ankle and working his way up, as she laughed delightedly.

"You cannot hide from me, Marchioness."

"I never shall, my lord."

He rose over her, a hand on either side, ready to swoop down and kiss her.

"Are you carrying our child?"

"I believe I am."

She watched him take a deep breath.

"Are you happy?" Jane asked.

In answer, he claimed her mouth with his, a deep, loving kiss, better than any she'd ever had before.

Why? she asked herself. *Why better?* Because it was replete with absolute tenderness.

Tears filled her eyes, and when Christopher finally pulled back to let her take a deep breath, Jane saw a moist sparkle mirrored in his own blue eyes.

Taking his hand, she brought his fingers to her cheek so he could feel her tears spilling over.

"We are both so happy," she said, "so why is this a moment for weeping?"

"There was a moment," he told her, "when I considered taking my own life rather than living alone in darkness. I thought only sad lonely years stretched ahead of me."

He stroked her cheek with his thumb. "You wouldn't let me give up. And now, we have created a new life. It's a miracle. *You* are a miracle, Lady Jane."

"Every day, I am thankful you finally noticed me that night at Marlborough House. Do you know what it felt like finally to be *seen?*"

He shook his head with the irony. "And then I was blinded.'

She held his face between her palms. "And yet you are still the only person who has ever truly seen me. *That* is my miracle."

He kissed her again, and the fire smoldering inside her burst into delicious flames of desire. She parted her legs and let him settle between her thighs.

"We shall know happy times and painful ones," she murmured. "But one thing is certain, I shall always love you."

"And I, you." He paused, then grinned down at her. "Speaking of which, can we . . . ? I mean, should we . . . ?"

"I consulted some books."

"Of course you did!" He threw his head back and laughed, and she punched him in the shoulder.

"I also asked your family's physician. And Lady Cambrey, who has experience in these matters." Jane loved her firm friendship with Margaret.

He ground his hips against hers. "I hope the answer is yes. Tell me at once."

She nodded. He waited. She nodded again.

"Are you nodding?"

"I am," she said, then giggled.

"You *are* a saucy minx!"

CHRISTOPHER PROCEEDED TO MAKE love to his wife, to worship every inch of her capable, intelligent, sometimes reserved—although *never* with him—sensual, adorable self.

In the afterglow, lying side-by-side with the woman he adored, he proclaimed, "I am the luckiest man alive."

ABOUT THE AUTHOR

USA Today bestselling author Sydney Jane Baily writes historical romance set in Victorian England, late 19th-century America, the Middle Ages, the Georgian era, and the Regency period. She believes in happily-ever-after stories for an already-challenging world with engaging characters and attention to period detail.

Born and raised in California, she has traveled the world, spending a lot of exceedingly happy time in the U.K. where her extended family resides, eating fish and chips, drinking shandies, and snacking on Maltesers and Cadbury bars. Sydney currently lives in New England with her family—human, canine, and feline.

You can learn more about her books and contact her via her website at SydneyJaneBaily.com.